Readers Love Amy Lane

The Rising Tide

"If you're looking for a well-written urban fantasy with hot sex, this one will do it. Nicely."

—Sparkling Book Reviews

All the Rules of Heaven

"All the Rules of Heaven is an intriguing, whimsical, and sometimes dark story. I particularly enjoyed the development of the primary and secondary characters."

—Love Bytes Reviews

Shortbread and Shadows

"Lane deftly builds a world where magic feels both plausible and inevitable, and inserts this magical world seamlessly into our own."

—Roger's Reads

Shades of Henry

"Shades of Henry is a beautiful character study and I can't wait to read more in this series."

—Rainbow Book Reviews

Fish Out of Water

"Fish Out of Water delivers an intense plot as well as a sizzling relationship between Ellery and Jackson."

—Gay Book Reviews

By Amy Lane

An Amy Lane Christmas
Behind the Curtain
Bewitched by Bella's Brother
Bolt-hole
Christmas Kitsch
Christmas with Danny Fit
Clear Water
Do-over
Food for Thought
Freckles
Gambling Men
Going Up
Hammer & Air
Homebird
If I Must
Immortal
It's Not Shakespeare
Late for Christmas
Left on St. Truth-be-Well
The Locker Room
Mourning Heaven
Phonebook
Puppy, Car, and Snow
Racing for the Sun
Hiding the Moon
Raising the Stakes
Regret Me Not

Shiny!
Shirt
Sidecar
Slow Pitch
String Boys
A Solid Core of Alpha
Three Fates
Truth in the Dark
Turkey in the Snow
Under the Rushes
Weirdos
Wishing on a Blue Star

BENEATH THE STAIN
Beneath the Stain
Paint It Black

BONFIRES
Bonfires
Crocus

CANDY MAN
Candy Man
Bitter Taffy
Lollipop
Tart and Sweet

Published by DREAMSPINNER PRESS
www.dreamspinnerpress.com

By Amy Lane (CONT)

COVERT
Under Cover

DREAMSPUN BEYOND
HEDGE WITCHES LONELY
HEARTS CLUB
Shortbread and Shadows
Portals and Puppy Dogs
Pentacles and Pelting Plants
Heartbeats in a Haunted House

DREAMSPUN DESIRES
THE MANNIES
The Virgin Manny
Manny Get Your Guy
Stand by Your Manny
A Fool and His Manny
SEARCH AND RESCUE
Warm Heart
Silent Heart
Safe Heart
Hidden Heart

FAMILIAR LOVE
Familiar Angel
Familiar Demon

FISH OUT OF WATER
Fish Out of Water
Red Fish, Dead Fish
A Few Good Fish
Hiding the Moon
Fish on a Bicycle
School of Fish
Fish in a Barrel

FLOPHOUSE
Shades of Henry
Constantly Cotton
Sean's Sunshine

GRANBY KNITTING
The Winter Courtship Rituals of
Fur-Bearing Critters
How to Raise an Honest Rabbit
Knitter in His Natural Habitat
Blackbird Knitting in a Bunny's Lair
The Granby Knitting Menagerie
Anthology

JOHNNIES
Chase in Shadow
Dex in Blue
Ethan in Gold
Black John
Bobby Green
Super Sock Man

Published by DREAMSPINNER PRESS
www.dreamspinnerpress.com

By Amy Lane (CONT)

KEEPING PROMISE ROCK
Keeping Promise Rock
Making Promises
Living Promises
Forever Promised

LONG CON ADVENTURES
The Mastermind
The Muscle
The Driver
The Suit
The Tech

LUCK MECHANICS
The Rising Tide
A Salt Bitter Sea

TALKER
Talker
Talker's Redemption
Talker's Graduation
The Talker Collection Anthology

WINTER BALL
Winter Ball
Summer Lessons
Fall Through Spring

Published by DSP Publications

ALL THAT HEAVEN WILL
ALLOW
All the Rules of Heaven

GREEN'S HILL
The Green's Hill Novellas

LITTLE GODDESS
Vulnerable
Wounded, Vol. 1
Wounded, Vol. 2
Bound, Vol. 1
Bound, Vol. 2
Rampant, Vol. 1
Rampant, Vol. 2
Quickening, Vol. 1
Quickening, Vol. 2
Green's Hill Werewolves, Vol. 1
Green's Hill Werewolves, Vol. 2

Published by Harmony Ink Press

BITTER MOON SAGA
Triane's Son Rising
Triane's Son Learning
Triane's Son Fighting
Triane's Son Reigning

Published by DREAMSPINNER PRESS
www.dreamspinnerpress.com

AMY LANE

A SALT BITTER SEA

DREAMSPINNER PRESS

Published by

DREAMSPINNER PRESS

5032 Capital Circle SW, Suite 2, PMB# 279, Tallahassee, FL 32305-7886 USA
www.dreamspinnerpress.com

A Salt Bitter Sea
© 2023 Amy Lane.

Cover Art
© 2023 L.C. Chase
http://www.lcchase.com
Cover content is for illustrative purposes only and any person depicted on the cover is a model.

Trade Paperback ISBN: 978-1-64108-575-5
Digital ISBN: 978-1-64108-574-8
Trade Paperback published August 2023
v. 1.0

Printed in the United States of America
∞
This paper meets the requirements of
ANSI/NISO Z39.48-1992 (Permanence of Paper).

As I get older—and my body gets more and more irritated at the dumbest things—I am frequently forced to rely on my husband and family for everything from a hand up from the couch to volunteering to do laundry because my knees aren't going to make it today. I couldn't do what I do—in any capacity—without my family, giving me their strength and their humor. Thanks, guys.

Acknowledgment

I need to thank Andi, my senior editor, because I adore paranormal romance, and plunging back into it with the Hedge Witches and now with the Luck Mechanics has been an adventure, and I think she's been my greatest cheerleader. Thanks, Andi!

Rude Awakenings

MILLER ALDRUN knew he was asleep, but the dream was always so real. It wasn't even a memory. Miller hadn't been there when the whole thing had gone down, but it was like, in the dream, he could remember being there. Remember the look on Brad's face.

"Just a milk run," Brad had said, one foot out the door.

Miller frowned. "Don't take this call for granted," he said, the feeling crisp in his belly, in his chest, where this premonition usually gathered. "It's not a milk run."

Brad scoffed gently. They'd come up in the same academy class—Brad had seen Miller's gift bail him out of trouble a thousand times, and each time he'd laughed and praised Miller for his luck.

"Good luck seeing that guy, Milly!" or "Ooh—lucky man, making a bust like that!"

Not once had he acknowledged that the pull, the *drive*, in Miller's stomach was something worth listening to, even when it caused Miller to take the shot that saved his life.

But Miller wasn't going to be out on the streets today. A twisted ankle of all things, running down a suspect. Brad had been in front, and Miller had gone down, calling out that he couldn't follow.

Brad had gone anyway, running the guy down on foot with the speed of somebody who'd lettered in track during college and hadn't stopped training.

Miller had barely been able to walk—he'd needed an ambulance, and Brad had taunted him as he'd arrested the suspect. "Pulled a hammy to avoid chasing a purse snatcher. Classic gag!"

Miller hadn't yelled at him then for going into a dangerous situation without backup, but he'd been sorely tempted. After shift, Miller had been put on desk duty while he nursed his ankle, with three days mandatory medical leave before he returned. Brad had let him catch a rideshare home, because he had paperwork to do and Miller wasn't *that* badly hurt.

He'd shown up at Miller's apartment that night, flush with a few beers with the guys, and Miller...? Miller gave in.

Usually he wouldn't have. He'd spent the entire relationship calling Brad out for being a condescending bastard, and Brad, charming, funny, the darling of the small New Jersey precinct, had told Miller repeatedly that the reason he needed Miller was that Miller didn't put up with any of his shit.

Also because Miller had as much to lose as Brad did if they got outed. Miller didn't need to be told that. He was a police officer after all.

But Miller had given in this night because... because he'd kept dreaming of Brad falling down a big black hole, and then he'd wake up shaking.

So Miller had given in, and Brad was running out the door wearing yesterday's uniform, rolling his eyes as Miller tried to tell him *not* to go running ahead.

That's how it had happened in real life.

In the dream, Miller was there, running down the suspect, twisting his ankle, and Brad was running ahead, scaling the chain-link fence at the end of the alley.

In the dream, Miller heard the shot.

He woke up in his little bungalow, far away from New Jersey, body dripping sweat, and tried to catch his breath.

The sound of the Atlantic Ocean surrounding his apartment on the little peninsula that reached out for Spinner's Drift masked his short breaths, and he had to calm down to hear the sound of his own thoughts over the sound of the surf.

He felt the pull then, something headed his way.

Something dangerously armed. Something a little crazy. Or a lot.

Something his least favorite combination.

Recognizing his gift—his "mechanic" as his new friend, Scout Quintero, called it—Miller took several deep breaths and tried to center himself, tried to feel what his mechanic was telling him, what it was asking him to do.

He closed his eyes, and the face that popped up behind them almost made him sit up in bed again.

Long, aristocratic, with an aquiline nose and almond-shaped brown eyes, the face of Piers Constantine, who was about as far away from small-town New Jersey cop as Miller could possibly imagine. Of course, they were in Spinner's Drift, a tidal archipelago off the coast of the Carolinas, now, so *Miller* was pretty far away from small-town New Jersey cop as well.

But Miller had gotten the job as local law enforcement—one of a force of four—on a fluke. His ankle had still been healing, and he'd still been grieving his partner and closeted lover when his sister had sent him the ad she'd seen pop up on Reddit. Clary had claimed she only went on the site for the knitting postings, but apparently she'd been job shopping for her big brother on the side.

Miller had been… heartsick at the time. He had no outlet for his anger at Brad, or for his grief, and the idea of walking back into the squad room and looking across his desk to see a stranger's face had made him queasy.

He'd take this job, he thought. A set of quiet little resort islands with free room and board? And not merely a one-room flat, either, but an entire bungalow, with a guest room and kitchen. It was like taking candy from a small township government, but he'd attended the academy, and he had the criminal justice degree. He was a real cop; he just didn't want to work in New Jersey anymore.

And now, three years later, his guilt and grief had faded, but his sentiment for New Jersey remained the same. He'd come to love Spinner's Drift, had come to love the idea of taking a boat to his worksite, or a bicycle. A solitary commute among the wind and the sea or the sky suited him. Most of his job was helping out the locals when they couldn't pay their rent or had too much to drink or, temporarily delusional about torque, got their vehicle—boat or auto—stuck in one of the many places the tide went in and out and traction or flotation varied from moon to moon.

But the people here knew him, and he fit in nicely. With the locals, anyway.

Piers Constantine was *not* local. He was one of the resort residents, and he was rich, educated, and snarky. He was also funny and—much like Miller—strangely gifted with his own "mechanic" of luck and magic, and having his face pop up behind Miller's eyes was a combination of worrisome and, uhm, *arousing*.

The first time Miller had seen Piers, back in October, he'd been cool, composed, and generally insouciant, and Miller had felt grubby and blue collar and… and *inferior* to the worldly Piers.

But that hadn't stopped Piers from giving him that bemused, almost sweet smile whenever they met at The Magic of Books for coffee and "magic lessons" with the other luck mechanics and magic users on the island.

Miller felt a flutter in his chest—intuitive, not physical, although it was sometimes hard to tell them apart—and then it intensified to a cramp.

Oh hell.

He closed his eyes, took a deep breath, and tried to zero in on a location. He had a vague ping of off the islands. Probably Charleston, since that was the closest place on the mainland with a ferry to Spinner's Drift, and he let out a sigh of relief.

He had a minute. He squinted at the clock and saw it was 4:00 a.m....

Well, the ferry loaded at nine and landed at 10:00 a.m. In that case he figured he had three hours before he had to wake everybody with a red alert.

He sat up in the bed of his cozy little bungalow, chewed his lower lip, and tried to assess the threat again. Yeah, yeah, it was holding in Charleston for the time being. He'd get a flutter—or a cramp or a screaming premonition—if it was getting nearer, but he didn't want to just leave his friends without warning. He knew that Piers's young cousin, Larissa, had been running away from a very dangerous man before they'd shown up in the islands, and the young barista at The Magic of Books was also on the run. So was Scout, the wizard, and his magically gifted sister. Spinner's Drift tended to attract people who needed sanctuary—Miller included—so the idea that he'd know innocent people on the run from dangerous psychopaths didn't surprise him, not when he'd been sensing weapons and bad intent since that one kid in the first grade had brought his pocketknife to school to cut a little girl's braid off.

Of course, like Brad, nobody had believed him then either—not even when he was a policeman and guys were banging their chests about "hunches" all the time. Nobody had believed him when he'd begged his father not to stop at the gas station late at night during a family trip and the guys knocking the place over for a few measly dollars had nearly ended Fred Aldrun's life.

To this day, Miller's father refused to believe in Miller's absolutely true, never proven false foreknowledge of people who were armed and crazy.

Miller had started to think he'd get shot and die while everyone around him was going, "But why would that person with the gun shoot *you*? You're imagining things!" He'd believed that right up until the day he'd knocked on Scout Quintero's door (or rather Lucky the barista's door, but Scout had been asleep inside the tiny apartment) and had not only been believed but had been given an absolutely magic cupcake by Scout himself, because Scout had wanted to cut through the "That's not possible!" crap and tell Miller he was not only believed, he had a peer group he'd never dreamed of.

The cupcake had been delicious, Miller's premonition regarding psychopaths with guns had been absolutely true—Scout had magicked them away to their violent home spawning grounds—and Miller had been meeting his new peer group once a week for coffee and discussion for the past six weeks. He liked it. Whether they were wizards like Scout and his sister Kayleigh; witches, like their bosses and local business owners, Marcus Canby and Helen Verde; or luck mechanics, like Lucky, Piers, and Larissa, all of them had been predisposed to believing Miller. And because Miller had been honest with *them*, they'd told him their own problems so he'd be game to help.

Sitting up at 4:00 a.m. and then leaving their problems until morning didn't feel right.

Frustrated, he grabbed his phone from the battered end table and rolled over to his side, texting to the group he had labeled Luck Mechanics on his phone.

Armed and dangerous coming in from Charleston tomorrow on the ferry, I think. Possibly aimed at Lightning or his sister. I'll be at the bookstore at eight.

Helen's coffee and bookstore, where Lucky worked and they met, opened promptly at seven, but he had to ride cold and choppy seas in his little skiff, and he'd rather do it when the sun was up.

Bad dreams?

Miller took a deep breath and looked at the text with relief. It was from Piers—whom he'd designated Lightning in his phone because he could control light sources with only a thought—and knowing someone was out there to hear his warning made him feel better.

Piers's text had been to Miller exclusively, not on the group chain, and Miller had no problem responding to him in kind.

Yes—I wanted everyone to know as soon as possible.

Appreciated. There was a pause as the text bubbles appeared, erased, and then reappeared. Then the phone rang in Miller's hand.

"What?" Miller asked gruffly, partly to mask how relieved he was to hear a friendly voice on the other end of the line.

"Just wanted to make sure *you're* okay. You said you got premonitions. I mean, we're talking deadly and crazy. That can't be much fun for you, right?"

Miller laughed shortly. "It's like having rats trapped in a bag under my sternum."

Piers's laugh was more like a bark. "Yikes! Okay, so, yeah. I'm just making sure you're okay."

Miller let out a breath and leaned his head against his knees. "Yeah, Lightning. I'm fine. But it's kind of you to ask. I keep wondering if I could look up travelers to Charleston to see if I can figure out who it might be, but then I remember that this is real life. Magic is real. Computer searches that can be done in five minutes on a laptop with no special features… not so much."

This time Piers's laugh was warmer and genuinely amused. "Sadly true," he said. "But we *do* happen to know the guy who owns the resort on the island and, you know, pretty much half the island. Did you ever think of calling Callan?"

Miller's low whuff of air was not so much a sound of annoyance as it was a sound of rejection. "Look, I know he's doing that thing… the body thing…."

"The moving the body of one dead lover to the island to relieve the suffering of the other lover's ghost thing," Piers said dryly.

"God. You know, I can't complain that nobody listens to *me* when I find it so hard to believe in *that*, right?"

Piers grunted. "I keep telling you, we need to have Scout take you to the spirit trap so you can feel all that grief congealing. It's…." Miller could hear the shudder over the phone. "It's important. And the reinterment might not solve the whole problem, but I'm with Scout. Easing that much suffering has got to be a good thing. Karmically speaking."

Miller groaned. "You know, it's great that you guys believe me and all, but… but…."

"But getting used to magic is tough when suddenly we're talking about it like it's no big deal," Piers stated. Miller could picture him, sitting up in what was probably a big fancy bed at Callan's resort and looking out a window that could take in the entirety of the main island of Spinner's Drift. Maybe he'd be shirtless, all smooth tanned skin and broad shoulders, with a tapered waist—uhm, maybe he'd be wearing silk pajamas. Either way he'd look rich and at home. Piers and Callan were distant cousins or something, and Piers's people were loaded with cash. The guy was made for luxury and refinement, and—

"Piers, is that Miller?"

Miller's eyes popped wide open. "Was that Scout?" he squeaked, the idea of Piers alone in his luxurious king-size bed in a five-star resort hotel suddenly rudely displaced by the idea of Piers in an IKEA-framed twin bed in Scout and Kayleigh's apartment.

"Lucky's got a couch now," Piers said on a yawn. "Remember? Me, Scout, Lucky—we were going to watch movies tonight, and you had a late shift."

Miller blinked. God, he was stupid, and it was late, and apparently he had a jealous streak he'd never known about.

"Yeah, yeah," he muttered. "I remember *now*. Weren't the girls with you?"

"They went back to Kayleigh's apartment," Piers said. Then, obviously not to Miller, "Yeah. He got woken up with a premonition. All he knows is that they're in Charleston, but he doesn't know who armed and crazy is here for."

"Gimme a sec" came a grouchy voice. Great. Now they'd awakened Scout's boyfriend, Lucky. Scout Quintero had thick, curly black hair, cobalt blue eyes, and the long, slender body of a dancer. In contrast, his boyfriend, Lucky McPherson, was midsized, stocky, with sandy blond hair and hazel eyes. Scout was lovely, right down to his dreamy smile and guileless charm. Lucky was grumpy, skeptical, and fiercely protective of Scout. Lucky was *also* a very gifted mechanic, and his medium was a magic coin that was never, ever wrong.

"How's the new couch?" Miller asked, curious. He'd been one of the people to help move the new piece of furniture off the ferry and then into Lucky's apartment. It had occurred to him as he'd done so that it had been a long time since he'd been a part of a friend group that did things like that for each other, and he'd missed it.

"Absolutely comfortable," Piers muttered, sounding disbelieving. "I mean, add a pillow, a couple of blankets and a space heater, and we're talking the Dreamland Express."

Miller's chuckles dispelled some of the lingering anxiety of his own dream. "You sound surprised."

"I was never much of a couch surfer," Piers admitted. "In fact, I'm sort of a spoiled baby about where I sleep."

"The prince and the pea?" Miller asked dryly.

"Not in *my* bed," Piers retorted, and it sounded like he meant both entendres unequivocally.

"A little personal," Miller hedged, and Piers's low laughter started a different anxiety buzzing.

"But I'm pretty sure it's nothing *you* have to worry about," Piers said. "You wear bike shorts a lot, Miller. Have seen no signs of peas."

"Oh God," Lucky's voice growled in the background. "Stop sexually harassing the guy—we've got business."

"What's the business say?" Miller asked, not wanting to answer Piers's flirting. He'd been doing it—subtly and not so subtly—since they'd met, but Miller wasn't a flirty guy. The most flirtatious, adventurous thing he'd done in his entire life had been to eat the cupcake Scout had produced out of thin air when he was trying to convince Miller that magic was real.

"Business says there's more than one scumbag," Lucky told him, having apparently wrestled the phone away from Piers. "Flipped the coin, said, 'Heads, Larissa's stalker is in town, tails, it's someone else.'"

"And?" Oh God.

"And it hung up there spinning, which is what it does when the answer is Yes. Yes to all the things. Yes."

"Crap," Miller breathed.

"Give me the phone," Scout said calmly, and of course Lucky would because Scout sort of led that way. "Miller, can you tell any of your fellow law enforcement people? I mean, you know, grab someone by the collar and say, 'Look, I've got a hunch about someone coming in tomorrow?'"

Miller's grunt was semiembarrassed. "Scout, I don't make friends that easy," he hedged.

There was a moment of puzzled silence on the other end. "You knocked on my door and said, 'What did you do with the armed and crazy,' and then you were our friend. How is that not easy?"

"You believed me," Miller said bluntly. "You were destined to believe me. You knew what I was when I knocked on the door. You can't tell a bunch of policemen that, even the—" Losers. Incompetents. Arrogant jackasses. "—the, uh, people who work on the island," he finished, knowing it was weak sauce. He hated speaking ill of other people, law enforcement or non-law enforcement alike. But the guys working on the island were a combination of locals with no education and a guy who'd failed the sergeant's exam in a bigger precinct in Wilmington and was now the proverbial medium-sized fish in a tiny pond. He was Miller's technical superior, but given that Miller had a better service record, more education, and had *passed* his detective's exam right before he'd left New Jersey, well, Leo Kowalski had a boulder-sized grudge against Miller on general principle.

Scout grunted. "Miller, you could have told us." He made another sound. "Piers, did he tell *you*?"

"Tell me what?" Piers sounded grumpy.

"That he's lonely and has no friends at his job," Scout said, and Miller grimaced because although it was true, he didn't think Scout had meant it to sound quite so… so *bald*.

"But he's such a nice guy!" Piers protested. "Give me that—"

"No, we're planning. Butt into his personal life when we're done," Scout replied shortly. "But not tonight. Look, Miller, come meet at the bookstore at eight, like we said. Come… dressed, I guess. Like you're on serious duty. That Kevlar stuff and your helmet—have that."

Miller gave a grim laugh. If he hadn't seen Scout pull various disparate information out of thin air and turn it into a way to protect the people he loved, he would have told Scout to let professionals handle things.

But in this case, they were *all* professionals. Miller's strength was in law enforcement, but that didn't mean the others didn't have their strengths too.

"I'll come prepared," he said. Then, because it meant something to him that he'd sent out a text and gotten a confab, "Thanks, Scout."

"Course," Scout said, super casual. "Now you talk to Piers and explain to him why the people you work with are stupid-heads and we should all hate them."

Miller was still gasping like a fish when Piers took the phone.

"I'm going to assume you're not going to do any of that," Piers said softly, and Miller wondered if everybody was settling back into bed—or in Piers's case, the couch.

"No, because I have a job here that I like," Miller said, smiling because Piers got it. He wasn't sure on all the details, but Scout and Kayleigh had been relatively sheltered when they'd grown up. The concepts of politics and compromise were not really bonded to their souls. And Lucky had grown up in a shitty part of Philly; if he hadn't been able to fight, Miller wasn't sure he would have lived to escape.

Miller had grown up knowing that nobody would believe him, even when he was telling the truth. It meant he'd had to learn to live with authority that didn't understand him and learn to work around it.

"Well, you deserve colleagues that don't try to bully the locals because they're not rich," Piers said tartly, and Miller groaned.

"Who told you about Leo?"

"Nobody had to. I was out at John's Thumb the other night, and there was a fight. You were probably on the other side of the Drift, because that guy—Leo you said? Kowalski?—yeah, he showed up. The local had been protecting the waitress from being harassed, but guess who Kowalski sided with?"

"The rich guy with his hand on her ass," Miller muttered. "Because he's just that awful."

"Yeah," Piers murmured. "You're worth ten of him."

Miller's ears burned in the dim confines of his room, and he felt like he had to change the subject. "What were you doing at the Thumb?"

John's Thumb was a truly tiny island—maybe three miles in circumference, and its one establishment was a bar/dance floor with a small nest of cabanas that were available to resort patrons for a fee. Essentially it was the kind of place where you could party with your friends, find a hookup, and then take a dip in the morning to wash off the walk of shame. The idea that Piers was there to get laid suddenly congealed in Miller's stomach like a knot.

"Wishing you were there," Piers murmured quietly. "Everyone else was sort of boring."

"Be serious," Miller muttered, embarrassed. It was such a smooth line—he was never sure if Piers was for real or not when he said things like that.

"I am," Piers replied, and God help Miller, he *sounded* sincere. "I asked you, remember? But you had to patrol the other side of the islands."

Miller remembered. In particular he remembered the mix of relief and depression that had washed over him when he realized he'd had a legitimate reason to turn Piers down. Relief because guys like Miller didn't hang out at John's Thumb—and they certainly didn't dance, right? And depression because… well, because Piers had asked him, and he… he liked Piers.

Was starting to like him more and more as this night went on, actually.

"Well, it's not like you'd want to join me," Miller said, not sure why he'd even mention that.

"It's not like you'd ask me to find out," Piers returned, so quickly it felt like a trap.

He sighed. "Piers, what are you doing?" He was tired, and he was worried, and there were so many uncertain variables in his life right now. He suddenly needed some clarity.

"I'm *trying* to flirt with you," Piers retorted crossly. "I could have sworn I was better at it than this."

Miller smiled a little. "Why?" he asked. "Why me? I've been out to the Thumb on patrol before. There's lots of guys there, and a lot of them would take you up on that offer in a minute."

"Because you're interesting," Piers said softly. "You're genuine. You want to save the world—or at least Spinner's Drift. And"—his voice dropped even more—"there's something in your eyes… something that says you have a me-shaped void in your life. I've never been the person who could fill exactly the right spot before. I thought we should give it a try."

Miller swallowed, trying to beat back a vision of being held close in Piers's arms while they danced slowly, a dazzling spread of stars above their heads, the beat of the waves pounding through their blood.

Piers lowering that handsome, arrogant face down to his and….

"I'm cursed," he choked out before he could finish that thought. "People die around me."

"Maybe," Piers replied archly, "that's because they don't believe—" A yawn punctuated the end of the sentence. "—you," he finished.

Miller yawned back and looked at the clock. A half hour had passed, and they all had to be up early. But something about the conversation— all of the conversations—had cheered him, settled him.

Made him feel heard and seen and as though he was not all alone in the world, fighting the forces that were.

"I'll let you go," Miller murmured, scooting down in the bed and pulling the comforter up to his shoulders. "But Piers?"

"Yeah?"

"Thank you."

"For what?" Piers was falling asleep, but then so was Miller now, and that was okay.

"For hearing me. For believing." He paused. "For asking me to John's Thumb."

"Next time," Piers mumbled, "you'll be able to come. I really want to dance with you."

"Night, Lightning."

"Night, Cassandra."

And with that they signed off.

When Armed and Crazy Comes Calling

THE MAGIC of Books was the kind of place Piers would have loved if he was attending school right now. It had deep shelves that extended back into the store, complete with little coffee tables and chairs not only in a pocket toward the rear but scattered in nooks and crannies, the better to sit alone and do homework and drink coffee in peace. The books were eclectic, with a combination of battered used hardbound books and brand-new bestsellers, and the coffee....

So good. There-oughta-be-a-law kind of good, that would have had Piers a raving, pot-a-day addict if he hadn't had to ride a bike or a golf cart across the island to get some on the days he didn't stay with Kayleigh or Scout and Lucky. As it was, he always got the ginormous size, with a little fresh cream and a teeny bit of raw sugar, and he nursed that baby as long as he could because it was *so* perfect.

The only defect, as far as he could see, was that the back of the store was surrounded by bookshelves that blocked off the natural light from the big window at the front of the store, and as such, was a teeny bit dim for all of that studying he and his new peer group did. The shop had a big not-for-sale collection of books just for them it seemed, and they spent an inordinate amount of time peering into the old and sometimes garbled texts on magic that Helen kept on a special shelf. They needed more light.

But then, light was his specialty.

He hustled to the back of the store, holding the tray of drinks Lucky had given him, and fixed the light just a fraction, barely thinking about it.

He needed light, and there it was. That's the way it had always been.

"Thanks, Lightning," Scout said absently. He was sitting in front of an outspread map and tossing a little wooden spinning top over it, his lips moving in quiet thought.

"What's that?" Piers asked, setting down a sweet coffee drink next to Scout's left hand.

Scout took it appreciatively with a brief smile, his cobalt eyes focusing for a moment underneath a fall of black dandelion hair.

"Thanks, Lightning," Kayleigh Quintero echoed, taking her own coffee drink from the tray, as well as his cousin's, and giving him a much more *present* sort of grin. "And that's a divining top. Our brother Macklin sent us a batch of them as early Christmas gifts. Here, set the tray down and I'll give you yours."

Piers gaped. "Mine? Your brother, whom I've never met, sent me a present?"

Kayleigh was Scout's *half* sister in fact—the only feature they shared was the brilliant smile and a certain slant of their eyes. And the magic of course. Other than that, Kayleigh had sun-streaked brown hair and brown eyes, and now they lightened with what seemed to be honest joy.

"Yeah. Macklin's fiancé is the leader of a coven of witches in California. One of them is a woodworker, and he made these little divining tops for everyone in his coven, and they're sort of awesome. So Macklin asked us to describe the people we hung out with—you know, power, vibe, aura, personality, that sort of thing—and then their friend made us tops!"

Piers stared at her, still perplexed. "That's… uh, *really* generous. But why?"

Kayleigh shrugged. "Well, once Scout sort of handed Alistair's ass to him on a platter and the coven could gather and have a life again, Macklin and Jordan—Mack's fiancé—wanted to give us something we could use to protect ourselves. I think they really want to come visit, but, you know…."

Piers nodded. He knew. Alistair—Kayleigh and Scout's father—*had* had his ass handed to him on a platter, but he was also a dangerous, spiteful man. Just because Kayleigh and Scout had removed his reason for wanting Kayleigh back in the wizard's compound they'd been raised in didn't mean he might not get a wild hair to come after them again for spite. Piers's father wasn't *quite* that bad when it came to being drunk on his own power, but he wasn't that good either. Their danger wasn't quite over yet, and it wasn't the only risk out there.

Lucky, Scout's boyfriend, had escaped from mobsters and run where his own magic had directed him—and ended up here in this tiny archipelago. Those mobsters had been one of the reasons Miller had texted everybody the night before. There was no guarantee they weren't going to show up and try to drag Lucky back into unwilling servitude in order to use his lucky coin to make profitable guesses for them.

And that wasn't even the scariest option.

Piers glanced over at his cousin, Larissa, who was sipping her own caramel latte and watching Scout use the divining top with wide eyes. God, she was so innocent. She'd just turned eighteen that summer, and in spite of the fact that her parents and Piers's parents were massive power brokers in the human world, she'd managed to remain relatively untouched by the spite and entitlement that seemed to suffuse so many of their peers. Piers adored her, and watching her spirit get viciously crushed under the fear of a stalker—one who had no problem accessing her privacy or harming her pets *or* her plants—had been awful. Piers had swept her away to Spinner's Drift, partly because the owners were distant cousins, and partly because nobody they knew outside of family had ever heard of the place.

But then, as Piers had begun to learn, the island was like that.

Seated off the coast of the Carolinas, and only accessible by a ferry from Charleston or a helicopter that could only land on a pad at the main resort, the Drift was a tourist paradise. Long stretches of white sandy beaches in the summer, moderately nippy temperatures in the winter, and lots of peaceful jungle paradise in between, the place attracted old money on the resort side of the island, young money at play places like John's Thumb, which was a bar and party zone, and old hippies and young beatniks at the merchant venues, because every tourist destination needed a retail trap, and there were some amazing ones on this end of the island.

In addition to The Magic of Books, which Lucky's boss, Helen, ran with a mixture of kindness and no-bullshit practicality, Scout and Kayleigh worked at Gestalt, a magic shop. Also on this end of the island was a fudge shop, Donut Do Dat—which served the best donuts Piers had ever tasted—a kite shop, a tarot shop, a crystal shop, and a place with all sorts of plant clippings and vitamin packs that could be slipped into smoothies so you didn't know you were drinking health food with your peaches, yogurt, and sugar. And that was only the beginning.

Piers had stopped by Doggy Duds so many times in the past three months since he and Larissa had arrived on the island that he was starting to want a dog to buy clothes for. Or a cat. Or a snake or an iguana. In spite of the name, it really was an equal opportunity companion apparel showcase.

So the retail end of the island was eclectic, tasty, and interesting. There were restaurants and dessert shops and sportswear and a thousand different things Piers had never thought of buying, and each and every proprietor came with their own interesting, often secretive, backstory.

Piers could really love it here if he hadn't been so afraid Larissa's stalker would find them. The idea that a complete stranger would send them help and magic was like a little beacon of hope—and beacons were sort of Piers's thing!

"So how do the little toppy things work?" Piers asked, and Larissa and Kayleigh almost spit out their coffee.

"Uhm, Piers, wouldn't *you* know that?" Larissa asked slyly after wiping her mouth.

Piers stared at her and then felt heat sweeping over his face and neck, cursing the rather candid conversations he'd had with his cousin over the years. Larissa had, as of yet, not ventured into the lands of sexual exploration, but Piers had been active at sixteen. Larissa had grilled Piers unmercifully about sex since she hit the same age, and, well, she knew what "toppy" meant.

He was, uhm, rather toppy himself.

"Not the time or place," he mumbled.

"For what?" Miller Aldrun said from behind him, coming to the back through the shelves.

"To discuss Piers's sex life," Larissa said blithely. "But definitely the time and the place for looking at these little toppy things."

Miller snorted, and Piers shot him a glare.

Miller shrugged. "It's been a long time since I've seen a little toppy thing," he deadpanned, and Piers had to look away to hide his grin.

The young policeman—and the biking pants and helmet did nothing to dispel the basic athletic competence and situational awareness that screamed *policeman*—could have been so very irritating. He had no reason to believe Scout was a wizard beyond his *own* Cassandra's gift of knowing when someone armed and dangerous was in the vicinity, and yet all Scout had needed to do was offer him a hand of friendship—and summon him a cupcake from midair—and Miller had been willing to believe. He'd still been all business—he'd taken down Piers and Larissa's details about Larissa's stalker, had checked in with the mainland to see if the guy had been apprehended, and had put his own staff plus that of Charleston on alert—but when he'd met with them on Tuesdays he'd been… open. A happy part of their little group, relieved—so damned relieved—to share his own stories of his gift, or "mechanic," that he'd been willing to work at believing everybody else's.

And he'd never minimized anybody's power. Not even Larissa's when apparently she was meant to never, ever let a refrigerator go without somebody's favorite drink. In fact, he'd looked at Larissa and grinned and said, "You are apparently destined to be everybody's best hostess. That's delightful."

Larissa had beamed all day, and Piers? Well, Piers didn't have a sister he'd defend to the death, like Scout would Kayleigh, but Larissa had been the first person he'd come out to, and while she'd been twelve and he'd been sixteen at the time, she'd kept that secret and had been Piers's staunch defender at all of the family reunions since.

Yeah, Piers was already predisposed to like the guy, but once he was nice to Larissa? That had sealed Miller's fate.

Piers was now *interested* in him, and Miller just kept giving him these, "Nice to be a part of the community, sir," smiles that made Piers want to jump into the ocean—or back Miller up against a wall and prove that "toppy" didn't have a thing to do with little wooden divining disks and they both knew it.

And his occasional burst of self-deprecating humor didn't hurt. In fact, knowing that Miller hadn't seen a top for a while did a whole lot to help Piers's mood. *Look* at him—compact body, brown hair, hazel eyes, and a sort of earnest American boy face, complete with an almost pug nose and what might have been freckles as a child.

And ears that turned red when he was embarrassed.

Piers wanted to eat him up, but Miller, as of yet, had not shown interest. Or rather, he'd not shown interest he seemed willing to act on.

In fact, Piers rather suspected Miller was either shy or heartbroken. There seemed to be a part of him that was held in reserve, and Piers was getting a little desperate to know him better.

He returned that self-deprecating smile with a sort of predatory grin of his own. "Would you *like* to see something toppy?" he asked, tilting his head in invitation.

In response, Miller looked away, but Piers noticed his ears turned red.

"What are you divining, Scout?" Miller asked, focusing everybody's attention back to Scout, his little top, and the map.

"Well, I've been asking the top where our armed and crazy is, and so far it's landing directly on Spinner's Drift, which is strange. Miller, wouldn't you have known if it was already here?"

At that moment Miller's face, normally a little ruddy after his trip to the main island and the bike ride to get there in the morning, went so white it was almost gray. Piers saw his knees wobble and was the first one there to catch him, putting his arm gently around Miller's waist and guiding him to a chair so he didn't crumple to the floor.

Miller looked at him helplessly. "Here," he whispered, looking so queasy Piers feared for his shoes. "It's *here*."

And at that moment they all heard the bell at the door of Helen's place jangle—a loud, discordant sound that made his skin crawl, when normally it was the usual cheerful little tinkle of most businesses.

"Oh God," Piers whispered, and they heard a voice, flinty with a Philly accent, snarling at someone in the front.

"Don't move, asshole. I can shoot you as easy as him!"

"Scout, don't move," Lucky said, his voice surprisingly calm. "He's here for me."

"There y'are, ya little pissant. Did ya think ya could escape the Shanahan gang after you took off last time?"

"Scout, no…," Lucky said warningly, and Piers, Miller, Kayleigh, and Larissa all looked wildly around the back of the library and realized that while Piers had been keeping Miller from passing out, Scout had all but teleported to the front of the shop.

They rushed to the counter to see a nightmare come to life. The young man with greasy black hair and a hawk-sharp nose wasn't dressed like a tourist. He was wearing camo clothing—a gigantic pair of camo pants, held up by a belt around scrawny hips, and a big army surplus jacket draped over his shoulders.

And an ugly gun in his hand, aimed straight at Lucky the barista, who was glaring back like he'd always known this was coming and was just sorry he couldn't drag the guy to hell with him.

"Stevie, no…."

The voice, frightened and pleading, came from a slender young man standing next to their camo nightmare.

"Shut up, Ciaran," Stevie snarled. "This isn't your business."

"You said he was a friend!" Ciaran protested. "You promised! I said I wasn't tracking down your enemies for you, and you swore he was a friend!"

Stevie sent the young man—a remarkably pretty boy, maybe Larissa's age, with a long fall of curly black hair and green eyes—a fulminating glance that promised a beating or worse when he was done with this more important errand.

"You did what I told ya," Stevie snarled, and Ciaran grew before their eyes.

"I did a favor for my cousin," he said. "And I did it on condition. You violated the condition, Steven, and I will not let you harm another with my gift!"

"Don't need ya now, do I, ya puny little fa—*God*!"

The harsh epithet never got a chance to land because as the extremely unlikable Steven-with-the-gun argued with his cousin, a spinning disk of light opened up behind him.

Piers and the others had seen this spinning disk before—it looked fire-edged, and the center of it held a landscape full of pines and beech trees and, this time of year, snow. Just as Steven had opened his mouth to drop the damning word, the disc, or portal, swept toward him, engulfed him, closed like a camera aperture, and he disappeared.

Ciaran was left standing, staring at the empty cousin-shaped space where Steven had been, his eyes wide and face pale with shock.

"Jesus, Scout," Lucky muttered. "You scared the shit out of me."

"Where'd he go?" Ciaran asked, looking to Scout for help.

"Upstate New York," Scout said without compunction. His mouth fluttered. "I think. My, uh, father lives there, and he's sort of an asshole, so, you know, it's like relocating an animal with its herd." He scowled. "But then, I was a little pissed. I might have missed. We'll have to check."

Piers hid his mouth with his hand and met Miller's eyes, because it was funny. They hadn't met Scout's father so much as helped *rescue* Scout from his father—with a lot of help from Lucky and Scout himself. To his surprise, he found that Miller wasn't registering amusement or even relief.

"What's wrong?" he asked, moving closer to the man. He smelled like salt air and exertion, and Piers edged a little nearer and fought the temptation to bury his nose in Miller's neck to see how warm he was there.

"The armed and crazy isn't gone," Miller muttered, his eyes turning inward like he was reading a map behind his eyeballs. "I… I mean, I felt that—I knew it was here, but it wasn't the most dangerous part. Scout got rid of it, and it's like losing a chocolate button off a cupcake. Some of the sugar's gone, but the biggest part of it is still there."

Piers widened his eyes. "But that guy was *scary*. What's still out there?"

Miller shook his head unhappily. "It's…." He rubbed his stomach. "It's got me queasy as hell," he admitted. "It's bad—"

At that moment, poor Ciaran, who had simply stood, gaping like a fish while they were muttering to each other, opened his mouth and, out of nowhere, started screaming, a wild, hysterical, unhinged sound that almost sent Piers stumbling to his knees in visceral reaction. It was like the kid wasn't even connected with his own body. His eyes rolled in surprise and fear, and he simply stood there, mouth open, that banshee wail coming from his diaphragm, until Scout grunted, waved his hand, and snapped, "God, please sleep!"

And then he fell to the floor of the bookstore in a little puddle, and the luck mechanics were left staring at each other in surprise while the few other patrons in the shop tried not to hyperventilate with shock.

Helen, who had been standing, stunned, at the counter, lowered her brows and said in a singsong voice,

> *Lethe, sweet river, sing to their senses of sleep*
> *Let them forget, let them dream, let this memory skate*
> *The surface of their minds, never to sink or to slumber*
> *But to drift far, far away.*

Almost as though in a dream, every other patron in the coffee shop turned toward the counter and stared at the menu as though the gun-toting psycho had never been there and the traumatized kid on the floor was no more than a sleeping cat.

All of the luck mechanics blinked, and Scout said, "Miller, Piers, you guys grab poor Ciaran there. Larissa, Kayleigh, you help Helen clear the line. Lucky, you're with us."

Larissa gave a little groan, and Scout winked at her. "Of all times, sweets, they can't afford to run out of coffee or whipped cream, you hear me?"

At the mention of Larissa's almost frivolous gift, a simple mechanic of a constant flow of drinks, she dimpled, and Piers loved her so fiercely in that moment he could hardly breathe. She wanted to help because she had a good heart. Oh heavens, they had to keep her safe.

"Can we just leave her up here?" Piers asked quietly as he crouched to the tile floor, ready to lift with his legs.

Miller joined him on the other side, and together they managed to get the young man—boy?—up between them and haul him behind the counter and into the space in the back of the kitchen occupied by the giant walk-in refrigerator, sink, sanitizer, and washing machines. To the left of the washing machines was a rail, the better to help someone walk up and down a narrow staircase that led directly below the book/coffee shop to Lucky's apartment.

Piers and Miller got their gangly knee-and-elbow burden to the stairs and stopped, grunting.

"Suggestions?" Piers asked, wondering how they could get him down that thing without the three of them wiping out to become a bones-broken pile in Lucky's tiny studio space.

"Let me go down first," Miller muttered. "Then slide him down feet forward, watching his head. When his head's about to start bouncing on the stairs, you sit, rest his head in your lap, and boot-scoot until you can stand."

Piers thought about that, placing all the players in the appropriate spot in his mind, and then blinked. "Okay. Yeah. Very clever."

"'Do you wanna hide a body' is the number one stupid game cops play when they're bored," Miller confessed, walking down the stairs until his head disappeared. "Now start sliding him forward!"

It took some hefting, some swearing, and some grunting, but eventually they had the kid downstairs and lying on top of Lucky's comforter, with his shoes off and another blanket thrown across his chest for good measure.

Scout was pacing around the small apartment, and the only way he could get any distance was to start at the bathroom, do a small loop around the kitchen island counter, and end up by the sliding glass door that led outside to the downstairs patio before turning back to cut in front of the bed and reach the bathroom. Piers and Miller sat on the bed, one on either side of the kid, and Lucky sat, knees drawn to his chest, on one of the overstuffed couches in front of the TV.

After a few nervous minutes, Lucky spoke up from the chair. "Uh, whatcha thinkin', Scout?"

Scout grunted. "Well, first and foremost, I'm trying not to freak out about that asshole pointing a gun at you," he said crossly. "All the times I've sent someone cross-country and that was the closest I've come to throwing someone in the middle of the Atlantic and wiping my hands of the whole affair."

"Thanks for not doing that," Miller said humbly, and Scout grimaced in his direction.

"Well, you do tend to keep us honest, Miller," Scout replied grimly. "And no real wizard wants a death on his hands. So that asshole is gone. I need to know where the other one is. Miller?"

Miller closed his eyes, and two bright spots of color appeared on his cheeks. As Piers watched, all the other color bled out of his face and he shuddered, the sort of groin-deep shudder someone gives if they're about to throw up a bar's worth of tequila, with the lime thrown in.

"Stop," Scout ordered kindly.

Miller swallowed hard. "I'm sorry. It's just… it's gross. It's huge and it's scary and…." He shuddered again, looking green. Piers reached across the bed for his hand, and Miller gave him a sad look before pulling away. "I'll try again," he said with more resolution.

But Scout shook his head. "I think whoever this version of armed and crazy is, he's deeply disturbed, and it's gonna hurt you too much to find him through your gift." Scout reached into his pocket and pulled out a handful of the wooden tops. "Here." He walked deliberately to Miller and pressed one into his hand and then did the same for Piers. "These are yours. I give them to you to use as you will."

The words had an intonation of ritual to them, and when the tiny object started to buzz and hum in Piers's hand, Piers wondered if he hadn't bonded to the little magic implement for life.

As if in response, the little top gave a tiny jump, and Piers held out his palm and watched it dance in the center.

"Hello, little friend," he murmured. "So nice to make your acquaintance."

"Hiya," Miller said across the bed from him. "You and me, I think we're gonna do good together. Whatya say?"

Piers grinned, because it was such a Miller thing to want—the greater good. Like Scout said, Miller's upright heart kept them honest, or at least it kept Scout from dumping armed assholes to their deaths in the middle of the Atlantic.

"Miller, come over here," Scout said, and Miller looked up from his new toy to where Scout stood over the kitchen island counter with a map he'd pulled out from one of the drawers. "Lucky, you too." He gave a wink. "Piers, keep an eye on poor Ciaran there. I think the kid got a shock, you know?"

"I'm not sure which was worse," Piers agreed, "finding out that his cousin was a scumbag or watching him disappear into thin air."

"He used me," came a quiet, tired voice from the bed, and Piers turned toward the young man.

With a sigh, Ciaran Shanahan curled up on his side and pulled the covers tightly over his shoulders. Piers looked up at Scout, who, surprisingly enough, nodded to Lucky.

"Be gentle," he said to his often-gruff boyfriend.

"Yeah, yeah, I get it," Lucky muttered. "You were right."

"About what?" Piers asked, curious as Lucky stood up from his chair and stretched before coming to the side of the bed.

"Scout had this idea that the reason the guys who showed up on the island looking for me seemed really surprised to be here—and could never remember that they *were* here—was that they were using another mechanic. The island protects us, so the only way to find me would be to have someone with *no* bad intentions look." Lucky gave the rather fragile Ciaran a surprisingly gentle glance. "And that's what happened, isn't it, kid?"

Ciaran closed his eyes, and two silver tracks slid out alongside his nose. "He said he was looking for a friend—someone who had money coming. And we sent two guys in October, but they disappeared for, like, two months. They finally came back and... it was weird. They didn't remember where they'd been, why they'd gone. So this time, Steve said I could take him." A bitter smile twisted his full lips. "I was so excited," he murmured. "It was the first time I'd been out of Philly. All those years of being nobody in the family and I was gonna go somewhere."

Lucky sighed. "That sucks, kid. Seriously. If it helps, we're all, like, no harm no foul."

Ciaran stared at him with lifeless eyes. "Thank you," he whispered. "But... what do I do now?"

"What do you mean?" Piers asked curiously.

Lucky, Scout, and Miller all went very still, like they knew the answer to that and it was almost too painful to voice. It was Miller who answered.

"Lightning, he can't ever go home. You realize that, don't you?"

Piers stared from Scout to Lucky to Miller and then back at Ciaran. "I don't understand," he murmured.

"His cousin was gonna kill me," Lucky said slowly, like he was explaining to a child. "The leader of the Shanahan gang was going to *kill* me. Ciaran was supposed to help him do it. Not only am I walking around breathing free air, but Ciaran here didn't get sent wherever Scout sent Stevie Shanahan. Once Stevie surfaces, Ciaran's gonna be next on the hit list, am I right, Bones?"·

Lucky turned to Ciaran, and Ciaran gave him a half smile.

"Right." He sat up in bed a little, like something Lucky had said gave him heart. "Bones, 'cause it's like rolling the bones, right? That's why you called me that?"

Lucky gave him a fierce sort of grin. "Yeah. What'd your family call you?"

Ciaran grimaced. "Spooky," he said with disgust. "Or Finder. I like Bones better."

"Sounds more badass, right?" Lucky confirmed, and watching Ciaran nod was gratifying.

"We'll find you a place to stay," Scout said in that dreamy, out in left field way he had sometimes.

"Why not here?" Ciaran asked, sounding forlorn.

Piers glanced around and gave a soft snort. "'Cause it's a studio apartment, and you're in the only bed," he said, and there was some gentle laughter. "And I usually have the couch, although…." He bit his lip.

"He could have the couch in Kayleigh's apartment," Scout said, and then he grimaced. "Since, yeah, I've sort of moved in here."

"One article of clothing at a time," Lucky added dryly. "Starting with your underwear."

Piers chuckled. "Which I guess means I need to go back to the—"

"My flat," Miller said, and then blinked as though he couldn't believe he'd said it.

"I'm sorry?" Piers had been *going* to say "the resort," because he and Larissa had a suite there that they visited every day or so for clothes and the like. His cousin's family ran a *very* nice place—the sheets were clean, the views were unparalleled, and the amenities were damned posh, including the option of keeping the sliding glass door to the patio open and letting the high ceiling fans import fresh air. Piers would go there in the afternoons sometimes to work on his computer and continue his education online—he'd deferred his last year of law school to help Larissa stay safe from her stalker, but he'd invested a lot of time into Chapel Hill, and he liked to keep up. He would download the reading from the courses—he'd done a decent job of knocking that out and keeping up with the papers so he wasn't too behind or out of practice for next year—and generally make a little noise so nobody forgot he'd been at the top of his class, and then….

Then he returned to the tourist side of the island to swim when it had been warmer and the sea had been less like a people-processor, or to hang out with Scout and Lucky or Larissa, or sometimes even to help them at their jobs, just because he liked the company. Since Scout and Lucky had gotten together, Larissa had all but moved into Kayleigh and Scout's old apartment, and Piers found he got a little lonely without her. Besides that, these people were *fun*. Fun in ways the trust-fund bunnies on the other side of the island were *not*, and that good feeling included Scout's boss, Marcus, and Lucky's boss, Helen, as well.

Why would he want to hang out in a bar and try to hook up with another kid going to law school who wanted to talk about money or his next vacation or his political aspirations when he could go to Helen's coffee shop and watch Scout *make somebody disappear*. And even if things like that didn't happen regularly, there was always practice with their gifts or practical jokes or general banter, because these people were smart, quick, and fun. And if there wasn't that, there was the island mystery, which Piers was *very* interested in. In fact, he wanted to take Miller there and show *him*, because he thought Miller's mechanic or talent might give them some insight into the mystery itself.

No, in general between the company and the preoccupations, this side of the island was much more exciting. Piers had been going to school full-time—summer school included—since the first grade, when his parents had sent him to poetry camp at the tender age of six. He had eaten, breathed, slept, dreamt, *crapped* academics and his important future as a politician or businessman for his entire life, and it had rankled putting that last year off to get Larissa away from their family environs in Charlotte.

But he'd had no choice.

That last time... ugh. Larissa's room had been torn apart, and her underwear(!) had been slashed to ribbons. All of her plants had been killed—almost like they'd been sprayed with bleach or herbicide, although the detectives hadn't been able to find a trace of anything there. And her cat....

Piers shuddered, thinking about what a near miss it had been.

Her cat was a psychotic little bird-murderer who masqueraded as a handsome black-furred gentleman. Larissa adored the deadly bastard, even when he left birds splayed out in Hannibal Lecter fashion on her floor. Well, Freddy (as in Kruger!) almost met his match the night the stalker had finally invaded Larissa's bedroom. Before then she'd known the guy was following her to class or to her job at a clothing store on the weekends. She'd seen him around, had told the family about him, had marked him on her radar.

Then came one day when her car—always perfectly maintained because Larissa was a truly responsible kid—wouldn't start. It's hard for cars to do that when they've got sugar in the gas tank.

Piers remembered that day. She'd called him at school in tears because she was afraid her father would yell. It wasn't fair, but he probably would have if Piers hadn't stepped in and gotten the car towed and had the auto technician write out the assessment first. Larissa was the youngest of four and the only girl, and Piers—who had an older sister—had seen the favoritism the boys had gotten. It wasn't fair, but then, neither was his sister's place as jewel in the family crown because she was both heterosexual *and* already working as a political attaché in the Middle East.

Piers—gay and more interested in criminal law than political law—had worked harder and longer for his entire life, and he'd been grappling with the fact that he was never going to be his father's favorite son, even if he was the only son. Watching the same thing happen to Larissa, who was as gentle as a rabbit and twice as adorable, had made Piers even more intent on protecting her.

Especially that day when he realized somebody had vandalized her car to make sure she was stranded and vulnerable.

It wasn't until he'd called the tow truck and made Larissa call rideshare so he could deal with the vehicle that he even thought to have her look around to see if anybody was watching. Her parents had been gone for a week, so he'd had her go to his folks' place—the staff let her in all the time. After dealing with the car, he took her to her house so she could get some clothes and come stay with his parents since he used the dorms at school.

So he'd been at her side as she'd walked into her own home and found the staff members unconscious. It hadn't been gas or violence—in fact, the police hadn't been able to figure out *what* it was that had put them under—but every plant in the house was dead too. Not just dead, as though all the leaves turned brown, but shriveled and desiccated, as though plants that had been green and healthy and thriving for the plant service *that morning* had been dead for a year.

And he'd been right next to her as she'd found Freddy, bloody and pitiful, panting on her white eyelet comforter, so close to death Piers *still* couldn't believe he'd survived.

Piers had wrapped the animal in a towel and put him in Larissa's arms, taking in the rifled drawers and the savaged clothing. Then he'd hustled Larissa through the house, where the cook and the maid and plant service guy were all groaning and trying to remember their own names, talking on the phone as he did so. He'd stopped to talk to the cook quickly before they ran for the vet's, and he'd given her his cell phone number so the police could contact him, and then they'd been gone.

Larissa hadn't been back to her house since, and his parents, for all their flaws, had taken her in, as well as her recovering pussycat, for a frantic, heart-beating week as she'd managed to disentangle herself from what would have been her first year at Chapel Hill.

Piers had managed—barely—to do the same thing, and then, guided by some instinct he couldn't even name, he'd taken advantage of the standing invitation issued to the Constantine family by the Morgensterns. He'd taken Larissa to Spinner's Drift for a long-term stay in the resort. He'd enjoyed himself a lot, actually. Had even gotten laid once or twice after hanging out at John's Thumb. But as autumn wrapped up, he and Larissa had started to hang out at the touristy side of the island from sheer boredom, and they'd discovered the Great Gestalt.

He'd been the worst stage magician Piers had ever seen. Tall, slender, with a dancer's grace and a curling dandelion of dark hair, Gestalt had fumbled, bumbled, and smiled shyly into the hearts of his audience, one slowly mastered trick at a time.

Piers and Larissa had become regulars at his shows—and had been excited to see him improve—when Piers had accidentally revealed the one tiny special thing about himself that had cemented his and Larissa's place on the far side of the island forever.

He'd seen the Great Gestalt peering into an old book on magic in the back of the bookshop and had given the poor guy a little light.

And that's when the Great Gestalt had revealed himself to be Scout Quintero, an *actual wizard*, and Piers and Larissa had been sucked into a world of more fun—and more magic—than either of them had ever dreamed of.

And also friendship and camaraderie.

And Piers would say more danger, but he'd seen Larissa's room that late August day, and something about it—the injured animal, the dying plants, the pillaged drawers—all of it left a dank miasma, an acidic taste of evil in his mouth that he was finding difficult to shake.

Sleeping on Scout and Lucky's couch—or on Kayleigh's couch, while Larissa slept in what had once been Scout's twin bed—in the two absurdly tiny apartments had felt safe.

And they'd kept Piers in the same circle of friends that had included Miller Aldrun, and that had been exciting too.

Piers wasn't sure he'd ever met anybody as… as *earnest* as Miller. As dedicated to doing his job, even on a bicycle and a tiny skiff in what was mostly a resort island area that didn't seem to need a decidedly small police force.

Piers, who had been getting a steady diet of the jaded art of "let's make a criminal defense deal," had come to treasure Miller's company and dogged determination to make a difference. Nearly every week since October, they would meet at the bookstore, and Piers would prod at Miller to talk about his week.

"Armadillos in the trash cans again," Miller had muttered one morning, looking like bottled hell. "The Little Island to the Left—you know the place? Three houses on it, spitting distance of John's Thumb?"

Piers had nodded, amused because the locals had been *very* quirky about their island names. A lot of them were yarn themed—Spinner's Drift was the name of the archipelago as well as the main island, but there was also Weaver's Wharf, Knitter's Tangle, and Tatter's Tot. Piers had asked Helen why there wasn't an island named Crocheter's Cottages, and she'd told him that crocheting hadn't been as big a thing in the mid-1800s when the islands had been populated, but that Little Island to the Left had a good chance of being renamed.

Then he'd asked about John's Thumb, and she'd grimaced. "I have it on good authority," she'd said conspiratorially, "that a weaver named John actually *lost* his thumb, and that spit-spot was sort of a community joke."

"I'd like to rename it Crocheter's Cottages," Piers told Miller on this day, remembering that conversation, "but yeah, I know the place."

"Not Hooker's Hollow?" Miller had replied, a glimmer in his eyes at the whimsy, but then he'd gone back to his story. "Anyway, little bastards got into Audrey Swanson's trash can, and she called my boss in his cozy house in Charleston, and he called me because I'm on Copper's Island in the apartment there. And you know what I got for my trouble?"

"An armadillo-skin cloak?" Piers hazarded.

"A trip to Charleston with an entire family of armadillos that now need to be humanely relocated," Miller had replied grumpily. "But if you can make the cloak without killing the critters, I'd do that too."

And that was Miller—a combination of whimsy and earnestness that Piers couldn't resist tweaking. Miller was a policeman who believed in mankind and a human barometer who pointed directly at armed and crazy and looked it in the teeth.

And still wanted to help people and armadillos.

And God, he was cute. He couldn't have been cuter if he'd had a button nose and a cleft in his chin.

"Sleep in your apartment?" Piers said now, trying to keep the pleasure out of his voice. "Not the resort?"

Miller frowned. "No," he said, and something about his voice, his expression, told Piers this wasn't the flirting invitation he'd hoped for. "There's… it's there." He shuddered again. "The armed and crazy. It's on the resort side of the island."

"Shit," Scout muttered. "Kayleigh works there!" Kayleigh, in fact, worked two jobs—one at the magic store with Scout and another in catering service at the resort. Scout, Kayleigh, Lucky, and even Miller were nice enough not to rub it in Piers's and Larissa's faces, but the fact was, they worked for a living while Piers and Larissa could both live off their trust funds indefinitely. They were very careful not to either flaunt their wealth or infringe too much on their friends' time, because they had both admitted, to each other at least, that this was the most interesting and enjoyable friend group either of them had known.

"I'll go talk to Callan—" Piers began, because he and Callan Morgenstern, heir to the resort entrepreneurs' legacy, had family associations as well as, more recently discovered, magic connections.

"No!" Miller snapped. "You will do no such thing. Call him. Don't visit."

Everybody in the room—the young Ciaran included—stared at the normally mild Miller Aldrun.

"I'm sorry?" Piers asked delicately.

"No," Miller muttered. "I'm sorry. Look, you guys, please don't ask me to explain this. I'm not even sure I can. But the crazy, as dangerous as it is, is focused on Piers and Larissa. Not Kayleigh, not Callan. Although I do get a faint buzz about Callan, as though Callan is on its radar, but *they* are in danger from it." He swallowed, hard. "Now. I... look. It's not like an average, everyday psychotic stalker."

"There's an average everyday psychotic stalker?" Scout asked, sounding as naïve as he could sometimes be.

"Yeah, Scout," Lucky retorted. "Everybody has one."

Scout blinked at him and then grimaced. "Sorry. I—"

"Grew up in a wizard's commune in the woods," Lucky said dryly. "We get it. I think what he means is that *this* stalker is like us. He's a wizard, a witch, or a mechanic—"

"Probably a mechanic," Scout murmured, and just like that he'd gone from being behind them all in knowledge to ahead of them all in intuition.

"What makes you say that?" Miller asked sharply.

"Because Piers said he killed all the plants," Scout replied. "And he did it in a very short amount of time. And he went after the cat...." Scout paused. "Cat's okay, right?"

"Yes," Piers confirmed. "Driving my father a little crazy but is also his favorite thing right now, so yeah. Cat's okay."

"Good." Scout let out a smile like sunshine. "I was worried when you told me about the cat. But see"—he suddenly went almost as earnest as Miller—"cats are magic user's friends. Witches have familiars for a reason, and very often they're cats because cats are more in tune with the magic of the earth and the wind and the seas. They're less domesticated, so a magic user with... well, all the crazy, as we've been saying, he's going to be afraid of cats. Cats will protect their people, and they'll do it ruthlessly. My brother said that when his boyfriend's house was under attack by bad magic, there were nine cats that would sit in front of the house and... and *kill* any animal that approached with bad intent. So by the end of the day, there'd be this sad little pile of enchanted mice, birds, garter snakes, lizards—all these animals that had been out to harm his boyfriend because they'd gotten caught up in the spell. And the cats just sat there and took them out. So yeah, the stalker's mechanic is probably plants, both good and bad, and the cat probably gave him hell."

Piers felt a reluctant albeit fond smile quirking at his lips. "Freddy *is* a bird-murdering asshole, but I can see how he'd be protecting Larissa when he got hurt."

Scout nodded. "So I think Miller is right on. Armed and crazy is after Larissa *exclusively* and after you because he obviously either saw you help her out or knows you were the one who got her out of North Carolina. He may know of the connection between you two and Callan, or he may intuit it, because you *are* distantly related. So we warn *everybody*—Kayleigh in particular needs warning, and so does Callan—but we keep you, Piers, and Larissa away from that end of the island in case we find out our subject is on the move."

"So what?" Piers asked, disturbed by the entire scenario. "We just *leave* her stalker there? What if he develops another fixation? What if he decides to start killing the island wildlife? What if he stubs his toe and kills all the trees—"

"What if we find him and Scout sends him to Antarctica?" Lucky interrupted before Piers could freak everybody *and* himself out with the worst-case scenarios.

"That's acceptable," Piers said, sounding surprised.

"Can we maybe arrest him before sending him to his death?" Miller asked irritably, and Piers smiled because he was thinking, "Well *duh*," but to both of their chagrin, Scout shook his head.

"Maybe, maybe not," he said, gnawing on his lower lip. Scout had run his hands through his dark curly hair until it stuck out on end, and he hadn't ceased his pace/wander around the apartment, so he looked a little less... grounded than usual when he said that.

"We're gonna ice the guy?" Lucky asked, and leave it to Lucky to lay things out that bluntly.

Scout looked at all of them blankly, as though still occupied on the etheric plane or something, before shaking himself almost like, well, a wet cat and focusing on them.

"No, I don't want to kill him, but Miller, we're going to have to look into his background. If he's slipped out of law enforcement's clutches before, we may need to do something... something a little more magically permanent with him. I... look, I have no literature to back me up here, but I do have empirical evidence. My father is batshit crazy, and I think the magic helped fuck him up. Do we all agree?"

There were some nods and some murmurs of, "Fair," before Lucky interrupted. "Yeah, but Scout, your old man's sort of drunk on his own power, you know?"

"Well, yes, but this guy may be too. Maybe his mechanic isn't only plants. Maybe he thinks Larissa smells like jasmine and it's driving him bugnuts or something. Whatever it is, I think magic *amplifies* the bad and the crazy, just like it amplifies the good. Lucky uses his mechanic to help us, but we've got a scared kid lying *right there* who can tell you that his mechanic is making all the bad guys in Philly apeshit. Am I right, Ciaran?"

They all turned to Ciaran, who had been listening to their conversation with rapt attention. The boy nodded enthusiastically, as though Scout had put a voice to all his problems, and Scout took this as leave to continue.

"So my point here is this: Whatever this guy is, and however he got this sick, and I mean that in the nicest possible way 'cause his brain is diseased, the fact is we might not be able to magically cure him. And if we can't cure him, we need to get him the hell away from people, because even if we wipe his brain and he can't remember Larissa's name or her face or whatever, you can be damned sure he latches on to the next pretty girl who's nice to him and makes her life miserable too."

There was a quiet then, which Lucky interrupted with, "Scout, you're starting to sound like you come from Philly. You tryin' to do that?"

Scout's face, which had been hardened and sharp with purpose, suddenly became the face of their dreamy magician again. "No, am I really? 'Cause that's *amazing!*" He blinked. "But you all get what I'm saying, right? We might not be able to throw this fish back into the law-enforcement pool. We might be forced to do something...." He flailed.

"Magically permanent," Miller supplied dryly, echoing Scout's words from before. "I get it. We'll have to play it by ear. But first we need to make sure he—or she, but I'm getting very male vibes here, so I'm gonna go with my gut—doesn't get to them first."

"Right," Scout said. "So yeah. Piers stays with you tonight. Larissa stays with Kayleigh, and Ciaran, you're on our couch or on Kayleigh's couch, although...." He and Lucky exchanged beleaguered glances.

"It's worse than having kids," Lucky muttered. "But yeah, Ciaran, better you stay on the boys' couch tonight while we figure out what to do with you." There was a long pause. "Which, you know, should have been the biggest part of our day, if you think about it, but no. We had a nice couple of months there, all of us, but now...."

"We've got armed and crazy," Miller confirmed.

"How depressing," Piers murmured. Armed and crazy was *not* the reason he'd wanted to get closer to the earnest, sober, and capable young Mr. Aldrun, that was for sure.

"So," Ciaran murmured, "I get you guys have other stuff to deal with—I mean, armed and crazy stalkers is bad." He blinked. "Bad-der, I guess. Than my cousin. Who was also armed and crazy. I... why did he want to kill you?" Ciaran peered at Lucky a little tearfully. "I get that he lied to me." He snorted bitterly. "But why?"

Lucky breathed out a sigh. "Because I'm like you," he said quietly, and their entire meeting was pulled back to the beginning. "I have a talent, and his gang wanted to exploit it like the last gang did, but I...." He shrugged. "I ran, kid. I refused to be killed or used. I ended up here, and you probably picked it up, but this island—it protects people like us."

Ciaran nodded. "You refused to be used." A small smile flickered across his narrow, achingly young face. "I... I'm going to make that my mantra. Refuse to be used." He swallowed and drew his knees up to his chin and then turned his head so he could rest his cheek on them. "Will the island really protect me?"

Piers, Lucky, Scout, and Miller all exchanged glances. "If it doesn't," Miller said stoutly, "we will."

Ciaran gave him a grateful smile and then looked to Scout, the way they all tended to do. "I...." He suddenly looked surprised. "I'm *hungry.* We were going to get *breakfast.*" Then his eyes, a dark green surrounded by thick black lashes, widened. "I don't even have any *money!*" he proclaimed. "Stevie had it all. I... they won't let me work. They keep me busy finding people." Suddenly he paled. "Oh God."

Lucky and Scout met eyes, and they had an *entire* conversation this time.

"Okay," Scout said, coming to a stop for the first time since he'd started pacing. "A plan. Here's the plan. I go on in—" He glanced at the microwave. "—an hour. Lucky needs to go help Helen because it's getting really busy up there and Kayleigh has to leave and Larissa isn't quite up to speed yet. Lightning, can you—"

"Bring him some food and keep him company?" Piers said, seeing very clearly where he needed to help.

"Yes." Scout gave him a grateful look. "Yes. That would be *great!* And Miller, could you—"

"Call Callan and update him on the situation so he knows what to look for?" Miller offered with a nod.

Scout grinned. "You people don't need me at all! That's fan*tastic*!" He sucked in a breath. "I need to go brief Marcus and Kayleigh and get dressed and stuff."

"And eat," Lucky supplied dryly. "Piers, if I give you some cash could you get us *all* some hamburgers and stuff from Russian Tacos and Spaghetti? I mean, I love Helen's baked goods, but...." He waved his hands.

"Protein," Piers supplied. "And I've got this one."

"Get lots," Lucky said, giving him a bill anyway. "Miller, if you could watch Ciaran here until he gets back, I'll be forever grateful."

"Can do," Miller said. "You guys go jump back into the swing of things. We won't leave him alone."

Scout paused in the act of running back up the stairs. "Thanks, guys," he said gratefully. Then to Ciaran, he said, "Look, I know you sort of fell through the looking glass. I wish I could say the pace around here will slow, but, uhm, no guarantees. Just know that if you ask any one of us, we'll take the time to explain stuff to you if we can, okay? And, you know. Nobody in this room is going to let you wander off and be alone. What happened to you wasn't your fault. Your cousin was...." He grimaced because the obvious way to finish that sentence was *not* the most sensitive.

"An asshole," Ciaran said with a sigh. "I... I should have known better than to trust him."

Scout's attention suddenly focused on the young man in that way it did when he was about to say something really wise. "We all hold out hope for the best of our family," he said softly. "Kayleigh and I waited to get booted out of a situation that was never going to get better. My brother Josue—he's still there because he keeps hoping the people he put his faith in to care for us will eventually see that they're doing it wrong. Don't kick yourself because you wanted family to be good. That's what we all want. It's a fair wish to have."

Ciaran's face opened up, and for the first time he wasn't miserable or scared or worn out. He smiled, and he was beautiful, and Piers was suddenly filled with Scout's hope for the young man.

They'd help him find his feet here in the magical corner of the world. It should be what they were here for.

Consequences of Spontaneity

"MR. MORGENSTERN?" Miller had the CEO of MorgenStar Industries on his cell phone because the man was, technically, his boss. There was no island government per se, but there was a chamber of commerce, because much of the industry was tourism, and that pretty much provided everything from medical services to trash services to, yes, police services. And Callan Morgenstern was the leader of the biggest, most contributing company of the chamber of commerce.

Callan Morgenstern was, in effect, the boss of Miller's boss, and that fortuitous meeting a couple of months ago, when Scout dragged all his friends to Callan's office to convince Callan to become part of their quest to help the magic of the island, had put Miller on Callan's radar as a friend. Miller's rather awful commander had certainly gotten off Miller's back since that day, and Miller thought his acquaintance with Callan was the reason why.

"Yes, this is young Officer Aldrun?"

Miller rolled his eyes. Callan was late thirties at the most, so the "young Officer Aldrun" was all affectation, probably so he could run his father's company without dealing with condescension.

"Yessir. Uhm, we didn't get much of a chance to talk since that meeting with Scout and Kayleigh and such, but something's come up that you need to know about. Uhm, you *specifically*, sir."

There was a pause, and Miller heard shifting, as though Callan was walking from someplace to someplace. "Understood. Give me a moment to make this phone call private."

"Yessir."

Restlessly Miller paced the little porch off the back of Lucky and Scout's apartment. The apartments were built behind and a little underneath the shops on the street, thanks to architects who had wanted to use the natural cliffside to create a windbreak for the town square. Both Lucky's apartment and Kayleigh's could be entered through stairs from the businesses above them as well as through a sliding glass door that looked out onto the main road of the island. Barely two lanes, it stemmed from the ferry dock and wound through the foliage and into the hills and glades of the lee side of the island, the side with the protected swimming coves that the rich kids and natives used. On the windward side of the island, the road cut a fairly straight line, curving only with the island's curve, keeping the public beaches and the glittering blue water always in view on the way to the resort.

The ferry and the resort seemed to be the two poles that oriented the Spinner's Drift population. There were the tourists who stayed at the resort and the natives who made a living from them, and between the constant push and pull, the island population stayed afloat.

Miller's roots in the blue-collar world of law enforcement felt appropriate for the working side of the island, while Piers's family ties on the resort side felt like just Miller's frickin' luck.

What had prompted him to offer Piers a bed?

That thought, more than any other, was worming around in the substrata of Miller's brain, and he couldn't quite get a handle on it.

It only made sense, right? That poor Ciaran kid, brought here by his unscrupulous family to do something the kid found morally repugnant, and then Scout portals his cousin into the stratosphere—they *were* responsible for the kid, and sending him back to where he came from was obviously right out.

But Miller's little state-subsidized bungalow was tiny. It had a guest room, yes, but only one bathroom and a little kitchenette. It was just so… so *humble*, when Piers Constantine had class written all over him, right down to the subtle way he kept trying to pay for groceries and takeout when they ate as a group.

Nobody took him up on it, but he gamely kept offering.

Miller wanted to pull him aside and tell him that it wasn't his *money* they wanted, but his calm reasoning, his good humor, and his compassion.

But who said that to someone as self-assured, as smooth, as Piers Constantine?

"Mr. Aldrun?"

Callan Morgenstern's voice pulled him out of his musings on Piers and back to reality.

"Yessir. I'm here. We've got a concern that you need to know about."

"We?" Callan asked delicately.

"You know—uhm, the chamber of commerce people?" Oh, that was stretching it. Helen, Lucky's boss, and Marcus, Scout and Kayleigh's, were both leaders of the chamber of commerce, but Scout and Lucky were technically just employees.

"You mean the magic people?" Callan asked bluntly, and heat washed Miller's cheeks.

"Yeah, the magic people," he said, remembering that Callan was one of them. "I'm what Scout calls a luck mechanic. I've got one talent, and it's a whopper."

"Uh-oh," Callan murmured. "Am I going to like this?"

"No," Miller replied shortly. "Armed and crazy—or dangerous and crazy. I can sense it. In particular, I can sense when it's a threat to people I know. I sensed it this morning, and Scout portaled it to wherever he does, and that got rid of *one* threat, but there's another."

Callan sucked in a breath. "Do you know where—"

"It's on your side of the island, and it's...." He thought of the queasy darkness he'd sensed and shuddered. "It's aimed at Piers, Larissa, and—peripherally—you."

Callan grunted. "Larissa's stalker?"

"I'm pretty sure, yes. I...." He thought again of going to the resort side of the island, and the wave of vertigo threatened to knock him on his ass. He held out his hand to touch the rough rock wall of the outside of the apartment and breathed deeply. "It's ugly, and it's hitting me hard. I-I can't...." He was embarrassed and ashamed by the way his voice shook.

"It's overwhelming," Callan Morgenstern supplied, his voice soft. "I've had that happen before. The gifts are... sensitive."

Miller swallowed hard against a mouthful of spit and nausea and tried to get his shit together. "You are telling me. Anyway, Piers and Larissa are going to stay on this side of the island, but we wanted to warn you and Scout's sister. Keep an eye out. Right now he's focused on Piers's cousin, but if he switches his obsession, I'm not sure I'll know."

"Understood," Callan said. "I'll keep an eye out."

Miller got the feeling Callan had his own ways, much like Scout had his, since Callan was supposedly a wizard. Well, good. Having a little magic on their side could be a useful thing. Which reminded him....

"And Scout thinks he's a mechanic. Like me."

"Really?" For the first time Callan sounded shocked. "The stalker has a gift?"

"He kills plants," Miller said, remembering this from the first time he'd heard Piers's account of the day the stalker got into Larissa's room. "Scout's heard the story too, and he thinks the dead plants weren't a conscious thing. It's like the guy's so dark inside he kills living plants just by... I don't know. Thinking dark thoughts. So that's something you and Kayleigh can look for, right? Dead plants. We've all got Larissa's description—"

"From a distance," Callan muttered, obviously disturbed, and Miller grunted in frustrated sympathy because he'd heard that description too. Larissa *had* seen her stalker, but always from a periphery. From a block away or having just rounded the corner. The staff at her house had seen him before they'd passed out, and their descriptions had been the same.

White. Midsized. Dark hair. Male.

The end.

Which reminded Miller....

"Okay, so Scout said the guy was a magic mechanic, and I think he's got more than one gift," he said, wanting to bounce this off Callan before he scared all his friends. And also knowing that Callan's laughter wouldn't hurt as much as Piers's or Scout's.

"Do I want to know?"

Miller scowled. "Of course you want to know, but you're not going to like it."

On the other end of the phone, Callan let out a harsh laugh. "You're a fun guy, Mr. Aldrun. I think we should know each other better."

Miller's eyes went wide. "Are you flirting with me? Because Piers does that too and it's very confusing," he said crossly. "Anyway, I think he's got a whammy of sorts."

"A whammy?" Callan repeated, sounding confused.

"Yes. I think he knocked the staff out with his brain power or magic or whatever. I called the police department in Charlotte and asked them how the staff had all been unconscious, and they said they thought it was some sort of gas because nobody had bruises or anything. That's what they thought killed the plants. But then I called forensics, and they had no trace evidence of gas or drugs that could explain how the staff had been knocked out."

He hadn't told Piers or Scout this, and he regretted it now. So many years of being his own oyster, of keeping things close to his chest because he *knew* nobody would believe him. Instead, he simply fed nibbles of intuition to the people who could do something, told people about "a hunch" or "a rumor" or "didn't so and so say…," and hoped they could navigate the situation on that alone. And the one time—the *one* time—he'd let his guard down, Brad had ignored him anyway.

Cassandra was a damned lonely bitch, and he was tired of walking in her shoes.

But Piers would have believed him, he thought now. He should have told Piers first. And Scout of course, but somehow, Piers was more important.

"That," Callan was saying, breaking into his self-recrimination, "that's worrisome. Does everybody else know this?"

"I was going to tell them after I got off the phone," Miller said truthfully. "There was a *lot* going on today. I mean, did I mention this isn't the only armed and crazy we've dealt with this morning?"

Callan sucked air in through his teeth. "Yikes. Okay. If you can, have Kayleigh report directly to me when she gets to the hotel. I know you said the crazy…." He paused. "Is that all we've got to call this guy?"

"Uhm… stalker?" Millar hazarded. It's what the police were calling him. "It's just that 'armed and crazy' seems *so* much more accurate."

"I'm going with stalker because I'm an adult," Callan snapped acerbically. "But fine. Have Kayleigh report directly to me. I've got some protection spells I can teach her, and maybe she can pass them on to Scout and, uhm, the hedge witches, and, uhm, you guys."

"Us little people," Miller retorted, and he heard Callan sigh.

"Please forgive me," he said, and the humility seemed real. "I'm fighting hundreds of years of patriarchal indoctrination, and sometimes I fail."

"You're forgiven," Miller said. "And I'll have her report to you first. I don't even want her going over there, but—"

"She and Scout are damned fearless," Callan filled in for him. "I've figured that out."

"Do you suppose it's because they've never lost anything?" Miller mused and then shook himself. "Either way I'll tell everybody. Uhm, Piers is going to be staying on this side of the island, and so is Larissa, but you may want to have maid service in their rooms anyway. Make it look like they live there."

"Good idea," Callan said. "Look, I've got to go, but feel free to call me if you have anything else you want to talk about." He paused again and added meaningfully. "Anything. *Anything.*"

Miller blinked. "I am not that cute," he said, stunned. "But I'll call you if we've got any idea on the armed and crazy. Gottagobye."

And then he hung up before the super rich, super blond, and handsome Callan Morgenstern could hit on him anymore, because that was uncomfortable.

He stayed put for a second, shoring himself up for the discussion with Piers and the others about what he knew about Larissa's stalker, and turned his face to the gray sky. Winter was a lot of cold rain in this part of the Atlantic, with some passes of sleet. The skies were often gray for days at a time, and now an icy wind came off the salt bitter sea, and he closed his eyes and allowed himself to taste it.

You didn't get this sort of wildness in New Jersey, and he loved it. Every now and then he thought about going back to his old beat, his old precinct. He still had contacts there who remembered he'd been about to be promoted to detective and wanted him back. But then there was this…. Yeah, sure, he had to worry about armadillos and drunk crafters, and that one island that was sort of a permanent knitting orgy, but then there was this… open skies and fierce winds and waves that carried life and death in their brine.

So much mundanity could be overlooked when there was this promise of mystery and purpose in every gust of wind.

"You get hold of him?"

Miller's eyes flew open at the sound of Piers's voice, and he frowned, realizing that Piers had come in through the patio gate that lined the road. There were bags of burritos and burgers in his arms, and Miller hurried forward to help him so he could make it to the sliding glass door.

"So did you?" Piers asked again as Miller opened the door for him and followed him in with his load of the food.

"Get hold of Callan?" Miller clarified, keeping his voice low. Ciaran, poor kid, was still in Scout and Lucky's bed, and it looked like he was fast asleep. Everybody else had left when Piers had.

"Yeah. What'd he say?"

Miller grimaced. "He said to have Kayleigh come talk to him when she got to the resort to work. Apparently the wizards are going to come up with some protection spells, and the rest of us peons can wait for them to figure it out."

Piers grunted as he set his bag down on the counter. "Did he really say that?" he asked curiously. "Or do you have a chip on your shoulder? Because I'm saying, that does *not* sound like the guy we talked into literally moving a grave to help ghosts a couple of months ago."

"He's moving the grave in a couple weeks," Miller clarified sullenly.

"Yes, but he was really excited about doing it," Piers replied, keeping his own voice patient. "So, you know, maybe tell me what he said without editorializing."

Miller scowled at him, not wanting Piers to be the voice of reason. He was so unfairly attractive—tall, broad shouldered, gold-skinned, with that aristocratic nose and almond-shaped brown eyes. And cheekbones— gah! To die for. Miller had never realized that rich-boys' cheekbones could be a kink until he'd met Piers Constantine.

Piers regarded him calmly back, because apparently that calm good nature was his *real* superpower and the thing he did with lights was just an anomaly, and Miller gave in.

It was hard to stay mad at Piers.

"He said to make sure Kayleigh stopped by so they could make plans," he rephrased reluctantly. "And he said I should tell you about what I learned from my contacts at my old precinct about the break-in that spooked you both," he added. And then, for reasons he could not define, not in a thousand years, he finished with, "And I think he hit on me."

Piers had been reaching into the bag he'd set on the counter, and he almost fumbled a hamburger onto the floor. He caught it just in time and set it nicely on the counter next to the bag before glaring at Miller.

"What?" Miller asked, shifting uncomfortably with the bag still in his arms.

"Set that on the counter," Piers instructed. "And repeat that part about Callan hitting on you again?"

"I was probably mistaken," Miller muttered, but he did what Piers told him to. "I'm not used to having rich people pay attention to me. It's weird and… and…."

"Disconcerting?" Piers asked, his tone still sharp. "Because you've been 'disconcerted' around *me* for weeks, so I've barely even flirted with you so I didn't scare you off. And now you're telling me Callan hit on you?"

Miller screwed his eyes shut and tried to find a good answer. "He probably didn't mean it," he said finally, but his voice rose on the final word, so it sounded more like a question, and he realized that yes, Callan probably *had* meant it.

"Miller?" Piers said, his tone still enough to make Miller open his eyes.

"Yes?"

"Look, we're in the middle of some weird shit right now, so I'm going to say this very clearly so you don't forget or get confused or whatever. I've. Got. Dibs."

Miller scowled at him. "The hell?"

"Yes, I know it sounds juvenile, but I've been very patient here. I don't care how rich and polished Callan Morgenstern is, I've been trying to get you to talk to me for *two months*. So please do not go falling in love with Prince Callan when Peasant Piers is right in front of you."

"You're an archduke if you're breathing," Miller snapped back, not even sure how this conversation was part of his life. "And you're both toying with the dumb flatfoot who sort of wandered into your orbit. I mean, I like hanging out with you guys, and you've been really nice to the stupid cop who stumbled on your little secret, but I get it. You, your cousin, you come play Scooby Doo here on the island, and when this is all over, you go back to school to become the part of the legal system with the good suits and the nice house in the suburbs. And me? I'm still in my tiny cop apartment, grateful I've got a job somewhere you can't smell garbage burning twenty-four seven."

Piers tilted his head, as though Miller was speaking another language.

"Do you really think that about us?" he asked, and Miller couldn't escape the tinge of hurt in his voice.

Oh no, Miller thought wretchedly. No. No hurt feelings. That wasn't how this was supposed to go!

"I think," Miller said carefully, "that the only thing special about me is the ability to predict crime. If this wasn't a *very* small island, you and Callan Morgenstern would have more important things to do."

Piers's expression cleared up, became pitying, and suddenly Miller *wished* he was the kind of person who could hurt others at his own pride's expense.

"Miller, you're… you're fun. You curse out armadillos while you're shipping them to safety. You got my joke about the island's name without even blinking. You're funny, you're competent, you're kind, and you're not hard on the eyes. Why... why would you think you're not worth hitting on?"

Miller stared at him. "I'm not sex on legs in two-hundred-dollar deck shoes, Piers. I...." He flailed for a minute, and then, as Piers straightened up from his concerned hunch, Miller caught the almost enchanted gleam in his eyes.

"You think I'm sex on legs?" he almost purred.

Miller did everything but scramble back against the sliding glass door like a cat. He said very distinctly, "I have made mistakes," as Piers slid toward him, those long legs eating up ground while Miller tried to find his way with his shoulders alone.

It didn't matter. The hanging blinds clattered behind him as Miller backed into them. They clattered again as Piers flattened a palm on either side of Miller's shoulders, staring down at Miller from that imposing height and pinning him with those warm brown eyes.

"I'm not going to hurt you," Piers breathed, close enough for Miller to smell a little bit of coffee and a little bit of mint on his breath. "I'm not going to force you or coerce you or even urge you. I'm just going to ask you a question, and then I'll let you go."

Miller took a deep breath and realized—oh hells—that their chests brushed when he did that. The next breath was considerably harder.

"What?" Miller asked, his stomach shaking in anticipation. Not going to force him? If they were both lucky, Miller would keep himself from raising his head and capturing Piers's mouth with his own before he enacted some of his most cherished fantasies on Piers's lean, muscular body.

"Do you...." Piers paused and traced his lips along Miller's temple. "Think I'm...." He moved and traced the other side, fluttering little touches over Miller's now-closed eyes. His mouth—full and sensual—settled near Miller's ear as he finished the question. "Sexy?" he whispered. "You've put me off for months, Miller. All of that, and I just want to know if you think I'm sexy."

Miller's groin had started to ache with the first touch of Piers's lips against his skin. His stomach quaked, his chest was melting and taking his bones with it, and he had nothing in him but the truth.

"Oh dear God, yes," he whispered back.

Piers's mouth on his was warm and sweet, better than a cupcake or hot chocolate, fulfilling in ways Miller hadn't known it could be. He sighed a little and let the door support some of his weight as he opened his mouth and drank in the kiss, letting it sustain him, letting himself respond. Oh God. It had been so long since he'd been kissed, so long since he'd been warmed by another man's body. And this wasn't just any kiss! Piers Constantine had apparently been taking classes in kissing. His mouth was warm, coaxing without overwhelming, sweet without cloying—every rub of his lips, ply of his tongue, was designed to make Miller hungrier.

Miller twined his arms around Piers's neck and pulled him closer, wanting more, and Piers reached behind Miller and kneaded firmly at Miller's backside, urging him to move closer, to arch against Piers as the ache in his groin blossomed, flowered, grew wide and ravenous with need.

Miller made a sound of confusion, and Piers pulled away with obvious reluctance.

"What?" he whispered, once again in Miller's ear.

"This isn't private," Miller mumbled, not sure how he could remember that but suddenly very much aware. Miller moaned softly as Piers drew away, and he tried to stand up straight instead of sagging limply in his arms. He could barely look at Piers, embarrassed by his response to a simple kiss and by his prudishness and… gah!

Piers's strong fingers under his chin provided his only incentive to look Piers in the eyes.

"What?" he asked defensively, noting that Piers had a wicked smile on his face.

"You want me," he said simply, giving a little shrug.

"Of course I do," Miller muttered. He tried to look away, but Piers kept that pressure on his chin. "You're very easy on the eyes," he said defensively. "I never said you—"

Piers kissed him again, this time short and hard, and when he pulled back, he eyed Miller with what was obviously exasperation. "Why is it so hard to admit you like this?" he asked.

Miller let out a sigh and closed his eyes. "It never ends well for Cassandra, Lightning," he said with a little wobble in his voice. "I thought you had a liberal-studies education."

Piers pulled back and cocked his head, those warm, sexy, *intelligent* eyes suddenly sharp with questions. There was a clatter on the stairs behind them, but Piers didn't step away immediately. "I'll be staying at your flat tonight," he said decisively, as though it hadn't been Miller's cockamamy idea in the first place. "And you're going to explain that to me, and we're going to have this out. Do you understand?"

"Oh my God!" Kayleigh all but squealed. "Somebody went to Russian Tacos and Spaghetti!" Of course the running gag about the name of the place was that mostly they sold burritos and burgers.

Finally Piers stepped away, before Kayleigh could switch her laser-eyed gaze from the food bags on the counter to Piers and Miller in front of the patio door, and Miller breathed a sigh of relief.

Kayleigh rifled through the bag first and grabbed a carne asada burrito, practically moaning in delight. "Excuse me while I eat this over the sink," she said. "I didn't get any breakfast, and this is going to hold me over till dinner. I'm due on the other side of the island in half an hour!" She was dressed in her resort uniform—khaki pants, a white polo shirt, and a shell-pink hoodie with the resort logo stitched on the pocket.

Looking at her, Miller had a sudden vision—an odd one. It was bland, off kilter. Kayleigh, but not Kayleigh as a person with brown hair and brown eyes, but Kayleigh as a... a construct. Hair a blur of chocolate brown, eyes simply dark spots in a beige face. It was like a cartoon version of a character that wasn't developed. A stage piece, not Scout Quintero's very powerful sister.

"Whoa, Miller!" Piers cried, his alarm coming from far away. He placed his hand on Miller's elbow and steered him toward one of the stuffed chairs grouped around the TV in the corner.

"Miller, what's up?" Kayleigh asked from a full mouth. "Piers, he looks super pale. What happened?"

"Get him a soda for me, Kayleigh," Piers directed, with that casual authority that Miller had needed to work for once he'd made the force. While Miller sat down, blinking hard to keep the world in focus, Piers knelt in front of him, taking Miller's rough, saltwater-chapped hands in his own long, elegant fingers and rubbing his wrists. "Miller, are you with me?"

"Kayleigh's safe," Miller murmured, not sure when this had become such a big, frightening proposition for him but suddenly so relieved he felt tears burning in the backs of his eyes. "He doesn't see her. Not as a person. It's...." He swallowed, and suddenly Piers had a basic cold and frosty Coke to his lips, and he drank it down like a jonesing addict. Piers pulled it away and wiped Miller's chin with a napkin, and Miller opened his mouth to finish his thought and belched instead.

Piers's laughter was warm and kind, and Miller's throat thickened with reaction.

"I am not myself today," he muttered, taking a deep breath. "Here, Piers. Let me finish that off—it's helping." He drained the soda in a few quick gulps, sense, time, and place flooding back to him with every swallow. When he was done, he held his hand in front of his mouth politely and let out the gas before taking the napkin from Piers's hand and wiping his mouth like a grown-up.

When he looked around again, he saw Kayleigh sitting in the chair next to him, eating her burrito over a plate, and Piers still kneeling, clasping his free hand in his own.

"Better?" Kayleigh asked kindly. "It was scary there for a minute. I was going to fetch Scout, but you started to perk up."

Miller nodded. "I-I saw you, and then... I saw you as the stalker saw you. And you weren't *human* to him. You were background noise. But that doesn't make sense," he muttered. "How does that make sense?"

"What do you mean?" Kayleigh said. "It's my understanding that you woke up this morning and knew he was coming—"

"I knew two threats were coming," Miller said, his head hurting. "And one of them Scout took care of, but if this guy... if the vision I saw was how this guy sees you, that means *he's already seen you*. Where were you this morning?"

They all took a deep breath and stared at each other.

"Kayleigh," Piers said carefully. "Where were you just now? Where did you come from?"

"The coffee shop," Kayleigh murmured. "Just now. But...." She frowned. "I had to run to the resort super early this morning. I took the bicycle. We got voluntary extra hours for helping with the decorations for Christmas, and I had to go pick up my check."

Miller was almost light-headed again with relief.

"So he saw you in your uniform this morning, and I got a flash of *how* he saw you," Miller muttered. "And because his brain is just... off, it really sort of—"

"Fucked with you," Piers muttered. "Oh, I do not like this. What happens if he realizes you're getting brain flashes?"

"Wait," Kayleigh interrupted. "You mean he's *here*? On the island? The guy who's got Larissa terrified—he's here?"

Miller squeezed his eyes shut and remembered that Kayleigh hadn't been downstairs that morning after Scout had magicked Stevie Shanahan to upstate New York, or wherever he sent his unwanted guests, but he had heard her voice as they were dealing with poor Ciaran, after he'd passed out.

"Larissa and I were helping because Lucky bugged out," Kayleigh was saying, "and then Larissa went in back to do dishes and Lucky went upstairs to take over for me. I worked for a couple of orders and then ran down here."

There was another clatter on the staircase into Lucky's flat, and Piers and Kayleigh leapt to their feet.

Larissa was running downstairs, adorable and charming with her chestnut hair pulled back into a curling ponytail and her little freckled button nose squinched up in excitement.

"Russian Tacos?" she asked, her excitement for the food run palpable. "Right? That's what Lucky said when he came back to the dishwasher." She paused at the bottom of the stairway and stared at the three of them. "Why are you all looking at me?"

Miller closed his eyes for a moment and took a breath.

Nothing. He got nothing. It confirmed his hypothesis that the stalker had seen Kayleigh at the far end of the island and didn't know Larissa was here. Good. *Great.* Piers and Larissa were both safe for the time being.

"Nothing," he said, looking at Kayleigh and Piers. "Grab your burrito and come sit on the couch, and, uhm, don't wake the new guy."

"Too late," Ciaran said from the bed. He yawned and sat up. "I've pretty much been awake since you guys kissed. That was hot, by the way—is there always a show?"

"Wait," Larissa blurted. "Piers finally kissed Miller? Fan*tastic.* I mean seriously, Piers, it took you long enough."

To Miller's immense satisfaction, *Piers* blushed. "We're not going to talk about that," he said, a certain grim cant to his mouth. "But we *are* going to tell you what we've figured out about the stalker, because it's *really* important."

Larissa rolled her eyes and rifled through the food. "Borscht Burger, extra pickles, extra bleu cheese," she said with a little hum of happiness. "You *do* love me, Piers."

"My favorite relative," he replied, fondness in his voice. "Now come sit down so we can talk about how to keep you safe before Kayleigh takes off. Ciaran, there's a plain burger, a vegan burger, and a carne asada burrito in there that have nobody's names on them. Choose your food."

"Carne asada burrito?" Ciaran said hopefully, standing up and stretching. "Can I come sit on the couch like a grown-up?"

Miller estimated the boy to be around twenty. "Feel free," he said. "Although technically not our couch."

Ciaran let out a low laugh, and while Miller was not attracted— certainly not the way he was to Piers—he could suddenly see that the boy, with his sweeping fall of dark hair and large, haunted green eyes against pale skin could *be* attractive. In his peripheral vision, he saw Kayleigh and Larissa exchange glances and raised eyebrows.

Piers did too.

"Hands off, girls. I don't think you're his type," Piers said, voice rumbling.

Ciaran looked over his shoulder, and that brooding goth-boy image was temporarily ruined by his bashful smile.

"Uhm, no. Gay as an Easter Parade."

Kayleigh scowled. "You know, Scout keeps talking about how this island protects those who need shelter. I'm starting to think there's other criteria involved here."

Piers chuckled. "Well, given that the heart of the island's protection seems to rest with Henry Corey and Tom Marbury, maybe the island has a soft spot for us, but it seems to like you and Larissa too."

Kayleigh grunted. "Since it's gotten me out of an arranged marriage I was *really* not looking forward to, I'll agree with that." She smiled prettily. "Besides, there are a couple of bartenders who are looking *very* promising right now—"

Piers and Miller both cleared their throats meaningfully.

"—whom I will most certainly not encourage until we know who Larissa's stalker is," Kayleigh told them dutifully.

"You need to visit Callan when you go in today," Miller told her, glad to get this off his chest. "He says he's got some ideas for how you guys can keep Larissa and Piers safe. Piers is on his radar too, and honestly, so's Callan. So, you know, anything Callan can give you."

Kayleigh nodded. "Good thinking. I mean, it's weird having a direct line to the boss, but I'll take all the help I can get." She sighed. "Too bad he's as gay as the rest of you. I mean, that could have been the best arranged marriage in *history*."

"If it's any consolation," Piers said, a smug smile on his face, "he would have snapped your brother up in a heartbeat."

Kayleigh rolled her eyes. "Scout does that to everyone," she said. "Girls, guys—I think it's… you know. Special Scout magic. That way he has of seeing you at the same time he's seeing a thousand other things. The only person who can make Scout *only* see him is Lucky. Hence the name." She shrugged.

Piers *hmm*ed, probably because it was true. Miller himself had harbored a mild-stage crush on Scout to begin with, and then he'd seen that Scout and his friends were offering so much more than a few hours of pleasure. They were offering *community*, and that was something Miller had *never* had, not down to their toes the way Scout and Kayleigh offered it. And it wasn't that they were all soft and squishy. Kayleigh, at least, could fry the tail off a jackrabbit on the far side of any island in the Drift—and she would, too, if she thought the jackrabbit threatened her brother. Scout was surprisingly cold-blooded about things that threatened the peace in their little corner of the world. But once you were in Scout's orbit, well, you were *in*, as Ciaran had discovered when he'd awakened in the apartment that morning.

"I think Callan's fickle," Miller muttered. "And he likes to play."

Kayleigh finished her burrito, letting out a little sigh of happiness as it went down, then gave Miller a shrewd look. "You know, that is not the impression the staff has of him at all. You'd think they'd be all aflutter about him bringing in boy toys and stuff, but apparently he's had a few long-term, low-key relationships in the past five years since he's taken over, and even the maids who tend his rooms are closemouthed about them. And not out of fear or NDAs or anything. They were like, 'He's a sweet boy, and his business is his business,' so I'm guessing there's no ayahuasca ragers in his suites, you know? What gave you the idea Callan's a player?"

"Nothing," Miller mumbled, now completely mortified.

"Callan hit on him," Piers said, voice surprisingly sharp. "If you get a chance, please tell him not to do that. Look at Miller. He's been flustered and defensive ever since the phone call."

"Piers...." Oh God. Miller would never be smooth, but it would be *great* if he didn't have to be the damsel in distress either.

"Are you sure that's not the kiss?" Ciaran asked, his eyes narrowed just enough to tell Miller he had a little bit of the devil in him when he felt safe.

"The kiss is our business," Piers said primly. "But I would appreciate it if Callan found another pond to fish in, if that's okay."

"Nope," Kayleigh said decisively as she stood and took her trash to the kitchen. "I'm not touching this with a barge pole. I'm going to go visit the boss of the entire island and ask him how to protect my friends and myself, and I absolutely refuse to tell him that you called dibs on Miller."

Miller struggled with his tongue. "Would you people quit saying that?"

Piers leveled a look directly at him. "Dibs," he said with no obvious compunction or hesitation.

Miller could feel his face heat, and he apparently lost control of his tongue.

"So what do *I* do?" Larissa asked plaintively, and *that* Miller could answer.

"Nothing without one of us," he replied promptly. "Don't walk across the quad alone. Don't go from here to Kayleigh's apartment alone. Stay with somebody—me, Piers, Scout, Lucky, Kayleigh—"

"Marcus or Helen?" Larissa asked anxiously. "Because I was thinking, they've got all sorts of protective spells at their cottage. They've offered before, but I'm thinking...." She bit her lip, looking worried. "I'm not stupid," she said after a moment. "This guy almost killed my cat, and I know that sort of thing escalates, and he's scary. I know Kayleigh could probably break him like a twig over her knee, but my only talent is refillable soda—"

"We love that talent," Kayleigh said staunchly, going to kiss her on the forehead. "But I'm glad you're taking this seriously. I've got to run, but it will make me feel better if I know you're going to be safe."

"Thanks, Kayleigh," Larissa murmured, so much gratitude in her voice Miller wanted to wrap the poor thing in Bubble Wrap and a cedar chest to keep her safe. He could hear it in her voice—Larissa needed the community as much as Miller did, and she trusted in it like he was beginning to. Which reminded him....

"Shit," he muttered, aware that Piers had raised a sardonic eyebrow. "Kayleigh, look, I told Callan this, but you need to know too—Scout and Lucky think he can kill plants and maybe whammied the staff so they'd be unconscious while he was there. I tapped some sources in Charlotte, and they haven't found any traces of gas or chemicals or drugs, and I think Scout and Lucky are right. Just... you know. Be on your guard even more."

She scowled at him playfully. "You're a real buzzkill, you know that? By the way, after I walk out this door, could you guys maybe play with the divining tops so you can, I dunno, make sure I'm not walking into his room? I'm not stupid either, and what none of us is saying is that he probably looks like a very average, possibly cute and interesting guy. He can pass for not crazy, if you know what I'm saying. So I'd love to know if I end up cleaning his room, right?"

Miller's eyes widened, and his hand went immediately to his pocket, where the tiny divining top had gone after Scout and Lucky left.

"Good idea," he said weakly, wondering when the whole world had gotten better at his job than he was. "We'll do that after you leave."

"Then text me," she said. "And I'm grateful. You all stay safe!" And then Scout's irrepressible and terrifying sister was gone.

Miller let out a sigh as she left and then jumped a little, pulling his phone out of his pocket as he did so. "Fuck." Oh God, had he really just sworn in front of Piers's impressionable young cousin and that kid he didn't even know yet? "I'm sorry. I mean shoot. Guys, I actually work today. This is dispatch, and there's a disturbance on Knitter's Orgy Island—"

"Wait, is that a real place?" Ciaran asked, sounding *really* excited, and Larissa shook her head.

"They're nudists in the summer, and, well, I suspect they don't have a lot of sexual boundaries inside relationships, but most of their sex happens inside cabins. But the island is private, and they don't like to be disturbed." Larissa grimaced. "Which is too bad because once Miller told us about it and called it Knitter's Orgy Island instead of—what is it really, Miller?"

Miller had stood and collected his bicycle helmet and windbreaker, which he'd left near the foot of the stairs. "Tatter's Tot," he said, shrugging into his jacket.

"Yeah, Tater Tot—"

"Tatter's Tot," Piers corrected. "It's a kind of needlework. Larissa, you do sense a theme, don't you?"

She looked blank for a moment. "Oh my God. I feel so dumb."

Miller suppressed a chuckle, and he inadvertently caught Piers's gaze, both of them twinkling for a moment at Larissa's confusion.

The buzz in his pocket pulled him back to himself, and Miller turned to them. "You guys, I don't want to leave you here. Please, Larissa, Ciaran, Piers, you stay safe here until the others come back—"

Piers crossed his arms and glared at him before glancing pointedly from wall to wall, indicating the smallness of the apartment, and Miller sighed.

"Don't go anywhere alone," he tried again. "Any of you. Piers, I'll be back to get you later on this evening. You guys keep in touch, okay?"

Piers's shoulders relaxed, and he nodded. "We can do that. I thought I'd take them out to Tom's bench. Given Ciaran's relative strength, I thought Scout might want to know how much he sees."

"Tom's bench?" Ciaran asked, looking interested.

"It's sort of a local landmark," Miller said uneasily. "It's, uhm… well, like us, really."

"Magic," Larissa said smugly. Her face fell. "Except I can't see much because I'm only a little magical."

Ciaran smiled at her, and Miller was struck by the expression on his peaked face. He'd had a nasty revelation, and he'd pretty much been stranded here on this island with strangers, but looking at Piers's adorable, innocent cousin, Miller could see he was charmed.

It took a lot of kindness—a lot of wonder—to be charmed after a day like the one Ciaran Shanahan had endured.

"Maybe you're a lot magical," Ciaran said. "Sometimes you just don't know what kind of magic you have until somebody else sees it in you."

Okay. Miller felt a little better leaving them all on their own. "Maybe you can go watch Scout perform," he offered. "I think he'd love to see you all in the crowd."

Piers gave him a flat look. "Don't worry, Miller. We'll all be alive and well when you get back. You and I still have to talk."

Ciaran snorted. "If that's what the kids are calling it these days!"

And that was it. Miller absolutely had to leave before he found himself stuck there in Scout and Lucky's tiny flat, forced to talk about his feelings until he said something honest.

Without another word he ran up the stairs to the coffee shop, hoping he'd remembered to lock his bicycle.

Afternoon Blues

"I'VE GOT to know," Ciaran said after Miller's unceremonious retreat. "Pretty, pretty girl, what *is* your talent?"

Piers glanced at him and smiled and tried not to fixate on how he apparently had Miller Aldrun on the run. That wasn't actually how he *wanted* Miller. He *wanted* Miller all sweet and passionate in his arms like he had been after their kiss. Needy, yes. Terrified, not so much.

But Miller was off to Knitter's Orgy Island—or Tatter's Tot, but Piers didn't think that second one was going to stick—and Piers had one job, and it was the one he'd shown up on the island for in the first place.

Keep his cousin safe. Now that apparently extended to the sweet young man who'd been betrayed and, well, left in their care was the best way to describe it. Yeah. He'd go with that one, since Ciaran's cousin was apparently a user and abuser and possibly a murderer. Ciaran had been left in their care.

And now he was reaching out to make friends with Larissa, and she was responding by rolling her eyes self-consciously. "Never-ending beverages of choice," she said with a snort. "It's total weak sauce. If I like you and I'm in your house, you will never run out of the thing you like most to drink."

Piers looked at her quizzically. "If you like someone? I didn't realize that was a caveat."

Larissa wrinkled her nose. "Remember Grandma Klaus? How her favorite drink was orange Fanta and she was always running out?"

Piers blinked, remembering their least favorite relative as children. They'd *bonded* at Grandma Klaus's house, because both of them had hidden from the old woman in her late husband's library—the one place she'd be least likely to visit.

"I thought you drank it," he said blankly.

She made a face. "God no. I think I just made it go away."

Piers started to laugh, and then Larissa laughed too, and he found he was covering his mouth to keep the giggles from coming. He stood so he wouldn't dissolve into giggles, because Larissa really *was* a damned delight, and went to get his own food from the bags he'd brought.

He grabbed the mushroom swiss burger and suddenly swore.

"What's wrong?" Larissa asked, and it sounded like the giggles had gone from her voice.

"Miller didn't eat. He probably didn't eat breakfast either. Dammit, I should have made sure he took his burrito with him."

"Is he off the island yet?" Larissa asked, and then she paused. "Wait—we can see!"

She popped up off the couch, ran to the counter where Piers had left the food, and unfolded one of the three well-worn maps that Scout had left there.

This one was an artisan map sold at a local souvenir store, a print made from a local artist's sketch, with little icons drawn illustrating the island's names. With a smirk, Piers recognized the little tatting needle and the delicate lace that gave Tatter's Tot its name, and he pulled out his tiny top, thinking hard about Miller Aldrun, his wide hazel eyes, his incredible earnestness, and the complete surrender he'd fought with every kiss.

Then he spun the top and let it hop on the map.

It went directly to the boat launch of Spinner's Drift and began to move toward Tatter's Tot at a steady speed.

"Well, so much for getting him his burrito," Piers murmured, "but I've got to say, this is a nice little trick!"

Ciaran stood from the couch and came to join them, watching the top spin appreciatively.

"Neat!" he said, some of the sadness and stress falling from his pointed features. "Do someone else."

"Okay, then," Larissa murmured. "Kayleigh!" With that she took out *her* top—and Piers could definitely tell the difference, thinking that the one he'd pulled from *his* pocket was a little darker, a little heavier, and Larissa's was made with a lighter wood, or at least a lighter grain, with a slightly more curved spindle and a decidedly feminine flared base.

Unerringly, the top found the road around the island and moved at a steady pace toward the space clearly marked Morgen Star Resort.

"She must have the bicycle," Larissa said. "She's going pretty fast."

"Oh wow," Ciaran murmured. "Who else can it do?"

Piers and Larissa met eyes, and suddenly Larissa shuddered and looked away. "I…. Piers, I can't. I-I'm afraid if I even think about him while I'm doing this, he'll know where I am right *now*."

Piers shuddered, and he was about to volunteer to do it himself, but he remembered Miller's words about how the stalker felt a connection to Larissa—and a smaller one to Piers.

"It's not out of the realm of possibility," he muttered, his throat suddenly rusty and his hands cold. "I think we shouldn't look for him magically without Scout to protect us."

That sucked to say: he really hated being helpless like this, but the fact was, Scout and Kayleigh had the big guns, magically speaking. He and Larissa were small potatoes.

Ciaran grunted. "I wonder if we could figure out where my cousin went." He grimaced at them both. "It was nice for a few months there," he said softly. "I thought he needed me. You know, for something not awful. I knew… I knew he wasn't a great guy generally, but when he was nice to *me* it was sort of good." He finished off with a sad little shrug, and Piers realized the kid was going to have a lot more damage that a burrito and a nap *couldn't* fix.

"I get it, kid," Piers said, trying hard to listen, to see, which were two skills he'd learned from Larissa because nobody in her family ever gave her the same courtesy, and she'd been…. God. Such a delight. Curious and funny, kind and smart. They could laugh about anything—*anything*—even their vicious grandmother, who delighted in telling their families that those two kids hadn't been worth having.

"No, you—"

"Your family treats you like an embarrassment," Piers said bluntly. "And it wasn't anything you did. It was… I don't know. The order of your birth. Something you said as a kid that told them you weren't quite like everyone else in the family. Maybe you read too much or read the wrong books or—" He shot Larissa a compassionate look. "—*you* were the one who was always around when the orange Fanta ran out. But somewhere in there you got the label as the kid everybody could blame. And for an entire, what? Three months?"

"Six," Ciaran said faintly.

"For half a year, you were suddenly the bee's knees. Everybody thought what made you weird suddenly made you great. And these were the people you were *supposed* to love. The ones who were *supposed* to love you, and for a little while, you thought the world made sense and you belonged in it, didn't you?"

Ciaran nodded, and Piers watched a fat teardrop run down his nose. He looked to Larissa in a panic, and she produced a clean paper towel, which he passed to their new friend.

"Here," he said gently.

"Thanks," Ciaran murmured. "So yeah, I guess you do get it."

Piers shrugged. "Did you *want* to see our friend gunned down in cold blood?"

Ciaran shook his head adamantly. "I was so scared," he confessed. "And it was like suddenly he wasn't my cousin. Suddenly he was—"

"A monster," Larissa murmured.

"Yeah," Ciaran admitted.

"Well, let's see where the monster is," Piers told him. With that he scooped up the still spinning top that had been following Miller's path in the skiff toward Tatter's Tot and touched it, allowing his fingers to find the curves and points of the well-crafted object. "Okay, little friend," he said softly, cupping it in his palm again. "This won't be nearly so pleasant, but Ciaran here would like to know where his cousin is."

The top started spinning in the crease of his palm, and Piers gave a startled "Oh!" as Larissa scrambled to get a map of the world from the pile of maps Scout had left and spread it out over the counter.

The little point was really digging in, so Piers held his palm out over the new map and let the top jump onto the paper.

Where it promptly raced over the ocean and then over the land until it found the northernmost province in Canada.

"Nun-a-vut...," Larissa sounded out. She blinked and pulled out her phone, typing quickly.

"What are you—"

"The temperature in Nunavut, Canada, is currently minus forty degrees," she said, and then clapped her hand over her mouth. "That's... I mean, I shouldn't laugh. Your cousin could freeze to death. He was wearing cargo pants and a sweatshirt!"

Ciaran clapped his own hand over his mouth. "Serves him right," he said, caught between alarm and laughter.

Piers tried to digest that. "So, uhm, do you think he'll chill out?"

Larissa and Ciaran looked at him in horror. "That's...," Ciaran sputtered.

"Piers!"

"That's terrible!" Ciaran finished, but then he giggled, and Larissa did too. Piers didn't join the general merriment, but he did text Scout, because he thought Scout might want to know that apparently when he was aiming for Upstate New York, he went a little bit... north.

Nunavut? came the reply. *Wow. I... uhm, may have been a bit upset.*

Well, he was aiming a gun at Lucky.

Yes. Should I call someone? Tell them where he is?

Let me ask Ciaran.

Piers smiled bemusedly, thinking about what a good person Scout was. *Piers* certainly wouldn't have obsessed about Stevie Shanahan's health.

"Ciaran?" Piers said, interrupting their giggles but not, oddly enough, the spinning tops.

"Yes?" Ciaran asked.

"Should we... I don't know. Call someone about your cousin? Does he have money? A passport? His phone?"

Ciaran blinked. "All of the above," he said after a moment, and then he grimaced. "They wouldn't let me have a phone," he said, his voice small. "Told me I had to work in the family business to earn a phone. I, uh, think they just didn't want me to know the family business was mostly drugs and prostitution."

"What did they tell you it was?" Larissa asked, looking properly shocked.

"Nunyo," Ciaran replied, eyes narrowed.

"As in 'nunyobusiness'?" Piers asked to make sure.

"Yeah." Ciaran nodded. "I was... see, my parents died when I was in middle school, and I was... I don't know. Family. Stevie's actually my cousin. But my mom had run away from Philly to marry my dad, so...."

And Piers got it. "You were the family burden," he said, voice laced with compassion. "Until they found out that you could find things. And in the meantime?"

"Went to school, kept my head down, and listened when my peers talked about the Shanahan gang," Ciaran confirmed with a sad little shrug.

"I'm sorry," Larissa said, putting a hand on his wrist. "That sucks. And your cousin sounds like a real douchebag."

Ciaran's lips twitched. "All things considered, I think Nunavut, Canada, is probably the best place for him. I, uh, hope he doesn't do too much damage there."

"Then we'll leave him there," Piers decided, and a part of him was a little bit appalled because it was such a big decision to make about another human being.

But most of him was pretty okay about the guy with the gun not being a threat to the people he cared about.

"Who should we do next?" Larissa asked, scooping the incriminating little top up off the map.

"Ooh," Piers replied playfully. "The people we can check up on."

Larissa blew out a raspberry. "Want to see what my brothers are doing?"

"You mean they're not curing cancer, solving world hunger, and negotiating peace in the Middle East?" Piers asked acerbically. Larissa's brothers were decent enough guys, but he really thought Larissa's parents had missed out by dismissing her because she was a girl.

"Let's see. What's my brother Kyle doing?" And then she spun her top on the map.

The top found a little city in Kentucky to sit on, and Piers squinted to read it. "Promise Town, Kentucky?"

Larissa gasped. "Oh my God!"

"What?" Piers asked, suddenly intrigued.

"That's... well, his best friend came out in their freshman year of college, and his parents pulled his college money, and he moved to Promise Town because it's sort of... well, it's sort of an LGBTQ haven in the middle of, you know, Kentucky. And Kyle told my parents that he had nothing to do with Chaz, but...."

She and Piers locked gazes, and Piers said, "No."

"Oh my God, *yes*. Yes! Wait until Mom and Dad find out!"

Piers looked at her severely. "You can't tell them."

Larissa rolled her eyes. "Of course not. But I have to say, it sure is nice having that secret. The next time he asks me if I'm majoring in fashion, I can ask him when he was last in Promise Town."

Piers smirked. Larissa's interest in science and mathematics had been a long-standing bone of contention between of her and her parents, who didn't think she could find a husband that way.

Then Larissa sighed. "But… but now that I know this sad secret about one brother, I don't think I want to know any others. And apologies to Kayleigh, but I really don't want to use the top for the stalker. I think you're totally right about that, Piers, and we don't need to make the connection for him. But, you know, that leaves the question. What are we going to do?"

Piers smiled slightly and glanced at Ciaran. "Want to go be a tourist?" he asked. "Do the touristy things? Scout's act starts in fifteen minutes. Larissa and I go sometimes to be the shill—you know, the guy the magician calls from the audience who pretends they don't know how the magic is done?"

Ciaran smiled a little. "I, uh, have never seen a magic show."

"Then that's what we'll do," Piers announced, folding the maps. "We'll go get some super awesome coffee drinks from Helen and Lucky and watch Scout's magic show and introduce you to the tourist side of Spinner's Drift."

"Watch the ferry come in," Larissa said excitedly—she really loved to people-watch.

"Absolutely."

"And visit Tom's bench," she added, and Piers agreed, mostly.

"Sure."

"What's wrong?" she asked. "I thought you wanted to go?"

"I, uh…." His face heated, and he turned away. "We need to get our jackets. It's super cold out there." It was in the low fifties, but with the breeze, it felt colder.

"Piers!" she protested, although she was grabbing a sweater that Scout had left on the back of the kitchen chair for herself and throwing one of Lucky's to Ciaran.

"What?" He'd brought his from upstairs, a warm fleece jacket with a hat and gloves tucked in the pocket, and he slid that on now and checked to make sure he had his phone and wallet.

"Piers," she said, getting his attention. "I thought you *wanted* to see Tom's bench!"

His face—already warm—probably went nuclear. "I wanted to show Miller," he mumbled, and her impatience faded.

"You will," she said. "I think… I mean, he's so practical and all. I don't think he knows what to *do* with romance."

Piers remembered the almost starstruck expression on his face as their kiss had faded, and the way his forehead had furrowed almost immediately after. "I think you're right," he agreed. Then he smiled. "I'll have to show him."

"That's my boy. Now let's *move*!"

SCOUT'S MAGIC show had vastly improved from the first time Piers had seen it. He used Larissa as the shill, something she adored doing, and she was all wide-eyed wonder as he picked her card again and again and again.

What was particularly impressive was how he shuffled the deck from hand to hand, holding his arms out at a distance in the fierce wind.

How people didn't suspect real magic, Piers would never know.

At the end of the act, in tribute to the looming holiday, he took a piece of ribbon planted on four different audience members before the show started—one of them being Ciaran—and had the ribbons weave themselves into a wreath before everybody's eyes as he threaded bells through a bow on the top.

Piers was suddenly reminded that it was early December, and while he'd bought his parents and sister their gifts, he and Larissa weren't going to be home for Christmas, and he might want to do a little something for the people he'd be with when the holiday actually hit.

Ciaran watched the last trick wide-eyed and then turned to Piers and softly whispered, "How do they not know?"

It so closely echoed what Piers had been thinking that he couldn't help but smile.

"We never expect real magic," he murmured. "Did you expect your cousin to vanish today and disappear out of your life?"

Ciaran laughed slightly, buried in Lucky's Philadelphia Eagles hoodie, and shook his head. "If I'd known it could happen, I would have been praying for it for years."

Piers chuckled. "Maybe God hears what we're not saying sometimes."

Ciaran's grin was real, and at that moment Scout produced the wreath and presented it to Larissa with a bow. Her squeal of delight was as real as Ciaran's gratitude, and together he and Piers applauded the finale of Scout's show with all their heart.

When it was done, Scout waved to the three of them over a crowd of people and called, "Meet me in the shop!" while he and Marcus worked quickly to clean up so they could go inside and sell props to the customers who thought that since Scout made it look easy, anybody could do it.

While they waited for Scout and Marcus to get situated—and through the first wave of customers, excited about the Christmas sales—Piers, Ciaran, and Larissa wandered through the shop.

Piers pretended not to see Larissa purchase some tarot cards, and he wondered if they were for her or for himself—she'd said oftentimes that she wanted to learn how to read them, and these were so pretty, done in strong colors and lines, but with an intricate story told on every card.

"Levitating table," Ciaran murmured, picking up a box that had a table inside that folded like an umbrella, with a special tablecloth that could hold the light aluminum frame up when the wires in the edge had been "popped" like an umbrella. "Does it work?"

Piers laughed softly. "Not the same as Scout's does," he said, nodding significantly, and Ciaran laughed too before taking a look at the stainless-steel balls. Scout's line had died down from the register, and Marcus had taken over, leaving Scout free to walk over to them and visit.

"Okay," he said, looking earnest. "Marcus and Helen have a spare room in their cottage for Ciaran. They want to keep a special eye on him because I think their thwarted grandparent instincts are popping." He grinned at Ciaran, who was looking surprised. "We're meeting at Kayleigh's apartment for dinner. Lucky and I are cooking tonight—no, Piers, you can't buy ingredients. Give it up."

Piers rolled his eyes. "Fine. You should know that Kayleigh asked Larissa and me to use our little tops to find the stalker, but we up—"

"You didn't, right?" Scout asked, looking truly alarmed.

"No. Larissa and I had a bad feeling about it, so—"

Scout's sweet smile might have made Piers's stomach flutter if he hadn't yet met Miller Aldrun. "You guys are so smart. Yeah, let Lucky and me do that. You guys, don't think of him at all while you're using magic. I just... I'm so scared for you both." He nodded earnestly, and Piers had a moment to think Lucky really was true to his name before Scout continued. "Okay, so that's us. Where'd Miller go?"

"Knitter's Orgy Island," Piers said without thinking. He grimaced. "Erm, Tatter's Tot. He's on call today, so I'll try to have him stop by."

"Okay. Check in with him throughout the day." Scout glanced at his register and sighed when he saw the line forming again. "What else have you got planned?"

"Showing Ciaran here how to tourist," Piers said, "and visiting Tom's bench."

Scout smiled softly. He had a fondness for Tom's bench. "Maybe ask Ciaran if he'd be interested in getting a job while you're out. A lot of places lose their summer help and are overwhelmed over the holiday season." He glanced at Ciaran. "Is that okay with you?"

Piers was not prepared for the boy's smile. "A job? Would I be able to keep a cut of the money?"

Piers heard Scout breathe carefully through his nose. "Well, all of it," Scout said. "Although you might want to offer to chip in on rent and groceries, depending on where you end up. But yes, Ciaran, you're, uhm, free. I mean, you don't have to stay here if you don't want—"

"I want!" Ciaran said a little desperately, and then he winced when a few people turned toward him in surprise. "Please," he whispered. "I… I don't have anywhere else to go."

Scout gave one of those sublimely gentle smiles.

"Of course. Let's get you a job and cement where you're going to sleep and—hey, do you have any luggage?"

Ciaran grimaced. "It was all in the backpack Stevie was wearing when… you know."

"So it's in Nunavut," Piers muttered.

"Hopefully guaranteeing he's not freezing to death," Scout added staunchly. "So let's get you a job and maybe a shopping trip to Charleston and a discount store so you can get some of your own things next week. After your first paycheck. That'll work."

He scanned the gathering line in front of the register again and grunted. "I'm officially out of time. Do me a favor, guys, and wait to go to Tom's bench until Miller and I can go with you. I… trust me. I think we're both needed, okay?"

Piers nodded and thought that was probably best. Job hunting with Ciaran promised to suck up the rest of their afternoon.

MANY HOURS later, he, Larissa, and Ciaran retreated to the back of The Magic of Books, cradling steaming mugs of hot chocolate in their hands. They'd no sooner ensconced themselves in the stuffed chairs in the corner of the shop by the window than Helen, the shop's proprietor and hedge witch, came back to visit.

"Lucky, join us. The bell will tell us if someone else comes in," she called, and Piers hadn't realized it, but the second ferry of the day must have left, because that was usually the signal for the daytime businesses to shut down, leaving the specialty restaurants that overlooked the harbor to turn on their lights.

This time of year, the lights were accented with garlands of holiday twinkles, and Piers spent a moment appreciating the contrast of the lit-up stores against the last lavender of the setting sun.

"So," Helen murmured, sitting down next to young Ciaran. "Did we find a job?"

Ciaran grinned fiercely. "I found *three* of them!" he crowed. "See, everybody needed *a little* help, and I...." His grin turned to a grimace. "I don't have a bank account or any of my ID, so I needed cash."

Helen nodded, seemingly unperturbed. "So you got a job with three vendors—"

"The souvenir shop as an afternoon stock boy," Ciaran said, "and Russia Burger, or whatever that place is called, to unload stock in the mornings, and the fudge shop to wash dishes at night. So each job is about two hours, and I get an hour break between each one." His smile returned. "I'm going to know *everybody* on this side of the island before I'm through!"

Helen laughed softly. "And that's important to you?" she asked, and Piers recognized the purpose of the question. What would this boy need, now that he'd been suddenly displaced and alienated from the family that had abused him?

"See," Ciaran said, "where I grew up, you could walk to the grocery store and take a bus to school and walk to the pharmacy or Walgreens or whatever. So even if things weren't... *great* at home, you still knew everybody in your neighborhood." The eyes he turned toward Helen were suddenly luminous and needy. "I-I figured that I would know all of you and then everybody at the other places, and I would... you know."

"Know your neighborhood," Helen said softly. "I think that was very wise of you. Piers, what do you think?"

Piers chuckled. "I think better him than me. I haven't been this exhausted since law school." But law school had been more of a spiritual suck, hadn't it? The thought occurred out of nowhere, but he wanted to curse because he could *tell* it wasn't going to leave him alone.

"I think it's a fantastic idea," Lucky said, coming over from the front. He had a pitcher of hot chocolate in his hand, and he used it to refill their mugs. "'Cause I learned the island from the coffee shop, but you know. Everybody wants their coffee in the morning."

"Piers and I were tourists," Larissa said ruminatively, cuddling her freshened mug of chocolate. "I... I don't think we'd made any friends until Piers spoke up to Scout that one morning."

Had the bell tinkled? Piers frowned. He wasn't sure if he'd heard the bell tinkle, but he *sensed* somebody in the store. Frowning, he met Lucky's eyes, and Lucky glanced down all five of the book aisles, moving quickly. Piers's paranoia relaxed a smidge when he laughed softly.

"It's Scout and Kayleigh," he told Piers. "They came up from the back—"

At that moment there was a tremendous *crash* against the safety glass of the front window, which, true to its nature, didn't shatter but did *crack* with a resounding *kkkkkk* sound, and Piers stared in horror as the body of a man wearing a bicycle helmet slithered down the window as though he'd been launched through the air against it.

Miller!

He wasn't aware that he'd moved, but suddenly he was *sprinting* through the bookstore, and the darkness outside was glowing bright, brighter, brightest as he tried to guess what was out in the merchant's square that had attacked.

Confusion at Tatter's Tot

Earlier that day....

MILLER GAZED around the landing of Knitter's Orgy Island, erm, Tatter's Tot, and wished heartily for Scout or Lucky by his side.

There was something definitely magically *hinky* about the island.

Miller's "armed and crazy" alarm wasn't going off, but the residents—and he recognized most of them, although, well, it was cold and they all had their clothes on, so that was different—were aggressive. Openly hostile. Angry.

But he couldn't get them to say at what.

"Hey, hey, hey!" Miller cried out for the third time since he got to the island. Angry voices rose again—he hadn't been able to get them to calm down enough to make sense—and in desperation, he put his thumb and forefinger in his mouth and whistled loud enough to shatter a wineglass.

The silence was sudden and offended—how *dare* this stranger make us stop yelling at him! But it was also refreshing, and it gave Miller a chance to take over.

"Julius," he said sharply. "You're in charge of the radio to dispatch." Cell service was spotty at best. "How about we start by you telling me why I got called over here."

Julius was a sixty-something teddy bear of a man, and he suddenly looked puzzled. "To stop... to stop all the fighting," he said, as though trying to remind himself. "Yes. That's it. I needed to stop all the fighting."

"Okay, good," Miller encouraged. "Roxie, can you tell me who was involved in the fighting?" Roxie was the unofficial port master of the island. There were only about a hundred or so residents on Tatter's Tot, and they all lived in the double row of houses that lined either side of the street that marked the boat dock. They tended to go in groups to the mainland, maybe once a month, to get supplies, and some forward-thinking soul had invested in underground power lines that led to a small power station on the far side of the island. There was a coffee shop that doubled as a post office and sundries store, but for the most part, the people there were the epitome of "work from home." Artists lived here, as did writers, spinners, smiths, weavers, knitters, crocheters, potters, and a poet named Otto who had yet to speak an intelligible word to Miller, as he was most often drunk.

In the summer, when the air was warm and no tourists were there looking to buy the rare and handcrafted items offered for sale at the island's one tourist-oriented store, most of the island could be found on the beach, naked and possibly frolicking since there wasn't a single resident under forty, and the standard rules of marriage, monogamy, and propriety seemed to have been shed with the rest of civilization when people moved here.

So Roxie's job as the port master basically controlled the valve that allowed the outside world to the inner world of Tatter's Tot. If she didn't know somebody, she'd make them sit in their skiff at the dock until she discovered who they belonged to. If the fight had broken out near the harbor—which was the one thing everybody could agree on— then Roxie would know about it.

Except now, when lines of confusion wrinkled her tanned, freckled forehead. "I... young Miller, I swear I don't know," she said softly, and her quiet seemed to bring the mood of the island down a notch, so that was fine.

"Can you remember at all?" he asked, surprised.

Her frown deepened. "Well, I was at my post, cursing Vern there because my space heater had died and it was fucking cold." Her voice grew sharp, and Miller grimaced.

Fortunately, Vern was her husband, fiftyish like her and comfortably worn. Usually when Miller visited Tatter's Tot, Roxie and Vern provided him with their homemade fudge, which they made copious amounts of during Christmas season and kept in the freezer to break out and thaw for special occasions. Vern had not been heard to speak a cross word to anybody, either at the Tot or on one of the bimonthly trips he led in his cabin cruiser, which he'd take to the mainland and fill with supplies. Anybody who needed to could go with him, but much of the island simply placed orders and paid him out of pocket. Miller—during a long fudge-and-coffee session with Roxie the summer before—had learned that their lives had become infinitely better with the advancements made in grocery ordering and curbside service during the pandemic.

Usually the people on Tatter's Tot could find the silver lining to any cloud and the pot of fudge at the end of any rainbow.

The angry voices Miller had heard when he'd arrived had been quite a shock, and he wasn't looking forward to breaking up that melee again.

He needn't have worried. "Sorry, Roxie," Vern murmured. "I knew the thing was going, but I was hoping it could make it until Christmas." He looked sheepish. "'Cause, you know. Christmas present."

The look she gave her husband was fond. "You're always thinking about me," she said, her comfortably lined face softening. "I'd love to get that early." She looked at Miller. "So I was freezing my ass off and unfairly cursing my husband's name, it seems, and then I looked out and saw a smallish cabin cruiser. One of the resort ones, right?"

Miller nodded. Since boats were the main source of transportation between the islands—unless you wanted to brave the tidal road that tended to flood even without the tide to help it—Morgen Star Resort provided reasonable boat rentals for all their guests. Most of the room packages mentioned boat use, Miller had been told once, and it was not unusual for guests to make a day or two of going from island to island to find specialty items to purchase. Miller himself had bought his sister a gorgeous pot from Anselm, one of the most talented ceramic workers on the East Coast, who sold his wares at the Tatter's Tot Trading Post with the rest of the artisans in the colony.

"Did they dock?" Miller asked.

Roxie bit her lip. "Now, I couldn't rightly say," she said. "Vern, do you remember? I... there was a little bit of fuzzing on the radio, and then...."

Vern frowned back. "And then I absolutely had to sock Cal Epstein in the face," he declared, before glancing at the balding man next to him who was looking at him with reproach through a blackening eye. "Sorry, Cal. I don't know why I did that."

"Me neither," Cal said, but then he shrugged. "I guess it was catching, though, because I...." He turned to his wife, Greta. "Sorry, Greta."

"You spanked me!"

"You poked my gut with your elbow! Sharp elbows, Greta!"

"Sorry, Cal."

"Yeah, I'm sorry too."

As Miller watched and listened with growing concern, nearly half the island—the half that had been out and about that morning as he and his friends had been talking—turned and apologized to each other for stunning acts of petty violence, all of it unprovoked.

On the one hand, it was nice to see the slightly bruised residents of Tatter's Tot were getting along again, and *really* nice not to have to incarcerate any or all of them in the tiny two-room jail that sat in the bungalow next to Miller's home. But on the other hand, *what the hell happened*?

"It was a presence," said a rusty voice near Miller's ear.

Miller turned his head in surprise and found himself face-to-seamed-face with Otto, the drunken poet, who did not, in fact, smell like rum or any other sort of alcohol once he got this close.

"Otto?" Miller asked uncertainly, suddenly aware that the man's eyes were a stunning, crystal-clear shade of ocean green.

"C'mon to my flat," Otto murmured, giving a nod to the rest of Tatter's Tot. The residents were continuing to hug each other, the hugs becoming more and more familiar and the sweet words of forgiveness becoming more and more laced with innuendo.

Miller grimaced. Give them half an hour and they'd be scattered among the houses, fucking like bunnies in big bunny piles. Good for them, really. Miller wouldn't begrudge a thing to anybody getting laid more than he was, but, well, not really his scene.

"Sure," Miller said, his voice revealing his doubt. Otto dressed like a bird's nest—ill-fitting, rumpled business clothes, shoulder-length graying hair going off in a thousand directions—and most of the time he wandered around the island with a flask in hand, eyes flitting to corners and shadows nobody else could see. He still *looked* like that now, but this was as close as Miller had ever come to the man, and he had to admit, the absence of odor was piquing his curiosity. It had never occurred to him that the unkempt appearance—and the flask—had been a front.

Together they skirted the crowd of affectionate crafters, and Otto led Miller behind the line of houses to a tiny cottage that Miller had barely noticed in his previous visits here. The main drag off the dock was paved to facilitate deliveries of bigger things, such as building supplies, but this cottage sat far enough back that the road to it from the paved part was a small bumpy footpath that barely cut through the lush preforest undergrowth that served as a precursor to the lush forest on the uninhabited side of the island. Miller was given to understand there were footpaths on that side of the island, and a couple of hidden beaches, but there were also enough rocky outcroppings and submerged obstacles to make approaching from that side impossible—and potentially deadly.

So one side of the island was Knitter's Orgy Island, and the other side was Dreamy Artist Rock. When he wasn't rescuing armadillos from Vern's inexpert clutches (because the Little Island to the Left did *not* have a monopoly on armadillos), Miller could admit it was almost a perfect balance of community and isolation. Unfortunately, after seeing the odd influence of a ship nobody could remember docking, he also saw the island and its inhabitants as worryingly vulnerable.

Were the other islands this vulnerable?

The thought made him shiver. Three thousand residents and another thousand tourists may not have seemed like a lot of people to care for—until you spread them across ten to twelve small islands and added in transportation and manpower. *Unlike* his supervisor, Miller took the safety of the citizens of Spinner's Drift seriously, and he refused to kick back with a beer and say, "Let the batshit crazies figure it out," which was exactly what his sergeant had told him when he'd first gotten the job.

So now he followed the one man seemingly not bewildered by whatever had happened at the dock to his tiny little cottage and hoped that the resident poet wasn't a fan of chainsaws, antimony, or firearms.

But as Miller followed Otto up the steps of the cottage, he realized that maybe he'd been too hasty in his assessment.

From a distance, the cottage looked rickety. The boards were weathered, and the roof—which appeared to be built with palm fronds and spit—was, in fact, *treated* to look that way. As Otto led him up the porch and through the door, it was obvious that the boards had been stained gray, and the "palm fronds" were made of the same tough vinyl that made up siding, only it had been cut and "distressed" to look like vegetation. Once inside the doorway, the cottage proved to be… well, amazing.

"Wow," Miller murmured, looking through the giant window that wrapped around the far side of the cottage. It ignored the harbor and the little town, but instead showed the drop-off to the seemingly untouched vegetation on the far side of the island, with a little twinkle of the ocean behind. Miller turned in a slow semicircle and saw the view obstructed by walls, but he thought that the window might actually wrap around so that the ocean could be seen from the bedroom that the walls obscured.

And speaking of walls—the wall and floor paneling was a deep, rich maple color that had been varnished and sanded until it shone. The furniture—a couch, a bookshelf, and a surprisingly modern entertainment system—occupied the part of the front room *not* illuminated by the window, but the kitchen table, made of the same wood as the paneling, enjoyed a healthy dose of natural light.

As did the sleek laptop set up on top of it.

Miller's breath caught as he looked around, and he fought the temptation to say, "Otto, you're a fraud."

But Otto knew, apparently, because he was cackling to himself as he took in Miller's reaction.

"Not what you thought, right?"

Miller let out a chuckle. "Not even a little. This is amazing!" He turned to Otto, who was busying himself with a teakettle on a gas stove. "Are all the houses this nice?"

Otto grinned at him over his shoulder, and Miller realized that he had a full set of white teeth involved in a very nice smile. "Most of them. I know they seem like a bunch of crazy sex-starved old people, my boy, but you have to understand. When we got together to form this artist colony, we were all, in fact, *very* successful in our fields." He let out a pleased cackle. "You don't believe me? Go check out the bookshelf!"

Miller did as he was told, but by now he had an idea what to expect.

"Michael O. Coogan," he said, shaking his head. "Wow." The bestselling crime novelist was a known recluse, but the dapper, clean-cut gentleman in his Oxford tweed coat with the leather patches on the elbows was a far cry from Otto, with his bird's nest hair, frayed polyester slacks, and rumpled button-down. If Miller hadn't seen the fine-boned face behind that bright smile, he might not have believed it.

As though to seal in his belief, farther down on the shelf sat three slim volumes of poetry—by Otto Rausch. The picture on the back of those books was exactly the same, and Miller wondered how many people in the literary world knew they were the same person. Otto Rausch had won literary awards, and Michael O. Coogan had won mystery awards, but neither gentleman, it seemed, occupied the same space on the mainland.

And this crazy-eyed individual in the heavenly little cottage was in a whole other world.

"Fun, right?" Otto said, coming to stand by him. He was laughing like a naughty child. "I mean, the people on the island know about Otto, but very few of them know about Michael. And my editor could give a crap as long as I turn in two manuscripts a year, on schedule."

"So," Miller said, keeping a straight face, "which one am I talking to now?"

Otto's cackle was infectious, but when the laughter faded, Miller felt the urgency of the matter at hand.

"So," he repeated softly, "what happened at the dock today?"

Otto nodded toward the table. "Come here, boy. Sit down. Have some tea."

Miller did as requested, bemused, and Otto bustled around him, setting out cups and saucers and little bowls—artisan made, of course—of cream and sugar.

Miller sat, loving the graciousness and simplicity of the cottage. As fine as everything was, it had also been *used*. There were faint rings on the kitchen table, as though Otto set coffee mugs down when he was distracted. The table runner was a very pretty woven cloth, but a few of the ends were frayed, because he obviously used it a lot. This cottage was loved.

"Would you like something to eat?" Otto asked, and Miller tried to say no, but he'd left his untouched burrito at Scout and Lucky's, and it had been breakfast. Now it was past lunch. His stomach growled loudly, and Otto gave a gentle smile.

"What would you like?" he said, and the way he said it caught Miller's attention.

"What do you have?" he asked, puzzled and trying not to think about a giant sugar cookie because *damn* his sweet tooth.

"Never mind," Otto told him, and he picked up the once empty plate and offered it to Miller.

It was overflowing with iced sugar cookies now, and Miller took one in bemusement.

"Oh," he said, apprehension dawning. "You're a luck mechanic."

Otto gasped, looking delighted. "Is that your word for us? Luck mechanics?"

Miller nodded and took a bite of the cookie. Ah, magic cookies—for some reason they always tasted better. "I have a friend who's a wizard. He thinks there's three kinds of magic. Big magic you're born with, the kind that wizards or sorcerers have. Hedge witch magic, the kind that comes with being in tune with the world and knowing the things that give you power to change it. And mechanical magic. One or two talents, sometimes small, sometimes larger, that simply aid in everyday life. They're like an extra tool you can use, and lucky you for having one."

Otto was gazing at him rapturously, as though Miller was giving him the secrets to the known world. "Luck mechanics—that's... that's *amazing*. And hedge witches? Are there really such things? Wizards too?"

Miller grinned at him, glad for once to be the one giving out this information instead of mulling it over doubtfully. "I know them all," he said, and then thought about what had awakened him that morning and brought him to Tatter's Tot in the first place. "In fact, I think one of them is the reason I'm here."

Otto's enchanted smile faded. "And what's *your* mechanic, boy? Mine is simple: I've never been a starving artist in my life. It's the only reason I could afford to keep writing in the beginning, you see? If I could find a hole in the wall to sleep in, I could always find a sandwich. But you look damned serious, and I don't think you came for the sugar cookies."

"Armed and crazy," Miller said softly. "I... I can sense armed and crazy. Not just armed, mind you—"

"Because a letter opener can be a weapon," Otto said, nodding.

"Yes, exactly. But someone who has a weapon and is unhinged. Planning to use the weapon out of malice. Unable to control themselves. I know when there's a dangerous person nearby, particularly one who threatens people I know."

Otto stared at him, considering. "Not always a comfortable gift," he said softly.

"No," Miller conceded. "And I am concerned that this morning I awoke thinking the armed and crazy was in the tourist section of the main island. That threat was addressed, and I felt another threat at the resort section. I left that threat sitting there to come *here*, where something damned odd has just happened, and now I am more worried than ever that my friends, whom I care about, are in danger, but my gift is still telling me that armed and crazy is sitting back at Morgen Star Resort, getting drunk on piña coladas!"

He blinked. "It is. It *is* getting drunk on piña coladas." He glared at Otto, feeling a little bit of desperation. "So if the armed and crazy is back on Spinner's Drift, what in the hell happened here?"

Otto cocked his head. "What kind of armed and crazy?" he asked in return.

"My friend's stalker kind of armed and crazy. Kills plants with the miasma of his soul, I guess." He swallowed. "Almost disemboweled the family cat. I understand the cat survived, but…." He shuddered. "Poor thing."

Otto gave him an absolutely precious look over the kitchen table. "You are too sweet for this world, aren't you, Officer Aldrun."

Miller gazed flatly back. "Animals are helpless," he said grumpily. "It's a coward's violence."

Otto nodded slowly. "Nicely said. I may quote you in my next book and not tell you or give you credit. You're welcome. So in order to explain what happened today, I need to ask you something. I take it you've been to the main island, right?"

Miller nodded. "Yeah. Hard not to. I mean, I patrol the whole Drift, right? Or all four of us patrol the Drift, I should say."

The sound Otto made was both inelegant and derisive. "I've only ever seen you and your sergeant—what's his name?"

"Leo Kowalski," Miller said dryly. "I had no idea he'd been out here."

Otto snorted again. "Not since you've been hired. He used to try to participate in our beach parties. It was like one of those comics where the dog farts and everybody gravitates to the far end of the room, except it was on the beach, and there were a bunch of suddenly very self-conscious middle-aged people who enjoy a good time after the tourists go home."

Miller gave a shudder. "That's horrifying," he said with deep conviction. "And I'll try to protect you from him in the future. But in the meantime…."

"Oh, oh yes." Otto fortified himself with a sip of tea. Miller usually was more of a coffee fan, but he appreciated the hospitality, so he took his own sip and waited.

"So," Otto said carefully, "if you've been to the main island, have you ever, perchance, noted the bench in the clearing just off the beach that fronts the main drag?"

"Tom's bench," Miller said, nodding. At Otto's rather depressed look then, Miller added, "I haven't actually been to the clearing, though. All my friends know about it. They… well, the more powerful of them have seen things there. They describe it like a play, with different shadow boxes acting out different tableaux. They keep telling me I need to go see it, and I just haven't squeezed in the time."

Otto harumphed, but he did look less depressed. "Well, I'm relieved to know there's still a possibility you can see the shadows of Tom's life, but really? How long have you known about Tom's bench?"

Miller frowned. "Late October," he said thoughtfully and then grimaced because the two-month gap really was odd.

"So...." Otto made little motions with his hands. "Explain."

Miller scowled at him. "I... well, all my friends go and hold hands and look around and try to figure out the puzzle. They already figured out some of it, you know. They've found Tom's body. They're going to bury it with Henry's, which is in a little grave behind the bench. You knew that, right?"

"Ooh—no, I did not!" Otto's depression had turned to delight. "But why haven't *you* gone yet?"

Unbidden, Piers's handsome face floated behind his vision. "It always seemed very... intimate to me. You know? Go to the bench, hold hands with people, look around? I mean, I *know* the magic is real, but I didn't want to do that with just anybody."

It sounded stupid when he said it.

"Never mind. I'll go tonight. My friends have been begging me to go—it's like the secret of the islands is sitting there and I'm waiting for the perfect moment." And the perfect man.

"Who *do* you want to hold hands and look at ghosts with?" Otto asked, seemingly fascinated, and Miller took a deep breath and tried to control his annoyance.

"It's not important—"

"A pretty young girl? A handsome young man?"

"An old geezer with bird's nest hair and a plate of refillable goodies," Miller retorted, not wanting to talk about Piers right now. "What does this have to do with a bunch of chubby, horny crafters almost starting a riot on the dock right before Christmas!"

Otto tilted his head back and laughed—not a cackle this time, but a full-blooded, jolly-old-Saint-Nick laugh. "Oh, my boy. You're just so wonderful. I can't believe I haven't brought you to my cottage before. It's the uniform, I think—rather puts one off. But you really are a treasure," he finished with a chuckle and wiped a tear from under his eye. "Oh my, that was precious." He sighed, took a sip of tea, and was suddenly all business.

"Whomever you want to take to Tom's bench, you need to do it soon. In fact, I may hitch a ride back with you. Because I'll tell you who got off that boat, but you're not going to believe it."

Then Otto did. And he was wrong. Miller believed every word.

But that didn't stop Miller from having Otto gather a change of clothes to throw in a knapsack and hustling him out of his cottage to Miller's little skiff, frowning at the sun as he went.

The day had flown by so fast! It took an hour or so to get from Spinner's Drift, the main island, to Tatter's Tot. There were a few smaller islands along the way. Miller had left around eleven, and after he'd spent an hour getting everybody's story straight and nearly three hours at Otto's cottage, the thin winter sun was already hinting at the horizon. The wind was a bear today, and they'd be spending a lot of their time back fighting the waves. Miller could feel urgency pressing at his breastbone the entire time, but that didn't keep him from checking periodically on Otto to make sure he was tucked behind the center console and staying dry and warm under the heated tarp he kept charged under the passenger's seat.

It was hard enough making this trip when you were used to it, but Miller had gotten the feeling that Otto took his pleasures *very* seriously, and freezing to death on board a police-issue center-console skiff was not one of the things he wanted to do in his old age.

The last glimmer of light left the sky as Miller pulled up to the reserved law-enforcement slip. He hopped out and tied the boat off before getting back in and helping a dazed Otto onto the uncertain footing.

Very carefully he escorted the older gentleman, who was good-natured about all this attention.

"I've spent the last ten years pretending to be toasted out of my gourd, and now that I'm doing something important, I actually *can't walk* to save my life!"

"Why did you do that?" Miller asked before giving the harbormaster a wave. "Why did you pretend to be cross-eyed drunk for all that time?"

"I don't like most people," Otto told him frankly. "And I *hate* explaining my gift, or my mechanic, to people. Most of the folks on the island know, and they give me a wide berth, but that's about the extent of it. If nobody's there but my happy naked crafters, I'm as sober as a judge."

They'd hit dry land by now, and Miller was well on his way to hustling Otto up the walkway toward the town center. The restaurants were open, with their blinking holiday lights, and the coffee shop was still—thank heavens—lit up. The last ferry had already left, and Miller suspected that most of the patrons had gone with it. He hoped—oh, he so hoped—that Scout and the others would be in the back of the coffee shop, chatting, brainstorming, coming up with possibilities and solutions. He'd seen them do it so many times since he'd first encountered Scout in October, and now he *really* needed them to do their thing.

Otto's knees looked a little wobbly, so Miller walked him to the other side of the town square, which used the gentle slope of the harbor hill to create a ramp up to the shop level. But even as they neared the brightly lit shop, Miller could feel it. A building menace in the pit of his stomach. A looming threat from down the beach.

Instinctively, Miller glanced over his shoulder and tried not to gasp.

He'd seen this before.

Tom's bench was located about a hundred yards off the beach on what had once been the side of the main road that wrapped around the island. The road had changed since it had been erected in the late 1800s, and the bench now sat in a clearing, with the sad little copper grave marker behind it so hidden not even Scout had known where it was located until after one of the many supernatural presences around Tom's bench had tried to kill him near the end of October.

Miller had been there for that, had seen the darkness from afar as it had engulfed Scout and his father, who had been more than happy to see his son die in its clutches as long as it meant that Alistair Quintero came out on top.

Scout had escaped both of them—his father, Alistair, and the great and terrible blackness, the star-stealing grief that worked as a high-pressure front over the other supernatural presences by the bench—but he had needed *everybody's* help, including Miller's, to do it.

Miller would never forget that night, Alistair practically throwing himself into the blackness that had seemed to open up from nowhere, and Scout being caught in a lasso of shining light that had dragged him in after his father.

Miller hadn't understood the forces at work at the time, but he *had* seen Lucky's panic to get Scout back, and he hadn't hesitated as the lot of them had formed a human chain, each person with their arms around the other's waist, dragging Scout out of the darkness until he'd fallen, coughing up half the Atlantic Ocean, on the sand.

And he'd felt the darkness, the terrible presence, looming over all of them as they'd scrambled back, half-carrying Scout and Lucky to Lucky's apartment to strip them, dry them off, and get them warm.

The chill Miller felt creeping out of the darkness *was* the darkness, and it was bone-achingly familiar. He'd known this icy vise around his bowels the day Brad had darted out of his apartment, telling him he'd try to call that night after work.

It had almost swallowed him whole when he'd felt *viscerally*, as though it had happened to *him*, the shot that ended Brad's life.

And it was wrapping knotted tendrils around Miller's ankles, his thighs, his hips, and more than that, it was lifting him up in the air, leaving poor Otto gasping and shocked as the terrible force squeezed Miller until he couldn't breathe anymore and then *hurled* him at the front window of The Magic of Books.

Miller felt the hit and thought, *Didn't shatter! Yay!* before he was out completely, swimming in the chilly blackness with his grief.

Panic

OH MY God! Oh my God oh my God oh my God—Miller?

Piers was the first one out the door and into the shockingly chilly night, the air a breath-stealing, testicle-shrinking, spine-freezing cold. Piers skidded on ice on the walkway—*ice?*—and fell to his knees by Miller's prone form.

"Oh God," he muttered. "He's sopping wet. His lips are blue. *Scout*! *Helen*! Come help him!"

Piers grabbed Miller's hands and rubbed them, not daring to check his body for other injuries—he'd hit the glass *hard*. Not hard enough to shatter it, thank God, but there was a crack now, radiating from where the back of Miller's helmet had thunked—slightly above the second *O* in Books—outward in two branches. Oh Lord, the back of his head. Wasn't that where comas were born?

Miller!

Oh God. As Piers watched, his chest rose and fell a few times in a labored rhythm, and then he *stopped breathing*.

Piers was vaguely aware of a person—an older man—kneeling creakily by Miller's other side, and then a warm hand on his shoulder called his attention away from Miller's blue-tinged face.

"Piers," Helen said, "I'm going to have you all join hands around him. I've got some healing spells, and I need you to repeat what I say three times, yes? Don't argue. It's all Marcus and I have, you understand?"

Piers nodded, desperation sweeping over him, darkening the sky and turning his blood to ice. He took his place near Miller's head, wanting to defend him, *help* him, and was vaguely aware of Larissa fumbling her hand into his on one side and Kayleigh fumbling on the other. When Scout, Lucky, Marcus, Ciaran, and the odd little man who'd accompanied Miller joined them, with Helen in the center holding her hands over Miller's core, they formed a tight circle around their friend, and together they listened breathlessly as Helen spoke.

Sand and sea, wind and sky
Help our friend who helpless lies

Earth and water, fire and air
All his hurts we beg repair

Then she spoke quickly, changing her voice from that of someone chanting to someone urging others on. "Everybody now!"

Marcus joined her first, and the rest of them chimed in, the chant coming more easily as they found their rhythm.

In his belly, Piers felt the uncoiling of warmth, like an ember flower opening its face to the words and the healing, but it wasn't enough. It couldn't seem to break free of his chest, flood his skin. Helen led them in the chant a second time, and everybody's voices grew deeper, stronger, more assured. Piers focused his attention on the words, on Miller, as he recited. But there was something... something *out there*... an oppressive, malign force that seemed to be pushing back with cold intent.

Piers changed his focus from Miller's white, still features to the darkness beyond their little group.

The light from the coffee shop seemed like a tiny warm pool surrounding them, but outside the semicircle of that glow lay a darkness, blanketing everything around them in soul-sucking ice. In fact.... Piers squinted. He'd seen them, not five minutes ago. The lights from the restaurants across the harbor. Bright and twinkling holiday lights; they'd brightened the sky and reminded everybody of hope in the darkest part of the year. With a sudden push, a broad unfurling of that ember in his stomach, Piers wished for the one thing his gift gave him.

Light.

Light in corners of libraries, in darkened rooms, in the hallway when he had to use the bathroom at 2:00 a.m. Light. Such a small gift, usually only useful when you were reading in a dark corner or trying to study in a dim library, and suddenly it was at the core of existence. That darkness, that encroaching, blanketing darkness, needed *light*!

Their little circle began the third recitation of Helen's healing spell, and Piers felt that heat, that warmth, exploding in his chest, and he glared into the desperate black and thought *Light!*

And light sprang up, illuminating Miller first, then their circle as they all poured whatever power they had into Miller's still body, and then, shockingly, into the void itself, where it pushed as though against fog, and pushed and pushed some more until the void tattered, splintered, diffused into a thousand pieces, and the holiday lights from the bayside restaurants could be seen twinkling once again.

The healing charm ended, and while Piers was aware that all of his friends were staring at him in surprise, he was staring at *Miller*, who was pink now, whose eyes were fluttering open, who was *breathing*.

"Geez, Piers," Larissa whispered. "What did you do?"

And Piers sank to his knees and traced his hand along Miller's cheek in reply.

Miller's eyes finally opened completely, and he frowned into Piers's face as though irritated. "I saw that," he muttered.

"What?" Piers asked, his voice choked.

"You lit up the world." A small smile tilted his lips upward in the corners. "More than you already do, of course."

Piers bent down and kissed his forehead and stayed there, rocking back and forth on his knees and crying for more time than he cared to admit.

Suddenly there was a brief whooshing in his ears, and all the colors in his peripheral vision shifted amazingly fast, and when he looked up, he was kneeling on the bed that dominated Lucky's room, and Miller was stretched out in front of him as though they'd been simply teleported from one place to another.

In his gut he felt a deep tingling sensation, like magic had happened.

"Oh," he said on a little hiccup. "*That's* what Scout's portals feel like."

Miller groaned. "I am so confused," he mumbled. "How did you get me into bed again?"

Piers gave a snotty laugh and scrambled back to stand by the bed—but only long enough to take off his shoes before he started helping Miller with his thick waterproof parka and boots. Somebody had turned the space heater on in Lucky's flat, and it was warm enough to strip off the outerwear so Piers could wrap Miller up in the comforter on top of the bed like a sweet, earnest little policeman panini, because Piers was *not* okay.

Miller put up with his fussing, even to the point of letting Piers strip his waterproof hip-waders down off his legs and hips, leaving him in his jeans, but when Piers went to unsnap his jeans—because they were wet—he tried to draw the line.

"I still don't even know what I'm doing here," he said. At least that's what Piers thought he was *trying* to say—his teeth were still chattering too hard for Piers to make it out.

"You almost died," Piers said thickly. "One minute I was looking outside, thinking about you, and the next, the sky turned black and some sort of nasty supernatural crawly threw you against Helen's window. You weren't breathing, Miller, and your skin's like ice, and your lips are still really pale, so let me *take off your jeans* so I can wrap you in a blanket and feed you soup or chocolate or something, because looking at you makes me cold."

"Oh," Miller murmured. "Okay. Sorry."

He seemed dazed and out of it, and Piers took pity on him. His next attempt to unsnap Miller's jeans was a little gentler.

"Look, I'm not trying to take advantage of you, okay? But I have the feeling Scout portaled us down here so I could get you all warm and toasty while they're all up there making sure everything is safe. Let's work on getting you settled, and then there's going to be group stuff and talking and...."

He was working while he lectured, undoing Miller's jeans and tugging them down and then scooting Miller back so he was sitting on the bed and making good on his first thought of making a Miller warmth-panini using the comforter and the pillows. Miller still had a hooded sweatshirt on, with *Security* emblazoned on the shoulder and the back, along with the MorgenStar logo, and as much as Piers wanted that thing off his body, he wanted Miller to be comfortable more.

He was in the middle of tucking the comforter in around Miller's hips when Miller stopped him, grabbing his nearest hand and squeezing. "I'm okay," he said, clearly this time, and Piers found himself shaking his head.

"You weren't," he said from a thick throat. "I... I know you think I'm toying with you—with your affections—but I *care* about you, Miller. And seeing you like that scared me."

Miller swallowed, and Piers thought he was going to scatter a few crumbs in Piers's direction—something like "That's kind," or "All good, see?"

But instead he said, "I thought about you all day."

Piers gasped, stunned at the offering, and pleased—so pleased. "Yeah? What did you think?"

Miller's expression grew a little bit dreamy. "Otto—"

"The old guy?" Piers asked, to be sure.

"Yeah. He's a neat old guy, and he's got an *amazing* mechanic, but he asked me if I had… a pretty girl or a pretty young man who I needed to be home for." Miller shrugged and stared at their hands, which were now twined. "I just nodded, but…." His eyes crinkled. "There was that kiss," he finished simply.

"It was a good kiss," Piers whispered. "I've been dying to do that for two months."

Miller nodded. "I'm prickly."

Piers snorted. "God, that's being nice to yourself."

And that made him laugh for real. But when he sobered, his eyes were deep and fathomless. Hazel was such an underrated color. Could be brown, could be blue, could be green—could be any of a thousand things moving around behind Miller's eyes, tinting them with fear or sorrow or joy.

"It sucks being Cassandra," he said softly.

"Only when nobody listens," Piers told him, and Miller looked away.

"It's hard to get used to," he said after a moment. "Two months of you people listening to me, trusting me, is not going to undo all the times people *didn't* trust me… and got hurt."

Piers sucked in a cold breath. God, he was privileged, he thought dimly. How could it not have occurred to him that Miller's story could be hard and painful? He'd thought of Miller as "earnest" and "sober." Only now, looking at Miller's averted eyes, did he think that the word "wounded" could apply.

"I'm sorry," Piers said, "that people you cared about were hurt. I… that doesn't mean you shouldn't let anybody else care about you."

Miller gave him a brief bleak smile. "I don't think there's any 'letting' about it," he said with a certain grim humor. "I… you just told me you cared already, without my say-so. I don't remember what happened after I hit that window, but I get the feeling when I find out, there's going to be a whole lot of caring that I was unaware of. I… I could *smell* magic in the air, and people were standing around me in a circle, and if that's not protection, I don't know what is."

"Why's that make you sad?" Piers asked, keeping his voice low and not angry or accusing. Inside he was thinking, *C'mon, Miller—let us love you!* But that was exactly the sort of thing that would send the young officer scrambling for his clothes, doing something stupid like trying to pilot his boat back to the tiny dispatch island so he could do things by the book.

"I… all my life I've wanted to do that for people," Miller admitted. "I knew *right where* the threat came from, and nobody would let me. Not one person. My father almost died. My favorite teacher in school. My…." He made a frightening sound then, one that only happened when somebody was holding so tightly on to tears that they threatened to explode outwards, and Piers gave up on getting the story right now.

Instead he pushed his bottom onto the bed and wrapped his arms around Miller's shoulders and whispered, "It's okay. I've got you. Let go."

He wasn't sure if Miller would sob on him or brush him away or even run into the bathroom and try to tough it out on his own.

What he actually did was simply rest there, head on Piers's shoulder, and breathe. At first Piers was disappointed; he'd hoped for passion… or at least release. God, not more oppression! But then he felt them, the fine tremors in Miller's shoulders. In his still-cold core. And Piers realized those breaths were coming raggedly, with the little liquid sounds that meant tears falling in silent taps onto Piers's shoulder.

He was being trusted.

All he could do was sit there and hold on, stunned by the realization that some storms happened under the cresting wave.

THE STORM eventually passed, and Piers kissed Miller's temple, holding him, feeling honored.

"I need a tissue," Miller said after a moment, and Piers grunted and grabbed one off the bedstand, handing it to him and scooting back while he tried to mop up the damage.

Above them, they could hear the rattles and bangs that indicated cleanup and closing, and his stomach rumbled, telling him that whatever the plan was for dinner, it would be great if it happened soon.

His phone buzzed into a silence growing heavy and awkward, and he shifted on the bed to check it to see Larissa's message.

Bringing food over for a debrief. You've got five minutes—sorry!

He sighed and tapped in, *No worries. I'm starving, and he needs a pair of Scout's sweats. His jeans were wet.*

Get Lucky's—Scout has the right dresser; Lucky has the left. Lucky's shorter.

Will do. Give us ten?

Will try. Go away.

And so he did.

"Your cousin?" Miller asked, interrupting Piers's racing thoughts.

"Yeah. They're bringing dinner over. I've got instructions to make sure we're both dressed."

Miller rolled his eyes. "I'm *not* doing the thing in somebody else's bed."

Piers gave him a level look. "Don't be picky. Remember *I* haven't slept in my own bed since August."

Miller grimaced. "I'm sorry. I forget sometimes that you don't belong here like the rest of us."

Piers retorted, stung, "What do you mean, I don't belong here? Am I not working class enough for you? Because that's just snobbery right there." In a huff he got up and headed for Lucky's dresser, found clean pairs of sweats in the third drawer.

"Piers, don't be dumb," Miller snapped. "All I'm saying is that you and Larissa both have lives to return to. You've got one year left of law school—don't think I've missed that. And your cousin hasn't even *started* school. I know how much it meant to you two to have one year together on the same campus because you both *told* me that. The rest of us, for whatever reasons, are here, making the islands our home. I could get hired in a dozen places off the island. My old commander emails me twice a month to ask if I'm *sure* I don't want to go back."

"Do you?" Piers asked, suddenly burningly curious.

"No," Miller told him, the often-ferocious lines of his face relaxing, making him look as tranquil as Piers had ever seen him. "I like it here. I feel like I belong. Every time Scout talks about the island trying to protect us, I feel that in my bones. It's what I want to do too, and I feel… I don't know. Like I finally have an ally. But you? You have a life outside this island. It's where *you* belong. So no, I don't think you're toying with my affections, as you so quaintly put it, but I don't think you've thought out what's going to happen when I fall for you and we get rid of your cousin's stalker and you have to…."

His voice quivered then, and Piers rode that sound to a little bit of hope.

"And I have to what?" he prodded, coming back with the sweats and putting them in Miller's hands.

"Have to leave me like everybody else I've loved," Miller said, as if trying desperately to say something like that matter-of-factly.

Piers made a sound then, wanting nothing more than *time* to hash this out, but there was a bump from upstairs, and they both grimaced because privacy was about to become vapor.

"Turn around," Miller said gruffly, shaking the sweats to indicate he was putting them on.

"No." Piers knew he sounded childish, but he didn't care.

"Piers—"

"Put them on now, in front of me, let me see you, know I see you, and *still* reject me—or sit through this meeting in your underwear with a blanket on your lap."

Miller scowled and got out of bed and put the sweats on one foot at a time without making eye contact. "I'm not rejecting you," he muttered as he pulled them up.

"Then what is this?" Piers asked, frustrated.

"I don't know." Miller crossed his arms. "It's a wake-up call, I guess. I... we just need to know that you're going to leave me, uhm, I mean here. That whatever you think you're starting up, I'm going to have to be okay with you going away."

Piers took that as hope too. He moved forward, put his hands on Miller's hips. and tugged his passively resisting body closer. "How do you know I won't come back?" he asked softly. "There's people here who commute to Charleston for the week and come back for the weekend. It's not unheard of."

Miller glanced into Piers's face then. "Yeah, but Piers, you're meant for bigger things."

Piers moved a little closer. "You didn't see me ten minutes ago," he said, feeling triumphant. "I lit up the entire horizon with my power. It doesn't get much bigger than that."

Miller's expression intensified, those lines of ferocious concentration returning. "Why? I mean, I don't remember that. What— what did you do?"

Piers couldn't help it. All that earnestness, all of that good intent. He smoothed Miller's hair back from his face, feeling the salt from sweat and brine breaking and the soft hair beneath.

"The thing that tossed you against the window," Piers murmured. "It was trying to... to suffocate you. To suffocate us all. It was darkness, and I-I poured light on it because I was terrified for you, and it went away."

Miller's expression softened. "That was very brave," he said, and it sounded like there was wonder in his voice.

"I was very worried," Piers said. "Not the kind of worried you get for someone you're going to leave behind. Do you believe me now?"

Those fathomless hazel eyes went limpid, and the mouth—so often firm against any temptation—went soft, and Piers had to taste him, warm him, know he was there and real and safe.

Piers took him, took that suddenly soft mouth, possessed it, and Miller's soft sigh of assent, of surrender, sustained him. Oh, he was so sweet, the way he just melted into Piers's arms like he'd been dying to be there all along. Piers gathered him up, wrapping his arms around Miller's slim waist and pulling him close, closer, until Miller had no option but to twine his arms around Piers's neck and drink in Piers's kisses, responding with a hunger Piers had long suspected beneath Miller's practical, no-nonsense surface.

Piers kissed him some more, making a meal out of what had started as a simple meeting of the lips, and Miller groaned needily, doing his best to feed that craving.

The footsteps clattering down the stairs finally broke them apart, but Piers wouldn't have moved to separate them if Miller hadn't practically leapt backward.

"Someday," Piers said, "we're going to finish that."

Miller stared at him, his hand on his mouth, as Larissa and Kayleigh went to the kitchen island and started unloading the groceries in their arms.

Lessons from Otto

"THIS PLACE is rather tiny, isn't it?" Otto asked, ensconced in one of the stuffed chairs that had been directed away from the television in order to make the entire one-room studio into a conversation pit.

The chairs and the couch were turned toward the kitchen island, and the island was set family style so people could come fill their bowls with the giant cheese and pasta concoction that Larissa and Kayleigh had put together on the fly as Piers and Miller watched.

There was hamburger, canned sauce, shell noodles, and cut up sausages, all thrown in with handfuls of shredded cheddar and stirred together in a giant pot with some crushed garlic and mushrooms.

When Miller had asked doubtfully what they thought they were making, Kayleigh had said cheerily that Helen called it "goulash" but that it didn't really have a name. "It's delicious, it's filling, and it takes about half an hour. Everybody else should be down here by the time it's done. And I think Helen is baking some fresh bread she's had rising to serve with it, and that should fill everybody up, okay?"

"Sure," Miller said, nodding. What did he know about food? He knew the basics—chicken breasts, omelets, mac and cheese. This was homemade and hot, and he was a fan. "Can I help?"

Larissa gave him the evil eye. "Get back under the covers and warm up and stop worrying Piers," she said. "Your lips are still white around the edges. Seriously, whatever just happened out there is going to have us all spooked long after Scout and Lucky try to explain it. I mean, I love how into magic and everything they are, but I've had organic chem classes with more mystery."

Piers chuckled, and the sound rumbled in Miller's stomach. God. Twice now they'd kissed. And each time Miller had given Piers more and more of his past, his story, of who he was at his heart.

And Piers kept taking it and asking for more, and Miller was so afraid... so afraid he would give it. God. It had taken him the last three years to get past Brad and the shot Miller still heard in his sleep. How was his heart supposed to survive falling for Piers when his entire future centered around leaving? Leaving Spinner's Drift, leaving the island, leaving Miller's heart in the dust?

But if Piers kissed him even one more time, Miller wasn't sure he could resist. He'd been Cassandra for so long, and Piers already believed him. The idea of being with someone, even for a short time, who knew Miller, all of him, and believed the things he said—that was a heady drug right there, and Miller didn't think he had the strength to turn it down.

And Piers was so damned charming. Yeah, sure, it had probably gotten him laid plenty—Miller had seen the rich young people who liked to hang out at John's Thumb and use the cabanas. But as much as that wasn't Miller's scene, he couldn't deny that when Piers turned his warm brown eyes on Miller, Miller felt wanted and singled out. Special. Piers was polite and funny, and coupled with his belief? Miller wasn't made of willpower. Who could fault him for falling?

It might even be worth the time and the pain it would take to dig himself out after he fell.

"I, for one, *like* their approach to magic," Piers told them, moving toward the bed as he did so and making little shooing motions to Miller. "I'm with them. Get under the covers and get warm. I'll help them. Now go!"

And Miller had felt the wobble in his knees then, the absolute exhaustion that had hit him when he'd awakened in the bed in the first place, and obeyed. He was still wracked with shivers, and his hands and toes were aching like he was out in the snow. He'd love to be able to get up in Piers's face some more and give him shit, but the hard truth was he still had to take the boat back to his cottage that night, and he needed to warm his core temperature and get his strength up to make the trip.

It wasn't such a bad thing, really. Piers put himself at Kayleigh and Larissa's direction and rearranged the furniture, set out the bowls and silverware on the island, and mixed a green salad from ingredients in Lucky's fridge. By the time the others started arriving—Marcus and Otto first after obviously having a long, happy conversation between peers—dinner was out, the coffee table was in the center of the room, and there were enough seats for everybody, provided Piers sat on the bed next to Miller.

He did, on top of the covers after tucking his discarded deck shoes in a corner by the bedstand so they wouldn't get in the way and crossing his stockinged feet.

Miller had a passing thought that Piers was very nearly house-trained, which his last relationship had *not* been, before Scout and Lucky walked in with a big box of pastries—obviously for dessert—and Helen came in with two loaves of bread wrapped in foil and tucked under her arms.

Piers went first and returned to the bed with two bowls full of the "goulash" or whatever it was, with two big hunks of buttered bread resting on top. He gave one to Miller and made himself comfortable with his, and both of them started eating without ceremony.

Miller, who hadn't eaten since the iced sugar cookies at Otto's cottage, was suddenly ravenous, too hungry to think, and for a moment his only objective was food. When he slowed down enough to pay attention to the room, he realized that Piers had done the same thing—in fact *everybody* was starving, and when Larissa said—through a full mouth—that there was enough for seconds, Piers grabbed Miller's almost empty bowl and went.

Finally, *finally*, everybody had eaten enough to actually set their bowls down—Piers took Miller's to the sink—and Miller could feel the room take a breath.

Marcus was the one who spoke first, his voice holding a tint of humor. "In case nobody knew this, using magic takes a fan*tastic* amount of energy, and food is fuel!"

A polite laugh echoed off the walls, but Miller was, in fact, relieved. For a moment he'd doubted his sanity, but apparently being healed counted as wielding magic, and it made sense that it would take calories to sustain it.

Otto spoke next, looking around him in surprise to remark upon the tiny apartment, and Lucky was the one who replied.

"Well, it's plenty big enough for me and Scout, but people keep wanting to sleep on our couch!"

Scout chuckled. "Well, today the whole world seems invested in our bed. I'm starting to think we should make like Marcus and Helen and build a cottage in the woods."

"Not a bad idea," Marcus said, but then he tilted his head and gave Scout and Lucky an inscrutable look. "Perhaps we want to solve the mystery of the ghost trap first. These apartments under the stores are sturdy—the walls are literally made of granite. But the supernatural forces have proved themselves quite adept at destroying property, and it would be a shame to get situated there and end up living in the island's biggest pile of kindling."

"Gee, Marcus," Kayleigh said, making her eyes extra wide, "tell them some more stories about how being a grown-up sucks. Tell them about health insurance and *taxes* next—it's inspiring."

There was some more laughter, and Marcus gave Kayleigh the sort of droll look you'd give a much-indulged granddaughter. "I'm not saying they shouldn't build a cottage, dear. I'm just saying they should wait until it won't get destroyed."

"The ghost trap?" Otto asked softly. And like that they were to the meat of the matter. "Is that what you call it?"

"We *call* it Tom's bench," Lucky said. "And we've sort of made it our...." He gestured at Scout, trying to find words.

"Quest," Scout said without embarrassment or irony. "It's our quest. The ghosts there—the spirits—are trapped. Stuck in the cycle of the worst moments of their lives, I guess. We... well, we've made plans to sort of, I don't know. Resolve their lives. Find a way to right the wrong that got them stuck in the first place."

Otto opened his mouth in shock, then placed his hand over it in obvious emotion. "Really?" he whispered from between his fingers. "Can it be done?"

"It's all about solving a mystery, isn't it?" Kayleigh said with a tart little smile. Scout's sister didn't have the brilliance of her dreamy, magnetic brother, but she did have a certain asperity, an attitude that with a little work it could be done, and that sort of thing was catching. "What went wrong in their lives. How can we try to make amends to the dead."

"Like what?" Otto asked, his voice aching with an unseen thread of tragedy.

"Well, like Tom and Henry," Scout said. He glanced at Lucky, but Lucky rolled his eyes because Scout was obviously the best speaker. "Tom went away, and the boy on the bench looking out to sea was his lover. Henry's the one who built Tom's bench, and he got... stuck, I guess. He never got over losing Tom, and when he died of a broken heart twenty years later after never finding another lover—"

"Wait!" Otto said. "How do you know all this?"

"We researched," Scout said with dignity.

"And the ghosts gave us their wedding rings," Lucky reminded him.

"And the ghosts gave us their wedding rings," Scout conceded. "But there's more to the tableau than that—we've always known it."

Otto looked around then. "Has everybody seen it?"

"Except Miller," Piers spoke up, giving Miller a reproachful look, and Miller looked away. What he'd said to Otto earlier that afternoon was still true—there was such a mystery, such an *importance* to the ghostly hollow that Miller didn't want to go alone.

Dammit, he wanted to go with Piers.

Whether he and Piers ever made love or not, he wanted Piers to be the one to hold his hand and walk him through the mystery. The ghosts felt so *personal* to the core of friends in this room. Miller wanted them to be personal to him too.

Gah! Who was he kidding? Miller wanted *Piers* to be personal, which made his whole entire speech about Piers leaving meaningless— and worse, *hypocrisy*.

Otto nodded and then gave Miller a meaningful look before flicking his eyes to Piers and back. Miller shrugged sheepishly, and Otto arched his brows in sympathy.

"I've seen the ghosts too," Otto said softly. "Not in as much depth as it sounds like you have, but then I wasn't in any shape to meet them as you did, Scout."

"Why not?" Helen asked, and while the older woman could often be sharp, she'd lowered her voice, made the question as unobtrusive as possible, and because Miller had heard the story earlier this afternoon, he was grateful. Otto deserved some gentleness.

"When I first came to Spinner's Drift," Otto told them, his voice falling into the rhythm of a practiced storyteller, "I was very much *a*drift, if you get my meaning. My wife and teenaged son had died in an automobile accident the summer before, and I had just enough income and fame to figure I'd go to an obscure little island paradise and drink myself to death. I mean, I *was* a writer—my liver was probably well seasoned, and I figured all it would need was a bottle of scotch a day to take myself out in less than a year."

There was a quiet intake of breath around the room, and in spite of the youth and inexperience that Miller had frequently marked among the group of friends, he'd been right that compassion was not among the qualities they lacked.

"That *is* a low place, my friend," Marcus said. He was sitting on one of the kitchen stools next to Otto, close enough to squeeze the man's shoulder, and Miller saw Otto squeeze his hand. Friends already, he thought, although he wasn't surprised. It had seemed to him that afternoon that Otto had been hiding among the sexually insatiable tangle on Tatter's Tot. He pretended to be drunk so nobody would hit on him, and when he wanted companionship, he put down the flask and talked to his neighbors. Marcus and Helen were intelligent, funny—and they believed. Otto didn't need his flask to talk to them.

"It was," Otto agreed. "And one day about a week into my plan, I wandered into the hollow with Tom's bench and actually sat on the bench. I'd barely cracked the seal on my bottle when I saw the first ghost: A young girl being whirled about by an adolescent boy—her brother, I was sure of it. And for a moment, I was caught up in such joy…." Otto's voice choked, and he gave them all an apologetic smile, pulled a tissue from the pocket of his suit coat, and wiped his eyes. "And then it faded, and the girl was sobbing inconsolably, staring out to sea. I looked about me, and seated on the bench was a young man also gazing to sea, and he had such shining hope on his face. But as I watched, he grew colder and thinner and sadder, and the hope died." Otto shook his head. "I saw them all that day—the young couple in love and the young couple in terror, the happy mother hugging her son and the grieving mother keeping the moss and the age away from the bench itself. All of it—*all* of it. And the more I watched, the more it seemed that a blanket fell on me, heavy and comforting at first but then cold—so, so cold—and while I tried to fall into the comfort, the cold sucked away my breath."

He paused.

"And after a few moments without breath, my vision began to darken, and that was nice too."

"What saved you?" The voice wasn't a familiar one yet, and young Ciaran looked up from his place sitting cross-legged on the floor in front of the coffee table, a sort of hunger in his gaze.

"I was never sure," Otto said gruffly. "A sort of light, a twinkle of them, a gathering of light particles rolled over me, washing me in an ambient warmth, and I barely staggered out of the clearing, gasping for breath and covered with sort of a black mange, an actual coating of slimy mung that had attached itself to my coat, my face, even my skin in places." He held up his hand, and to Miller's surprise, he could discern a white patch on the back, near the base of the thumb, when much of the rest of his skin was a deep tan. "My drinking hand," he said with a trace of bitter irony. "And it's that mange, that coating, that brought me here today."

He looked around and saw that his audience was riveted, and then he gave Miller a faint smile. Miller had assured him that he'd be believed by this group, and now, as they proved true to the test, Miller wondered why he couldn't have as much faith in Piers as Otto seemed to have in Miller.

"As I stumbled out of the brush, a couple of young men helped me up—big, strapping young men who spent a lot of time swimming or hauling stock for the merchants in the square, depending on the day. And they were amiable as the sun and rain most of the time—sweet as Labrador retrievers. I maintain to this day that they were deeply in love and were just too dumb to figure it out. And as they helped me to my feet, they started brushing the black *gunk* off my clothing and... and it was the oddest thing. Suddenly, for no reason at all, they'd forgotten all about *me*, and they were brawling, right there on the beach. Of course they were both strong as oxen, and within a couple of punches, they were sitting on the sand, bleeding and stupid, and one of them turned to the other and said, 'What the hell, dude?' and the other said, 'Seriously.'"

The burst of laughter was very much needed in the little flat, and Miller joined in. Otto hadn't added that detail when he'd told Miller the story earlier—for all Miller knew, he'd made it up at this moment, when he saw the raptness of his audience, but it didn't matter. The man knew how to tell a story, that was all.

"It's true!" Otto insisted, making Miller doubt it even more. "But as they stared at each other, that... that presence, the buzzing light presence, washed over all of us, and when it was gone, the gunk was gone, and the young men were sleeping in the sun, and I...." He gave a bitter smile. "I was stone-cold sober. And frankly, I haven't really had the urge to drink since. It was as though the presence—the dark one, the one that had coated me in mange or mold—had so thoroughly crushed my spirit that my will to die was completely driven out, and the light, the sweetness that had revived me and cleaned me off had left me with the faintest glimmer of hope."

"Grief," Scout said, making eye contact with Lucky, who nodded. "That black presence around Tom's bench—it's grief. It... it feeds on mourning, on the death of hope. You must have made it a very tasty lunch that day."

Otto nodded. "That may be true, and I'm sure we'll discuss it further, including that buzzing light—"

"We've met," Lucky said dryly. "We call it a Wisp, and it's not always sweetness and, well, light."

"Well, it can be," Scout amended, giving Lucky a reproachful look. "But it can't always protect us from the blanket of grief. It means well."

Otto gave a chuckle of bemusement. "Good to know. But about that black sticky stuff that made the young men fight...."

Marcus and Helen were the first to exchange alarmed looks. "Oh my word. Is that back?"

"Yes," Otto said simply. "Young Miller there was called out to Tatter's Tot, erm, Knitter's Orgy Island, because frankly all those middle-aged orgy participants almost had a riot. As I told Miller, we were going about our day when a ship signaled it needed to come in. I wasn't in a particularly social mood today, so I was hiding, if you will, in a little spot in the underbrush. I had my chair, my book, and a view down to the harbor with both rows of houses in my sights. And that's where I was when the boat docked and a young man got out. The boat itself was covered in gunk, and the young man... he was practically swimming in it. Of course the good folks of Tatter's Tot all gathered around him to see if he was going to be all right, and suddenly...."

He shook his head. "It was quite fearsome. And then the young man dove off the dock into the water, and for a moment I thought all was lost, because it's damned cold, as you all know. But as he hit the water, the black mange washed off, and the young man...."

"Became the Wisp again!" Scout said excitedly. "It... it was the Wisp! But what was he doing on the island?"

Otto sighed. "If I had to guess," he said after a moment, "it was to get a message to me. Perhaps *this* message, so I could pass it on to you." He shrugged. "I do know that the moment Miller arrived and was unaffected by any remaining hostility, I figured he and I possibly shared a few things."

"Like what?" Larissa asked suspiciously.

Otto twinkled at her, and Miller got a glimpse of the charming public man he must have been in his prime. "Are you quite finished eating, my dear? Would you like, say, a roll to fill in the corners?"

With that, the plate on the table that had held the bread, sliced and warmed and ready for butter, filled with four or five crusty, heated dinner rolls.

Larissa grinned at him. "Oh, I would! How about you, sir? Would you be interested in a cup of coffee to go with your dessert?"

Otto's gasp was pure delight, and Miller glanced at the counter to see that Lucky's coffeepot—which had been unplugged, he was sure of it—was suddenly plugged in, and the carafe was full of fresh coffee with just a hint of cinnamon.

Otto closed his eyes and inhaled and then grinned back at her. "Oh, young lady, you do an old man good. Indeed, I would like some coffee. And I suspect everybody else would like a chance to mull over my story in discussion, and I"—he grimaced charmingly—"would love the restroom and a hand to help me up."

"I think we can do that," Larissa told him, and she and Marcus gave Otto a hand while the rest of them lapsed into excited conversation, because what Otto had told them was indeed worth talking about.

For his part, Piers turned to Miller and said softly, "You heard his story, I take it?"

Miller nodded, remembering the charm of Otto's kitchen as they drank tea and Otto spoke. If there hadn't been so much danger and madness in the story, it would have been an enchanted moment. Otto reminded him a lot of his father, even after he'd been injured, when every day had become a fight against bitterness and despair. "Yeah, I knew I had to bring him here so the rest of you could hear it. It… I'm not sure what it means, but it's obviously damned important."

"Mm." Piers nodded in return. "It must be," he said, his voice completely sober. "Because the… the darkness, the 'blanket of grief' or whatever Scout calls it—it attacked you. On purpose. And it singled you out, Miller, much like it singled out Otto, I would bet. I was looking across the quad to the restaurants by the harbor just… just *seconds* before it found you and tossed you at that window. What did that thing find so tasty it had to reach out into the void to try to eat *you* for lunch like it tried to eat Otto?"

Miller swallowed and looked away. "I'm not great with the whole crowd looking at me, Piers. Can we… can I tell you this later tonight?" He had to, he realized. He wasn't looking forward to it, and he *really* didn't want Piers to pity him or give him another chance or any of that other bullshit. He didn't even want to *admit* he was a meal for something like a supernatural grief blanket, or whatever that thing was.

But the thing was dangerous, and Miller's job was to protect people. And these people were special to him. They'd reached out to become his friends when he'd been almost certain it was his lot to be lonely for maybe the rest of his life. He *owed* them an explanation.

But maybe, if he told Piers first, it would be easier to give.

DESSERT WAS served—the cookies and pastries Scout and Lucky had provided were supplemented by Otto's offerings of whatever treat somebody asked for. He seemed genuinely happy to do it for them, handing out plates of Russian tea cakes and chocolate chip cookies with aplomb. Miller wondered if this was the first time he'd had an audience who would believe him and accept his gift without fear or hesitation.

Piers left the bed and returned with a small plate of sugar cookies—slightly warm because Otto apparently remembered from their conversation that afternoon—and Miller gazed at them longingly. *I should get one*, he thought, and was *still* thinking it when Lucky walked up to rummage in the drawers next to the bed and throw stuff into a knapsack he'd pulled from a closet.

"What's up?" Piers asked, and Lucky rolled his eyes.

"Me and Scout are taking Helen and Marcus's guest room. Otto's taking their couch. Larissa and Kayleigh get the girl's flat, and Ciaran gets *their* couch."

Miller frowned, shivering a little because he really *hadn't* warmed up completely. "Why aren't you sleeping in your own bed?" he asked.

Lucky laughed a little. "Because you've been staring at a plate of sugar cookies for five minutes and haven't moved. Miller, you were out, but we all saw you...." He bit his lip, uncharacteristically for the stoic Lucky. "You weren't looking good, brother. It's cold, and we're not going to send you back out there in your little boat to sleep in your own bed. Even if Piers was with you, it would still be a bad idea. You stay here and"—he cut a sideways look at Piers—"stay warm." He gave a quick smile then, self-conscious but genuine, and then went to Scout's dresser and started throwing in *his* clothes.

Piers's warm hands closed over one of Miller's and thrust a cookie between his fingers that Miller ate automatically. Each bite seemed to carry a little bit of Otto's magic in it, and he relaxed into the bed's mattress for the first time. He didn't have to leave, he thought, and as much as he'd longed to have Piers in his own apartment, with his own stuff around him, he realized that Piers didn't have to leave either, and that gave them privacy. Self-containment. Warmth and a place to sleep.

It gave them everything, and he wasn't going to take that for granted.

"I've got a knapsack," he said out of nowhere. "In the cockpit of the skiff. It's got…." He swallowed, thinking about a toothbrush in the morning and clean underwear. "It's got clothes and stuff. So I don't put anybody out."

Piers scooted a little bit closer, still on top of the covers, and lowered his mouth to Miller's ear. "You're not putting anybody out," he murmured. "Lucky's right. You still look cold. This is their way of taking care of you."

"And you?" Miller asked, hating himself a little.

"I could take *such* good care of you," Piers told him, settling in for that closeness. "If only you'd let me."

Miller sighed, and a sudden exhaustion beset him, the kind that came with a day out in the elements, of his body fighting off cold.

"For tonight," he murmured, relaxing against Piers. "I need to call in—"

"Kayleigh called Callan," Piers told him without compunction. "Told him to call your supervisor and tell him you'd be out tomorrow too."

Miller opened his mouth to protest, but Piers shook his head. "As much as I'd like to claim credit, to say this is all to spirit you away to this tiny little apartment to use as a love nest, the fact is, this is really bad, Miller." Piers pulled away far enough to meet his eyes. "You and Otto are both tired and need to rest, but it took *all* of us to chase the darkness away. And out of you! And that thing that happened at Knitter's Or—erm, Tatter's Tot was terrifying. The timing can't be coincidental, and the boat with the resort logo on it can't be either. It's *got* to be related to the, uhm, armed and crazy on the resort side of the island. It's a big puzzle—and a big tangle—and we can't do it all tonight. It's all hands on deck." Piers shrugged. "And like it or not, you're part of the crew."

Miller sagged against him a little more, feeling weak but, just this once, giving in to yearning. "I like," he admitted. "I've never been in the crew before." Not even on the force in New Jersey, when he'd always had a little bit more knowledge that he had to hide, a little bit of himself he couldn't show another human.

"Me neither," Piers admitted, sounding like a naughty schoolkid. "Fun, isn't it?"

Miller let out a low chuckle and fought off the wave of exhaustion. "I should go get my knapsack," he mumbled, and Piers's arm came up around his shoulders.

"Later," Piers murmured in his ear. "Later."

"Okay, later," he said. Or at least he *thought* he said it. But he was finally warming up, and Piers's arm was *so* comforting, and for once in his life, he let go of himself and slept.

"BRADLEY, NO!"

As usual with the dream, the gunshot woke him, terrified and sweating. He struggled to sit up, tearing at the hooded sweatshirt he'd somehow fallen asleep in, desperate to figure out where he was.

The sweatshirt hit the floor, and he sat, panting, staring wild-eyed at his surroundings, waiting for his vision to adjust. Dimly he became aware of a warm presence under the covers with him, sitting up and swearing before a soothing hand found that spot between his shoulder blades and started rubbing.

"Miller?" came a confused voice from the shadows. "What's wrong? Did you have a dream?"

Piers. Oh God, he *wasn't* alone. Piers was with him, and they were... they were....

"Where am I?" he asked, knowing the answer was right there, teasing his brain, but he was too disoriented to find it. "What—what are we doing here?"

"It's me. Piers," he said gently, sitting so they were shoulder to shoulder but keeping up that soothing motion with his hand on Miller's back. "We stayed the night at Scout and Lucky's, remember? You fell asleep while everybody was still here, but Lucky fetched your knapsack, and everybody left."

"You stayed," Miller said wretchedly, hugging his knees and shivering. "You stayed."

"Yeah, baby. I wouldn't have left you here alone. Not when you didn't know where you were."

"Don't leave me alone," he begged, feeling pathetic. "Don't... oh God." He leaned against Piers, seeking help in the aftermath of the dream as he wouldn't have under any other circumstance, and Piers draped his arm over Miller's shoulders and pulled him close.

"Oh, baby," Piers whispered. "I wouldn't leave you in the dark. I promise."

"You can't promise," Miller told him, his own quaking voice almost his undoing. "Nobody can make promises with armed and crazy around. Just... just listen. Listen to me when I warn you. Listen!"

"Of course," Piers said. "I'll always listen. Who didn't listen, Miller? You're terrified for somebody who didn't listen."

"He didn't listen, and he never came back," Miller whimpered, and then—oh please, no—the first sob tore through his throat, and the second shoved through right behind it. The third had an easier path, and by then, Miller's head was against Piers's chest as he lost it, truly lost it, for the first time since he'd been eleven and his father had almost not come home.

The sobs eventually quieted, and Piers brought him a cup of water and some ibuprofen.

"Thanks," Miller said through a raw throat after washing the painkillers down with the water. His head ached like a beaten gong, and his nose was still clogged with sobbing. "How'd you know?"

"Bad breakups through college," Piers said, mouth twisting as he took the cup and set it on the bedstand. "Looking after Larissa these last six months as she dealt with fear and grief. Take your pick."

"Who'd break up with you?" Miller asked almost involuntarily. "I mean, I get blindsided by armed and crazy all the time, but dumping you is just stupid talk right there."

Piers let out a chuff of laughter as he scrambled back under the covers with Miller. Miller realized he was wearing boxers and a T-shirt and was probably freezing like any other mortal would be in this almost subterranean apartment. The blankets and comforter were thick and warm, but the space heater must have been turned off because it was too cold to sit around in their underwear and have an adult conversation. Miller threw his pride to the wind and snuggled in next to him, turning to his side so they could see each other in the darkness.

"Not all the rich, gay young men like to come out," Piers said into the secret hollow of their breath. "The second or third time you get told that you're a great passing phase but he's got to marry a rich young lawyer or congressman's daughter, you get to cry about it."

"I'm sorry," Miller said, and his heart was in the words. "You're a decent guy, Piers. You didn't deserve that."

Piers's shoulder rose and fell in the shadows. "Thanks for that. I happen to agree. But that doesn't mean it didn't hurt when it happened. All three times."

Miller sucked air through his teeth. "That really sucks. You didn't expect it?"

Piers let out a huff of air. "Well, I did grow suspicious the third time, but when I called him on it, he lied to my face. Honesty—seriously, it's an underrated trait." Piers's hand came out to cup his cheek in the dark. "You've got it in spades. Damned sexy."

Miller felt a shaft of guilt. "I've lied about a thing or two," he muttered.

"Sure you have." Piers clearly didn't believe him. "Now lie to me about tonight and tell me it was just a dream."

Miller couldn't do that, though. Not now. "I promised I'd tell you the truth," he said. "When we were talking about grief."

"Ah."

Miller had to smile. None of this sounded like it surprised Piers in the least.

"I told you it sucks being Cassandra," Miller started, and Piers nodded. "Who didn't believe you?"

In all the times Miller had practiced telling this story to someone so he'd have words when it was time, he hadn't counted on that someone actually understanding why this sucked so bad. The relief flooded through Miller with the painkiller, and for a moment, he felt strong and able to stand against anything—even the powerful emotions that rocked him.

"Lots of people," he admitted. "Starting with my father when I was eleven. My sister and I were waiting in the car, and he was going into the gas station to get some snacks. We were on a trip to the ocean, if you can believe that, and... and I felt it. I *felt* this force of malevolence, of irrationality and cold metal, and all the thoughts were of blood and bullets and...." The shots from the convenience store echoed in his brain, and Miller's next breath was shaky at best. "It took ten hours of surgery and months of occupational therapy, but he was all my sister and I had. To this day I'm more grateful they could save him than I am for anything else in my life, but...."

"You're still bitter," Piers said.

"I'm *pissed*!" Miller burst out. "I told him. I *begged* him. And I was so scared, my sister, Clary, started to beg with me. But he just laughed at us both and told us not to be silly and... and then walked in to almost die. And I was so mad. If he'd just *listened*, none of that had to happen. And two years later, my eighth-grade teacher…. She was young, and I told her to get somebody to walk her out to her car after school that day. And I felt it. I was at home, doing homework, and I felt her fear as she heard the footsteps behind her and her panic as the guy grabbed her hair and yanked her down." His voice shook. "I passed out as she was assaulted, but I woke up and it was like I was in her head. I *felt* her pain, her violation, her absolute fucking terror. She never came back to teach after that, and I was so over not being listened to. I became a cop so I could defend people from deranged gunmen. I know that sounds stupid, but I told myself, 'Hey, if it's my *job*, someone's *got* to believe me.'"

Piers sucked in air through his teeth. "Not so much?" he asked, as though afraid of the answer.

"Not even a little," Miller snapped. "I couldn't keep a partner. I'd try to tell them what we were dealing with, and they'd ignore me or laugh at me or call me a coward—that was my favorite. And then shit would go wrong, and they'd be like, 'Hey, good guess!' and then they'd ask for a transfer." Miller shook his head, the bitterness still rank in his throat.

"That's awful," Piers murmured soothingly. "I mean, truly. Awful. Larissa and I had each other and our little abilities that just, you know, made life easier. We always sort of yearned for something bigger, something that could help protect people, like yours. It never occurred to either of us that the people in our lives just wouldn't… wouldn't believe what we said."

Miller snorted. "I don't know. Did you ever tell anyone besides your cousin?"

Piers grunted. "Now that you mention it, no. I guess Larissa was enough until we got here."

"Yeah." Miller sighed, some of the bitterness draining from his body, his voice, as he did so. "I was working with cops—some of the least imaginative people on the planet and definitely the least empathetic. The stupidest thing I ever did was start sleeping with one."

"Oh my God," Piers said, sounding as surprised as Miller had ever heard him.

"Yeah, I know. Makes me the dumbest asshole on the planet, right?"

Piers gave a weak chuckle, and Miller abruptly wanted to move closer to him, tangle their legs, feel his skin. Without questioning his own motives, Miller did that, and Piers *hmm*ed before saying, "Remember,

Miller, three guys. *Three* dumped me because they'd been planning to marry a nice girl their family picked out before we even started dating."

It was Miller's turn to chuckle. "So neither of us wins any genius awards," he said, and something—not his grief, certainly, but his self-recrimination—started to erode with the sound. Miller hadn't been dumb; he'd been trusting. He'd thought he'd been in love. But he hadn't been the stupid one. He could have some pride about that.

"What was he like?" Piers asked, and to his credit he *tried* to keep the jealousy out of his voice.

Miller found he sort of liked the jealousy. Not that he thought Piers would be a possessive prick or anything like that, but that he *mattered* enough to this handsome, kind man for Piers to want Miller to himself. He realized it had never mattered to Brad. But then Brad had never claimed he was exclusive, because for Miller, beggars couldn't be choosers.

There was a reason Cassandra had chosen to join Agamemnon in bed, where she knew death awaited. The prospect of living alone with only terrifying thoughts for company could derail the stoutest heart.

"He wasn't a prize," Miller said, and it was the first time he'd ever said such a thing out loud. The mourning he'd done in front of his department had been for a friend—and good ole Brad had been the best of friends, always brought beer to the party, always ready to take a brother out for a drink, always had his buddy's back.

Piers's choked laugh told him he might have been a bit blunt. "That's… I mean, I expected sainthood if you still miss him after… what? How long's it been?"

"Three years," Miller said, feeling foolish. "But, you know. Not a lot of guys in my past. This one stuck for over a year. He was sort of larger than life. Everybody's favorite bachelor. All the wives were trying to fix him up with their sisters, and nobody could figure out why he'd only make it to two dates."

Piers grunted. "Ugh."

"Well, yeah, but not all bad. If someone needed help moving, he'd show up and only expect to be paid in pizza. If you needed someone to take your shift 'cause your kid had a recital or something, Brad would jump right in. He wasn't even a bad cop. He was the guy who hooked the homeless man up with the shelter or the domestic abuse victim up with the counselor. He once pretended to arrest a woman to get her out of her husband's clutches, and then got a bunch of us to go in and get her stuff when he found a safe space for her. I mean...." Miller shrugged. "A good guy, really, if you weren't his booty call."

"But you *were* booty call," Piers said gently. "Why? I mean...." In the darkness, Miller saw a brief glint of teeth. "You're sort of a long-term guy, Miller. Why let yourself be booty call? You, uhm, don't seem the type to fall for a charming scoundrel."

Which is sort of what Miller thought Piers might have been at the beginning. It was only after two months of being a solid presence here on Spinner's Drift, eager for the camaraderie of the other magic users on the island, that Miller began to see him as more than a hard-core flirt.

The kisses helped. Solid, thoughtful, ravenous, controlled. Piers didn't kiss like a man who was in a hurry to go anywhere. *Maybe you should give him a chance?*

"I was lonely," Miller admitted breathlessly. "I knew better than to come out to anybody in my department, but we were partnered up. And one day, he... he took me out for a beer, walked me home, asked to come in and use the head, and that was it. He left before dawn, and I thought, 'Okay, that was neat. Maybe it'll happen again?' And that was our relationship. Some nights he'd show up, some nights he didn't."

"For the record," Piers muttered, "after we make love, if you think 'that was neat,' you need to tell me so I can change my name, abandon my fortune, and become a monk."

Miller tried but couldn't control the snort of laughter that took over his body. "Awfully confident, aren't you?" he asked, and in response Piers locked their tangled legs even closer together.

"Tell me in the morning," Piers murmured, and he trailed his fingertips under the covers, brushing Miller's shoulder, his ribs, his hips. "I frankly don't see us leaving this bed without making the earth move."

"Moving fast—"

Piers kissed him, long and hard, and Miller barely managed to stay in the present.

"Okay, fine," he moaned, wanting to drown in the warmth of Piers's kisses. "But let me finish."

Piers pulled their mouths apart but left their bottom halves tangled. "Deal," he said, and Miller could hear the resolve in his voice. "I don't want to hear the evil ex's name in bed with us again, okay?"

"I don't even *know* your ex-boyfriends' names!" Miller protested.

"Chad, Kevin, and Murray," Piers snapped off smartly. "Yes, they were all as white, entitled, and bland as that sounds like. Not a Miller among them. Now finish your story."

Miller grunted, reassured on some level because what he said next surprised even him. "I'd sprained my ankle the day before he got shot. He said I wasn't hurt that bad and told me I should take rideshare home. And I did. And then he showed up that night, a little buzzed, and he didn't apologize, or ask me how my ankle was. Just got all boozy and charming and handsy, and I let him. And the next morning, I felt it, knew it was the day. Knew I'd been afraid of this day since we'd been assigned together. And I tried to tell him, and he put on yesterday's uniform from his backpack and ran out the door, laughing about how nervous I was. And he didn't come back. Ran into danger without backup, just like he'd done the day before when I rolled my ankle."

Miller's voice was getting thick, and he hated that. Hated that he couldn't tell this story dispassionately. Brad had been a fun if dangerous partner and a shitty boyfriend—and Miller couldn't seem to wall off his emotions, to listen to the side that said he would have broken Miller down eventually, wrecked him and his confidence and his self-esteem in the worst ways.

"I'm so sorry," Piers murmured, and Miller refused to cry again, attempted to explain.

"We wouldn't have lasted," he said. "He was horrible for me—you get that, right?"

"Well, yeah," Piers said softly, cupping Miller's cheek. "But whether he was a good bet as a lover or not, he was still your friend. You're allowed to miss him. To be mad he's gone."

Miller nodded, and Piers's permission for him to be hurt was almost like magic. It was also permission to heal, and Miller wasn't sure when he'd begun to need that, but Piers's kind words washed over him, a balm, an emotional analgesic that eased the pain enough for Miller to breathe.

"He just… just didn't listen to me," Miller whispered. "He never listened."

"*I'm* listening," Piers whispered back. "Doesn't that count for something?"

"Yeah."

Piers's mouth on his was gentle at first, but Miller was aching for his taste. He opened his mouth and invited that kindness, that healing, inside, and Piers's groan told Miller all he needed to know about suppressed hunger.

Piers pulled back and spoke then, fumbling for words. "I want you," he said, voice ragged. "I want you so badly. If you have any objections, please raise them now, because I don't want to stop."

Miller closed his eyes, and every pretense of being strong crumbled. Refusal was probably the right thing to do—probably the self-protective thing to do—but Miller was so tired of being careful, and so damned lonely.

A night with Piers. Two nights. A week. A month. He'd been so kind, and in two months of flirtation had shown more constancy than Brad ever had.

And that luxury of faith—how could Miller turn that down? This man had poured light into the darkness to protect him. What kind of fool would he be to not taste that brightness when he had the chance?

Particularly when it felt so good. "Don't stop," he whispered. "Please. Please don't let me fall."

"Not while there's breath in my body," Piers promised, and from anyone else, it would have sounded silly and melodramatic, but not from Piers, whose every act, from generosity to agency, was filled with such substance and purpose. "Come here."

Miller pushed himself into Piers's embrace, and Piers kissed him again, hotly, with a kind of openmouthed carnal joy that left Miller breathless.

His hands were insistent and everywhere, pushing under Miller's T-shirt, cupping Miller's chest, his shoulders, his ass. Miller couldn't get enough, arched against Piers begging for more. Their tangled legs untangled as Piers shoved Miller's briefs down and then his own, and for a moment Miller couldn't breathe at all as their naked bodies moved silkenly together.

"What?" Piers asked, stripping Miller's shirt over his head.

"We're naked," Miller almost moaned. "I forgot how good it felt to be naked with another human."

Piers chuckled roughly and stripped his own shirt over his head. "I've wanted you naked almost since I first saw you," he confessed. His hand came up to cup Miller's chin. "All this earnestness, this honesty—I couldn't devour it fast enough."

Oh Lord. "Who says these things?" Miller asked almost frantically as Piers rolled on top of him. Miller wrapped his legs around Piers's hips, urging him closer as they frotted, yearning for Piers to do more than grind against him—yearning for Piers inside.

"I do," Piers growled, and then he took Miller's mouth again in a kiss that obliterated time, laid waste to space, and left Miller's consciousness, his words, to float around in the ocean-roaring darkness while Miller's body lost itself in sex.

Piers tore his mouth away and started kissing down Miller's throat, taking his time to nibble, to tickle, and to lave. He broke the lock of Miller's legs and kissed his way down Miller's chest, sucking a tight, aching nipple into his mouth and flicking the end with his tongue. Miller moaned and knotted his fingers in Piers's hair, holding him tight against his skin while his body, long asleep, long blanketed in grief he hadn't wanted to give voice to, remembered how to demand ecstasy.

A wave washed over him, not quite the peak, but it left him shuddering, muscles easing against the mattress, fingers loosening in Piers's thick blond hair, as he tried to control his reactions, tried to get hold of himself.

"Relax," Piers murmured, skating his lips across Miller's tummy—too firmly to tickle, not hard enough to make him suck in his gut. "What's the worst thing you can do when I'm making you feel good?"

"Get loud," Miller said breathlessly, and Piers was low enough that his deep chuckle blew air on the end of Miller's stiff and aching cock.

"Good," Piers said, flicking his tongue over the bell.

"There's people," Miller complained, and Piers pushed himself up on his elbow, wrapping his warm hand around Miller's cock and stroking slowly while he spoke.

"Where, Miller?" he asked, and Miller's eyes had adjusted enough to see the crinkles in the corners of his eyes. "There's a big chunk of granite between this apartment and the girls' bedroom, and Ciaran's on their couch. Everybody else is out in the forest in the middle of the island, and Lucky and Scout are probably wishing *they* were here in *this* apartment so they could have sex without worrying about who would hear. What are you worried about?"

Miller stared back at him and tried to pull in his lower lip, which wanted to mutiny. "I could be loud and embarrassing," he said, wishing he had enough experience to even *know*. Every encounter he'd had so far, including his relationship with Brad, had been about the other person's needs. This—this *thing*, where Piers stroked his cock and teased his cockhead and oh, oh God, tickled his cleft down by his taint—wasn't part of Miller's sexual repertoire.

"Nobody to be embarrassed about," Piers said wickedly before sucking the bell of Miller's cock into his mouth and swirling his tongue a little.

"You—ou!" Miller moaned, falling back against the pillows.

Piers bobbed his head a couple of times before pulling up and flicking his tongue across the slit. Miller was fighting not to make noises then, but he knew a few broke out.

"Miller," Piers said throatily, forcing Miller to look down his body to where Piers lay, propped up on his elbows, squeezing Miller's cock some more.

"What?" Miller panted.

"Don't be embarrassed to enjoy yourself," Piers said, and this time, when he swallowed Miller down, Miller's cockhead hit the back of his throat.

This time Miller cried out, spreading his legs and allowing Piers to clamber between them as Miller gave Piers carte blanche to continue.

"That's more like it," Piers practically hummed. Then he swallowed Miller down again and squeezed Miller's base, and Miller lost track of himself, of his noises, of the things he said urging Piers on.

Then he felt it, Piers's spit-slick finger probing his cleft as Piers sucked Miller's cock farther down his throat. Miller's knees fell apart, and he heard himself begging, begging to be penetrated, begging to be fucked.

Piers thrust his finger inside, and the rough burn of it had Miller thrashing around on the bed, whimpering, *pleading* with incoherent syllables, needing possession as he'd never dreamed of needing anything sexual before in his life.

Another finger joined the first, and now Miller felt the synthetic slippery texture of lube.

"Where'd you get tha'?" he slurred as Piers pulled his fingers out. "Oh God, more," he begged.

Piers shoved his way up Miller's body and pushed his legs and his hips up, opening Miller like a wishbone ready to be torn apart.

But that's not what he did. Instead, Piers placed his cock—oh wow—right at Miller's gate. Was *that* his cock? Miller hadn't had a chance to stroke it, to taste it, and he wanted to. He wanted to know it like a friend so when Piers left he could remember everything.

But Piers's cock was at his entrance now, and it was big and slick and throbbing and—oh... oh wow.

Miller remembered this and closed his eyes, willing himself to relax, to embrace the offending intruder, to welcome... oh! Oh! It was past the tight ring, and Miller went completely boneless, shaking with need and pleasure and the invasion of his body.

"How you doing?" Piers asked as he sank into Miller's ass with all the assurance of someone who belonged there, was meant to be a part of Miller's flesh.

"Yummy," Miller said, and Piers's rough chuckle told him that was probably not the right thing to say.

"Excellent," Piers said before pumping very slowly—out, out, out—innnnnnnnnn. Miller keened when he was all the way seated and then groaned as Piers began to pump out again. Out, out, out—

"Oh my God!" Miller cried in surprise as Piers snapped his hips forward hard and fast. "Oh yes! Oh hell—more!"

The sound Piers made then was positively evil. "Oh yeah," he growled, and then... oh wow. Oh jeez. Oh heavens oh hells oh glory fuckin' hallelujah! He began to fuck Miller powerfully, that incredible cock stretching Miller out, pleasuring him, thrusting hard on his sweet spot and making him gibber with ecstasy to the point of pain.

But never over.

Never rough.

Masterful. Piers Constantine took control of Miller's body and used it thoroughly while Miller cried out in complete surrender beneath him.

One... more... time... and Miller felt it. The rising torsion of climax, tightening all his muscles, popping sweat out on his face, on his chest. He couldn't bear it. Couldn't sustain the pressure. Couldn't live with the joy of it! He started shaking all over, and Piers kept fucking him, kept pounding inside him, claiming him, making Miller the focus of all his powerful ego, his powerful sex, his powerful possession.

"Piers!" he cried, the first real word he'd said in a while. "I'm frightened!" Through the tensing of his body, the inescapable, building full-body shatter of orgasm, he heard his own words and quailed. Who said that? Who was afraid of—oh! Oh Lord! Piers had pushed back on his knees, his hips still thrusting at speed, but he'd taken Miller's cock in his hand and was squeezing.

"Fall apart," Piers demanded breathily. "Come for me. Don't worry, Miller. I'll catch you!"

The final wave crested inside him, and he exploded. He bore down on Piers's cock, shaking violently, and his cock spat come between them. Piers let go of him to catch his own weight on his hands as he continued to thrust, sweat running down his forehead even in the chill of the apartment. With a low roar, his hips stuttered, and Miller could feel him, *feel* the pour of come in his ass, and the combination, the combustion of the physical and the emotional, drove him up one more time.

He shouted, a hoarse, incoherent sound, and his body came completely undone. He quivered all over, rocked to the core and overstimulated to the breaking point as Piers groaned heartily and kept coming inside Miller's body.

Miller closed his eyes and let the trembling take him over, abandoned himself to the things his muscles, his pleasure and pain centers, needed. The things Piers had done to him and was still doing, feathering kisses down his temple, bumping his nose along Miller's jaw.

Miller's body went limp, and Piers sighed, apparently replete, and rolled to the side.

The spend that coated Miller's thighs brought him a moment's embarrassment.

"We'll have to," he panted, "change the sheets."

Piers's throaty laughter surprised him. "*That's* all you've got to say?"

Miller let out a breath of a chuckle. "It's a good thing," he said, "you told me I could be loud."

This time Piers buried his face in Miller's neck and really let himself laugh while Miller reached across his chest and palmed the back of Piers's head.

Finally Piers's laughter died down, and they both reached for the blankets to pull over their bodies, which were no longer sweating in the cold.

With a sigh they positioned themselves—or rather, Piers positioned them—with Miller as the little spoon and Piers draped over his shoulders, lacing their fingers together over Miller's stomach.

Miller found himself snuggling back against Piers's warmth and his powerful body, feeling protected and safe as no other lover had ever let him feel.

"How you doing?" Piers asked softly, and Miller closed his eyes against the dark, against the warnings his brain tried to whisper, against the guilt for enjoying something so thoroughly when he didn't know where it was supposed to go in the end.

"You've wrecked me," he said dreamily. "I appreciate it."

Piers's low chuckle was his reward for being funny. "You were worth the trouble," Piers told him, nuzzling his shoulder. "That was amazing. *You* were amazing. Thank you."

"Don't see how I was so amazing," Miller confessed. "All I did was lay back and let you have your way with me." He paused and then added, "Loudly," in the interest of full disclosure.

Piers chuckled again. "Next time, I get to be the lazy one. I'll lay back and let *you* make love to *me* until I can't stand it anymore, and then I take you again."

Miller grunted. "Sounds great. Am I supposed to top anytime soon?"

"No," Piers said, so decisively Miller had to laugh. "No. You have been alone too long. You get to top when you remember you deserve pleasure too."

Miller *hmm*ed. "What about you? Don't you deserve to be pleasured?"

"Oh, Miller," Piers all but purred. "I have pleasured myself beyond climax on your body. Don't worry about me. I'm going to do it again and again and again, and it's never going to get boring."

What a lovely fantasy. "Sure," Miller agreed, eyes closing, Piers's warmth at his back still protecting him more than he'd ever felt sheltered before.

"Maybe, after the fiftieth, sixtieth time," Piers said philosophically, "you'll believe me."

Miller groaned. "Low blow, Agamemnon."

"Then believe in me, Cassandra," Piers finished pertly.

"Maybe I will," Miller mumbled, and then he was too tired for banter anymore. He closed his eyes in sleep.

Clean Sheets

PIERS WOKE up early when his phone buzzed on the nightstand.

Sleep in 'til ten, it said, a text from Lucky, and he blessed the guy because that gave him and Miller some time.

Miller was still sleeping soundly. Limp and replete, he hadn't moved since their last muffled words. Concerned, Piers propped himself on one elbow and feathered his fingers through the hair over Miller's ear, wondering what he needed more—sleep or sex or soothing.

"Whatcha doin'?" he slurred, and Piers settled down at his back again.

"Watching you sleep."

"'S creepy. Stop."

Piers let out a breath of laughter. "Sure." He tightened the arm around Miller's waist, his entire body contracting and expanding in that morning stretch that signaled he could possibly wake up now, even though it was barely 6:00 a.m....

As the stretch ended, his bare groin made contact with Miller's bare bottom, and Miller shuddered in his arms. Ever so subtly, Miller moved his top leg forward, opening himself up again, and while Piers wasn't sure if that was a conscious or unconscious invitation, he suddenly wanted to take it—take *Miller*—in a more than casual way.

Piers stretched again, this time grinding up against Miller, his cock hardening and balls swelling in reaction to that taut, smooth backside.

"You didn't ask," Piers growled in Miller's ear.

"About what?" Miller responded, arching backward against Piers in another unsubtle invitation.

"About my HIV status."

Miller's entire body tightened, and Piers wanted to curse himself, but this was important.

"It's negative," he hastened to say, relieved when Miller relaxed again. "I'm on PrEP. And you haven't been with anyone in three years, so I figured you're probably negative too."

"Tested after he died," Miller muttered—more in embarrassment than sleep, Piers was certain. "Wasn't sure he was exclusive."

"Mm…." Piers pushed up against Miller's naked body again. "Good. Don't want to worry about that." His cock slid into the cradle of Miller's ass, and he thrust some more.

"I didn't," Miller said, arching back against him. "It's the only good part of being Cassandra."

Piers was so surprised he stopped. "You know when someone's…?"

"Armed with bad intent," Miller replied breathily. "Keep wielding your weapon, soldier. I need to be impaled!"

Piers buried his face in the back of Miller's neck and gave a strangled laugh. His cock was hard, and Miller's flesh was warm, willing, and still stretched from the night before.

"Gimme a sec," he pleaded, scrambling for the lubricant he'd found under the pillow earlier. Bless Scout and Lucky; he wasn't sure if they'd meant to facilitate his sex life, but he was grateful anyway.

His oily hand on his own cock ramped up his arousal, and when he was back in position, Miller had propped one leg up, giving him perfect access to—

"Ah…." Miller sighed in abandonment, and the stiffness Piers had sensed from the night before, the fear of someone who hasn't done something important and huge, had faded. In its place was a wanton enjoyment, and Miller thrust back against him, opening and accepting as Piers penetrated him.

"Mm…." His body, hot, slick, tight, wrapped around Piers's cock like a satin vise, and Piers shuddered in the sheer hedonism of fucking an eager lover.

"Okay?" Miller asked, arching his back to allow Piers in farther.

"Perfect," Piers moaned, accepting that inch and taking a mile. "Gah! *So* perfect."

Miller let out a sweet sigh of his own, and Piers skated his hand over Miller's chest, spending a moment pinching a stiff, excited nipple.

"Stroke yourself," he whispered in Miller's ear, his hips never losing rhythm.

"In front of you?" Miller squeaked, and his body tightened in surprise.

"Shh…." Piers spent a few strokes calming him down, relaxing him again, getting back to their even keel, before trying another tack. "So pretty," he murmured, running his hand down Miller's flank to his hip. He wasn't lying. Miller's body was well defined by an active life of work outdoors. His hips were lean, as was his waist, and his chest had enough developed muscle for Piers to get a good handful when he went to squeeze a pectoral. "Look at this body," he purred, keeping his strokes even, just enough to tantalize, not enough to satisfy, not yet. "Sturdy, clean, made for hard use…."

"I'm not a… oh God…. Faster. Racehorse."

Piers laughed in his ear and stayed at exactly the same speed. "You're my lover," he murmured. "And I've been waiting for you. Why can't I watch you stroke your cock?"

Miller gave a low moan, and Piers gave an inward fist pump. "Embarrassed…," he breathed, and Piers moved his hand over Miller's and laced their fingers together.

"Hot," he corrected, moving Miller's hand toward his cock. He'd have to break his stride, hunch his back to get it all the way there, and he wanted Miller to *want* it, to *want* to please himself, to please Piers. He kept his hips set on "tease" and reached down as far as he could, waiting for Miller to move on his own.

"Don't you wanna?" he baited. "Don't you wanna stroke yourself? Let me watch you?"

Miller's hand moved hesitantly, and Piers threw in the kicker. "I'll go harder if you touch yourself," he urged, slowing down even more.

Miller's tortured groan was music to his ears.

"Please?" he begged, and Piers lifted himself up enough to watch as Miller's bony, roughened hand closed over his cock.

"Yesss!" And Piers snapped his hips forward as hard and as fast as he could.

Miller practically screamed, and his fist tightened, turning the end of his cock into a weeping plum, and Piers shuddered in excitement.

Miller liked a little bite, just a little, to his sex, and now Piers knew that about him.

How delicious.

He kept thrusting, as hard and as fast as he could, hampered a little by their position. Then Miller moved, temporarily dislodging Piers from his asshole but rolling to his stomach and pulling his knees up to his chest in a blatant, carnal invitation.

"I like," Piers told him, lips brushing Miller's ear. "Now adjust your position and keep fucking your fist."

Miller's answer was another breathy moan, and Piers scrambled into place behind him. He paused for a moment to run his hands over Miller's backside, along his back, taking in the leanness and wishing for maybe a little more weight. It wasn't a deal breaker, but more Miller seemed to be Piers's flavor, and Piers wasn't losing his taste for him anytime soon.

Ah! Traction.

Piers didn't hesitate, throwing his back and his hips into the job at hand. Miller's body shook, and Piers could feel his strokes, strong, a little hard, probably squeezing his cock until it wept some more. Beneath him, Miller began making the most decadent sex noises, a greedy mewling, demanding more, begging for more, *pleading* for release, and Piers was exhilarated by this new Miller, this self-pleasuring, greedy, wanton Miller who didn't hesitate to let Piers know he was enjoying himself.

To open his body to Piers's invasion, to expect ecstasy, to reach for climax.

Abruptly, almost too soon, Piers felt the contractions rippling through Miller's tight bicyclist's ass, yanking Piers's climax from him before he was ready. He cried out, completely in the moment, pouring himself into Miller's body again, collapsing onto Miller's back, his hips pumping viciously as Piers's orgasm roared through his muscles, his sinews, his blood.

Miller collapsed beneath him, shaking, all control gone from his movements, and Piers tried to shelter his narrower shoulders with his own broader body.

Miller was so vulnerable right now.

So vulnerable all the time.

The thought flashed behind Piers's eyes, his mind unexpectedly naked in aftermath, that Miller was alone most of his days, lost in his own thoughts and solitary in his own heart.

As Miller shook beneath him, trembling again in comedown, Piers wrapped his arms around Miller's lean shoulders and held him tightly, probably too tightly, but he was damned if he'd ever let Miller—*his* Miller—out into the world again thinking he was alone.

FINALLY THEY were situated, Miller with his head on Piers's shoulder, watching through the blinds as the sun touched the porch behind the sliding glass door. Piers had his arm wrapped around Miller's waist, and they were lacing and unlacing their fingers together as they rested on Piers's stomach. Piers didn't want to stop touching him, ever.

"What time is it?" Miller asked drowsily.

Piers glanced at his phone. "Seven thirty."

Miller grunted. "We should wash their bedding."

Piers's lips twitched. "I know where their spare sheets are," he said. "If we wake up at nine, we can have it all changed out, and I can have the load in the washer upstairs before we meet."

"You spend a *lot* of time here," Miller remarked, and Piers was unabashed.

"So much better than the hotel," he said. "And when I get the feeling I'm cramping their sex life, I sleep on Kayleigh's couch instead." Was the hotel more luxurious? Definitely. But he loved this side of the island. He helped Scout and Marcus sometimes when they needed it, or Lucky and Helen. He liked feeling useful and liked that his company was wanted.

Miller *hmm*ed. "I feel so… floaty. I don't remember ever feeling this good after sex."

"I don't think you ever had good sex," Piers said and then wished he had a hand free to clap over his mouth.

"What's that mean?" Miller asked, his shoulders tightening again, threatening to hunch forward. Piers was starting to hate it when he did that. It meant that Miller had remembered to be… constrained. Trapped in a role or a past or a set of expectations that he'd let define him. The Miller who hunched his shoulders was the Miller who wasn't believed. It was the Miller who thought he only got to be booty call because of his job or his gift. It was the Miller who was used to being mocked for trying to keep people safe.

And it was the Miller who, for one reason or another, was too shy to have had really good sex with another man until Piers.

"Because I'm the only one who's heard your noises," Piers said, and he didn't have to ask—he knew. "I'm the only one who's ever watched you touch yourself. Or seen you come apart, or heard you beg." He tightened the arm around Miller's waist. "Don't argue."

"I'm not," Miller murmured.

"I'm honored," Piers told him, dropping a kiss on the top of his head. "You need to believe me when I tell you that I don't want to let that go."

"Okay."

He sounded on the verge of sleep again, but Piers couldn't let him go without knowing what that meant. "Okay what?"

"Being Cassandra sucks, Piers. I won't make you do it. I... I want you too. I've dreamed about you. I'll believe you when you say I'm important. I'll hope when you say we'll find a way. I'm tired of being alone. I'm tired of grieving. Right now"—his fingers tightened on Piers's—"it's like being held by sunshine. I almost died of cold last night. Keep holding me."

Piers caught his breath and realized it was close to a sob. He squeezed Miller's fingers back and closed his eyes against the burning behind them, the overwhelming rush of relief.

"Okay," he said, his voice thick. "Thank you."

"Mm...."

And that was apparently all Miller had in him for now, because in a moment, he drifted off. Piers checked his phone to make sure it was set to go off in an hour or so, and then he pulled Miller tightly to him for a moment before relaxing and joining Miller in his dreams.

MILLER STILL looked exhausted after they'd showered and changed the sheets. The clothes he'd brought in his little knapsack were civvies— jeans and a sea-green T-shirt with Spinner's Drift on the chest, done in a fanciful script, with a burgundy hoodie with some sort of gaming character on the front. It was the first time Piers had seen him not wearing his Morgen Star Security uniform.

"What?" Miller asked, yawning as he stood in front of Scout and Lucky's coffee maker, staring at it in hope as it began to drip. He'd made the brew especially strong, Piers had noticed, and thought that maybe Miller was *perpetually* tired, between the job and his own demons.

"You like color," Piers deflected, padding into the kitchen in his stockinged feet. He kept a change of clothes in Lucky's drawer because he slept over often enough, and they were standard. Blue jeans, white briefs, blue fleece. Only the name brands betrayed their price, but Miller didn't seem to care about that. His socks, Piers noticed, were a deep purple and green, with the same gaming character on the side. "What is that... that thing on your sweatshirt?"

"*Bloodborne*," Miller said with a smile. "My sister, Clary, plays it all the time. Last time I went to visit, we spent practically all three days playing that stupid game. It... made the visit easier. She sent me the hoodie for my birthday that year."

Ooh! So much to choose from. "What was so hard about the visit?" Piers asked, not sure when Scout and Lucky would get there and wanting to know something important before they did.

Miller lifted a shoulder. "My dad," he said, like it was nothing. "He lost a lot of mobility when he was shot. It… it left him bitter. He's angry at the world, you know? Drove Mom away. She kept us for a couple of years but got sick, and we were back at Dad's, and he was…."

"Bitter," Piers said softly. "Does your sister live with him?"

"Naw. She went away to college, got a degree in accounting. Runs her own business. Which sounds all buttoned down and stuff, but she works it from her home office on her own time and spends the rest of her life doing whatever she wants."

Piers grinned. "Sounds awesome. You're not jealous?"

Miller breathed a soft sigh of relief when the coffee drip started to increase in volume. "Nope. She takes dance classes, spends time volunteering with disabled children, plays on a local volleyball team. Dates when she feels like it, sleeps alone when she feels like it, goes dancing when it suits her. Has a solid core of girlfriends who sit and craft and bitch and drink wine at least once a month. She lives a good life." He shrugged. "I do too, really. It's only when we have to go visit Dad for holidays and such that we bury ourselves in video games. This sweatshirt was, like, her way of telling me to protect myself, I think."

Piers's antennae sharpened. "He's hardest on you." He knew that as certainly as he knew Miller would drink that coffee deeply saturated in cream and sugar.

Miller gave him a bleak look. "I think he blames me. He tries not to. In fact you can see him visibly *trying* not to be a bitter old man, but everything hurts, and I'm the one who begged him not to go in the convenience store. So yeah. The sweatshirt was nice. Not having it blue or black was nice. I wish I could think of something really cool and in-depth to ask you, but…." His voice quivered at the end, and Piers had to laugh.

"I'm grilling you without coffee," he conceded, moving to block Miller's view of the coffeepot and pull him into his arms instead.

"So cruel," Miller admitted, leaning his head on Piers's shoulder. He shivered there, and Piers felt the chill that had maybe faded from his bones during their lovemaking the night before but had never really gone away.

"Sorry, baby," Piers whispered, trying to warm up a heart that had gotten far too cold in the course of Miller's life.

"What *is* your family like?" Miller asked, snuggling in a little tighter. "I know Larissa is your cousin. Any brothers or sisters?"

"A sister," Piers admitted. "A perfect sister who has the perfect politically mobile job and makes the perfect amount of money to satisfy our parents. And isn't gay—that's a fun thing."

"Mm...." Miller desultorily stroked Piers's back through his fleece zip-up, and Piers had to admit the comfort was nice. "Is that why you're in law school? To be the perfect son?"

"It *was*," Piers admitted. "But, you know. The problem with school is you get an education. A couple of humanities courses, a social justice course with a really passionate professor—female, I'm not that kind of student—and suddenly I want to do criminal law, defense attorney, the kind who doesn't make a lot of money but, you know, helps people."

Miller sighed, which Piers liked because every time he did that he seemed to sink farther and farther into Piers's arms, into the protection he'd longed to offer from the very beginning.

"Everything you say makes you easier to... like," Miller said against Piers's shoulder. "That's not fair."

Piers sighed too, but his was sad. "You only think that because you're waiting for me to leave you," he said.

"A lawyer for the little people?" Miller stepped back to peer into his face. "Do you understand how important that is? It's not like you're going to be a lawyer to make money and gather all this power. No. You're going to be a lawyer for the people that my asinine supervisor wants to put in jail. The waitress who doesn't want her ass grabbed or the tourist who spent all his money to get here and gets his wallet taken. I mean, how awful would I be if I took you away from that?"

"You don't have to take me away from anything," Piers whispered in his ear. "First we fall in love, then we figure out how to make it work. We're still in step one. It's like sex. Enjoy it. Let it happen. Respond to it. It'll all be good."

Miller squinted at him. "Are you sure you're a rich man's son? That is *not* the philosophy of a type A personality."

Piers shrugged. "I think I broke that part of myself when I deferred law school to take care of Larissa." It was his turn to sigh, and he relaxed more into Miller's space, realizing that this trick of setting your burdens down could be amazing and freeing at the same time. "It was like suddenly the rat race, the 'I'm on the top of my class, look at me, old man, who's the loser now!' was not so important. I mean, you've met Larissa. If her parents weren't going to rise to the occasion—and they weren't—somebody had to."

Miller laughed a little. "You're practically a superhero," he said, and Piers was going to laugh, but suddenly Miller straightened.

"Do you hear that?" he demanded. "The coffee's *done*!"

Piers leaned back against the center kitchen island and chuckled as Miller got out two mugs and began to pour. His pocket buzzed, and he checked his phone, thinking the timing couldn't be better.

"Larissa's bringing pastries," he said. Then he gave Miller a severe look. "You need to eat them. You don't eat enough."

Miller rolled his eyes and handed Piers a mug of coffee. "I'm usually busy," he said. "Six days a week—"

"Is that even legal?" Piers scowled, and Miller held his hand out and tilted it back and forth.

"Legal, not legal. What really matters is that Leo isn't running around the islands making things worse."

"No, that's not what really matters!" Piers snapped, suddenly cranky for Miller, who apparently had no way to be cranky for himself. "What matters is you and your fellow peace officers—"

"Just me," Miller told him mildly. "Those other two guys wouldn't put themselves out to save a granny in the way of a runaway car."

"*Why haven't you said anything?*" Piers burst out.

"Wow—you really *are* starry-eyed if you think that's how law enforcement works," Miller said, chuckling to himself.

Piers stared at him, and Miller gazed happily into his coffee cup, apparently content. Piers cocked his head and tried to decide how to handle this.

"Miller?" he said, eyes narrowed.

"Yeah?"

"Sex was pretty good last night, right?"

Miller glanced at him shyly, his cheeks pinking up like clockwork. "I thought so," he mumbled to his coffee.

"You'd like for us to do more of that, right?"

Miller did a little head-wagging thing over his coffee, a very self-satisfied gesture that had Piers clutching his chest—or would have if he didn't have a goal. "Wouldn't mind," he said.

"So, uhm, if I go back to school and come to visit on the weekends, I want you to think about this. There I am, driving five hours and taking the ferry or spending my trust fund on a private plane or helo for my cousin's resort landing strip so I can visit all my friends here for the weekend. And I spend the morning with our little gang of witches and wizards, and then I take a skiff for an hour to get to your little island, and I'm primed. I'm dying to take you to bed and make you screech like a barn owl, and you—you've been *dreaming* about it. But because you didn't bother to rock the status quo and ask Callan, who's like your *real* boss, because we all know Leo's an ignorant sack of shit, for some reinforcements you can count on, I have traveled all over the goddamned eastern seaboard, and you are out *answering a call*. And there is no sex. And I have to go back the next night. With no sex. And it's another two weeks of us talking on the phone at night, *with no sex*."

Miller was scowling at him. "You are ruining a perfectly good cup of coffee," he complained.

"And *you* are exhausted, and not just from supernatural stuff either."

Miller grimaced and stared longingly at his still-steaming mug of what was, apparently, the thing that sustained him. "If I promise to think about it seriously, could you promise not to nag me for ten more minutes?" he begged almost pitifully.

Piers relaxed a little. "Sure," he murmured, taking his own mug and moving to lean against the counter with Miller. "Sorry for nagging."

Miller moved a little closer so their arms touched. "Sorry for being an asshole without my coffee."

Piers laughed softly and took a sip of his own, and he had to admit, the world looked a little less intimidating when it hit his stomach. Together they stood in a tranquil coffee haze until Kayleigh and Larissa ran downstairs with a big box of pastries and the sugar-rush portion of their day began.

Tom's Bench

MILLER WAS only a little disappointed to find himself at the Tom's bench clearing with a crowd. After breakfast—and Piers had made him eat a sausage muffin in addition to a donut, so he was feeling quite sustained at this point—Helen and Marcus had urged them to go to Tom's bench in the lull before lunch. It was Monday, and Scout and Lucky usually took it off, but the holiday season was busy enough for both shop owners to need the extra help.

But an hour they could spare.

Otto and Ciaran came with them, and at Scout's instruction, everybody paused on the sand before they took the path through the island vegetation to the carpet of crabgrass that formed the apron in front of Tom's bench. The bench sat under a canopy of trees, but the grass faded into sand, so it looked out directly into the sea, facing Charleston, although the mainland wasn't visible on the horizon. It was as though, Miller thought, the bench looked out into infinity, into all the possibilities, into the hope of forever.

A whimsical thought for a man not used to whimsy, but Miller could feel the clearing calling to him. It hummed, resonating in his stomach and up through his chest, the sort of hum that could push a man over when he was trying not to cry or that drove a person to watch a melancholy movie because there was something healing about the sadness. The sort of hum that was a favorite song, forever marred by a terrible memory.

In the back of his mind, Miller heard an old Killers' tune, the one about being young and in love, playing on his phone while he and Clary watched their father walk into the gas station convenience store, and his eyes burned with the tears of a wasted moment, a wasted life, of inevitability.

"Miller!" Piers snapped, grabbing his hand. "Miller, breathe!"

Miller consciously sucked in a breath and then another and desperately tried to center himself.

"This place is cold," he said, and his voice seemed to come from far, far away.

"Larissa, grab his other hand," Piers ordered. "He's freezing."

In a moment, he was surrounded, Piers on one side, Larissa on the other, but the rest of the group—Scout, Lucky, Kayleigh, Otto, and Ciaran—surrounded him too.

Scout met his eyes grimly. "Okay, Miller. I guess it's a good thing you didn't come here alone, isn't it?"

"Guess so," he said weakly. Already assaulted on all sides with sadness—with grief—he couldn't believe what he said next. "But I need to go in. God, you all are right. This place is important."

"Okay, then," Scout said. "We all join hands—I lead, Kayleigh takes the caboose. We link up into a circle when we all get in. Nobody take action. *Nobody*. We're observers here only. We'll compare notes when we come out. Understood?"

Miller nodded, reassured by Scout's boot-camp approach. Scout and Kayleigh were some of the most powerful magic wielders in the world—they had to be. Scout beat his father in combat, and from what Marcus and Helen said, that was unheard of. They'd take care of the people in their charge just like Miller had shown up on the beach two months ago to form a human chain to drag Scout out of darkness. That's what they took on when they decided to help Scout on this quest—not only the determination to help heal the psychic wounds of the souls in this very place, but the determination to protect each other from whatever the supernatural world threw at them.

Still, he'd never felt so brave as he did when Scout got them all in a line, Miller, Piers and Larissa in the middle, and began to tow them in, one at a time.

His feet moved, though, and the buzz of the transition from the plain old beach to the supernaturally protected area of Tom's bench caused the hair on his legs to rise and abraded his skin like a flurry of sand.

They made it to the center of the clearing, and Miller could see… well, ghosts. Translucent forms of people he'd heard about, presences moving about in this place, locked in moments of hope and moments of despair so solidly that not even death could dislodge them.

Their outlines teased his vision—he knew they were there, and even knew who they were, but only because he'd heard the others talk about them, had heard the stories of what they looked like. The hair on the back of his neck rose up, crackling with electricity and apprehension in equal parts, and then the circle shifted, and Scout and Kayleigh joined hands.

The *whoosh* of power that detonated from the center of the circle threw Miller backward, and only clinging to Piers's and Larissa's hands prevented him from breaking the bonds that kept him on his feet. As he fought for his footing, he saw everybody else lacing fingers and squeezing hands tightly, grim determination on their faces until Scout said loudly, "Our breath becomes our shield, so may it be!"

On instinct alone, the rest of them echoed, "So may it be!" and that quickly, the pressure throwing them outward from the circle eased and they were standing again, their hands still linked but without that panicky force that had tried to pull them apart.

"Yikes," Lucky muttered. "How long's that gonna last us, Scout?"

"Not long. Everybody, look around and observe. But remember, don't follow anybody! I've done it, and I needed Lucky to pull me back. There's too many of us to keep track of, okay?"

Miller nodded, and so did everybody else, and he began to glance around the clearing, taking in figures he knew so well by this point they were practically iconic.

But, like with anything live and in person—a band, a play, a work of art—*hearing* about something secondhand, even reading the script or singing along or seeing a replica, is not nearly the same as being there.

Scout and Kayleigh had closed the circle with Tom's bench at their back—which meant Miller, Piers, and Larissa had the best view.

Miller could see Henry, Tom's beloved, sitting on the bench and looking out to sea, the longing on his face so poignant it made Miller's eyes burn and his throat tight. Next to Henry—and sometimes *through* Henry—was Tom's mother, laboring with a scrub brush and bleach Miller could *smell* to keep the marble of the bench clean and free from algae or the encroaching growth of the greenery that surrounded it. In real life, to the ghost-blind, the bench looked well cared for, the ghostly efforts paying off in a granite bench that shined like marble. In the ghostly world, the woman went from a healthy middle age to a worn and haggard cronehood, the despair and sorrow on her face etching itself in terrible lines.

Miller knew to expect those figures, and the figure of the little girl as well. In one place she could be seen whirling in Tom's arms, and in another sitting, her legs crisscrossed under her skirts, staring out to sea, much like Henry, in sorrow and grief and longing. And then in the far corner of the glade, a grown version of the child could be seen kissing a young man, the look on her face one of such wonder and joy Miller's heart ached with the very hope that she could have found a soulmate to comfort her after her brother's death.

But he didn't even need to blink for that vision to change. In the place of the two young lovers discovering a whole new world of kindness in each other's eyes, there was suddenly two cowering victims, kneeling in the face of utmost cruelty, clenching hands and crying out from a terrible blow that Miller absolutely had to stop.

He wasn't even aware he'd broken free from the circle until the warmth that had sustained him from the moment Piers had grasped his hand drained away, leaving him trembling and cold and leaping around the circle of surprised people, over the bench, and into the corner of the clearing to stop the violence, stop the knife from slashing down, stop the inevitable conclusion of that shadowy figure threatening the two innocent victims in his reach.

In the span of a heartbeat, he'd gone crashing into the most haunted corner of the Tom's bench glade, and in an instant, he was swallowed up by the darkness within.

HE KNEW this darkness, he thought vaguely as he rushed the menacing figure looming over the two terrified lovers. This was the darkness that sang ugly songs to his soul when he was least expecting them. This was the darkness that spoke of violence and the madness that spawned it, the darkness Miller had known from a very early age must not be allowed to spread.

Blessed be the light bringers, for they illumine our souls.

The source of darkness became clearer as he vaulted the bench and pitched forward. Lit by some ambient illusion, it took on the subtle curves and hollows of what had once been a human being, now consumed by hatred—hatred and a certain disease of the mind.

He looked normal enough. A man in his midtwenties, with pale skin and rotting teeth and clothes that were thick and heavy and costly for an island that was close to tropical in climate. Wealthy.

"He doesn't know you, Ellie—not like I do."

"Percy.... Percy, we're going to the mainland to marry. I told you that this morning. I... we've saved for a year—"

A pale, limp hand emerged from the miasma that was Percy and caressed Ellie's cheek. She shuddered but took the hand in her own work-roughened fingers and set it gently between her palms, where she held that pasty, limp hand like one would hold a friend's.

"He can't have you," Percy snarled. "I want you. You're... you're perfect."

Ellie, bless her, must have had a pure, kind heart. "Nobody's perfect, Percy. But William and me—we're perfect for each other."

William stepped forward, and in the light, he was a big, plain man, with wide working hands and a broad face. But he smiled kindly at the snarling Percy and extended his hand.

"Ellie and me, we've waited to be married," he said. "We thank ye for her job at yer place. We have money for our own now."

Percy glared at the man and stepped back before giving Ellie one last searching gaze.

"It's nothing," he said, and Ellie and William looked relieved, but Miller heard it. Heard the escalation of madness in Percy's voice. Miller had been caught, frozen in time—frozen even in midair, body suspended in a moment, hovering between the forest canopy and the tiny corner that housed this drama beyond the bench. But with that jangling note in Percy's voice, Miller began to descend, his legs extending toward the ground, his hips shifting backward so he could hit the ground without rolling.

"Nothing?" Ellie asked, only curiosity in her voice.

"Nothing at all to me," Percy said, his voice distant, distant and detached, and Miller's feet were still stretching, reaching for solid earth when he saw the knife. Ellie screamed, and the knife rose and fell, and William yelled, and the knife rose and fell, blood flowing like black water as Miller finally touched down and crashed to his knees, the bodies of the two lovers lying in a pool of blood before him, surprised and gory, their wounds masked by their clothing but unmistakably mortal nonetheless.

"No," he whispered, and reached his hand toward Ellie's open eyes to shut them.

As soon as his fingers made contact with her cold flesh, he was somewhere else.

He was sitting by a heated pool, looking over a chaise at a cold ocean beyond. The sun was bright on the waves today, and there were people all around.

Sort of.

The people were distorted, cardboard cutouts, badly animated cartoons of what people should be, and as soon as Miller's hand made contact, he became one of those people, as real inside a killer's head as the other cardboard cutouts were, walking toward the pool or swimming or serving him drinks.

Killer. Yes. He liked the sound of that. He had killed before. The pretty dark-haired girl was not his only beloved. He'd had other women he'd loved like Larissa Constantine, but Larissa had that tang to her. That smell. The unmistakable smell of money, and the killer craved it. Had stolen it. Wanted to be surrounded by it when he and Larissa finally had their night together, became one under the stars—

MILLER COULDN'T breathe. He was covered in slime, in mange—black gunk coated his face, his hands, his mouth, his skin. He shivered, freezing, and gagged, falling to his side as he struggled for oxygen, and from far away he heard an older voice scream, "Water! He needs water! Don't touch him, does anybody have water—"

Without warning, a deluge of cold water, pure as a mountain stream, drenched him from head to toe, surging into his mouth, pouring over his face, and for a moment he sputtered, trying to breathe, but he realized the deluge was rinsing away the black gunk, healing his skin from the burn, keeping the morass of it from his lungs, and he quit fighting. He held his breath and persevered until the torrent had ended and he was alone, lying on his side in the small bare patch of land behind Tom's bench.

"Piers," came Larissa's voice. "Piers, don't—"

"He's clean," Piers said, his voice choked. "Larissa, you… you cleaned him off. How did you do that?"

Miller took a gulp of air and then another. When he was no longer hauling in air like he was afraid he'd be denied with his next breath, he had barely enough energy to smile.

"What?" Piers asked, his hands gentle as he pulled Miller up to a sitting position. "Why are you smiling?"

"Favorite beverage," Miller muttered. "Just lucky it wasn't coffee."

Piers let out a choked laugh, and Miller managed to focus on his face. He was pale, and his eyes were red. His hands shook as he passed them over Miller's sopping wet hair, pushing it back from his face.

"That was smart," Piers murmured, peering into Miller's face like he could find the answer to what had happened.

"Tell *her*," Miller mumbled, wanting nothing more than to sag back across the ground and sleep.

"Larissa, Miller wants you to know that was pretty quick thinking with the water."

"That's great," she said, her voice ringing with sarcasm. "I'd tell him thank you, but first I want to beat the hell out of him for scaring us all shitless!"

"Sorry," Miller mumbled, not sure he could stay conscious for one more moment. "Trying to keep her safe."

His eyes closed then, and there wasn't a thing he could do to stay awake.

Shadows in the Glade

PIERS REMEMBERED the times Lucky had needed to half drag Scout back to the apartment, because Lucky was midsized at best and Scout was pretty damned tall.

Never in his life had he been prouder to be tall and strong than when he lifted Miller Aldrun into his arms and began the suddenly vast trudge up to the sidewalk that would lead back to the apartments. He'd just gotten to where the sidewalk began to rise a little, become the seawall that swept around the beach to the harbor, when Miller started to shift.

"Put me down," he said distinctly. "Please, Piers. Put me down. Let me sit for a sec. We all need to talk."

"Inside," Piers said gruffly. "You're freezing again."

Miller shuddered in his arms and then struggled, this time freeing himself so Piers had to let him stand. Piers kept his arms around him until he knew for sure Miller's knees were going to hold, and then for one heartbeat more.

"I'm okay," Miller said, and for a moment, he did that thing where he rested his head against Piers's shoulder, that trusting, setting-his-burdens-down thing, and Piers was afraid to open his arms at first, in case Miller needed him.

"Here's a bench," Piers said. It was the last one on the walkway before it tapered to the beach, and Piers walked him to the bench, almost relieved when the others gathered around him. Otto sank down beside Miller and patted his shoulder.

"That was an experience full of wonder and terror, my boy. Do you care to brief us on what happened?"

Miller gave a weak smile and looked to Larissa in supplication. "Do you think you could conjure some hot chocolate for me, sweetheart? I'm—"

"A little shaky," she filled in for him. "Here, hold on." She closed her eyes and cupped her hands, and a large-sized paper coffee cup appeared. She grinned at all of them, so pleased with herself that Piers wanted to hug her. "Look! I can actually *do shit* with my mechanic! Sweet, right?"

Miller reached for the cup and took a deep drink, and then Otto held out a gloved hand with a steaming pastry sitting on his palm.

Miller reached for that and gave a quiet smile, raising his eyebrow at Piers. "Want to take bets on what you think it is?"

"Hot pumpkin pie?" Piers hazarded, equal parts mad at Miller for trying to flirt him out of his anxiety, and relieved because the flirting really *was* taking the edge off.

Miller took a bite and smiled blissfully. "Custard," he said. "Although it was a toss-up between custard pie and chicken pot pie. I would have loved either one." He took another bite, and Otto produced another pastry. Smiling another thank-you, Miller passed the rest of the dessert pastry to Piers and bit into what looked to be exactly as advertised—a chicken pot pie.

After a few moments of blissful eating and drinking—and having Otto supply snacks to everybody else surrounding the bench—Scout broke the silence.

"Okay, Miller, I get that you, you know, completely disobeyed orders, but I'm going to assume you saw something really important to make you do that. Let's hear it. What did you see?"

"I saw how the couple died," Miller said baldly, and there were some gasps around them. "The shadow—you saw it as a shadow, right?"

Everybody nodded, but it was Piers who said, "I always saw a man, but with a shadowed face."

Miller gave him a tired smile. "You… I think your light was what let me see. But the reason I broke away—the thing that made me break the circle—was that I felt it. A resonance. It was familiar and scary, and I was maybe the only one who could identify it. I got close to the couple, and I *saw* them, back as they must have been in their day. The girl's name was Ellie—"

"That's Tom's little sister," Lucky said excitedly.

"That's what we thought," Kayleigh said. "Remember, Scout? The little girl grew into the adult woman—"

"She and her lover were going to get married," Miller told them all, looking earnest and heartbroken. "They were so happy. And they told her… boss? Her young man thanked the other one for the job. They were trying to, I don't know, disengage themselves from him. Gently, it seemed. She seemed to have been made of kindness. But he…." Miller shrugged and glugged down a good portion of his hot chocolate. "The core of him was my specialty," he said, his lips twisting unhappily. "It was armed and dangerously unhinged. He… I watched him detach from the two young lovers completely, become something else than human, and then he killed them."

Miller shuddered again, and Piers leaned over the back of the bench and eschewed the niceties, wrapping his arms around Miller's shoulders. Miller reached up with one hand and clung to Piers's arm, squeezing.

"But that's not all," he said, and this time Piers could *feel* the shudder that rocked Miller's sturdy frame. "The murder—it created a link. A terrible one. Suddenly I could feel armed and crazy on the other side of the island. I could *see* people as he did, and I heard him thinking about Larissa. People, this is so important. She's not the only person he's stalked. He's stalked others. He's *killed* others. And he's planning on doing the same thing to her."

Piers stood, keeping one hand on Miller's shoulder, and drew his young cousin near. Larissa went easily into his embrace and held him tightly.

"Oh Lord," he muttered. "Larissa, I thought you'd be safe."

Miller reached to his shoulder and squeezed Piers's hand again. "I think it's time I did some police work," he said soberly. "I've got some of the fingerprint programs and such at my flat, but we've got to come up with a plan and find this man. He's terrifying, and Larissa, I'm feeling a bit attached to you and Piers here, and I want to wrap you up in a cushioned container and ship you somewhere safe."

"He'd just find me again," Larissa said. "He's not the only one with gifts, just like Ciaran isn't. No, I like your idea. Some of us go to your apartment and you do some research, and others of us do some, you know, sneaky work and see if we can figure out who it is."

"You're going to the apartment with me," Piers said, sounding panicked.

Larissa rolled her eyes. "No," she said adamantly. "No, you and Miller need time alone."

"This isn't about our relationship," Miller said frantically. "This is about your safety!"

"I have guardians here," she told him, and her big brown eyes were completely adult. "I do, Miller."

"I don't think the island's protection extends to the peninsula that keeps your little cottage and the dispatch office," Lucky said, and Piers looked up to see him pocketing his coin.

All eyes turned to Lucky, who shrugged. "I thought I'd ask it," he said nonchalantly. "It's important that we keep Larissa safe, but Miller's right. We need your police contacts now that we've got some more information, and I'm going to assume you've got copies of the island's birth and death records, am I right?"

Miller shrugged. "I do, but I also have a direct link to Charleston, because they only go back so far."

"Which we can't do from here," Scout said, as though this had only now occurred to him. "Yes, you and Piers are better at research than we are anyway, and you've got the resources. I promise you, Piers, we won't let her out of our sight, okay?"

"But the whole reason I'm *here* is to protect her!" Piers protested, feeling like his heart was being ripped in two.

"But you can do it better with your laptop at Miller's!" Larissa said. Then she grimaced. "Your laptop, though. Is that still at—"

"The hotel, yes," Piers muttered. "And you and I can't go there."

"I've got more than one computer," Miller said with a small smile. "But, uhm, maybe have Kayleigh grab your laptop just in case…."

They all shuddered. Yeah, the idea of Piers's personal stuff—even if it was the brands he shopped and the paper he'd recently finished on the hidden benefits of retaining counsel—in the hands of their stalker was too horrible for words.

"I can do that tonight," Kayleigh said. "Callan said my first priority is to check on Piers and Larissa's suite to see if anybody's intruded. Callan and I are the only ones with keys right now besides Piers, although…." She grimaced, and Piers could read her mind.

"Yeah," he acknowledged. "I don't see not having keys as a deterrent either."

"So far the plants are fine, though," she said brightly. "At least they were this morning."

"Any mysterious plant deaths in the rest of the resort?" Scout asked, and Kayleigh sighed.

"Not the right time," she said, her face set in grim lines.

Which meant that somewhere on the other side of the island was a gardener tearing his hair out because the foliage was being decimated at a fantastic rate with no apparent cause.

"I…." Miller swallowed. "You guys, I don't know if our perp felt me looking into his brain or not. I just… I am *afraid* for you all, do you get it? I've felt a lot of different kinds of violence coming from many different criminals, but this is a very special, very *demented* kind of smell, and I hate that it's got its sights set on people I care about."

"Aw, Miller," Larissa said, bending down to kiss the top of his head. "We worry about you too. And not just Piers 'cause he's crushing. We'll stay in touch, but first we need to get you back to the apartment and warm you up, and then we need to fill Marcus and Helen in on the plan." Her voice dropped. "I may get to spend the night at their place with Ciaran tonight, and he says they're like the good kind of grandparents you see in movies."

"I've had the crappy kind," Ciaran confirmed, nodding his head. "Marcus and Helen are better. But I need to ask a question about the ghosts at Tom's bench when somebody has a moment."

Miller had been about to stand up, but even through his hand on Miller's shoulder, Piers could feel the wobble in his knees.

"Ask us now," he said, meeting Lucky's and Scout's eyes. They nodded, so he continued. "I think we need one more minute before going back."

"Okay," Ciaran murmured. The boy looked so much more comfortable now than he had the day before, and Piers wondered which of his jobs he was taking a break from to do this with them. It didn't matter. He seemed to be 100 percent committed to their side, and Piers was pleased.

"So," Ciaran continued, "I saw the shadow advancing on the boy and girl, and that was terrifying. But as that was unfolding, I had to look away." He gave them all an apologetic glance. "It was terrible. I… I didn't want to see."

"That's fine," Kayleigh told him, with a hint of gentleness in her ordinarily crisp voice. "The whole little area is scary—"

"Not all of it," Ciaran told them, suddenly too excited to hold still. "I mean, most of the glade was just… saturated in sadness, right? But didn't you see the boy in the corner, all covered in sunshine? He was watching everything happen, and he was devastated, but he was, you know. Covered in sunshine. And he knew we were there too. He looked out and watched us watching the… the stories unfold. As soon as Miller broke free he, well, he looked *relieved* is what he did. Like he was pretty sure Miller was going to make it all better."

Piers's lungs stopped working for a moment, and he was not alone in gaping at the boy.

"You saw that?" Scout asked, sounding happy and surprised at once. "In the same glade we were in?"

"Well, yeah," Ciaran replied, his narrow face pinching more in apprehension. "You *didn't* see it?"

"No," Scout replied, like the mystery was the most amazing thing in the world. "Did anybody else?"

There was a puzzled chorus of "No," "I didn't," and "That's super weird," from around the group.

"That is *so* interesting," Scout muttered, starting to pace. "Because a boy covered in sunshine sounds *very* much like our friend the Wisp. According to lore, they're the spirit of somebody who is trying to guide the living to not make the same mistakes of the dead. And *this* Wisp has gone out of his way to send us messages."

"His trip to Tatter's Tot," Miller said, his shoulders straightening. "He wanted us to know that our stalker is on the island and he's very similar to the evil we can see in the ghost glade."

"And he wanted to warn us of that clinging grief moss, or mange or whatever," Larissa added. "The gross stuff. And…." Her eyes shifted to Otto, who was listening to them all in wonder. "Otto, I think he wanted us to meet *you*, because you'd encountered that. The residue of the evil presence, you know?"

Otto nodded. "I think you're right, my dear." He looked to Ciaran. "And I think it's very important that *you* saw him, when the rest of us could only make out the features on the shadows because of Piers's gift. I think our Wisp has taken a liking to you, young man. Best be careful—"

"I don't think he's dangerous," Ciaran said quickly.

"I don't think he is either," Scout told him. "Remember, he led me to the bench to see the big black soul-suck that's covering the place. He's been really good at trying to warn us and let us know what we're dealing with. It's just…." Scout looked to Lucky like he thought Lucky would find words when he couldn't.

"He's not really in our world," Lucky said bluntly. "He doesn't always realize that what he's doing can hurt us in the living world. Like when he brought the ghost mange to Knitter's Orgy Island. That could have killed somebody if those folks hadn't been apple-pie and sugar-cookie grandparent types. Miller said there were a few bruises at most. But it *could* have been much worse. Like when he introduced Scout to the big soul-sucking blanket and Scout almost drowned. We're not saying don't make eye contact," Lucky concluded. "We're saying try to make sure someone's got your back when you do."

"Yes," Scout seconded, sounding relieved. "I think our Wisp is all good intentions and not so great at unintended consequences. Just be aware. And that goes for all of us, all right? The island's trying to show us stuff, and I think the Wisp approves of our quest to put the spirits to rest. But we need to tread very carefully." He glanced behind him at the glade, which seemed quiescent for the moment. "There are beautiful and tragic stories in there," he said, his voice growing singsong. "We must be careful not to lose our way as we wander their paths."

"I'll be careful," Ciaran said soberly. Then he smiled. "And thank you, everybody, for worrying. That's sort of awesome."

There was some gentle laughter, and Piers felt Miller attempt to stand up again.

This time Piers let him, and Miller rose to his feet and stretched, then shivered because he was still wet from Larissa's dousing. "Let's get back to the apartment and set up shifts for Larissa before Piers and I take off," he said. Then he pinned Kayleigh with a gaze. "And you—be careful during your shift tonight. I hate the thought of anybody being there, particularly somebody gifted with magic. After getting sucked into this guy's head, I think Scout was right—I think he's magically gifted too. I think the power of it sort of wrecked the guy's head. I worry for us, okay?"

Kayleigh nodded soberly. "Understood. We're taking this seriously, Miller. Remember, we all almost saw my brother die."

"And now you," Piers muttered.

"Did you hear that, Miller," Scout announced. "We're part of a club."

"Better than the Cub Scouts," Miller said, smiling bemusedly at Scout. "Now let's hurry before I need to sit down again." He yawned and shivered some more. "If I hadn't seen what that sort of thing did to you and Lucky two months ago, I'd be *ticked* at how tired it's making me now!"

THE CROWD mostly dispersed when they got back to the apartment. Otto was spending the day helping Marcus and Scout in the magic store, Larissa was in the coffee shop with Lucky and Helen, and Ciaran had at least two other jobs to work before the end of the day. Only Kayleigh was there with Piers when Miller allowed himself to be shooed into the shower, and she left when he emerged ten minutes later, looking exhausted and fragile, wrapped in the set of Lucky's sweats they'd laundered when they'd done the sheets.

"I'm going to have to buy him a new set," he said, wrapping his arms around his middle and shuddering hard. "Your turn."

Piers gave him an unhappy glance, not wanting to let him out of sight again. "I'll only be a minute," he said apologetically.

"Give me your clothes so I can put them in the washer upstairs. That way Lucky just has to move laundry to have last night's clothes back."

Piers smiled slightly. "You're very good at everyday things. I had to be reminded to help Lucky clear the tables in the coffee shop. Larissa and I were really showing how spoiled we are."

Miller shrugged, and Lucky's clothes—made for someone his height but with a wider chest and stockier build—swung a little on his body. The effect was of a kid in his father's clothes, and Piers thought for the umpteenth time how vulnerable he looked.

"Did your father want you to be a policeman?" he asked abruptly.

Miller made a raspberry. "No. Why?"

Piers shook his head, frowning. "No reason. Just… just be here when I get out, okay? Just wait for me to go out to the boat. Please?"

Miller blinked at him with those hazel eyes that could be *so* sharp, *so* astute, but there was nothing about him now but bewilderment.

"Sure, Piers. What's wrong?"

Piers shook his head. He wanted to engulf Miller in his arms, to squeeze him tight against Piers's own chest until he knew for certain Miller would never be threatened, never be cold, never be alone and unable to reach safety, never be out of Piers's reach *ever* again.

But Miller wasn't the only one who was practical. Piers was wet and shivering, and while the black gunk had washed away, it left a sort of residue, like water in a puddle in a car repair shop, and he had one last change of clothes left.

"Nothing," Piers said and held out his hands as Miller drew hesitantly near. "And I'm grungy and wet and gross. No touching me until I'm clean, okay? Go do the thing you were planning with the laundry. I'll be out in ten."

"Okay," Miller said, looking hurt.

Piers sighed. "I'll fall apart on you then, okay? Promise."

Miller rolled his eyes, the hurt look going away but the skeptical look he'd maintained over the last few months returning. "Whatever," he said. "I'll be back before you're out."

He was true to his word, Piers saw when he emerged, dressed in his clothes from the night before, which they'd put through the wash that morning. He wondered if he'd be pushing his luck to ask Kayleigh to bring him an extra change of clothes from his room and decided to send her a text in case she could manage it. He knew Larissa had an entire drawer full of things in Kayleigh's apartment, but then, after Scout had sort of migrated over here, Kayleigh had been alone, so it only made sense.

He came out of the bathroom, ready to make a beeline for his phone on the nightstand, and was brought up short by Miller, who had apparently done laundry and then curled up on Scout and Lucky's bed to wait for him.

And had fallen asleep.

With a sigh, Piers sank down next to him and watched him for a moment. Miller Aldrun was so vulnerable. Piers had fallen in love with his practicality and his sort of flat-eyed whimsy. His capable nature, and the way he had of not backing down from a task, even if it tested the bonds of what he'd previously known to exist.

But he hadn't counted on Miller's position in the world as an outlier. Even down to his living situation, off the main island on a tiny peninsula within sight of the mainland. The only police officer who took his job seriously in Spinner's Drift. The eternal Cassandra who was heartsick because the people he cared about most wouldn't listen.

So eager to have a tribe who believed in him that he'd been a part of their numbers from the moment Scout had first produced a cupcake with his initial on it.

He could sense armed and crazy—and would pursue it even if it made him dizzy and weak—but also felt for the victims with all his heart.

Piers pushed Miller's hair back from his brow and thought miserably that he wished they hadn't pulled the young man into their midst. It was like putting a watermelon in front of a tractor. But then he'd think about how much information Miller had gleaned from that encounter and thought maybe the tractor should swerve around to avoid Piers's sweet little watermelon, because Miller could do some damage.

But not now. Now Miller had Piers as his guardian, and Piers would do his best.

"Time to go?" Miller said, obviously trying to get his feet under him.

"You can nap for another hour," Piers told him, kissing him on the temple. "Then when we get to your place, we can go right to work."

Miller searched his face. "Lay down with me?" he asked, and Piers felt a stab of satisfaction that he *would* ask. "You looked so odd before you got in the shower. I… uhm, was wondering if you had second thoughts."

Piers did as he asked, reaching down to the foot of the bed to pull up a wool throw to cover them with. "No second thoughts," he said firmly. "I was just thinking."

"About what?"

Piers tried to choose his words carefully. "That you need me," he said, scooting in close to Miller from behind and pulling him tight. "Not only because I listen to you and believe you, but because… because you've needed me your whole life, and you've got scars for not having me when you were younger."

"That's silly," Miller said, but his voice was indulgent, not derisive. "You're so big I had to wait to be Piers-sized before I had you in my life."

Piers gave a rusty chuckle. "That might be true," he whispered. "But I wish you had let me in sooner anyway. I could have kept you from so many bad things."

"No bad things here," Miller murmured. "Just us."

Piers let him sleep then—and for two hours, not one. When they got up, they made the bed and finished the laundry and departed, Piers shouldering their knapsacks and insisting on stopping for hamburgers from Russian Tacos and Spaghetti.

The trip to the tiny peninsula containing the dispatch center and the officer apartments took about forty-five minutes. Miller made sure Piers was snug and secure behind the center console, out of much of the wind, and Piers—who hated to be bored—was expecting a long slog of staring out into the flat blue ocean and wishing for his computer or cell service, which was spotty on the water, or anything to do.

Instead, he was treated to Miller's running commentary about the small islands they passed—who lived on them, what their general problems were, what the families were like. Piers ditched his snug and secure little niche and chose instead to stand up next to Miller, listening to his stories and enjoying them very much.

"Small dog rescue?" he repeated, surprised, as Miller pointed at Kate's Thimble. "Like, you know, Chihuahuas?"

"And Frenchies and Doxies and Boston terriers," Miller said, laughing. "There's two couples, and their shelter has twenty-three dogs."

"I don't *see* any dog enclosures," Piers murmured doubtfully, squinting at the harbor. Beyond the boat dock by about 200 yards were two houses across a small path that had probably been used by a construction crew to build the places. Each house had a large fenced-in yard—some sort of carefully mowed island grass—with big water bowls and some food pellet dispensers but no kennels as Piers thought of them. How odd.

"That's because there aren't any," Miller replied, laughing. "The houses are prefab—you can see them, right?"

"Yes."

"The island's a mile, end to end. Do you see any cars?"

Piers frowned. "Cars? But what do they do with the garage—"

Miller's raised eyebrows stopped him.

"Oh."

"Wall-to-wall old couches with ratty blankets. There's crates—all the dogs know the command, and most of them sleep in the crate voluntarily. There's a few who are... well...."

"Crate resistant?" Piers tried.

Miller shook his head and grinned. "Ten-pound Labrador retrievers," he corrected, laughing. "They stick their noses into every crate, every night, check on all those *other* dogs, you know, and then make their way to the bed where *they* get to sleep, after having minded all the furry children."

Piers laughed. "Seriously?"

"Definitely!" Miller's chuckle came up from his stomach, rolling out as though from a much larger man. "It's precious. Anyway, there's two couples, and they all have telecommute jobs, so I can stop there whenever I need Wi-Fi. They've fenced off a couple of acres and sort of shaved it down so the dogs can run without getting lost in the undergrowth, and there's always somebody out there at all times. One of the women knits, and so does one of the men. When they're not disposing of waste in an enzyme pit or washing the squirming buggers, they're out getting their ankles licked while knitting. Every one of those dogs has a sweater. Can you believe that?"

By now Piers was laughing outright.

"It's true!" Miller told him, a smile still creasing his face. He sobered for a moment. "I, uh, really want one of the dogs. Charleston dog rescue knows about them and ships dogs out here, as well as kibble and wet food. They've got a veterinarian friend who trades free service for a month's worth of vacation in a guesthouse on the far side of the island. Anyway, they brought this pregnant mother dog out, and she had five babies—all of them some bizarre mix of shih tzu and, God, anything else. I swear there's one that's golden retriever, so I guess that would make it a golden shih, which sounds sort of dirty. And she's such a good dog! She's already a caretaker—runs around, licks ankles, sticks her nose in the backs of people's knees to make sure they don't need anything. One of the knitters told me that she actually tells time. When they've been outside for too long and need to go start their evening chores, like dinner and such, she starts to headbutt their ankles. I mean, she's a baby—she weighs maybe two pounds, and she might make it to ten—but she's already bossing these people around." Miller gave a happy smile, and a teeny bit of sun peeped out and graced his cheeks while bouncing off his sunshades, and the wind tossed his hair under his tan baseball cap. It hit Piers, rather hard, that having this man in his home every day would be... wholesome. Like a filling meal after a hard day's work. Not fancy. Not involved. Hearty. Those big loaves of crusty bread with butter. Wonderful. A prelude to sweetness, but a meal all by itself.

Piers's stomach cramped with the wanting of him, with a *yearning* to have Miller in his life on a daily basis.

With need.

As unobtrusively as possible, he settled his hand on the small of Miller's back with more than a hint of possession. Miller's smile went shy, and he had to fumble for words for a moment, but beyond that, he didn't object.

Good.

"Will you get her?" Piers asked softly.

"She'll be ready in a couple of weeks," Miller told him. He gave Piers a small, hopeful smile. "I, uhm, might ask you to ask Callan to clear having a dog at the apartment. It sure would be nice to have a companion when I'm on the water."

"I can't wait to meet her." Piers kissed his cheek, and for a few moments, until the next island brought its own set of questions and stories, there was a thick, companionable silence.

Dots of Connection

"WHAT ARE you still doing here, Patsy?" Miller asked as he led Piers into the small dispatch office. The front of the office held two shared desks with basic computers, a coffeepot and Patsy, their receptionist, because a four-man police force didn't require a staff sergeant. The hallway led to the one-seater bathroom and two jail cells. If two employees needed to pee at the same time, it was understood that Patsy got the one-seater and the men took their turns at a jail cell stainless-steel john.

In order to access the employee barracks—Miller's apartment and two single-room bungalows—they had to pass Patsy and go through the hallway to the back door. Miller had anticipated needing to unlock the building himself—Patsy was a full-time receptionist, but her day ended at three o'clock.

"Leo made me stay," she said, wrinkling her nose. "Something about he had to work an extra shift so I had to stay until it's over. Asshole."

Patsy actually lived on the mainland, in Charleston, a middle-aged mother of two college students who had wanted a job to stave off the boredom. She'd ended up being their dispatch center, and while she loathed Leo, she'd confided to Miller that she enjoyed the work. The cases were often interesting, and the quirks of island life, from plumbing to animal incursions, were often funny and challenging. Plus, she'd told him, she had the best work stories when she and her husband talked about them over dinner.

She was a warm, friendly presence, and Miller had the feeling the other two members of the force—Lonnie Kerwin and Caspar Getz—were more interested in using this job to boost their resume for bigger districts like Charleston or, in Caspar's case, to go cruising for dates. Before he'd met Piers and his friends, the closest thing Miller'd had to a social life was sharing a cup of coffee with Patsy.

"Amen," Miller told her with a smile, and he was suddenly aware of her scrutiny.

"You look tired," she said, that practiced mom thing coming out. "What's up? We got a call last night from Callan Morgenstern himself that said you needed a couple of days off for a special project. Leo's been bitching about prima donnas and their 'specialness,'"—she used air quotes—"but you don't look like a guy who's been hanging out at the resort being special."

Miller gave a weak chuckle. "I, uh, sort of ran into a nasty customer last night. Callan and I are trying to figure out how to get him off the island without making a stink, and that means…." He waited for her to finish the thought.

"Not telling Leo," she hazarded, but her concern didn't waver. "Did you get *hurt* last night?" Patsy asked. "I know you left before I got here yesterday, which, you know, happens, but only with you. So you got *hurt* at the end of your shift?"

Miller winked at her, knowing he was tired and pale and about wrung out after the encounters of the last two days but not able to fix any of it. He'd become very aware that something huge had happened to his body. A lingering tenderness at the back of his skull and in his shoulders and spine told him that whatever his friends had done to warm him up had probably also saved him a hospitalization—or worse.

"Yeah, darlin'. Got smacked around and fell in the drink. Spent the morning warming up again. Don't tell Leo, okay? He's going to jump in, thinking this is some sort of way to get glory and a promotion, but it's… it's a real bad guy, okay? The kind I don't want you near and that Leo can only make worse."

Patsy nodded soberly. "Is he after you?" she asked, and to her credit, there wasn't a hint of titillation in her voice.

"Naw, I just got in his way. Me and my friend here have to figure out how to make that work better next time."

"Oh!" And for the first time she noticed Piers. Her eyes got big when she took him in, because Piers *was* that pretty, and Miller found his own smile crinkled the corners of his eyes. "You *do* have a friend. Who's this?"

"This is Mr. Constantine," Miller said. "He's a friend of Callan Morgenstern's, and he's got some law in his background. We're going to do some research at my place tonight and see if we can't get this bad guy out of Callan Morgenstern's hair, right?"

Patsy's eyes raked Piers and then raked him, and although he'd never really talked about his love life, he got the feeling in that moment that he was fooling *nobody*.

"Riiight," she agreed, drawing out the syllable. "Law research. Ookaay…."

Miller grimaced. "Patsy, if Leo hears you—"

She scowled back at him. "I'm not telling Leo fucking Kowalski shit. Certainly not about Mr., uhm, Lawyer Man staying in your guest room." She glanced at Piers again, and Miller wasn't sure what expression was on Piers's face, but Patsy made a little "Ha!" after the words "guest room," so Miller thought he'd better not look Piers in the eye. "Uhm, your grocery delivery got here last night before I clocked out, so you've got food. And, uhm, I added a bottle of wine and some cookies to your order. You can thank me later."

Miller felt his cheeks heat. "I'll thank you now," he said, wondering if Patsy could make this any more awkward. "That was kind."

"Well, I had no idea how necessary it was," she said, her tone a mirror to his. "But I'm glad to know you're not alone after your scary experience yesterday." She sighed and stood. "Which reminds me, I'm not waiting for Leo. If I don't get a move on, I'll miss the ferry to the mainland and I'll have to wait until low tide and hope I don't end up swimming home. It's the world's longest half mile."

"Let me know if you need a lift to the ferry dock," Miller offered. He'd done it many times before.

She shook her head. "Naw. By the way, Leo's planning on leaving tonight. He's on his private skiff, so he'll probably call in and go straight home." She gave him a devilish grin. "You and, uhm, Mr. Constantine can study all you want."

He compressed his lips so he didn't respond, but he was pretty sure she knew the color on his cheeks wasn't from the sun. "Patsy…."

She giggled just like a teenager, like Larissa or Kayleigh, and Miller realized a sudden truth then, that all women had a little bit of naughty child in their makeup. He wondered if it was the same with men. That had certainly been one of Brad's most endearing qualities, right?

And it was probably the reason Piers enjoyed flirting so much.

But right now, Piers only flirted with Miller.

"See you in the morning," she called, grabbing her jacket and scarf from the post by the door. "This thing's already locked, so just go on through to the back. Bye!"

And with that she whirlwinded out of there, leaving Miller to push on the door behind her to make sure the mechanism had engaged.

It had, so he turned toward Piers and nodded him through the rest of the tiny police station.

"Wow," Piers said as they walked out the back and into the little quad that separated the two night bunks from the permanent residence. "She's, uhm…."

"Sharp," Miller said dryly. "And she likes to poke that sharpness into my business."

Piers laughed a little and followed Miller as he made his way along the concrete walkway toward his apartment. The place was small, a double-wide trailer that had been set on a permanent foundation. It had two bedrooms, two bathrooms, a kitchen, and a dining area, with a sitting area complete with a widescreen on the wall.

"It's not quite a hut in the woods," Miller, looking around proudly, admitted as they went in. "I've replaced the crappy seventies paneling and the nasty-assed tile in my spare time. The green appliances were still functional, so I couldn't sell them off, but I figure they look better in a kitchen painted white with daisy-yellow trim."

Piers's laugh was warm and not mocking at all. "It's nice," he said, sounding surprised enough to make Miller feel his praise, but not shocked or anything that would have been insulting. "The curtains are a nice touch."

"Thanks," Miller said, his cheeks growing warm. "I told my sister about the daisy yellow, and she got those pretty white things with the daisies on the bottom of the valance. The bedroom is a boy's space, thank God. I mean, the walls are white, but the bedding's blue and green, and the curtains too. Don't tell Leo. Patsy told him *she* did the redecorating, to get him off my back. I swear the guy would be happier if I decorated with beer cans on my window."

Piers grunted and shook his head. "That man sounds more and more like a prince whenever you talk about him."

"Well, I'd rather you not find out how wrong that assessment is," Miller told him. "Two words. Ass. Hole. And he'll hate you. He hates anybody with money that's not him. Which is funny because he'd spend it all on cigars and mistresses—the guy wouldn't know how to fix his own home if a genie walked up to him with a list of home improvement wishes to choose from."

Piers's rolling laughter warmed him again, and he felt that sort of triumph he got when he was interesting enough to make Piers laugh.

"So my regular laptop's in my knapsack," Miller said, after clearing his throat. "Hook it up to the charging station at the kitchen table and boot up the one that lives there. We can work for a couple of hours before I'll have to cook dinner. What sounds good, by the way? Grilled cheese? Omelets? Broiled chicken breasts with baked potatoes? I'm a one-man grill, here."

"What kind of omelets?" Piers asked, grinning.

Miller started going through his stores, boosted from the grocery delivery. "I've got some onions, some Canadian bacon, some cheese, and some mushrooms. How's that sound?"

"Delicious," Piers said. "Particularly if you break out those potato chips I see in the back of the cupboard and share them while we work. And do you have any soda?"

"Well, not like your sister does," Miller told him regretfully. "Basic cola, some root beer, and some of that fizzy water, which is what I usually drink so I can offer the cola and root beer to Patsy."

"Think she'd mind if I took one?" Piers needled.

"Naw. She seems to like you."

"Good. Break that out and let's get started." The good-natured teasing dropped from his eyes. "I want to get this stalker thing taken care of so you and I can start planning how we're going to be together while I finish law school."

Miller felt his own teasing smile fail a little. "Sure."

"Miller?" Piers said softly, moving in two smooth steps from the table where he'd been setting up the electronics to the kitchen where Miller was rounding up their snack.

"Yeah?"

"You and me can build a life around this island," Piers told him, drawing near. "Law school will be a test, don't get me wrong. But I haven't met anybody more worth fighting for than you."

Miller nodded and then gave him a quick smile. "Let's get rid of the bad guy first," he said decisively. "Everything's less dire when scary stalker people aren't out there, waiting to pounce."

Piers nodded, and Miller almost relaxed, relieved that Piers was so easily distracted from the topic, when Miller's mouth was suddenly taken in a messy, all-consuming kiss. Piers took no prisoners, mauling his mouth with skill and passion and leaving Miller reaching to the counter to support himself because his knees weren't up for the job.

Piers pulled away, leaving Miller to try to stand up and remember what he was doing while Piers—looking kiss-mussed but definitely still purposeful—gathered the chips and the sodas and the glasses of ice that Miller had been rounding up and took them to the table.

"Miller?" Piers said over his shoulder.

"Yeah?"

"Do you believe me yet?"

Miller gave him a rather grim smile. "I guess I have to," he said, conscious that Piers's habit of not taking no for an answer was pretty much working for him.

"Good. You're right. Sucks to be Cassandra. I think both of us should work at believing the other as much as possible. Now sit down. We've got work to do."

MILLER BOOTED up the websites with the birth and death records on them, as well as the newspaper archives that had been transferred to digital from microfiche in the last few years. Those were on his regular laptop, and he wrote a list of passwords to help Piers get in and search more thoroughly.

Miller took his stationary laptop and started looking up crime statistics, as well as forensic records that contained the very specific items that indicated *their* bad guy as opposed to other criminals, of which there were a depressing number.

They worked in companionable quiet for an hour or so. Piers had to place a couple of phone calls at one point, and he left the room so as not to distract Miller, and Miller did the same thing. When he came back, Piers was sitting at the table, giving a leonine stretch, and Miller found that his tongue had cleaved to the top of his mouth and his heart was beating triple-time, seeing the man's flat, corrugated abdomen peeking out from under his long-sleeved shirt.

"So what do you have?" Piers asked. Then he frowned. "Miller? Miller, what do you have?"

Miller shook himself and swallowed and tried to recall his attention to where it belonged.

"Okay," he said with a final shake. "Here's what I got. I called the lab again, and we've still got zero chemical residue on the plants or in the humans from your cousin's house after the attack, which I'm going to take as confirmation of Scout's theory that this guy has a gift. He's a plant-killing zombie maker who stalks girls, which if you think about it, is about one of the scariest sentences I've ever said."

Piers grimaced and nodded. "True story," he agreed. "Is that all?"

Miller shook his head. "No, because it gets worse. I started searching crime databases for crimes in which all the plants died, and/or there were animal attacks."

"That, uh, doesn't sound like a bear market," Piers hazarded.

"No, it is not." Miller's kitchen table had three chairs, and Miller sat in the chair nearest Piers to show him the map he'd just printed out. "And I got two hits—one in Winston-Salem, one in Charlotte."

Piers sucked in a breath. "That's pretty close," he said. "And mine and Larissa's families live right outside of Charlotte."

Miller nodded. "He's picking families in the area, and he's here in Spinner's Drift."

Piers narrowed his eyes. "What does that mean?"

"Well, we all agree that the island seems to protect its own, so the question is, how does our attacker *know* about it. It's not like Nag's Head or Martha's Vineyard if you're looking for East Coast island paradises, right?"

"No," Piers said slowly. "And it's not like the mobsters from Philadelphia could find Lucky without Ciaran's help."

"*Exactly.*" Miller's toes were starting to tingle—he hadn't felt this much buzz since the time he and Brad had busted a theft ring on their beat. "*Nobody* knows about this place except for locals—and upper-middle/lower-upper locals at that."

Piers gave him a droll look. "Are you saying I'm lower-upper?"

"Upper-upper doesn't vacation locally," Miller said dryly. "I think if Callan Morgenstern hadn't been a distant relative or friend of a friend or whatever, you and Larissa would have been in the Bahamas or the Seychelles or in France or something. The Drift is a local attraction, really. It's like the San Juan Islands off Puget Sound. Yeah, they're a tourist attraction, but you've got to look them up specifically to find where to vacation."

"Or be related to the guy who owns the hotel. I see what you're saying here," Piers conceded.

"I'm saying that this guy is one of you," Miller said. He stood up abruptly and started to pace. Now, if he'd been Scout, he'd be wandering a pattern around the kitchen and the front room and the hallway, but Miller was more straightforward than that. He went from the table, across the living room to the bedroom, and straight back, tapping the couch for luck.

"He started near Chapel Hill," Piers said softly. "In Winston-Salem. He works that area. Maybe he knows...." His voice rose with supposition. "The school? Do you think that's it? Larissa would have made several trips to Chapel Hill. Winston-Salem is really close."

Miller whirled in midstride. "Don't *they* have their own school?"

Piers snorted. "Try eight—" He stared at Miller. "Where were the other crimes with the similar MOs? I mean, *who* were they targeting?"

Miller didn't have to look at the paperwork; he'd practically memorized it. "They were both young women Larissa's age," he said. "I put that into the database. One of them woke up in a cornfield." His voice sank. "She'd been badly beaten and sexually assaulted, Piers. It was no joke."

"And the other?" Piers asked.

"She was never found." Miller swallowed. "I… I *heard* his thoughts. She wasn't the only one. I think if we look back over the database, we'll find a couple of others that might fit his MO, but not everybody was going to notice and report the plants or the pets. Not every police force holds those kinds of standards."

Piers shuddered. "I know I'm going to be defending some bad people," he said softly. "I *know* there are going to be some ugly cases. I just *hate* that this has to come so close to my cousin, you know?"

Miller nodded, thinking about Larissa's irrepressible smile, her bounce, her gentleness. The gods gave her the gift of *favorite beverage*, for heaven's sake—she was strawberry-lemonade levels of sweet and refreshing.

"She's a great kid," he said, meaning it, and then he remembered her dousing him with water to save his life. "And stronger than we give her credit for," he added. "We'll keep her safe. I mean, Marcus and Helen, Kayleigh and Scout—we're talking record levels of protection, you know?"

Piers nodded, still looking troubled. "I wish we knew where he originated. If he followed these girls from school, he's got to have some sort of official capacity. I mean, even the timing. He showed up yesterday, which is when a lot of winter breaks start. He's a student or a TA or a professor or something close—"

"Which means he's working on a deadline," Miller said, taking another pass by the couch. "I've felt him all today on the resort side of the main island—" He stopped short and closed his eyes, his internal compass giving him a little map of the archipelago with a dank black/red miasma where their perpetrator was. "And he's still there," he said with a whoosh of breath. "Thank heavens. Anyway, he's still there, but he's probably planning to search the rest of the island soon and…."

Miller paused and frowned. "He... we connected today," he went on. "He's probably... I mean, I can't say this for certain, but he's going to be looking for Tom's bench. I mean, I'm *sure* of it, but I don't know how."

"Could we set a trap for him, do you think?" Piers asked.

Miller grimaced. "That ghost I saw—Percy what's his face...?"

"Hampstead," Piers told him, and Miller stared at him in surprise. "I was busy too," Piers said, laughing. "But go on."

"He... he had the same soul," Miller said absently. "But you can't leave it there. What happened to him? How do you know it was him?"

Piers raised his eyebrows a few times, as though trying to assimilate what Miller had just said, but Miller couldn't put it any better, and they were on to something.

"Well, I figured that this person had to be on the island between ten to twenty years after Tom left. I couldn't see how old the little sister was as an adult—"

"Late teens, early twenties," Miller said, realizing how much information he really *had* gleaned. "So ten to twenty years after Tom died of cholera was about right."

Piers nodded as though he, too, was putting together the different ages they'd seen Ellie's specter pass through. Eight or so before Tom left, in her early teens when he died, young womanhood when she and her William had been killed. It made sense.

"Yes. So I looked up deaths or departures." He grinned. "Isn't that wonderful? They had *departures* listed, as separate from deaths as people left the island to go find their fortune. They also have *arrivals* in their census. Whoever was in charge—"

"The Morgensterns," Miller said dryly. "Just like today, they ran law enforcement and the chamber of commerce and probably the newspaper as well."

Piers frowned. "Do they run it today?"

"Nope. The newspaper is run by the people who run the map kiosk. They also have an online paper and a once-a-week flyer that gives locals discounts." He grinned. "I understand their paperboy/delivery person works for a spot in their spare room and food because he's so happy to be out in the boat every day."

Piers chuckled. "Maybe Ciaran can take over for him, give him a day off."

"It's looking like he'll do every job on the island at least once," Miller agreed, eyes crinkling. He sobered. "I'm so glad he landed, though—or it looks like he will. He didn't belabor it, but if you're thrown into the dead center of a group of people and an off-the-wall situation and you adapt to it like that kid did, I think he really *needed* a place to land."

Something disconcerting about Piers's level gaze caught his attention, but he didn't want to explore it right now. "Anyway, what did you learn from the records department and the press?"

"Lots," Piers said. "Elizabeth Marbury and William Abbott applied for a marriage license in Charleston the day before their bodies were found in the glade with the bench, back in the foliage." His face hardened. "The island's one police officer said it looked as though 'The young man attacked the girl and then turned the knife upon himself.'"

The heat ran out of Miller's body as he remembered the savagery with which Percival Hampstead had fallen upon his two victims.

"Only an idiot would think that," he said grimly.

"Or a man paid to have that opinion," Piers told him, his voice flat. "Because having the police look into the affairs of the man who was about to save Spinner's Drift and the Morgensterns from bankruptcy would have been quite awkward."

"Wait a minute." Miller frowned. "Bankruptcy?"

"Oh yes. See, the cholera epidemic that killed Tom had far-reaching consequences. Tom wasn't the only islander buried in that graveyard in Charleston, and the young people who had been hired to work the resorts were leaving at a dreadful pace. The departures column is bigger than the births, deaths, and arrivals columns combined. The Morgensterns took to putting advertisements in the Charleston papers and beyond to attract young people, and they'd arranged for a—and I quote—'propitious' marriage for Percy Hampstead and one Alice Morgenstern, the youngest child of the original Morgenstern scion, Richard Denning Morgenstern."

"Oh God," Miller said, horrified. "They married her off to him? After he killed Elizabeth and William? That's… that's awful!"

Piers shook his head. "No…. No, they're bad, but, well, not monsters. I mean, not entirely. There were no charges brought against Percy—not even the hint of suspicion. But there was no engagement listed for Alice until nearly three years later, to an iron mogul from Chicago, bless her soul. But Percy is listed in the departures column four days after the murder. What does that say to you?"

Miller caught his breath. "That the Morgensterns didn't want their baby married to a monster," he said, feeling relief for a woman long dead whom he had never met. "But they still needed the cash until they could find some workers for the resort. So they took Percy's money, but not for the marriage."

"Exactly," Piers said, nodding. "It was hush money so they wouldn't get him arrested or I don't know my rich people or their back-alley deals. But here's the thing." Piers called up another screen and directed Miller's attention to it. "See here? This column marked Arrivals?"

"Yes," Miller said, curious.

"I wanted to see how the resort continued to function. I mean, Percy's influx of cash was enough to float it for a little while, but not forever, right?"

"True," Miller said. "Where did they get their workers?"

Piers grinned. "You're so damned quick. *Yes*, that's where I was going. In the arrivals column, people had to list where they'd come from. Look here."

Miller followed Piers's pointed finger. "Winston-Salem, Chapel Hill, Charlotte—" He turned to Piers in surprise. "From the universities. The Morgensterns started to recruit from the universities. That's… that's interesting," he said, mind racing, because this obviously meant something.

"Mm-hmm. Which brings me to where I'd just gotten when we stopped. I checked Percy Hampstead's arrival column, nearly three months before his departure. Took me forever. I feel like I should get the very special omelet."

Miller grinned and patted Piers's knee. "As special as I can make it. Go on."

Piers pulled up another screen. "See here? This is what he listed as where he was from."

"Winston-Salem," Miller said in wonder. "He's… he's related to the university somehow."

Piers nodded. "And that's where I was when we took a break. I mean, it *might* be a coincidence, but…."

"But it can't be," Miller said, frowning. "Yes. Definitely. I'll cook dinner, and you run that down. We can discuss the very interesting history of Percy Hampstead when I'm done."

Piers turned his head and unexpectedly kissed Miller on the mouth. "You're so much fun to work with. We're going to find a way to make us happen. Mark my words."

Miller bit his lip and looked away. "Omelet," he mumbled, getting up to go cook. He didn't dare look at Piers with hope in his eyes, not even when he heard Piers's low laughter rumbling out from his stomach.

A HALF HOUR later Miller had two passable omelets plated, along with some baked Tater Tots because he felt like they needed more carbs after the day they'd had. A little hot sauce, a little ketchup—voila, they were ready to go.

He set the table around Piers, moving his own laptop to the counter, and then brought more soda and glasses filled with ice to the place settings. After one more trip to the kitchen for napkins, he returned to find Piers was scowling at the ice glasses.

"I thought you liked soda?" Miller asked, surprised.

Piers shook his head. "You don't want wine?" he asked, and Miller blushed.

"The wine is, well, Patsy usually has a glass if she comes over for a chat after work. I, uhm, I didn't think you would...."

"Oh, come on, Miller," Piers murmured. "Are you really that afraid of a real date?"

Miller's face heated. "All we've got are water tumblers," he said. "The, uhm, dishware came with the bungalow."

Piers arched one eyebrow, and Miller swallowed hard.

"I'll be back," he said, wishing hard for some class. He walked past the counter to the kitchen and went fishing in the back of the cupboard; then he grabbed the souvenir corkscrew that was schwacked to the hood of the stove. He came back with the promised water tumblers and the bottle of wine, which Patsy had put in the refrigerator.

"Pinot grigio," Piers said, taking the wine and corkscrew from Miller's hand, "and not from a box. It's fine, Miller. Sit down."

Miller sat, self-conscious and clumsy, and watched as Piers smoothly used the point of the corkscrew to break the seal on the bottle.

"I, uhm, come from a beer after work kind of family," he said, and Piers winked at him.

"My parents are all about scotch and soda," he said. "But I had a date or two who wanted to impress me in college, and I've come to really enjoy a glass of wine."

"Well, it's sort of fancy for my omelet and Tater Tots," Miller admitted, taking the tumbler from Piers's hand. "But thank you."

"How do you know?" Piers recorked the bottle, sat, and took a sip of his own wine. "That's really good!" He peered at the bottle again. "And local! Wow. I'll have to get a couple of bottles of that to give to my parents." He looked at Miller again, as though waiting for an answer, and Miller scrambled to remember what he'd asked.

"Oh! How do I know it's fancy for my omelet and Tater Tots?" Miller snorted. "Because they're Tater Tots." He popped one in his mouth, and his entire body relaxed with the taste of crispy, salty comfort food. "They're better paired with beer," he practically moaned.

Piers laughed and ate one of his own. "Or maybe a good Spanish red," he teased. "Something with body."

Miller laughed, and his embarrassment faded. He forked up a bite of omelet and sighed with pleasure. "Okay, I'll admit it. There are probably people out there who could make this a delicate dance of flavors, but I like me a good old-fashioned egg, cheese, ham and mushroom carbfest."

"You stress about carbs a lot," Piers observed, tucking into his own omelet. "Any particular reason?"

Miller shrugged. "I was a pudgy little kid. My growth spurt hit...." He chuckled. "Not much of one, I own it, but it made me skinny, and I started to watch my weight so I didn't go back to pudgy. It's second nature now. Besides, when you're on the force you have to keep fit to do the job." He grimaced. "Brad made it some sort of contest between the two of us. Who could maintain the best BMI, that kind of thing. I swear, it was a year after his death before I could eat so much as a donut without feeling unfaithful, which is sort of the dumbest shit I've ever heard of, given how faithful he *wasn't* to me."

Piers nodded. "I'd love you pudgy," he said, his eyes lighting up a bit. "Or thin. Or ripped. I'm not in it for the beefcake."

Miller's face heated. "That's fortunate for you—I mean, you *are* the beefcake."

And those warm brown eyes went molten. "You think so?"

Augh! "I can't eat my omelet thinking about... sex, or your body, or... nungh!" He shoved his face full of omelet and tried to swallow the massive bite in little bits.

"C'mon, Miller." Piers started playing with the lip of his water tumbler as though he was fondling cut crystal and flirting at a fine eatery, the kind with an expensive wine list and white tablecloths. "Aren't you going to play with me, just a little?"

Miller gazed at him with tortured eyes. "You know you're beautiful," he said, taking it all in again. Golden skin, warm almond-shaped brown eyes, blond hair, square jaw, flirty, full mouth. "I just… I look at you and my tongue tangles. What am I supposed to say that will make you keep looking at me like that?"

Piers took his hand from the table and pulled it up to that sinful mouth. Very slowly, he sucked Miller's finger between his lips and laved it with his tongue, then scraped it with his teeth as he allowed it to slide out. Just as deliberately, he placed the finger on the edge of the tumbler of wine and then put his own finger in that same position.

"Nothing," Piers told him throatily. "Nothing of importance." Desultorily, he played the edge of his tumbler with his finger. "Just talk. Start with why you have no wineglasses and no dog."

Miller swallowed and tried. "I have no wineglasses because when I moved here from New Jersey, I had to put a lot of my stuff in storage. Moving things out here isn't easy, and since the bungalow was mostly furnished and I wasn't sure how long I'd be here, I figured easier that than paying moving costs, right?"

Piers nodded. "But you're staying here now, aren't you?"

Miller gave a half smile and nodded. "Yeah, but I didn't know that until October."

Piers raised his eyebrows. "Until you met the lot of us, you mean?"

Oolf. That was something to admit, wasn't it? "Yeah," Miller said, looking away. "I… I loved the islands. I did. But three years is a long time to be in love with a place with just Patsy for company." He paused. "Not that she's not good company, mind you, but she's got a whole other family."

Piers laughed softly. "I'm sorry it's been so lonely for you," he said, and Miller couldn't meet his eyes.

"Well, you know. It'll pick up once the puppy's old enough," he said, trying to make his voice sound effortlessly teasing, like Piers did.

"Yeah. That's what's missing. The dog."

Miller *had* to get the subject off himself; he really did. "What...
I mean, I suppose you have lots of friends back in North Carolina," he
said. "Besides the three bozos—"

Piers laughed outright, and Miller grinned cheekily at him and then
continued on.

"Yeah, I remember. Bozos. Anyway, besides those guys, anyone
else I should know about?"

Piers shrugged. "Friends—yes, I have them. Truth to tell, Larissa's
my best friend, and yes, I realize how sad that is because she's a teenager
and I'm supposed to be close to grown. But we both shared something,
right? Something nobody else had. It's hard to beat that as a bonding agent."

Miller nodded in understanding. "I told you about my sister. We
talk or text once a week. Every now and then we'll call when we know
the other one's going to be home and not busy, and we talk for a dog's
age, and when we do it again, it's like we were never apart. I get it."

"Does she know about your gift?"

Miller held his hand up and wobbled it. "I think so? She believed
me when I knew something awful was going to happen to our dad—
even tried to help me convince him not to go into the gas station. But I
haven't actually talked about it with her." He frowned. "What about your
parents?"

"What about them?" Piers asked, and for the first time the snide,
bored party boy that Miller had always feared sounded in his voice. *A
front. This subject hurts him.* He wasn't sure where the thought came
from, but he listened.

"I guess they don't know what an awesome son they have," Miller
hazarded, and Piers managed to look sheepish.

"They're not excited about me being gay, for one. I told you that.
And... well, they love me and my sister, and they've been nothing but
supportive about this thing with Larissa. It's not that I *don't* want a
relationship with them, I just don't want an *involved* relationship with
them."

Miller was holding his hand over his mouth now to try to hide his
laughter.

"I sound awful," Piers groaned, hiding his own face with his hands.
"I know. I just... I learned I had my gift when my mother refused to
put a night-light in the bathroom. She felt we should be able to hold it
overnight, which, you know—"

"Twisted," Miller agreed.

"So I walked down the hall one night and thought, *light*! And light appeared. And about a year after I figured I could do that, the power went out in the house, and my father ran downstairs and was tripping about in the dark, and it never occurred to me, not once, to give him some light. But Scout was holding a book on island lore to his face because he couldn't see, and Larissa was like, 'Piers!' and I called the light automatically. I've done it for other people too—nobody who figured out that it was magic, but people who seemed to need it. The law librarian at Chapel Hill, for example. There's always corners she's trying to see in. She's always so grateful. She looks around the corner for the light and then frowns and then puts the book away. It's cute. But it's like I can't make myself summon light for anyone who's going to be snide or rude or ungrateful." He shrugged. "I haven't wanted to see what my folks would make of it, that's all."

Miller found he was gazing at Piers adoringly. "But you used it to save my life," he said.

And it was Piers's turn to blush and stammer and look away. "I liked you," Piers murmured.

"I'm so glad," Miller told him, feeling like he might be getting the hang of the flirting thing after all.

SURPRISINGLY, THE rest of the conversation was neither awkward nor embarrassing. They talked about school and what they'd loved and what they'd hated. Miller confessed to his love of literature, and Piers remarked on the bookshelves lining the living room walls. Piers tried to explain his love of BBC TV, and Miller managed to hold on to a straight face as he postulated that the BBC version of the show *Ghosts* was better than the American one, and how *Midsomer Murders* was an addicting cornucopia of aging British actors that he could watch all day.

By the time they'd finished their dinner and washed the dishes, retiring back to the kitchen table with a plate of cookies and two glasses of milk, they'd laughed more than Miller could remember doing with any date previous, and his chest had a warm, glowy sort of sensation that he couldn't describe.

It wasn't until their second cookie—Patsy had ordered the good ones in the bakery box, soft and squishy and delicious—that a companionable silence fell, and Miller was forced back to their original subject.

"So," he said with a sigh. "I hate to do this to us but...."

"Percy Hampstead," Piers agreed. "Yeah. We need to hash this out so we can go to bed tonight and not have it in the air."

Miller was caught unprepared for that statement, and Piers actually laughed out loud.

"Did you think I was sleeping in the guest bedroom?" he asked, eyes twinkling. "After I got you to drink wine and had deep, meaningful courtship conversation with you?"

"No!" Miller retorted, annoyed. Then, truthfully, "Maybe. You know. I thought you might be... I don't know. Satisfied. After, uhm, last night."

Piers gazed at him with a look of such patience that Miller's ears grew hot.

"No?" he asked, making sure.

"No," Piers told him, nodding soberly as though Miller would need the reinforcement. "Last night was wonderful, Miller. I for one want more. What about you?"

"Well, *yeah*," Miller burst out before he could censor himself. "I just...." He let out a breath. "God, you're pretty. Ignore me when I'm being stupid. You could stand on Spinner's Drift, crook your finger at me as I stood out on the dock, and I'd be like one of those cartoon characters, putting on my full-body swimming suit and diving in to swim to you so I could get on my knees and...." He swallowed, his throat suddenly dry as he thought of what he'd do to Piers while on his knees.

Piers's eyes had grown wide and heated, as though the image had just occurred to him too.

"I wouldn't make you swim," he rasped before clearing his throat. "And I'd most certainly show up here in a skiff to beg for it."

"I guess you're here already," Miller said, suddenly grateful for the lesson on flirting. "No need to take the skiff."

Piers winked. "But I'll definitely beg for it." He looked over to the computer on the counter and sighed. "Later on tonight."

With that he grabbed the laptop, opened it, and patted the seat next to him so Miller could resume his spot and look over his shoulder.

"Okay, here's what we know about Percy Hampstead," Piers said. "His father was a clockmaker, and his mother taught school until she married because that was the law back then, unfortunately, and then she tutored the wealthy children in Winston-Salem afterward. She must have brought Percy along when she did so. He developed a taste for wealth, and one of the families that his mother helped gave him an education at Winston-Salem college and an introduction to society. He became a banker, and he was canny, bright, and from what I can see, *unmerciful* when it came to collecting debts. The bank loved him. He invested...." Piers let out a breath. "I have no proof, but everything I've read uses the words 'uncanny,' 'propitious,' and 'extraordinary.' If I had to guess, I'd say...." He bit his lip, obviously not wanting to be the one who said it.

"I think we have a luck mechanic," Miller guessed, and Piers nodded.

"I wouldn't be surprised. He made a fortune—eventually bought the house of the family that helped him and, from what I can see, did *not* return the favor. So now he's rich, he's cold, and he apparently needs a wife."

"Why not take one locally?" Miller asked, frowning. "There had to be lots of young women on the marriage market at the time. I understand it was practically a family industry, right? Turning out eligible young women to catch a rich young man's eye."

"Well, yes," Piers agreed. "But there's that whole 'bought the house of his benefactor' thing. If he was that cold to the people in his own backyard, are they really going to be throwing their marriageable daughters at him?"

Miller grimaced. "I don't know, Piers. My family has cops and bohemians—we're not exactly marriage-mart people, you know?"

Piers nodded. "I can tell you this. Remember how Scout and Kayleigh's father was literally pursuing them across the country to make Kayleigh participate in an arranged marriage?"

Miller shrugged. "Yeah, I was here for that."

"Well, as insane as Alistair is, he was driven by a couple of traditions that functioned as absolutes in his world. One was that the marriage would benefit his family. The Quinteros are famous for their magic ability, and the Morgensterns are richer than the gods. That marriage was a business transaction for him, and yes it made him a bastard, but he was coming at it from the angle that he was trying to acquire wealth and stability for his family, and that's usually not a bad thing, unless of course you're that guy and insane."

"So that's one tradition," Miller prompted.

"It is. And the other tradition is that the Morgensterns have real-world clout. If Callan hadn't been so excited to not marry Kayleigh—"

"And seriously, it's too bad he's gayer than an Easter parade, because Kayleigh deserves someone as awesome as Callan," Miller said. He'd been very impressed by the young Morgenstern heir. When Callan wasn't hitting on him, he was a progressive employer with environmentally respectful policies and a habit of making reparations for all the douchey things his family did back in the days when there were no policies to stop them.

Piers gave him a flat-eyed look. "I told you. I have dibs."

Miller laughed. "Oh, as if. Callan doesn't want me—I'm inconvenient enough as a boyfriend for *you*. I'd be a disaster for Callan, and you both know it. Anyway, tell me about the real-world clout."

"So cute." Piers sighed happily. "So clueless." He shook himself. "Onward. If the Morgensterns wanted to, they could put all sorts of pressure on the Quinteros to cough over the reluctant bride because they are older money, older magic, and generally a bigger furry deal. Everybody in their circle would be now treating Alistair like he had the plague, only nastier."

"So," Miller said, suddenly getting it. "Percy pissed in his pool. He *had* to go to another dating pool to try to date poor Alice Morgenstern."

"Yes," Piers said, nodding. "But not only was she, from all reports in the local rag, 'cool' toward Mr. Hampstead, it became clear after the murder of Ellie and William that he was a frickin' monster, and the Morgensterns broke it off. Percy bought their silence and then ran back to his big house of money."

"To what?" Miller pondered. "Terrorize the maid? Kill small animals? Did he buy a herd of sheep and torture livestock? I was *in* his head, remember? That kind of crazy doesn't go back in the bottle. Did you look that stuff up after his return?"

Piers gave him a wounded look. "Do I look like an amateur? Two years of law school, my friend—I think I can scan some archives."

Miller laughed. "Yeah, you're smart. But I'm on the edge of my seat here."

Piers frowned briefly as though wanting to ask him something but then plowed on. "I did find stuff," he said, "but you've really got to read between the lines. Have you ever heard of Howard H. Holmes?"

Miller shook his head. "Nope."

"He… well, it's complicated. Some people say he was responsible for over ninety murders, and some people have it down to a measly ten or so, most of them mistresses and their children."

Miller stared at him. "Yuck."

"That's the point," Piers said. "He was convicted and executed for the murder of his business partner. Why?"

Miller had to rub his stomach because he hated the answer to this. "Because the women were expendable. The children too. The man's life had value, but the women's didn't."

Piers tapped his nose grimly. "Got it in one. So that's what I'm working with here. You asked if he tortured his housemaids. What if he had? Who would they tell? How would they get away? A housemaid who quit her job back then without a reference would end up on the streets. She couldn't get a decent position after that. How much would a woman put up with to not end up in the gutter?"

"Gah! That's awful. And if the housemaid disappears, the guy with all the money simply says, 'Haven't heard of her, old chap—so sorry. One of those things. Maybe she's a prostitute who's dying of the clap by now.'"

Piers nodded. "Exactly. But there *are* personal ads and employment records. And I've got *three* personal ads looking for young women who were once employed by Percy Hampstead. I couldn't find a death certificate for any of them, which could mean anything, including—"

"He got rid of the bodies," Miller said, shuddering. "Okay, that's what I'm doing on my next vacation. Got it."

"Finding bodies?" Piers sounded surprised.

"Solving this guy's mysteries completely. All the murder victims. The whole enchilada. We can't do it *now*, because we've got something else on our plates, but this needs addressing. This…." Miller shuddered. "I don't know. Those poor girls. Nobody would believe them, and if they did believe them, they wouldn't help. It's just… bwah."

Piers leaned close to him then, close enough to feel his body heat, close enough to slow time down.

"What?" Miller whispered, suddenly wanting to hide his face against Piers's chest.

"So many Cassandras," Piers murmured. "You understand them."

Miller swallowed, feeling like he'd gotten a compliment he didn't deserve. "I've never been that helpless," he said.

"No?" Piers's hand on the side of his face surprised him—such a tender gesture. Miller leaned into it without thinking. "You went to your lover's funeral and sat silent as stone, Miller. Am I right?"

"Yes, without the poetry," Miller argued, capturing that hand and kissing the palm. "I'm not good with poetry."

Piers's smile barely touched the corner of his lips and the crinkles of his eyes. "You'd be surprised," he said softly before pulling Miller into a kiss. Long and full, slow, gloriously slow, with no endgame, just kiss after kiss after kiss.

Finally Miller pulled back and rested his forehead against Piers's, trying to remember his own name.

"We have got to," he said on a breath, "finish what we're doing so we can—" He swallowed. "—go back tomorrow and try to catch our scary guy."

"And do what?" Piers asked, looking as dazed as Miller felt.

"Have Scout portal him to Antarctica," Miller said grumpily. "Yes, I know, officer sworn to uphold the law—but Piers, you're a law student. Can anything we've put together here be introduced into a courtroom?"

"Unless we get him rushing Larissa with a knife, I'm going to say no," Piers agreed. With a huge sigh, he pulled himself back to what they'd been doing before, well, they'd started doing other things.

"So about Percy," Miller said, taking control of things with an effort. "Did he have any children?"

Piers glanced at him curiously. "What are you thinking?"

"That unless you're a hedge witch and look at how to tune the natural forces with natural elements and such, like Marcus and Helen, the other magic—the mechanics and the wizards—they tend to run in families. You and Larissa, Scout and Kayleigh."

"Do *you* have any mechanics in your bloodline?" Piers asked.

Miller shrugged. "If I do, they're on my mom's side of the family, and we never met them…." He shrugged. "But I'm thinking that's a lot of evil there in our guy Percy. If one poor housemaid had to bear his child, that mechanic—and that personality—has somewhere to go." He let out a breath. "No, I don't buy that we're always guilty of the sins of our fathers. I'm saying that if raised kindly and loved, a Percy Hampstead grows up to be a moody guy who can accidentally kill plants."

"But if raised to be quiet or abused in rich people's homes…," Piers murmured to himself.

"Or thrown in an orphanage or brought up by addicts or a thousand other things that can happen in a family," Miller continued. "That, yes—we're looking at someone who inherited Percy's psychotic tendencies *and* a little magic twist. What do you think?"

"Aha!" Piers crowed, pulling up a page that looked like a pdf of a microfiche of an original document.

"Holy thirdhand source, Batman," Miller said dryly.

"It's Percy's household account book," Piers told him with a flounce. "And finding it online while you were doing dishes was one of the most magical things I've ever done. See here?"

"Gardeners," Miller said.

"Yup. Right down the line. He lost one every two months. Poor men—probably realized all the plants were dying no matter what they did and left in shame."

"So that answers that question," Miller mused. "Now how do we use that knowledge?"

"I don't know," Piers admitted. At that moment both of them jumped as their cell phones buzzed in their pockets. It was Kayleigh, and she'd done a mass send.

Guys! Guess what? I just spent three hours eating sushi in the security room with Callan and his chief of security. (Totally hot by the way, and he's got dimples when he smiles. I may keep him.)

She accompanied that with a shot of a guy with a pricey haircut and a linen blazer, with a hawk nose, sharp gray eyes, and a lantern jaw.

"He's cute," Piers acknowledged. "Go Kayleigh."

Anyway, Des, Callan, and I have been scanning video clips looking for dead plants and bingo! We've got one. We're trying to track the people in that video around to see if we can get a picture of the guy. Piers, I went into your suite to grab yours and Larissa's laptops—the plants were still alive, but I got a bad feeling, so I buggered out and had Des go get them and hide them. Callan knows where they are. I hope we're all on board trusting him. Definitely don't go back to your suite until this is taken care of.

I'm bedding down here in Callan's suite tonight. Don't worry about me, but everybody take care of each other.

Night!

Miller scanned the message and felt relief for a moment. Kayleigh was making progress, and so were they. Then he had a terrible thought. Without hesitating he pulled up Callan's number and was about to punch it when it started to buzz his phone.

"She's fine," Callan said shortly. "I could feel your doubt. It was like a flaming arrow in the dark. Are you sure you're not a wizard?"

"Very," Miller said, relieved. Then, hearing someone fumbling with the phone, "Kayleigh? Are you—"

"Fine, Miller. Wow. You're intense. So's Piers and Scout, by the way. Jesus. I type one 'I'm fine' text and everybody starts calling to make *sure* I'm fine. Go away so I can talk to Scout."

And with that Callan came back on the line and chuckled. "That really would have been a fun marriage," he admitted.

"We're just—"

"Worried," Callan said soberly. "I get it. Look, I understand you guys have a meeting time and place. Let's all plan on being there for that, okay? I promise Kayleigh's not going anywhere, and she swears Larissa's in the best hands."

Miller remembered Helen's strong, pure magic flowing through him before Piers's bright sunshine rolled down the same path. "She's got good people looking after her," he agreed. "And that sounds like a plan."

He looked over to where Piers was now on the phone with... who? Lucky? Larissa?

"I've got to go and pass the reassurance down the phone tree," Miller told him. "But thanks for watching out for us."

"Course," Callan said. Then his tone changed. "So I gather Piers got to you first?"

"I'm a dumb cop, Callan," Miller told him. "I would have embarrassed you at parties. Count your blessings on a narrow escape."

Callan laughed, and it was a good laugh, rolling and kind, but underneath there was a tinge of hurt. "I'll talk endlessly about the one who got away," he said, his voice tender. "Now go and have your alone time with Piers. Kayleigh very much didn't want to interrupt."

"Thanks, Callan," Miller said, feeling inadequate. He hung up and looked to Piers, who was trying to get a word in edgewise.

"Larissa," Piers mouthed. "Freaking out."

Miller held his hand out for the phone. "I spoke to her in person," he said, cutting through Larissa's five-star freak-out. "She's fine. Callan's fine. They're all fine. Callan wanted to make sure *you* were safe, so no going to visit her tonight, understand?"

"Yeah, Miller. I get it. But thank you. I just—it's easy to fake a text, you know?"

"I know," Miller said, laughing a little. "But I think we've ensured there will be phone contact from now on. Meeting tomorrow at the usual time and the usual place, like it was a regular Tuesday, okay?"

"I'll pass it on. Thanks."

"Stay safe, sweetheart." Miller swallowed, remembering everything they'd uncovered tonight. "Our bad guys aren't messing around."

"Will do." She called to somebody not on the phone. "Marcus, Helen, Miller wants to make sure I'm safe."

"She's safe," Helen said, sounding only a few feet away. "But her phone is dying because none of you young people know how to charge the damned things."

"Bye!" Miller called, and Piers added on to it, and they signed off, both of them breathing softly into the sudden silence now that what felt like a crisis had passed. Their phones buzzed some more, and they both fielded texts from Scout and Lucky, but eventually the message "back of the coffee shop, tomorrow at eight" was passed around without anybody actually *saying* the place or the time. It felt like saying it out loud might attract something nobody wanted, and Miller was prepared to honor that sort of thing, given that Callan had started it and was probably as powerful as Scout in his own way.

Finally they were done, and Miller felt the sudden lassitude of the end of the day catching up with him.

"Gah!" Piers swore, holding his arms above his head and stretching. Miller did the same thing but stood up to complete the stretch, and in a moment they were both moving back and forth in the living room, trying to get their blood flowing again. Piers did something at Miller's computer, and suddenly there was music coming out of it.

"You found my streaming service," Miller said, arching an eyebrow.

"And your playlist," Piers agreed. Something folksy and delicate came up, and Miller almost groaned.

"No... no. No man should get caught listening to this song."

"No, no," Piers murmured, kicking off his shoes. "Come on, get rid of yours."

Miller did, leaving them under the kitchen table like a heathen. But Piers was standing expectantly, and Miller knew what was coming. Piers stepped into his space and wrapped his arms around Miller's shoulders, giving him shelter like he'd never had.

Miller was out of fight. Out of "But we have work to do." Out of "But how's it going to work?" Out of "But you're a cute rich guy and I'm a dumb cop." All of that was true, but right here, in this moment, Piers was holding him, and even if they ended up in a place where they saw each other every day and made love every night, the truth was, they were human and mortal, and mortal humans got a finite number of hugs, of dances, of kisses. They might seem endless at the beginning, when people were made of hormones and hope, but Miller had lived to watch a lover—no matter how flawed or temporary—walk out the door and never come back.

Hormones and hope faded, and someday, sometime, there would always be a last hug, a last kiss, or a last dance.

Miller wanted to fit as many between now and then as possible.

They swayed to the music together, languorously, as though nothing was hunting them, not even time. Miller's body began to burn, slowly at first, like a heating pad on low, but as Piers rocked them around the small living room, Miller's temperature began to rise. Their chests pressed together, their groins. Piers's hands on his shoulders grew hot, scorching, and Miller wanted them on his bare skin.

Piers lowered his lips to Miller's neck, nibbling softly, and Miller clenched his hands against the back pockets of Piers's jeans.

Piers made his way up to Miller's ear and sucked on his earlobe, adding a nip that made Miller buck up against him in need.

"Should you show me the bedroom?" Piers asked, his lips brushing the whorls of Miller's ear. "Or would you like to undress here and dance naked in your living room?"

"Bedroom," Miller rasped, but barely. He grasped Piers's hand and hauled him past the couch and the recliner, around the kitchen island, and toward the largest of the two bedrooms in the cottage.

When he got there, he paused at the closed door and looked up at Piers, this move to a room of their own, a *bed* of their own, suddenly feeling very different from the lovemaking in Scout and Lucky's apartment.

That had been an interlude, and he'd needed it, would never regret that it happened.

This was a *choice*, and it was a decision to move forward with hope in his heart that Piers—beautiful, brilliant, rich, and gifted—could want Miller for the long term.

It was more than he'd ever done with Brad, and Miller felt the difference, the depth of this choice, to his bones.

"Miller?" Piers urged gently.

Miller slanted a look at him and opened the door.

Portals, Doors, and Gateways

PIERS WASN'T sure what he'd expected when he'd walked into Miller's bedroom, but what he got was much better.

Perhaps because he'd said he'd put things like glassware in storage when he moved, Piers had been thinking it would look more like a college dorm than a grown man's apartment, but he should have known. The bed frame had probably come with the apartment—it appeared to be made out of wood to match the paneling that Miller had claimed to strip—but the bedding was masculine and comforting in shades of sea and sky and sand.

The floors had been stripped recently—to a local wood, probably loblolly pine. The throw rugs that covered its varnished surface were ocean gray and sky blue with sand-colored designs, and if Miller hadn't been there, standing before him with limpid eyes waiting apprehensively for Piers's attention, he might have perused the room further. There was a desk that looked personal and battered, and a print on the wall by a familiar local artist, as well as wool throws on the bed that looked locally made as well.

Miller truly had made a home here, his lack of wineglasses notwithstanding. Of course he'd been worried about getting involved with Piers. He'd uprooted himself upon the death of his lover, moved from New Jersey down here to the Drift, and fought to establish himself among the locals. He watched over his people closely—the people on Tatter's Tot hadn't called Leo Kowalski, they'd called Miller. Helen and Marcus had accepted him easily into their sphere, and Piers wondered if they'd known who he'd been before he'd knocked on Scout's door, asking for an explanation for the suddenly missing tourists. Miller's toes were already dug in past the sand and into the bedrock of the islands, down below the sea.

If Piers tried to yank him off the Drift, it would be like yanking his legs off and carting him around, footless and mourning and trying hard to walk in Piers's shadow.

Piers would rather die.

"Don't look so scared," he murmured, feathering kisses across Miller's cheekbones, wanting to drink in the sweetness and the salt. "I love... your room...."

He brushed his lips across Miller's, and Miller opened just a tad, just enough to let Piers's teasing tongue in before he spoke.

"It's not the room," he said softly. "It's the choice. This time has consequences. Once can be a fling. After tonight, we're a *thing*."

"I should have had that on a T-shirt when I started college," Piers said, thrusting his hands under Miller's shirt at the hem and lifting it over his head. Miller held his hands up obediently and simply stood there, allowing Piers's scrutiny, while Piers glided his lips over Miller's collarbones, his neck, his chest, and tried to drink him in with little sips.

Miller's own hands had gone foraging, and Piers ducked his head to let Miller strip him of his shirt and fleece before starting his perusal of Miller's chest again.

"Isn't it my—oh!—turn!" Miller protested as Piers took his nipple in his mouth and sucked. "I need to—"

Piers let go of him with a satisfying pop. "Well, I did it first," he said smugly. "I want to taste all of you, and lucky me, you just melted and let yourself be tasted."

"I can top," Miller sighed as Piers went to the other nipple and started to suckle some more. "I can be aggressive—oh.... God, don't stop. Piers!"

He shuddered, not quite in orgasm but close, and this night, when it was them alone in this little house, alone on this tiny peninsula of land, Piers wanted more of that. He wanted Miller to beg him, to order him, to make his needs known.

To make them a priority.

"Show me," Piers whispered, standing and shoving his jeans down to the floor.

Miller caught his breath, and his hand—rough with work and saltwater—drifted up, almost of its own volition, to stroke along Piers's bare hip.

Piers moved closer, capturing Miller's hand and pressing it to his abdomen, the neatly trimmed area above his cock. "Aggressive?" he taunted gently.

Miller met his eyes with a shy little smile. "I really wanted to see this the other night," he admitted. His first touch to Piers's cock was hesitant and heavenly, the rough glide of fingers along tender skin.

"Mmm...." Piers moved a little closer and began to nibble on Miller's neck again and was gratified when those fingers closed around him, squeezing gently. "Keep going," he whispered in Miller's ear, and to his surprise—and delight—Miller fell to his knees.

Piers straightened and reached down with delicate fingertips to caress Miller's cheeks. "Know what you're doing?" he asked, and Miller gave him a sly little look.

"Only sometimes," he promised and flicked his tongue teasingly along the underside of Piers's cock, stopping short at the harp string and puffing soft breaths along the bell.

"Sometimes might kill me," Piers hummed, and he was rewarded by a slow stroke along the shaft and Miller's tongue teasing that sensitive underside, flicking with almost tickling touches.

Almost.

Piers raised a hand to the back of Miller's head for his own balance, and so he could keep touching, even as his whole body shivered.

"More?" Miller breathed.

"Please."

More stroking, more licking, more laving, and Piers barely kept himself from knotting his fingers in Miller's hair and thrusting his hips like a madman. With a more aggressive lover, he might have, but he wouldn't chance it with Miller. Miller might not tell him no if he didn't like it. Miller might simply accept it as his due.

Piers would die before he forced Miller to do anything he wasn't comfortable with.

Instead, Piers tilted his head back and made noises, encouraging him. He hummed quietly as Miller developed a stroking rhythm and cried out when he squeezed at the base of Piers's cock. His noises deepened, and urgency began to thrum through his bloodstream. After a particularly delicious stroke, followed by Miller's plying of his talented tongue, Piers *did* knot his fingers through Miller's hair, tugging his head back gently.

The sound of want issuing from Miller's throat was one of the most gratifying things he'd ever heard.

"Two choices here," Piers muttered harshly. "First choice, I come in your mouth and then pleasure you with mine...."

Miller moaned and stuck his tongue out, barely capturing a shiny drop of pre at the tip. Piers shuddered and tugged Miller's head back just a little harder, not missing Miller's sly glance upward.

The cheekiness absolutely undid Piers. "Choice two," he grated. "Stay right there."

He turned toward Miller's bed and dragged the covers back, then fumbled in Miller's drawer for lubricant. He brought out a tiny bottle, almost completely filled, and suppressed the urge to roll his eyes. *Miller, you'd better make time for our sex life in the future.*

Then he lay back against the pillows completely nude and looked at Miller kneeling on the carpet, watching him in the lamplight with hunger and curiosity written plainly on his face.

"Don't just sit there," Piers teased. "Get naked and get over here!"

Miller stood hesitantly and began to strip off his jeans and briefs. Piers turned to his side and grinned as Miller fought the elastic of his briefs over his springing cock.

"You don't have a clue what I have in mind, do you?" he asked.

"No," Miller told him, finally winning the battle and scrambling over to the bed. "What do you—ooh...."

Piers held up the lubricant and squirted some on his fingers before lying back down again and oiling his cock.

"What, uhm...." Miller stumbled over his words, so Piers decided to help him out. He took two of Miller's fingers and sucked them into his mouth, scraping their underside with his teeth before releasing them with a pop.

"I'm going to suck on you," he said patiently, "and you're going to stretch yourself. Then you're going to...." He raised his eyebrows devilishly. "Sit down," he finished, and was rewarded when Miller's face washed red before settling into a blotchy pink.

"Okay," Miller rasped, and then looked at his fingers in slowly dawning realization.

Piers added a dollop of lubricant to them and murmured, "Come here. I won't see what you're doing if I'm sucking your cock."

Miller let out a keen of arousal, but he did what Piers told him. Piers rolled to his side, moving his hand from his cock so he didn't make himself come as he sucked Miller down to the back of his throat. Miller let out a gasp, and for a moment, Piers wondered if he was going to come and they'd have to plan it all out again, but after a few moments of worshipping Miller's body with his lips, mouth, and tongue, he felt Miller shift his weight, and his sounds of arousal grew more pitched.

He was fingering himself, like Piers had told him to, and the thought made Piers giddy with desire.

It wasn't his best blowjob—he could admit that—but Miller was jerking, obviously torn between the pleasure of his own fingers in his backside and the pleasure of Piers's mouth on his cock, and knowing that was like an aphrodisiac. Miller paused for a moment to shudder, and the hand he put on the back of Piers's head wasn't gentle.

Piers pulled away and whispered, "Now it's time to sit down."

Miller whimpered and swung up on the bed, straddling Piers's stomach before reaching behind himself and squeezing Piers's weeping cock.

With shaking hands, he placed Piers at his slick, dilated entrance and began to shift downward.

Piers threw his head back and hissed, the pressure exquisite, and tried to control his breathing, his *body*, so he could listen to Miller alternatively gasp and moan as he slid down, down, slowly down, along Piers's length.

Finally, after a millennium, an *eternity*, Miller was flush against Piers's abdomen, and his head drooped on his neck as he pounded Piers's chest lightly with a clenched hand.

"Piers... I can't... I can't... I *need*.... God, help me out here—"

"Shh...." Piers gripped Miller's hips and locked him into place, thrusting his ass against the mattress so his cock slid out just a little before he thrust back in. Miller groaned and lifted up slightly on his knees to give Piers more room to work.

"That's my boy," Piers whispered and thrust upward again, glorying as Miller cried out. Piers picked up speed, the slapping of their flesh vying with Miller's sounds of desire as the sexiest things Piers had ever heard.

"Piers!" Miller gasped, shaking all over, and Piers knew what he needed.

"Touch yourself," he commanded, wanting to see it as his stomach muscles burned in exertion.

Then Miller did, wrapping that gloriously rough hand around his own cock. His head fell back, and Piers felt his groan down where they were joined, the sound vibrating through both of them, through the pit of Piers's groin, as Miller's desperate, hard strokes drove him higher and higher and his arousal clenched his asshole tighter and tighter around Piers's cock.

Miller's climax was a roar, from his stomach, from his balls, from his spasming ass, clenching against Piers's erection. Piers closed his eyes as Miller's come spattered his chest and stomach, and then his own orgasm coursed through his bloodstream, a lightning strike, igniting every nerve ending in a burst of pleasure so hot it was almost pain.

Piers kept pumping, rutting helplessly inside Miller as Miller fell forward, his hand still on his cock, and squeezed out one more scalding spill of come.

A long, slow aftershock rocked them both, and Piers pulled Miller closer so he could take his mouth, heedless of the rush of fluid that coated them both as his cock slid, still hard, from Miller's ass.

The kiss went on and on, hot, ramping to incendiary, until Miller was grinding up against him, moaning in mindless need. Piers was out of subtlety this time. Miller's naked sexuality, unleashed and unembarrassed, had him charged even higher than before. He rolled them both like a shark and plunged back inside Miller's body while Miller held his knees spread with abandon and begged to be pillaged.

Begged to be fucked.

This orgasm was feral and elusive. It had to be stalked, had to be chased, and when Miller finally caught it, his arms fell trembling to his sides, flailing as he lost all coherence and begged, a simple "Please, please, please…" issuing from his throat as Piers pounded inside him, chanting, "Yes, yes, yes—"

"*Augh!*"

Once again, Miller's spasms triggered Piers's climax, and this time Piers rutted into Miller's limpening body until his arms gave out, and it was the two of them, clenching each other as the final bursts of hot, then cold washed through them, their climaxes pulsing through their bloodstream and into the salt air around them.

This time when Piers slid to the side in a breathless wash of come, his arms and shoulders shook, and his entire body was coated in sweat, in fluids, in replete sexual satiation and a burning need to know what they'd just done meant as much to Miller as it had to him.

"Piers?" Miller whispered, right at the point when Piers thought he might be able to hear something over his heart beating in his own ears.

"Yeah?"

"I'm not embarrassed about that at all."

Piers felt a smile twitch at the corners of his mouth. "Good to know."

"I mean... I... I *need* that inside me."

Piers must have let out a sound of amusement—or shock—because Miller backtracked and tried again.

"I mean...." And now he hid his face against Piers's sweaty chest. "I'll do anything in front of you," he said. "For you. I...." The realization seemed to shock him. "I *trust* you," he said in wonder, and Piers's eyes burned.

"Good," he said thickly, knowing this was an honor, maybe one of the most important in his life. "Because I think I love you."

Miller's gasp told him he didn't take this lightly, and then Miller had pushed up, was taking Piers's mouth with his, was kissing him, hard and deep.

He pulled back enough to whisper, "I think I love you too."

And then Piers absolutely had to kiss him back.

Unexpected

PIERS VERY rarely showed his privilege, Miller had noted, but getting him up at the—his words—"furry taint and ball sac of dawn" apparently brought it out of him. It was Miller's turn to nurse him into the frigid dark morning with thermoses of hot coffee and an extra warm hat and scarf set that Miller's sister had knitted for him the year before.

"It *is* cozy," Piers had admitted after wrapping the oversized scarf around him several times like a shawl. "Why aren't *you* wearing it?"

"Because I have to pilot the boat," Miller explained patiently. He pulled the hat and cowl from the pocket of his jacket that he kept there for mornings like this one.

"You had that?" Piers asked peevishly as Miller thrust a thermos into his hand and threw a waterproof satchel containing his smaller laptop over his shoulder. "You had that hat and neck thing two nights ago when you had all the heat sucked out of your body and you're just putting it on now?"

Miller stared at him. "This is for morning chill! Are you looking at it? It's… it's like super wool with llama or something—I don't know. She's always going on about it. It will cook your brain if it's more than thirty degrees outside." He slipped the cowl over his head and the cap over his ears. "In this case, it should get us to the Drift in time for more coffee while you hunker down behind the console."

Piers scowled at him. "I can ride up top with you."

"Take the console and the heated tarp," Miller said patiently. "You'll be in a better mood when we get to the coffee shop."

"Not fair," Piers muttered, moving to the door as Miller opened it. "Who knew you had a superpower." He took a step to cross the threshold and gasped, "Who the fuck are you?"

Miller looked around his shoulder and groaned internally. "Hey, Leo. What are you doing here so early? I thought you went back last night."

Leo Kowalski looked awful. Already paunchy, his clothes were pulled tight around his thick frame as though he'd… he'd *bloated* inside them. His craggy face was melting, sliding off his skull, almost obscuring his mean blue eyes. His thinning hair stuck up in six places, and his jacket was covered with a suspicious kind of mung.

"Things happened," Leo said shortly. "There was a... a disturbance," he finished. "A *disturbance* over at John's Thumb."

Miller kept his polite attention on Leo, but inside he was starting to quiver. *Armed and crazy*, he thought. *Armed and crazy armed and crazy armed and crazy....*

"Did you put it in the report?" he asked, all business. "I've got a meeting with the chamber of commerce this morning—"

"Where?" snarled Leo.

"The resort conference rooms," Miller lied easily. "Ten o'clock if you want to come with us."

As though for the first time, Leo noticed that Piers was there, backing into the kitchen after almost plowing into him. "Who the fuck are you?"

Miller gave Piers a warning look. Normally his shyness was reserved for the people close to his heart who could actually hurt him—unless coming out at work could be dangerous. Given that Callan, his actual boss, was gay, Miller figured he was in a place to say, "Whatsitoya?" and blow Leo off like the asshole he was. But there was something odd, unhinged, about Leo, and right now all Miller could think of was getting to the skiff and getting the fuck away from dispatch as quickly as possible.

"I'm visiting from law school," Piers said, and his even tones told Miller he felt it too—something was decidedly off about Leo Kowalski. "I had some research to do last night, and Miller has good Wi-Fi."

Leo's lip curled, as though he was smelling something off, something rancid. "They don't got good Wi-Fi at the resort?" he challenged.

Miller knew his own eyes had gone round. Leo's voice had changed, the accent going flatter and stiffer, somehow. Old—or old-*fashioned*.

"I'm not staying at the resort," Piers lied, much as Miller had. "I'm staying with friends at one of the smaller islands—I'm sorry, I forget the name."

"Thimbleberry," Miller supplied, waiting for Leo's response.

"I don't got time for the big house," he snarled, his voice sounding more and more *old* and less and less *Leo*. "I'm looking for one of them *other* resort scum." His eyes narrowed on Piers again. "What'ya say your name was?"

"James," Miller said. "James Simmons." He gave a polite smile. "I'm sorry, Leo, but we really do have a meeting, and we can't be late."

Leo Kowalski—the *real* Leo Kowalski—would know that leaving now would get them to Spinner's Drift by around seven thirty, with some play for tides or strong winds. But *this* Leo Kowalski looked suddenly terrified, as though the idea of getting caught out, of being *caught* in some way, was the absolutely worst thing that could happen to him.

"Then I'll leave ya to it," he said, looking cagily left and right. "Do ya mind letting me kip over in your cot?"

It took Miller a moment to realize he meant *nap*, and the thought of this... *this* whatever it was, sleeping in his snug little cottage made him want to vomit.

"Did you lose your key to the overnights?" he asked. That was what they called the two small apartments on the other side of the little grassy yard they were standing in. "I've got a key. I'm afraid James left his room a mess. No place for you to sleep."

And with that he led the way to the snug one-room flat, opening the door for Leo-not-Leo and letting him in. "They've been stocked recently," he said. "You should be able to find soup and a can opener if you're hungry."

Leo nodded, looking around vaguely, and Miller pulled out one last burst of dissembling.

"I'll leave you to it," Miller said, using the same words in sort of a daze. "See you this evening." With that he shut the door and took Piers's arm to haul him down to the dock and the skiff.

"What the hell was that?" Piers asked as they hopped on board. "Don't bother with the ropes, I'll get them. Do we have enough fuel?"

"To get us to the Drift, yes," Miller said, following his plan and starting the engine. He hadn't asked about Piers's sailing background, but given the easy way he moved about the little skiff, Miller was pretty sure he had one. "Not much beyond. Are we ready?"

"Aye-aye, captain," Piers said without a trace of irony. He was obviously as invested in getting the hell away from the tiny peninsula as Miller was.

It wasn't until they had pulled away, a good hundred yards from shore, that Piers called his name, his voice strangling over the wind. "Look!" he said desperately, coming to stand next to Miller at the console. "The trees!"

The dispatch office had two palm trees—the short kind—flanking either side of the walkway into the office itself. Miller squinted against the salt spray and gasped.

Even from this distance, he could see that the palm fronds, usually a lustrous green, were brown. As they watched, a handful from each tree clattered to the ground.

"Fuck," Miller muttered. "We've got to get on the horn."

"That was your *boss*?" Piers asked as he crouched behind Miller out of the wind and pulled out his phone.

"No, that was Percy Hampstead," Miller retorted.

Piers sucked in a breath, and Miller waited for it. For the, "C'mon, be real. *That's* stretching it to the limit," but that's not what Piers said.

"How do you know?" he asked.

"Because nobody lives on Thimbleberry right now," Miller told him, his voice shrill over the wind. "It's practically underwater. But when it *wasn't* underwater, it was the original resort—sort of a big Victorian house with a whole lot of beach for the Morgensterns. Leo would have known it was unlivable now—but Percy wouldn't."

He peered behind him, and for a moment he and Piers made eye contact, the horror of the situation hitting them both full force.

"I'll text the group," Piers said.

"I'll get Patsy on the radio," Miller said. And then he had a terrible thought. Piers believed him. But then Piers was part of his world.

Would Patsy?

Miller powered up the satellite phone that was kept hooked to the console and hit the preset.

Only one way to find out.

"Whossis?" She was obviously still sleeping.

"Patsy, honey—it's Miller. I need you to do me a favor and don't come in today."

"Wha'?" Yup. She was waking up a bit. "Don' wha'?"

"Patsy, I need you to wake up, honey. This is important, but I can't explain why, okay?"

"Mmmkay." Miller waited as she yawned and stretched, keeping his eye on the horizon and his compass as he did. They were getting to the island waterways now, and it paid to be alert. "Go. Why'm'I no'coming in?"

"There is something—*someone*—dangerous happening today at dispatch. I… I can't explain it better than that, but I need you to not be near it, okay?"

"Wait." And *now* she was awake. "Are you saying the island's police center has been taken over? Like by *terrorists*? Because shouldn't we call somebody?"

Miller grimaced. "Not by terrorists," he said. "Just... something *really* unwholesome is there right now—"

"Does this have anything to do with the witches on the main island?" Patsy asked suddenly. "Because, Miller, they are perfectly nice people, and it's bullshit if you're calling them names!"

Miller caught his breath. "You know Marcus and Helen?" he asked, grasping at that straw.

"Yes. They're lovely. Helen sold me my first book on Wicca. Why?"

"Because they *are* lovely, and I'm one of their, uhm, witches. And there is something *evil* on the dispatch island. It *looks* like Leo Kowalski, but it's *not*, and we need to keep *everybody* away from dispatch so it can't... I don't know. Take over anybody else."

Patsy sucked in a breath. "Miller, that sounds crazy. You know that, right?"

Miller's heart sank. "Please believe me," he begged. "Please, Patsy? You've been so kind to me since I got here. Please believe me and stay away."

There was silence on the other end of the line, and the wind and buzz of the engine filled his ears. *Please*, he begged all the powers that were. *Please please please.*

"Okay, sweetie," she said placatingly. "Is it just me you want to stay away, or—"

"Everybody. The ferry, whoever's on duty today—call them up and tell them there's a hazard in the harbor or something. Tell them I'm taking the shift. Whatever you need to—"

"Should I call Leo?" she asked.

"No!" Miller almost shouted.

"Okay, okay," she said. "Why not?"

"Because he's dangerous," Miller said again. "He's... he's dangerous. He's not really Leo, and he can't know we know that." Oh God. He was going about this all wrong, and he couldn't seem to fix it. "God, Patsy, I know I sound deranged. I know it. I know this whole thing is unhinged. But could you... for me, honey, could you just believe I want you safe? I don't want anybody hurt?"

Another silence, and for a moment, Miller thought he'd lost her.

And he felt grief. Mourning. Because at this stage going into the dispatch office would be the end of this lovely woman who bought him cookies and wine and wished him luck with a date and who had made his stay here pleasant and his job worth doing.

But he didn't feel guilty.

This wasn't his fault, he realized in that heartbeat. It wasn't his guilt speaking because she wouldn't listen. He was doing his best—his human best. He had a gift, but he wasn't all-seeing or all-encompassing. He could point out the danger, but he couldn't restrain it.

"I believe you want me safe," she said at last. Then, "And seriously—who wouldn't take a day off, right? I'll contact the others. Don't worry about it."

He couldn't be sure if she was lying to make him feel better. For all he knew he'd gotten through to her—but with a sort of freeing finality, he knew one thing.

He'd done his best for the moment. He could call her later—or have Helen or Marcus call her—but the more he begged, the crazier he'd sound, and that would help nobody.

"Thanks, Patsy," he said, his stomach still cold with fear. "I'll call you when it's safe."

He hung up then, surprised by a warmth at his back. How long had Piers been there, up in the cockpit with him, listening to him beg?

"Do you think she believed you?" Piers asked into his ear, close enough to keep their words from the jealous wind.

"I don't know," Miller said, still grieving—but not guilty. God, not guilty. Not this time. "But she knows Marcus and Helen. Could you text Helen and—"

"On it." Piers had braced himself in the corner of the console and was texting frantically while Miller steered them through the deepest parts of the archipelago, keeping the skiff from foundering.

In a few quiet moments—moments Miller desperately needed as he worked the forward lamp and the helm at the same time—Piers straightened and assumed his position as Miller's human back-warmer.

"They'll call her," he said, his voice comforting.

"What about the others?"

"They're having a raging discussion right now," Piers said. "But the consensus when I climbed up here was that the spirit needed a body—or at least a focus to go body hopping again. For one thing, it couldn't cross saltwater as just a spirit. Also, Callan and Kayleigh have been looking and have figured out what happened at John's Thumb and how the spirit of Percy Hampstead was hiding before it hitched a ride in Leo Kowalski's skinsuit."

They both shuddered.

"It would be *great*," Miller said passionately, "if we knew whoever was left knew what had happened, or if he was a pawn."

"Or if he was both," Piers said. "If he was a stalker and a creep to begin with but Percy Hampstead hitched a ride sometime in the last few years and made him worse."

It made sense; Leo wasn't a good guy. In fact, he was a perfectly suited vessel for someone whose psychosis and superiority complex made him a merciless killer.

And if that was what they were dealing with, it was infinitely more dangerous than either of them had thought.

THE THING with this part of the commute was that it couldn't be rushed. Many of the smaller islands off Spinner's Drift used to be part of the larger island and could still be reached via land bridges during low tide in summer. That's why Miller piloted a skiff with a flattish bottom instead of a cabin cruiser. He needed something reasonably fast but not deep. He kept his attention on the waters ahead, watching the shadows of the darkened islands appear and recede from his peripheral vision as he kept the skiff on course, with Piers at his back. They'd exhausted themselves speaking over the wind, and the morning mist was rising, so Miller needed all his focus where it was.

But that didn't mean he didn't appreciate Piers's warmth, or the hand he kept at Miller's back, either.

It surprised him how good it felt to have somebody there. He usually gloried in his solitary job—he could listen to music or audiobooks during his time in the skiff, or sometimes just ponder the world in his own head. He loved those things. But having someone there, the silence companionable between them, that warmed him in ways he hadn't thought of.

And the fact that Piers poured coffee for both of them every so often was nice too. It was bitterly cold in the dark of early morning, and while Miller was grateful for his sister's knitting, even knitting needed the assistance of a good hot brew.

As they neared the dock of Spinner's Drift, he saw that the light was still on at the point, guiding in any night arrivals, but beyond that, the restaurants had left on their holiday twinkles, and the merchants lining the town square had also left on their light strings, and he wondered if that had been Marcus and Helen's doing, to help warm the square and make it harder for the darkness, the grief, and the cold to attack the unwary traveler.

It was the sort of thing people did when they wanted to welcome you home.

Miller's stomach warmed, and he leaned into Piers for a moment before he steered the skiff to the small dock and took the bay closest to shore. The ferry docked on the other side of the harbor. That side was considerably larger, and the road faded right into the water, so all a loaded ferry needed to do was drop its ramp and a smallish electric vehicle could add itself to the ranks of the island. There was another ramp of this sort on the resort side, but anything like a gas-powered jeep had long since been replaced.

Piers made quick work of the ropes, and Miller grabbed his satchel with all their work inside. He hustled up on the dock, allowing Piers to guide him as he read all the messages on the text chain Piers had started as they'd fled the dispatch peninsula.

"Oh my God," he muttered as Piers deftly steered him around a patch of ice and up the wooden stairs leading to the tourist quad. "Scout's brain—does it ever shut up?"

"Terrifying," Piers agreed. "But look at Kayleigh. She's getting tight with this Desmond guy. I hope he's not trouble."

"Lookit you getting all protective. Larissa seems to think he's hot—one picture and she's already maid of honor." Miller scanned the text some more, catching up by the time they neared the store. He checked the time on his phone and gave a whistle of relief. "We made good time—it's seven twenty. The ferry shouldn't get here for another couple of hours."

Piers's grip on his elbow tightened. "You don't think fake-Leo is going to be on the ferry, do you?"

Miller grunted. "What I think is sort of complicated," he admitted at last. "It all depends. If Patsy did like she told me and called everybody and told them to stay away from the dispatch island, I think Leo's skinsuit is going to be trapped on the peninsula. You can't travel the tidal road this time of year, and I don't think Percy Hampstead could swim. Just an idea, mind you, but not everybody could back then, and, well, he seemed like sort of a fucking coward, so it's a guess. Anyway, Leo's not that fit, so I'm gonna say no."

"Unless—"

"I don't know how he *got* to dispatch," Miller admitted. "If he parked a skiff or something away from the dock, that's a possibility."

"And…?" It was obvious Piers could read his very real fear.

"I need to see what Kayleigh's friend has to say. See?" He waved his phone around. "Kayleigh says they've got the moment on video. We get to see Percy Hampstead taking over Leo's body. I need to see what that looks like before I—"

Piers stopped him, standing a few doors down from Helen's. Warmth and *hot* coffee, not to mention breakfast, was yards away, and Piers demanded his attention. Reluctantly, Miller turned toward him.

"Miller, have I doubted you *yet?*" he asked, the hurt evident on his face.

"No," Miller admitted. "And you have no idea what it meant to me back there. You took my lead. You've been with me every step of the way. But that was something you could see with your own eyes. This… this is a feeling. A connection that I hate to even think about. It's everything I hate about my gift, and everything I've been afraid of all my life. I… I want some backup before I start making crazy talk."

"I *am* your backup," Piers said without compromise. "You tell me first so I can tell everybody else to listen if it sounds too damned bonkers."

Miller swallowed. He closed his eyes and felt Piers's kiss across his forehead.

"C'mon, Miller. You're one of the most pragmatic men I've ever met. If you think this is real, there's got to be some logic behind it, even if the logic is magic, right? Let's hear it."

"Tom's bench," Miller blurted, before he could second-guess himself. "It's a solid connection between the past and the present, between the world of magic and our own. And Percy Hampstead left a piece of himself in there. When I touched him in the clearing, I was *right there* in his head. I'm thinking if he's desperate, the first person who can contact him even a little in the clearing is going to have the spirit itself trying to worm his way in."

He glanced warily to Piers, waiting for the shoe to drop. Was this it? Was this when Piers broke his heart, broke his trust, left Miller behind with an "I'm sorry, man, I just can't follow you there"?

But that's not how Piers was looking at him.

"No," Piers whispered.

"No what?" Miller asked, failing to keep the telltale defensiveness out of his voice.

"No. Don't. I know what you're thinking, and don't."

Miller gave a shrug. "I'm probably wrong. You know that, right?"

Piers's lower lip crumpled, like he was about to cry, and Miller realized he had to take ownership, right now, of both his reasoning and his idea, the one Piers had seen right through to, the one that had been building in his head since they'd scrambled aboard the skiff and left the ghost of Percy Hampstead in Leo Kowalski's rotting body.

"If we can get this terror out of the world," he said, looking Piers in the eye, "it will be worth it."

"No!" Piers yelled, and Miller fought the urge to wince, to cave, to bend before Piers's formidable will.

"Let's see what they've got to show us," he said gently. "And then I'll propose it. I'm not planning to do this alone, sweetheart. I'll need the whole mechanic's garage to help me out, right?"

Piers's eyes closed tightly, and he dropped his head in defeat. "I was going to call you baby," he said softly, and Miller stepped into his space, leaning his head against Piers's chest and drinking in his warmth, his light, against the darkness.

"No law that says you can't," he whispered.

"You'd better be here so I can," Piers told him, enfolding him in those long arms and holding him close.

"I'll do my best," Miller promised. Of all people, he knew that was the best promise he had.

"That's not good enough," Piers whispered, but Miller had no answer to that.

"It's probably not even needed," he said, trying to be cheerful. "Let's go talk to everybody and see."

"Sure," Piers said, voice gruff. And then he didn't let go until the cold started to seep into their bones and they had no choice.

Sunshine and Sacrifices

HELEN'S TRUEST witchcraft lay in her coffee and hot chocolate drinks, and she and Lucky had made insulated pitchers of both and carried them to the big table in the back of the store. There was also a box of donuts from Donut Do Dat, bacon, egg, and cheese biscuits from Helen, and bread that Larissa and Ciaran had apparently made in Helen and Marcus's house that morning after Piers's text had hit the airwaves and before they'd had to come to the meeting.

"Still hot," Larissa confided proudly as she passed Piers a piping slice, replete with salted butter.

"Thanks, honey," he said, watching as Miller spoke seriously in the corner with Kayleigh and the sharp young man from Kayleigh's photo the night before. Desmond appeared to be all business until Kayleigh spoke, and then his eyes—sort of a piercing gray—went a little soft. "Have they figured out how to show us their video?"

"I think on Miller's laptop," Larissa said, not sounding particularly concerned. "Why do you look like you're trying to pass a lemon?"

Piers narrowly avoided sputtering breadcrumbs. "Oh my God, what a thing to say."

"Well, it's weird," she said defensively. "I mean, I get being terrified—your text got me out of a warm bed to *bake*, for God's sake. But you look… well, *terrified*, but worse."

"I'm not scared for myself," he said unhappily. "I'm scared for *Miller*. And you'll see why in a minute." Piers didn't need to see the video footage. He more than had faith in Miller's assessment of the situation. After the work they'd done the night before, the profile they'd been building on Percy Hampstead, and the way it seemed to mesh with Larissa's stalker, they'd been on their way to the conclusion of the ghost taking over somebody else's body already. But when the thing that used to be Leo Kowalski had shown up at Miller's door that morning…. Piers shuddered in spite of the warm mug of hot chocolate mixed with biting coffee that he kept cradling to his chest. What he and Miller had seen in that thing's eyes had been the stuff of nightmares. A dark, endless, malevolent void. It took Piers's breath away just thinking about it.

No, Miller's conclusions were right on the money—Piers felt them in the pit of his balls. And the thing he suspected Miller had planned was even more terrifying, and Piers didn't know how to stop him from doing it. Didn't know how to make him not try.

At that moment, Callan arrived, coming from Helen's kitchen with two more pitchers of refills, and Piers tried not to glower at the guy for being a better human being than he was. When they'd arrived at the back of the bookstore/coffee shop, Piers's only goal had been to get Miller in from the cold.

"What'd I do now?" Callan asked as he set the pitchers down near Piers. "I mean, you already got to my crush first, what could you possibly have to be mad about?"

Piers huffed a little and managed a smile. "Don't mind me. I'm just grouchy because we had to flee a possessed cop this morning. Makes me stabby."

Callan grimaced. "Yes, I can see that." He let out a sigh. "I mean, on the plus side, I was wondering how to *fire* Leo Kowalski, but I hadn't planned on this."

Piers slanted him a look, not sure whether to be shocked, appalled, or impressed. "You know that guy might not be dead for real, right? I mean, we get the ghost out, and maybe all the rotting…." He shuddered. He couldn't figure out whether he'd been seeing the metaphysical or the physical decay now that they weren't looking it straight in the eye.

"I'm kind of hoping he'll be permanently damaged from the possession," Callan said glumly, and Piers was now positive he was appalled.

"Oh my God!"

Callan rolled his eyes. "Look, I get that you have room for moral high ground, okay? But this guy was generally making an ass of himself—and *me*—and hiding behind the generous union benefits *my company gave him*. Grabbing asses, arresting townspeople instead of the entitled little pricks abusing them. He was a leftover from my father's administration, and Dad didn't see anything wrong with letting good old Leo handle stuff. Well, good old Leo is a psycho killer now, Dad, can we fire him *yet*?"

Against his better judgment, Piers found himself chuckling. "Well, you might want to let us exorcise him first."

Callan laughed outright and then gave Piers a shrewd look. "You never asked," he said. "Our families knew each other, and suddenly you find out I'm a wizard. You never asked about it."

Piers shrugged. "Do you know how awesome it was to find there was more than just me and Larissa in the world? Hedge witches, luck mechanics, wizards—I was just so happy that it wasn't all my imagination. That someone would believe me."

Callan nodded. "And I have to admit, this group is a lot more fun than the families themselves." He gave a mock shudder. "The patriarchy—my God, the patriarchy!"

Piers snorted. "Which, in a way, is why we're here. It's how Percy Hampstead managed to stay unrecognized in his lifetime, and how guys like Leo are allowed to keep jobs."

The sigh Callan let out was full of firsthand knowledge, and Piers had to remind himself that Callan had been fighting against two hundred years of patriarchy with every new company policy he pushed through.

"You can't solve it all today," Piers told him. "Today's got its own challenges."

Something in his voice must have alerted Callan to the strain he was feeling, because Callan's eyes were suddenly glued to his face. "What? Why are you looking at Miller like he's about to keel over? What have you done to my perfectly innocent crush?"

Piers raised an eyebrow. "He's not perfectly innocent anymore, if that's what you're wondering." Callan sent him an arch look, and Piers shook his head. "Just... just call the meeting to order and listen."

"You think this is *my* meeting?" Callan asked, amused. "Oh no, this is magic workings. The most powerful wizard leads, and that would be—"

"Everybody got coffee?" Scout asked. He'd been huddling in a corner with a book open in his lap, which was pretty much how he spent most of his time in the book side of the coffee shop, but he'd suddenly sat up, taken the cup of coffee Lucky had thrust into his hand, and realized time was passing. "I'm sorry. I was looking something up," he said to nobody who had asked. "Do we all have coffee?" He looked toward Piers and Miller. "Are we warm? Is everybody ready? Because we've got a very short time to work here, and we need to get going."

And that simply, what was normally sort of a coffee and chat about magic had changed to a strategy meeting, and Piers—and everybody else, including the island's most powerful and prominent resident—was all in.

"Okay, good," Scout said. "Now for starters, everybody, we've got a new person here. Kayleigh?"

Scout's sister spoke up, sending a radiant smile toward Callan's chief of security. "Okay, all, this is Desmond. You can call him Des or Desi, and his superpower—"

"I liked luck mechanic," Des told her.

"Dammit, Scout, it's sticking and I hate you. Anyway, Des's superpower is knowing when somebody is going to steal or has stolen something. Apparently he's saved Callan a fortune by stopping people getting into the safe before they've even broken the law."

"Not robes and towels?" Lucky asked curiously, although Piers had the feeling Lucky had never actually stayed in a luxury hotel.

"Robes and towels *make* us a fortune," Des told him seriously. "We take people's deposits when they disappear from the rooms."

Lucky's eyes widened. "Helen, we need to start selling coffee cups. I swear those things keep disappearing."

"I'll put it on the list," Helen told him, voice dry. "For now, on to other things."

Des nodded at her respectfully and continued. "I need to see the person face-to-face to know for sure. Over video I just get... well, it's like having a black marker highlight a person's outline. I know they've done something wrong but not what. Let's say security was a natural calling for me."

"Is that how you got the job?" Scout asked curiously.

Des and Callan looked at each other and snorted. "He's my first boyfriend's little brother," Callan said. "Too bad his brother's a cheating prick, but Des and I have always been friends. He saw me do something... odd, one day—"

"Walk down the street during a rainstorm and not get wet," Des said, shaking his head. "It was awesome."

"—and confided in me." Callan shrugged. "You're right. He's a natural for security work. I paid for his training so I could hire him."

"God, you're an ass," Des told him, and Callan winked.

Friends, Piers could see, but not lovers. Which was good because Kayleigh seemed a little smitten.

"Anyway," Des continued, "Kayleigh and I spent most of last night looking through footage of the hotel. It would have been ideal to start around the evening and morning from when Miller first got an intuition tingle, but the harbor on the resort side of things was sort of a madhouse that night. There was an extra ferry coming in anyway for a big convention, and the ferry after that one was delayed, and then the morning ferries were off schedule. It was a big mess that would take more security people than I've got to sort through. So instead of wading through that, we started with Piers's suite from the moment Kayleigh entered and felt like somebody had been snooping. First we worked backward to the last person who entered the place before Kayleigh, and that's where things got interesting."

"The first interesting thing," Kayleigh said, "was a nearly unconscious maid vomiting in the changing room. About an hour before I went in to check on things, we could see her enter the suite and stay for about two minutes, which isn't long enough to service the room. When *I* went in afterward, the laptop was open and booted, but the password wasn't entered. I'd been in the room before, because Piers had me check on it, and this was the first time it made my skin crawl. Anyway, after the skin-crawling thing, I followed the maid. For starters, she wasn't doing her job. More like knocking on doors and then moving on. At first I was like, 'Wait, maybe there's just a bunch of people in their rooms,' and then I realized it was the opposite. Somebody said, 'I need toilet paper' or something, and she went in. When she came out, there was a guy following her, and she looked dazed. They found their way down the freight elevator and into the linen supply closet, and then he came out without her." Kayleigh swallowed. "Des sent a team immediately, and boy were we glad she was alive. Watching all that on film was creepy as fuck, and I was so afraid she'd be dead by the time we got there."

"Why wasn't she?" Miller asked, sending Piers a sharp look. "All our information—and we'll get to it—says that shouldn't have been a problem."

Desmond and Kayleigh made the same kind of eye contact Miller and Piers had just made. "We have an answer," Desmond said. "But you've got to wait until we're done."

"We'll hold you to that," Miller said. "Go on."

"So after we found the maid," Kayleigh said, "we tracked the guy. He stole a boat, literally *stole*, as in shoved the actual driver of the boat overboard and roared it out of the dock. We picked him up about half an hour later at John's Thumb."

This time, Piers was the one who shot Miller the look. "We can guess what happened there," he said.

"We don't have to guess," Desmond told them. He held up a tablet with security video feed from the bar area of the party island. "Kayleigh and I spent an hour tracking our suspect's movements, and they were... conflicted."

Kayleigh nodded and started to point to the picture on the screen. John's Thumb was the resort's hedonistic center, with a giant swimming pool—designed for flirting—glowing like an Aegean jewel against the lit background of the night. Even in December there were pretty people in bathing suits standing waist deep, enjoying the warmth of the heated water and the propane heaters surrounding the space. It was sort of like sitting in a hot tub outside in the snow, Piers knew; he'd been one of those people in the fall.

Surrounding the pool was a series of dance platforms, each one lit with flashing lights and mirrors, and each one with its own small bar. Back beyond the reach of the lights were smaller and larger bungalows that could be rented for the night and catered to. There was no disguising what some of the bungalows were used for, but they were kept clean and tidy and elegant, with wet bars and personal products available.

Piers felt his face heat as he remembered his hookups on John's Thumb back when he and Larissa had first arrived at the island. He'd been trying not to be bitter about leaving his third year of law school— and about the last of those breakups he'd told Miller about.

Those furtive gropings of release in the bungalows, with the music pumping outside, his hookup's pleasured gasps in the dark—they all felt surreal now. Dim and shallow in the light of what Piers knew lovemaking *could* be. *Was* now that he'd had Miller in his bed.

Suddenly the thought of what could occur in one of those huts with somebody such as Percy Hampstead passed through him, and his mortification turned to revulsion.

"See here," Kayleigh told them, pointing to their possessed suspect—an average-looking white male with hair that probably was not cut to stand on end. "Here, he's scoping out the men. Not in a sexual way. He's not cruising, he's...." She bit her lip.

"Sizing up," Lucky said. "He's, like, evaluating the guys. You'd see the gang guys doing that. Who was up to rumble, who was too stoned to shoot straight, who was too much of a loose cannon. He's looking for someone to party with."

At that moment a girl walked by—voluptuous, her figure barely contained by a bikini and a sarong. The pretty brunet pattered by, turning to wave at her friends as she went. There was no audio for this, but Piers could imagine the exchange, as he'd seen a thousand of them. She could have been saying anything from "The music's too loud," to "I need a drink," to "I have to pee."

"Oh no," Larissa said, covering her mouth.

Their possessed suspect suddenly lifted his head as though scenting prey. As if in a trance, a cartoon character following an exotic perfume shaped like seductive hands, he swiveled his head, forgetting about sizing up the men and focusing on hunting the women.

A woman.

The pretty brunet with what was probably a captivating laugh.

She was oblivious as he began to follow her away from the lights, away from the people, off into the shadows where the restrooms probably were.

Incongruously enough, Kayleigh chuckled. "I love this next part," she said.

As if on cue, their suspect reeled out of the shadows, hands up in front of his face, and the young woman followed. He lunged at her, and she set her body in a perfect chambered position before letting another kick fly, this one nailing him in the jaw. He fell backward onto his ass, and before he even landed, two solid, muscular young people—one male, one female—emerged from the sidelines, both of them wearing the distinctive sea-green polo shirt with the resort insignia.

Callan's security force, ready and waiting.

"Wow," Larissa said, sounding mesmerized. "That was amazing! We should have brought popcorn!"

"It's not even eight in the morning," Helen admonished. "Croissants for the morning, popcorn for good TV."

"Of course," Larissa said, grinning at her. Piers wanted to clutch his chest. Apparently "good" grandparents were something that had been missing from Larissa's life.

Desmond, who had been holding the tablet up for everybody to view, was fiddling with it again. "That wasn't even the finale," he told them, eyes glued to the screen.

"Although I sort of wish it was," Kayleigh said glumly. "This next part...." She shuddered. "Buwah!"

"That's not promising," Lucky said, sounding truly alarmed.

"It's horrifying," Kayleigh told him, completely in earnest.

"See for yourself," Desmond finally said. "This was about half an hour after we called dispatch for an officer. She was about to go home, but she sent Leo Kowalski our way." He glanced up at Miller. "We actually asked for you, Officer Aldrun. Nobody likes the way Leo deals with things, but I guess you were busy."

"That was about fifteen minutes before we pulled into the dock at dispatch," Miller said, peering at the time stamp on the tablet. He grimaced. "I forget how early it gets dark in the winter—for some reason, I thought Piers and I got back when it was still light, but that was just because it was not quite five."

"You mean the cold as balls escaped your attention," Piers said dryly. As warm as it was in Helen's little shop, he was still wrapped in Miller's scarf, because he wasn't sure he'd ever feel his ears again after that jaunt on the skiff at taint o' dawn a.m.

"I keep telling you, there's a heated tarp behind the console," Miller retorted, and Piers smiled, warming a little. It was good to see Miller would poke back when baited. It was like seeing him grouchy without his coffee; it made him so much more perfect to know that he wasn't perfect at all.

"Well, given what you're about to see here," Desmond told them, "it was probably a good thing you missed out. Here." He pointed to the screen, where another camera angle had been pulled up. "Here they are at the security station. Note that the two bouncers aren't touching him. I asked them about it, and they said... what was it, Kayleigh?"

"That they'd sooner stick their hand in a sewer full of bloodworms," Kayleigh recited, looking disgusted. "Apparently you don't need to have any magic to know this guy's got bad shit going on. But wait—here comes the ultimate in bad shit."

Leo Kowalski swaggered up to the tiny kiosk, his thick body made clumsy by his attempts to browbeat or intimidate the two bouncers.

"What's he doing?" Piers asked, repelled by his body language alone.

"Asking for the name of the young woman who charged the man with assault. He claimed he wanted to question her, but...." This time he shot a glance at Callan. "We sort of have an agreement not to put any young female resort guest within twenty feet of him," he said apologetically. "I know that sounds terrible, but he's...."

"Terrible," Callan said flatly. "I get it. But give those two security officers a raise or a promotion or something, because he certainly seems to be throwing his weight around."

"Yeah." Desmond shook his head. "It's his basic MO. I don't know what he spends his days doing, because the resort certainly avoids calling him."

"Oh, that's easy," Piers snapped. "Miller answers all his calls, and Leo?"

"Is probably off in one of the inlets, fishing and drinking," Miller said wearily. "We all know it. But—oh my God!"

Because the terrible thing they'd all been promised had suddenly occurred on the tablet.

Leo had reached for their young suspect, and suddenly, everybody froze, arrested on the screen as though it had been paused—but it hadn't.

The picture began to shake, to pixilate, and then—for just an instant—a blinding light filled the screen before they were looking at the image from the security kiosk on John's Thumb again.

The two security guards were staring, heads cocked, at Leo Kowalski, while their erstwhile attacker was collapsed at their feet, handcuffs gone, as he vomited spasmodically, his body twitching.

The stillness that followed—for both the watchers and the participants—looked absolutely silent.

Then Leo turned toward the camera like he'd known it was there all along and grinned before turning his back and swaggering off, leaving devastation in his wake.

"Oh dear God," whispered Otto. "That's...."

"Did you see his face?" Miller asked, as though the residue of horror hadn't touched him. "Desmond, go back to his face and freeze it."

Desmond did as he was asked, and Miller jumped to his feet and pointed. "There. There—Piers, do you see it?"

Piers nodded. "Yeah. Yeah I do. Hand me your laptop, Miller. I know which file it's on."

Miller did so without question, and because it was already booted up, Piers was able to pull up the picture in no time.

It was an old-fashioned photo—not a daguerreotype but the ambrotype, which came later. It was exquisitely clear, featuring a distinguished man in the formal suit of his day, but one that fit badly, hanging too large at the shoulders and dwarfing instead of draping over his gaunt frame.

His face was hatchet thin, and with a smile or a relaxed expression might have been considered attractive.

But he *wasn't* smiling, and he *wasn't* relaxed. In fact, he appeared bitter, resentful, his lip curled up in a sneer that was supposed to pass as a smile, his eyes hard and flat and dismissive.

Piers held the picture of Percy Hampstead up to show everybody in the back of Helen's store, and then Miller pointed to the still frame from the security kiosk on John's Thumb.

"Do you see it?" he asked needlessly.

"Of course we see it," Lucky snapped. "It's gonna haunt my fuckin' dreams."

Superimposed over Leo Kowalski's paunchy, squat features with his tiny beady eyes and receding forehead was *this* face, thin and disdainful and bitter, and absolutely sure it was superior to every other form of life.

Leo Kowalski may have swaggered onto that island, but not a soul in that room doubted that Percy Hampstead was the one who left.

"HOW DID that happen?" Callan asked out loud when the shock had worn off.

"We have a theory," Piers said, glancing to Miller. Miller made "go on" motions to Piers to keep going, but Piers refused. "No, I'm not going to finish it. You made the leap, Miller. You're putting all the clues together. Stand up and take some credit."

"Credit's overrated," Miller muttered, but he did stand up and take the laptop. "Fine. Here's what we know."

And with that, he set about neatly explaining everything they'd discovered the night before, starting with the life of Percy Hampstead—and the deaths and possible cover-ups surrounding him—and ending with the origin of Larissa and Piers's stalker.

When he was done, he let the silence settle, allowed his people to make their own conclusions, and waited for the questions.

"So," Larissa said quietly, "you're saying my stalker had several more victims besides me."

Miller nodded, his jaw tight. "That's right, sweetheart. And I think you were the lucky one."

"And it doesn't matter who it is *now* because he was taken over by a ghost?"

Miller and Piers both grimaced. "No," Miller told her soberly. "No, we think that he was probably like Leo. He had potential to be an awful person. Maybe he would have grown out of it. A lot of school bullies regret who they were in high school and grow into the world's greatest philanthropists. But some of them grow into criminals—or worse, cops like Leo, who are harder to fight against and capable of doing far more damage. If we knew *when* he was hijacked, we'd have a better idea. Because he could have been a stalker or worse, and then he wandered into the Winston-Salem area, and Percy saw a great vehicle and hopped on board. But the fact that Percy couldn't keep a gardener—and your guy seems to be a walking black thumb—seems to tell me that your stalker was hacked before he got to you at the very least. And while I haven't discussed this with Piers, I think it's what made it possible for him to follow you here when the island kept you safe before. *Percy* has been here. Whatever magic overtook the island made it such a good haven for those of us who needed it, but Percy had already broken into the shelter. I...."

He hesitated, and Scout said, "Go on. You're thinking something. What?"

"It's just that Tom's bench is this terrible mixture of sorrow, both sacred and profane. I think Percy is a big part of that darkness. I've dealt with criminals, and the thing that seems to make the worst of them go over is... is a void inside. They don't get why hurting people is wrong. And whatever their drug—meth, power, violence—they always crave more. And it feels very... very familiar to me, as does that big black void that picked me up and threw me against the plate-glass window."

"Safety glass," Helen said dryly. "But we hear you. You're saying that Percy is a part of the island's legend."

"Yes," Miller said thoughtfully before shaking himself into the present. "But that's not what we need to deal with. He's here *now*, and he's vessel hopping, and we need to... I don't know. Banish him somehow. Or bury him until...." He bit his lip.

"Stop doing that!" Piers and Callan burst out at the same time.

"Good God," Callan continued. "We're hanging on your every word. Don't tease us like that."

Piers grunted, because he recognized the hesitation for what it was—an extension of the shyness that had so beset him in bed. A natural, self-protective reaction to a world that had too often hurled his gifts into his face as being not worth having.

"Fine," Miller snapped, ears turning red. "Here's what I think. I think it's great that you're getting Tom and Henry back together, but there are more stories at the bench than Tom and Henry's. I think that once we banish Percy—and yes, I've got an idea about that too—we're going to need to find his bones and do what it takes to rid the world of Percy Hampstead once and for all. Salt and burn the bones, hire a priest, do an exorcism—something. And there's more to it than that. We all know it. There's the hidden bones of Tom's little sister and her lover, and whoever poor Ciaran saw who probably turned into the Wisp, who was a real person once too. I get that the immediate threat is important—" He searched out Piers's gaze across the table. "—particularly because it's after people we care about, but...." He sighed. "Once we trap and eliminate the ghost of Percy Hampstead, I think we're going to have to have a long talk about how to manage the supernatural glen of Tom's bench."

There was a stunned silence, and then Piers's startled chuckle.

"You really took that speak-your-mind thing seriously, didn't you, babe?"

Miller scowled. "Am I wrong?" he asked.

This pause was longer. It consisted of everybody in the room thinking deeply, looking at the person next to them, across from them, next to someone else whose opinion they sought. And in the end, the people who spoke were probably the ones most qualified to speak.

"It's going to take a unification spell of epic proportions," Marcus said at last. "And it's going to take all of us. I think interring Tom's remains in the glade next to Henry's will give us an edge, particularly since we're doing it on the winter solstice—Yule. It's a moment of death and rebirth, and that combination of powers you're talking about? I think it might give the light, the rebirth, an edge. But after that, and after we get rid of this noxious ghost, I think you're right. There's going to have to be a reckoning spell."

"Probably cast on Litha," Helen said, as though thinking hard. "And I think Marcus is right. It will need to be all of us, and it will need to be thought out, combined." She heaved a sigh and looked at Scout with an apparent sense of resignation on her face. "And I may have to speak to your brother when we get closer. His fiancé's coven is very powerful and very resourceful, and we may need their help."

Scout cocked his head and looked at her oddly. "I never told you that," he said, obviously surprised.

"Later," she said with a faint smile. "It's a long story. Right now, young Miller here is right. And he's also right about us needing to get rid of Percy Hampstead—and us running out of time. Miller, you've managed to isolate Percy on an island. How do we perform an exorcism on him while he's there?"

Miller looked surprised and then a little embarrassed.

"We don't. We get Percy to come here—without Leo."

Helen and Marcus frowned. "Look," said Marcus, "I know you kids don't know much about witchcraft, but one of the things that makes Spinner's Drift work is that the island is surrounded by saltwater. Saltwater wards off evil spirits. The only way Percy could get here in the first place was by hitching a ride, or hijacking a body, as you all so violently phrased it. How are we supposed to get him off that island and here where we need him?"

Miller glanced at the clock in front of him. "Well, as for his body, I told him we were meeting at the resort conference room at ten o'clock. He said he needed to catch a nap, but we were leaving at six a.m. He's probably had time to nap and…." He closed his eyes, and unconsciously his hand rose up to rub between his stomach and his chest. "And he's moving. Like I sort of thought he would. So yes, he's going to be at the resort at ten, looking for us in one of the conference rooms."

Desmond's eyes went round. "Callan?" he asked, sounding panicked.

"Take care of it," Callan said crisply. "Make sure that nobody—"

"Touches him," Desmond agreed. "And lock up all the women and the plants—I hear you." He paused. "Are you sure he's not headed for this end of the island?" Unconsciously his eyes darted to Kayleigh, and if they weren't all so pressed for time, Piers would love to dish with Scout and Lucky about how exciting it was that Kayleigh had finally found a straight guy worth having.

"We'll let you know if it changes," Miller told him, "but right now, he's taking the eastern channel. He's got to do some fancy piloting to get to the north side of the island from there."

Desmond gave a little laugh. "You forget the waterways are that complex," he said. "You're so good at taking the quickest route, I forget the other officers aren't that adept."

Miller shrugged. "I study." Then he turned from Desmond with the simple assumption, probably, that he would do his job, and spoke to the rest of them.

"By the time he's on the island," he said, "we need to be at Tom's bench, and we need to be ready. I've got a plan."

Piers could remember having actual out-of-body experiences a few times in his life. When they'd found Larissa's cat, that had been a bad moment. He'd seemed to slip reality then. When he'd broken his leg skiing and had needed to be airlifted to the hospital. That had sucked, and the pain had made his vision blacken, and it had felt like his entire selfhood would vanish with each breath. One of the helicopter pilots had come back then to talk to him, have him breathe, convince him he could live through it if only he'd take one more breath. The morphine had kicked in then, but Piers would forever be grateful to that pilot for talking him out of the great beyond and into the present.

It would take more than a pretty helicopter pilot to talk him into his body now.

He'd known it was coming and thought he was prepared, but he wasn't. What Miller proposed he do, right there in front of their friends, in front of their magical family, was enough to frighten Piers right out of his flesh and into the great beyond.

Remembering to Breathe

"PIERS, BREATHE!" Larissa's voice echoed urgently through the back of the bookstore, and for a moment it was the only sound in the room. Miller strode urgently around the table to where Piers sat, staring into space, looking shell-shocked and terrified, and took his hand.

"C'mon, Piers," he cajoled. "It's not that bad. I mean, you and Larissa and everybody else will be around to help me. It'll be fine." He glanced over at the rest of the seemingly stunned group and gave them a green smile. "You all are seriously the best backup I've ever had. I've never felt so safe."

Larissa, who was standing next to Piers and shaking his shoulder, smacked Miller in the back of the head.

"Ouch!" he complained.

"Harder, Larissa," Lucky ordered. "Smack him till his eyeballs bounce out and maybe let some sense in."

"That's totally gross," Scout told him, and Lucky shrugged.

"Who cares. The theory's good. I mean, I get it—sunshine and clean water and you kill the infection, but I've *seen* zombie movies, Scout. Some infections kill the host."

Miller glared at him. "Lucky, you are *not* helping. I'm gonna be fine."

"You will not!" Piers burst out, showing life for the first time since Miller had dropped his bomb. "You've said that your entire life, but you're *not*."

Miller swallowed, not wanting the things he'd told Piers in the privacy between them to be blurted out among their friends.

"Piers," he said gently, coming to kneel before Piers's chair. "This is the *reason* I'm Cassandra. I connect with the armed and dangerous. It's the reason I became a police officer, a *protector*. So I could do something about scary people who threaten the people I care about. Finally— *finally*—I have backup, people to help me out when I'm dealing with something awful. Do you know how huge that is?"

"But *I'm* your backup!" Piers wailed. "What if I let you down?"

Miller stared at him. "Honestly, Piers, that never even crossed my mind. You're... you know. You."

There was a stunned silence, and Piers gaped at him.

"You know, Piers," Larissa said quietly, "he does have a point. You're... you know. You."

Piers took a deep, shuddering breath and seemed to get hold of himself.

"He *is* sort of awesome," Lucky said judiciously. "I mean, if he didn't have Scout as competition, he'd be the most awesome person in the room."

"And I am chopped liver," Callan muttered, which made Piers laugh.

"This is a terrible plan," he said, even though he was starting to see how it could work.

"It's the worst," Scout agreed. "Marcus, Helen, what can we do to make it happen?"

At that moment, the bell at the front of the shop rang, and Helen watched grimly as one of the temporary helpers she'd hired from the resort pool came in, looking around in puzzlement because the usual opening preparations weren't underway.

"Okay," she said grimly. "For starters, Lucky, Ciaran, you two need to keep my business running."

"On it," Lucky said. "Tell us when you need us for the ritual and we'll be there." He and Ciaran stood and hurried to help the college-aged young woman open.

"Larissa, you, me, and Marcus need to go to the cottage and gather some things to prep the Tom's bench area. Scout—"

"I need to keep Marcus's business open," Scout said, standing. "I got it."

"And me?" Kayleigh asked.

"You and Callan need to do wizard's work around the Tom's bench area," Helen said. "There are ways to set up barriers so that whatever we call into the place can't be let out."

"But shouldn't Scout do that?" Kayleigh asked in surprise. "He's the stronger wizard."

Helen shook her head. "No." She rubbed her stomach as though trying to put into words something she could feel there but hadn't voiced. "This man—this *monster*—consciously attacks women. We attack what we fear or don't understand. We need as much women's power in that glade as we can get. Larissa's power is necessary, but your power, mine, it's going to be stronger and more terrifying to this enemy than any man's." She glanced about the room in apology. "Not that I don't love men and think they're powerful," she said kindly, "but in this case, we need to be the thing that scares him. Remember, that young woman he went after was probably touched in the shadows, but she wasn't taken over. She fought back, and he was *stunned*. He doesn't expect that from his females. The maid was found sick, but not dead—Desmond, was that the reason you were thinking about?"

"Yes," Desmond verified. "The people he camped out in were, uhm, assholes. Katrina is one of our nicest employees—two kids, a doting husband. She was the exact opposite of the people who held the spirit for any length of time."

"Exactly," Helen said, nodding. "She was probably handy—however he got into her—but existentially anathematic. He could have been in her body for hours, but he hunted down a man's body because he understood it better. You, Larissa, and me are our secret weapons."

"Then why not Scout?" Kayleigh said, and Miller thought she was on to something, but this time Marcus shook his head.

"Because Callan has ties to this place," Marcus told her. "Callan's family was here back during the original incident. Callan has roots in this island. He'll be able to claim the part of the island that Percy's darkness is trying to take over."

There was a moment while everybody digested this, and then an unexpected voice spoke up.

"But Scout is the more powerful wizard?"

They all turned to Otto, almost surprised to see the older man there.

"They say so," Scout told him cheerfully.

"Then let me set up the magic store, son. I've worked retail a time or two in my life. Show me what needs doing, and then the rest of you go get ready. I'd like to help too, and snacks won't do it this time."

"Otto," Marcus said happily, "you are a treasure. I think Miller bringing you to us was a sign that the island works to protect its own."

There was a bit of laughter, and then everybody stood and gathered their belongings and took one last sip of coffee or ran to the bathroom.

It was time to work.

TWO HOURS later, Miller was pacing out the center of the clearing, trying to attach string to a peg in the ground in order to form a protective pentagram. Helen and Marcus had divined the edges of the power spread of the glade, and it went surprisingly wide, perhaps thirty yards in diameter—the energy of the ghosts, the magic, the protection, and the malice spreading out from the center of the bench into the sand, into the foliage, and even, for a footstep or so, out into the walkway that skirted the beach and approached the glade.

"I wonder how many people tripped over that," Marcus had pondered, "or felt a cold spot or changed their mind about an outing, passing that place."

"I feel like we need to mark it," Kaylcigh muttered, bending over the area with tape. "Maybe just a little bit—"

She put her hand on the ground, and it even began to glow a smidge before Helen called out, "Stop!"

Kayleigh snatched her hand back and sent Helen a hurt look. "What'd I do?"

"Child," Helen said on a huff of breath, "I get why you want to fix things, but we've built this spell on the way the grounds are *right now*. If you change it—if you heal the bad or even shore up the good, even on that patch of earth right there—you change the shape of what we're doing. Can we not make things more complicated, please?"

Kayleigh, who listened to very few people, actually blushed prettily. "Sorry, Helen," she murmured.

"It's fine," Helen said, obviously restraining what could be a hair-trigger temper. "You weren't trying to screw things up. I just really don't want to fry Miller's hair off or something because we changed a thing that we could have left alone."

"Understood," Kayleigh said and gave Helen a hesitant smile. Both women could be sharp-tongued, Miller knew, but something complicated and kind passed between them, and he thought that maybe there was a relationship forging there that wasn't his to understand.

He knew that Scout and Kayleigh had been without a real maternal influence in their lives—in fact he was beginning to think most of those who gathered in the coffee and bookshop and talked about magic were adrift that way. Their parents had failed somehow to catch the people they should have loved the most—and that included him and even Piers.

Helen could be abrasive sometimes, could speak sharply, but in that moment he sensed that she was trying very hard to fill that void.

Miller turned back to what he was doing, trying to create a physical manifestation of protection inside the circle, as everybody else felt out the boundaries of the space and tried to work within it.

Piers and Larissa were inside the circle by their own insistence. Their enemy was going to come after the both of them, and Miller was his gateway, his conduit. The physical spells—the pentagram of thread in the center of the glade, the circle of salt, iron, and silver chain that ran the perimeter of where the power radiated, and the healing wash of sage, rosemary, and saltwater that sat in five-gallon drums at a measured five points around the center of the power—were all to keep the spirit inside Tom's glade when it tried to burst out.

Kayleigh, Callan, and Scout had been working for the last two hours, trying to decide how to handle the ghost of Percy Hampstead if it got out of the shields, while Marcus and Helen were working on ways to handle Percy's three intended victims on the inside. The first thing they'd done had been to etch a pentagram into the sand in front of the bench, which would keep Miller safe from the shade reenacting that cold-blooded murder in perpetuity. Miller, Piers, and Larissa had been reinforcing it with thread in myriad colors ever since.

Healing had been mentioned so much, Miller had been tempted to ask if he should take a couple of Advils beforehand, just in case.

Miller scowled as the thought hit, and he shook himself, trying to walk the pentagram again. He was having trouble focusing; something was bothering him—a sickness, a restlessness, a feeling of approaching danger—that he couldn't shake.

"Give me that," Piers snapped, taking the thick cone of cotton thread that Helen had given Miller to outline the pentagram with. "What's wrong with you?"

Piers had been focused since they'd started working on the spell together, but hurt. Miller had tried—more than once—to take him aside and explain that this wasn't a personal affront to Piers, and it wasn't a death wish either. This was the paranormal equivalent of one cop going in as point and the other following up when it was a weapons-drawn situation.

Miller was working point in this instance because he had the appropriate weapon. Piers and Larissa had weapons of their own that were pretty useful, but they wouldn't be able to access those weapons if Percy was inside their brains, their souls, their bodies.

They needed Miller to call the ghost and Piers and Larissa to push him out of Miller's body.

And Scout, Callan, and Kayleigh to fry him to vapor.

"Even vapor can build to something dangerous," Callan had warned, and Helen and Marcus had both agreed.

"He'll be trying to come back," Marcus added. "Like Miller said, burying Tom and Henry together here will increase the strength of the protection around this place, but it's going to need that protection to keep Percy in check."

"I used to worry about Scout stirring things up," Helen said thoughtfully. "But now I think he arrived here to protect us from things that had waited too long to change."

Miller had caught Piers's eyes then. "Maybe like someone else I know," he said softly.

Piers frowned, as though trying to fathom the meaning of that, but they were busy filling the buckets of healing wash, and they didn't have much time to talk.

Now Miller wished they'd had the time, because the thing in his stomach... it was getting worse.

Frustrated, he stopped dead still in the middle of all the activity and put his hand on his stomach, closing his eyes.

He felt it. It was here. Not at the far end of the island, like he'd anticipated, but *here*, probably at the dock, having felt its way like the big dark void of grief had, scenting its prey with the same supernatural compass Miller had been born with.

It was coming.

He opened his eyes and looked toward the harbor, not sure if the black miasma he saw smudging the distance was actual smoke or magical haze but knowing with absolute certainty that it was real and it was dangerous.

For a moment he quailed.

All of these people, adept in magic, secure in their loved ones, in the family they'd been forging, and who was he to tell them their jobs.

But then he looked from that smudge, that haze of evil, to Larissa, who was working, her lower lip between her teeth, to lay the thread in exactly the same trail as the rest of the pentagram, and his heart squeezed. *She* believed him. *She* was counting on him.

And then he felt Piers's gaze on him, and he turned his head, locking eyes with the man who had found him worthy, believable, interesting, and *love*able from the moment they first met.

"What?" Piers asked, and Miller's newfound confidence returned in a rush.

"He's *here*," he shouted, loud enough for everyone working at the glade to hear. "Look toward the harbor. He's *here*."

"How did he find us?" Larissa whispered.

"I don't know," Miller replied, leaping over the thread to the center of the pentagram. "But we need to be ready to start now—"

"Wait," Scout said from the beach side. "Oh my God, is that Lucky and Ciaran?"

"Who's minding my store?" Helen asked, but it was a reflex, and they all knew it.

"*He's here!*" Lucky cried out, his voice carrying across the beach. "*He's here!*" He drew closer, and Scout ran to meet him. Lucky bent down, holding his knees and gasping for air. "He's here! Spring the trap! He went to the square first. He's screaming for Larissa and Piers, and people are running away. Spring the trap now. He's gonna hurt somebody!"

"Shit!" Scout turned toward Miller, Piers, and Larissa, but they were all in the center of the pentagram, as protected as they'd ever be.

"Set the shield now, Scout," Miller called, and whatever magic Scout, Callan, and Kayleigh had conjured up, the low hum, just under the sound of the breakers crashing, just above the breeze through the trees, was reassuring, as was the glow that surrounded the clearing, carving its way in a perfect circle along the boundaries of power that had been seeping through the ground all along.

Miller took a moment to search his surroundings, swallowing a little as he did that.

The shield shimmered against the thin blue of the winter sky, the glimmer reminiscent of the Wisp Ciaran had claimed to see overlooking the tableaux as they unfolded.

But over that, on the south end of the clearing, supported by a massive old loblolly pine tree, was the roaring void, the seething darkness of grief, fighting the shield with everything it had.

Miller swallowed. Two enemies here: Percy and the soul-sucking grief that permeated this place. Suddenly he wished they could have done this after they'd reunited Henry and Tom, allowing their dust to mingle in the love-consecrated ground, but it was too late for that.

"We good?" he asked, wanting to touch Piers badly but knowing that as soon as he did, their real battle would begin.

"Call him," Callan ordered, his natural authority giving Miller some badly needed confidence.

"All right, then." He looked at Piers and Larissa on either side of him and said, "Cover the pentagram."

As a unit, they started kicking sand over the colored threads. The protection of the pentagram remained, but some of its potency would be dimmed.

Miller stood straight and scanned the glen in front of Tom's bench, and his breath caught.

He could see them. This was the one thing they'd worried about—contact with Piers and Larissa had to wait until he needed them. Would he be able to see the spirits in the glade without another magic user's power?

But the wizard's shield apparently gave *everybody* power, as did the efforts by Marcus and Helen marking boundaries, using herbs and small stones to add clarity and power to the edges of the dome.

"Can we all see them?" he asked, his eyes seeking out the shade of Percy Hampstead.

Uncannily, the shade stopped its preordained dance, locked in the tableaux of tragedy that surrounded the glade, and met Miller's gaze.

Percy Hampstead's eyes were a noxious shade of green.

"The hell," whispered Piers, and Miller could feel his movement, his instinctive reach for Miller's hand.

Miller wanted to take it more than anything, but he couldn't. He shifted a little forward so the temptation wouldn't be there.

Then he closed his eyes and felt for that thing he'd known all his life but had feared.

Power. Fear. Frenzy. Power. Fear. Frenzy. Coldness. Void.

Nobody is human but me. They're all cardboard cutouts, everybody. The rich men's sons who punish me. Who abuse me. Who laugh at me. Monsters. Monsters all. Cruel.

I can be crueler.

I can abuse. I can punish. I can rape.

Women are easier. Their fear is... delicious. Hello, little girl. Let me taste your fear.

Miller shuddered in revulsion, fighting not to disengage his mind from this most terrible of evils, the simple human monster.

"Hello, Percy," he said to the shade. At the same time he felt the ghost, the active, conscious part of Percy Hampstead currently using Miller's supervisor like a meat puppet, perk up.

"That's right. I'm here. Don't you want inside my brain? Don't you want to join the past and the present? Think of all the pretty girls, Percy. All that power. What would you do with all of that?"

And he heard the voice in his head.

"Slash it. Kill it. Drink its blood. Rape it. Skin it. Hold its beating heart in my hand!"

The awfulness, the terror—he had to put a hold on all of that.

"Come and get me, Percy. You can feel my heart beating. You know where I am."

"Yessssss!"

The darkness fell upon him like a ravenous beast. In a heartbeat, all he could hear in his head was his own screams.

PIERS HATED not touching him.

This plan—this harebrained scheme—all depended on Miller, with his connection to the vicious, to the insane, to become a willing vessel to all of that awfulness long enough for the wizards to trap the essence of Percy Hampstead in the power center of the glade.

And then it depended on Piers and Larissa to cleanse it from Miller's body until it seared itself into vapor on the protective shields the wizards had cooked up.

Cooked being the operative word.

It was crazy. Not "armed and crazy," which Miller claimed was his specialty, but "playing chicken at the cliffside" crazy, which Piers had never been stupid enough to do.

Miller was offering himself as a vessel, as a sacrifice, with the full knowledge that if Percy Hampstead took over, they'd be forced to kill him, simply to drive Percy Hampstead against the wizard's carefully constructed spirit net like a big bug-zapper for ghosts.

Piers couldn't let that happen.

Miller's eyes were focused on the dark doings at the forest end of the glade. His lips moved as though he was speaking. Piers couldn't hear the conversation, but Miller's preternatural stillness told Piers he was probably not entirely there, not entirely with them.

He wanted so badly to take Miller's slighter, shorter form into his arms and make this real-life boogieman go away.

Then Miller tilted his head back and yelled, "Come and get me, Percy. You can feel my heart beating. You know where I am."

"Is he crazy?" Larissa asked, meeting Piers's eyes as they stood slightly behind Miller, flanking him.

"Oh my God," Piers muttered, his gaze pulled upward. "No. Yes. Hang on, guys, here it fucking comes!"

A plague of locusts? A swarm of ashes? A flock of flies? What besieged them, hitting the dome of the wizard's shield, defied description. More conscious than smoke, with physical dots of something solid— ectoplasm?—it surged against the shimmer of the shields, searching with wizened smoky fingers to find a way in.

"Scout!" Kayleigh cried. "Need your help!"

"Make a chimney!" he shouted. "Callan, hold the borders."

Piers had no idea what they were doing, what sort of magical control they needed to have, what sort of spells they'd practiced since the cradle. All he knew was that a hole opened up directly over Miller's head as he stood facing the sky, his mouth open, like a baby bird waiting to be fed.

The swarm of ashes flocked to the hole in the shield and poured through the air, directly into Miller's throat.

"Now?" Larissa begged as they watched Miller's helpless body thrashing, listened to him gargling on whatever noxious thing was being forced past his tonsils.

"Not yet," Piers told her. His face was wet, and he fought the urge to scream.

LOSER. LUNATIC. Impotent coward.

Miller's worst versions of himself were shoved through his body on a cellular level, and he heard every taunting cruelty in a voice that sounded like his father's, like his sister's, like Brad's—oh God.

Brad's face appeared before his eyes, haggard, flesh rotting in strips.

You couldn't stop me from getting killed? What kind of lover are you? You fucking coward, sniveling in the kitchen as I left. Why would I believe you?

His father's face, worn with pain, his hair grayed by age and bad health, floated in front of his vision.

Mewling little bastard. Couldn't tell me? Yeah, sure, you cried like a baby, but you couldn't tell me? A fucking meth addict, waiting to kill me, and all you could do was beg?

His teacher. His sister, bitter over their father's anger. The faces of the women he'd told not to go back to abusive homes.

Couldn't speak up for yourself? Couldn't speak up for us. What kind of protector are you? Who would love you? Who would trust you? Nobody wants a freak!

Every word hit him in the vitals, draining his heart's blood, his confidence, his ability to trust, his ability to love.

Unconsciously he fell to his knees, and then there was Percy Hampstead, not just his face, his entire body, top hat, opera cape, cravat and all, looming over him, leering.

Pretty boy. Such a pretty boy. Women will fall all over themselves looking at those pretty, pretty eyes.

Piers liked his eyes.

Miller stared up at Percy, his own eyes blazing, and when he spoke, he spoke aloud.

"You can't have me," he growled. "I am my own man."

Percy laughed, and the construct of the man standing in front of Miller disappeared, and when he spoke again, Miller realized Percy was inside his head, had been there all along.

He opened his mouth to call for help and couldn't, his breath and voice stopped as though by syrup.

He sucked in a breath and couldn't breathe, and tried to force out the air in his lungs but couldn't.

He clawed at his throat, screaming, *Piers! Piers, help!* inside his head but not making a sound, not one.

He'll never hear me. I can't breathe. I'll die in front of him. Piers—Piers, I'm sorry. I wanted so much more time.

He must have made a sound then—a sound of grief, a sound of protest—because in an instant of searing light, everything changed.

PIERS WATCHED in horror as Miller fell to all fours, his body heaving as he tried to retch, his hands scrabbling at his throat.

"He's dying!" Larissa shouted, and sure enough, Piers could see Miller's lips turning white as his body struggled for oxygen.

"Now!" he screamed, and he and Larissa dropped to their knees and wrapped their arms around Miller's shoulders, both of them pouring their power through his body, hoping their little gifts, their tiny abilities, their fun little conveniences, were enough to save Miller's life.

SUNSHINE, PURE sunshine, poured like water through Miller's consciousness. The ghosts from his past—bitter, accusing—tattered like old film, and a cleansing burst of pure water washed away the images, even from his memory, even from his mind.

He managed a gasp of air, and Percy spoke up from inside his head.

Make it stop! I'll let you breathe if you make it stop!

But Miller didn't answer.

He was turning his metaphysical face toward the sun, letting it warm him. Glorying in the fresh water that cleansed his skin, letting it purify. Piers and Larissa poured themselves into his body, into his soul, and he let them until they filled his lungs, flowed in his blood, ran the courses of his brain.

The essence of Percy Hampstead was forced out, violently, as Miller dropped his head and retched, for real, the thick syrup of Percy's consciousness, of his evil, pouring out of him. Miller's body, shored up by his friends' love, became an ultimately unsuitable place.

Dimly, through eyes blurred by a lack of oxygen, he watched as the darkness flew upward, searching for a welcome, and found instead the shield erected by three very powerful wizards.

The swarm of flies, that flock of ashes, hit the shield and flared brightly, like bugs on a zapper. Percy Hampstead's shriek of second death echoed through Miller's bones.

Miller gasped, secure in Piers's arms, and let himself be held, be comforted, Larissa's tears against his neck, Piers's cheek against his own, as he remembered that feeling from childhood, to be loved unconditionally for who and what he was.

OTTO WOULD relay what appeared to happen in the center of the merchant's square, and Scout and Kayleigh told those who'd been in the center of the storm.

"Leo Kowalski" *had* hidden his small patrol boat on the backside of the island. He hadn't needed the ferry. Instead he'd piloted his own skiff toward Spinner's Drift. The harbormaster would report that it "looked to have had a rough go of it." Leo must have left soon after Piers and Miller, had probably tried chasing after them, but Percy had been running the show, and Percy didn't know the waterways. He'd run aground a lot in pursuit.

His arrival at the harbor had been accompanied by the smell of decay, so strong it sent the few early morning patrons reeling from the stores, fleeing toward the resort side of the island as a stumbling, shambolic figure lurched its way from the dock to the square, screaming a young woman's name from a shredded throat.

Percy's ghost apparently burned its way through its hosts, and even Leo wasn't particularly accommodating to that much evil. Later that morning, Callan and Desmond would initiate an intensive search throughout the resort grounds and find the body of a young man, recently graduated from college, who would be tested to have the unmatched DNA markers of Larissa's stalker. The match was dead-on, and his friends and family would report that he'd been acting "especially frightening" over the past two years, but even someone who had once tortured the family cat was no contest for the ghost of Percy Hampstead.

Leo Kowalski lasted less than twenty-four hours before collapsing in the town square, vomiting what some thought was blood but what only the magic users knew was the brownish psychic mass that had ridden here on Leo's flesh and bone and tried to force its way into Miller's body when Miller called its name.

Miller, Piers, and Larissa would learn all of this when they woke up, miles away, in Miller's bungalow on the dispatch island, after Scout used a portal to transport them there, along with himself and Kayleigh to provide care for the three of them because the battle with the ghost of Percy Hampstead had, in Scout's words, "Wiped you guys out but *good*."

Piers was the first to awaken, bathed clean and wearing his own sweats, next to Miller in Miller's bed.

Miller slept, curled up in a self-protective ball, shivering.

Piers moved closer to him, wrapped his arm over Miller's stomach, pulled him in. Miller gave a little sigh and relaxed against his chest.

"Thank God" came a voice next to the bed, sounding exhausted. "We got him in and out of the shower, but he hasn't stopped shivering for the last two hours."

Piers looked over Miller's shoulders and saw Scout, curled in a stuffed chair he'd moved from the living room. He looked as tired as Piers felt.

"Did we do it?" Piers asked, trying to order his jumbled memories of the last few hours. Days? "What day is it?" He frowned, realizing the light coming in from the window was pale gray. Morning? Evening?

"Same day," Scout said reassuringly. "You three needed a shower—Larissa's power had washed the gunk off everyone, but it leaves a residue—and you needed your own bed. And frankly, there was so much chaos back in the square that it seemed best not to show up there with three unconscious people. It's a good thing Lucky and I visited Miller about a month ago—remember when he'd missed a day?"

Piers *did* remember that. Miller, who had seemed so eager to make their meetings, had gone no-show for a day without calling. He'd been out all night handling a drunk and disorderly, and his cell phone had gotten smashed in the fracas. Piers had been at the resort, working on a paper, and hadn't known about the trip until a few days later. And then he could have kicked himself. He'd wanted so badly to know where Miller lived.

Now he knew, and he never wanted to leave.

"You could portal us here," Piers murmured, his eyes already weighted. But first, "What happens next?" he wondered.

"Well, they bury Leo," Scout said, "and I do feel for his family, who might not have known what was in his heart or might have loved him anyway. And then you and Larissa can go back to your regularly scheduled lives, I guess." He shrugged and looked sheepish. "I mean, I like it here, but then, Kayleigh and I came willingly."

"But... but Tom's bench! You'll need help!" Piers said, a little desperately.

"Of course we will," Scout told him, his voice soothing. While Scout often sounded like someone who'd gone to gather ladybugs and had been called back to do nuclear physics, right now he sounded like someone who was very, very focused on the matter at hand—Piers's feelings and his fears. "We'd love to have you help here, Piers. Nobody wants you to leave. But you have so little time left in school. We all understand that you need to finish. We have phones and computers. We won't abandon you."

"But how can I leave?" he asked, unconsciously holding Miller even tighter. "This is where he belongs."

And that right there was the heart of it, wasn't it? Miller. Piers didn't want to leave him, not now, not when their relationship was so new and when Piers wanted to spend every waking moment with him.

But Scout didn't seem as concerned about that. "You'll figure it out," he said softly. "I don't see Miller breaking it off because things get hard, Piers. I get it, I think, about you and Larissa. Kayleigh and I had to work to be family. You both were sort of given it, but there wasn't a lot of effort made to keep you. Miller knows how to work for a relationship. He's had so few people listen to him, trust him, *believe* in him. He's not going to let that slip out of his grasp without an effort to save it."

"But...." Piers wanted to spill all of it then, Miller's shyness from a lover, his reluctance to believe he'd be cared for. Those things felt too unbearable to share, though, and he pulled back.

Scout hugged one knee up to his chest, an impossible act of human origami for such a long, slender man. "You'll figure it out," he said gently. "Right now, sleep. Kayleigh and I are cooking up something wonderful that we don't have a name for, and Larissa should be up in an hour or two. Don't worry. It's all taken care of."

Piers managed a small smile even as his eyes closed. "Says you," he murmured. "I still have to finish my Christmas shopping."

"I'd bet Miller has a couple of days off coming," Scout said cheerfully. "Maybe you two should go to Charleston for a weekend. I mean, Spinner's Drift is great, but it's not the *only* place on earth."

The idea floated like a feather and landed on the still pond of Piers's mind, leaving ripples. He fell asleep wondering how many of those shy, personal smiles he could get from Miller Aldrun as they were Christmas shopping in the historic old city.

A FEW HOURS after Miller heard the hum of Scout's voice talking to Piers, Scout and Kayleigh chivied them all out of bed and onto the couch, where they sat, Piers in the middle, and devoured a spicy tortilla soup and crusty fresh-baked bread. Scout and Kayleigh pulled up animated features on Miller's streaming service, and it was decided that cartoons—and discussions about cartoons—set the absolutely highest bar for conversation that night.

Larissa fell asleep first, leaning against Piers, and then Piers slouched into Miller's arms, and Miller was left watching the end of *Lilo and Stitch* with Kayleigh while Scout curled up like an awkward Chihuahua to sleep in Miller's recliner.

The movie's credits had run down when Miller reached for the remote control, found the home page, and then lay for a moment, staring at the screen blindly.

"Ready for bed?" Kayleigh asked kindly. "I can take Larissa, you shake Piers awake, and Scout will sleep on the couch. Someone's piloting your boat back tomorrow, and Callan and Desmond are working on getting reinforcements over the next few days. By the time you three are ready for the real world, we'll have a way to get you back to it."

"Thank you," Miller said softly. "The last time…." He closed his eyes. "The last time something like this happened, where the world felt like it ended and began again, I didn't have anybody. This is better."

"Mm." She nodded, looking very serious. "What happened?"

She didn't apologize for asking, and Miller was forced to remember once again that Scout and Kayleigh were very much like Stitch from the movie. They had a lot of power and a lot of good intentions—but they also didn't understand the world they'd ended up in 90 percent of the time. Miller thought that was probably why they were both so committed to helping the souls at Tom's bench and keeping the island safe. The island they understood—it was the first home they'd ever had that they loved.

So he told her everything. Things he hadn't told his sister; things Piers had figured out but he'd been too embarrassed to say. About being Cassandra, about Brad, about coming home from Brad's service and sobbing, unable to tell a soul what he'd lost.

About fear to show his true self to the world. Not his sexuality—that had only been a problem because Brad hadn't wanted it—but his ability to lead, his ability to fathom what he was up against, about the things he knew with no logical way of explaining how he knew them. His absolute belief that *nobody* would believe him had become a self-fulfilling prophecy. Who would believe someone who didn't believe in themselves?

"Until Piers," she said softly.

Miller leaned his cheek against the top of Piers's head. "Until Piers."

"So what are you going to do about it?" she asked.

Miller closed his eyes against the way they burned. "Work for it," he said, not sure what that would look like but sure it had to happen.

"You'll be okay, then," she said.

He glanced at her. "You think so?"

She gave a soft laugh. "You didn't see yourself today, Miller. You were giving orders like a general. It takes a lot of strength to get my brother to shut up and do something someone else is telling him to." She nodded to where Scout slept, his narrow, handsome face almost angelic in repose. "You ordered him around, you ordered Callan—*Callan*, who's used to being a god in his own little world, right? And Piers, and his confidence is one of the things that has guys panting all over him. You've got it in you, sweetie. You just have to let it out sometimes."

"Not all the time," he mumbled, yawning. "That's exhausting."

"Yeah. Now let's unstack you."

She chivvied Larissa off to bed, which made it easier to get Piers to move, and eventually they were back in Miller's bed again, this time with Miller as the big spoon.

"D'jou mean it?" Piers croaked.

"Mean what?"

"You'd work for me?"

Miller burrowed closer. "How could I not?"

"Good. Then this'll work jus' fine."

TRUE TO his word, Callan brought in reinforcements, and while Miller was busy for the next few days training them, giving them a cursory explanation of how to patrol the islands and, of course, getting used to his own role as captain—even to a small station nobody had heard of—Piers was busy too.

Part of that was accompanying Miller. One of his requirements for criminal law was hours spent shadowing a law enforcement officer. He figured those hours, standing next to Miller in the pilot's console, looking out at the wild greenery of the islands, the harmony of sun, sand, and water, were possibly the best use of his time law school had to offer.

The time he wasn't with Miller, he spent turning in as many assignments as he could for his semester work. With the addition of one class in the spring, his counselors told him that with his law enforcement follow, he was good to graduate at the end of the spring semester. Piers wondered how much of that was him and how much was Callan Morgenstern's money, but if he could pass the bar exam, he was happy either way.

Three days before the solstice, he managed to spirit Miller away to Charleston. The results were as delightful as he'd hoped.

Miller wandered the historic district entranced, looking for small gifts for their friends—a pretty tea set for Kayleigh, an area rug for Scout and Lucky, small herb jars for Helen and Marcus—all of which Piers approved of very much or helped with, because Miller had champagne taste and a Coca-Cola budget. They also got clothes and shoes for Ciaran—he'd shown a preference for black jeans and long-sleeved black T-shirts, but they were pretty sure that might change as spring came to the islands, so they also got him some basic island wear of his own. And a knapsack, since he seemed to spend his time between Kayleigh's couch, Scout and Lucky's couch, and Marcus and Helen's guest room.

Otto was a tough one to shop for, but after Miller had tugged Piers's hand and brought him into the bookstore, showing him the list of titles under Otto's pen name, Piers had a poster commissioned for his tiny cottage of all his collected works. After some furious texting to everybody else at the island, they made that a group gift, because Otto, it seemed, had everything else he needed.

Together they went in on matching luggage for Larissa—hard cases with cats on the front—giving her permission and hopefully incentive to travel between school and the islands as much as possible. The few days they'd spent recovering at Miller's bungalow had given Piers and Larissa a chance to talk, and both of them admitted that the Drift felt more like home than any place they'd ever known. Piers could see himself working in Charleston and taking clients from the Drift. Larissa could see herself telecommuting from a cottage on the island. They both were reluctant to leave the place in their rearview; it had welcomed them and sheltered them and made them feel cared for.

They wanted to return the favor with everything in their hearts.

When they were done shopping, Piers took Miller to a restaurant—a nice one, but nothing pretentious—where they ate delicately grilled fish and steak so tender it cut with a fork. Piers had spent his entire life learning how to be charming, but Miller, with his blunt observations and his almost perpetual good-natured surprise at people, on or off Spinner's Drift, was a joy. The conversation didn't flag until dessert, when Miller fell happily into a crème brûlée, closing his eyes and eating with almost orgasmic pleasure.

"You don't like it?" he asked, cleaning the plate with his finger.

"It's wonderful," Piers said, staring at him, starstruck.

Miller popped his finger in his mouth to suck off the last of the sweet and then realized Piers hadn't moved.

"What?"

"You," Piers said, feeling helpless. "Just… you."

Miller met his eyes then, and that gloriously shy smile appeared, and Piers had to fight to catch his breath.

"Now you know how I feel," Miller confessed, his ears turning red as he spoke. "Every minute of every day."

Piers signaled for their check then, and he hoped he'd left a whopper of a tip. He didn't remember anything between Miller's ears turning red and their bodies moving together in the hotel, every kiss a miracle, every touch a revelation.

When Miller cried out in his arms, his climax rocking him, spurring Piers to his own, Piers could swear the air about them sparkled with magic.

Maybe it was just love, in which case, that was magic enough.

Morning broke over them, coming through the snowy white curtains, blessing their bodies as Piers kissed the back of Miller's neck, pleased that he'd booked the late checkout so they might actually get some sleep.

"Piers?"

"Yeah?"

"I really am in love with you."

Piers's breath froze in his chest.

"Yeah?" he gasped.

"Don't... don't give up on me while you're trying to make it through law school, okay? I... I don't know how relationships work, much less over a distance, but if I know you're coming home to me, I'll body tackle anyone who gets between me and a day off with you."

Piers's eyes burned, and he gathered Miller to his chest, clutching him with joy and with hope. "I love you so much," he confessed.

"Good."

It must have been good—Piers had to call the concierge and book the room for another night because they weren't going to make the afternoon ferry.

They had to fill up on moments like these if they were going to survive until June.

THE WINTER solstice dawned cold and bright, and their little family of wizards, witches, and luck mechanics gathered at Tom's bench for a ceremony nearly a hundred and seventy years overdue.

They'd taken turns digging the grave the day before, next to Henry's marker behind the bench, and a new wooden casket—simple and unvarnished, as was only right—was lowered solemnly into the earth as the first gray of dawn breasted the horizon.

To all of the sensitive living souls in the clearing, what felt like a giant sigh—almost a moan—of completion rippled through the glade. The trees and grasses within the circle of power they'd divined the day they'd trapped Percy's ghost had all been withering, brown, not quite dead, but fighting the good fight since that day. When Tom's bones were placed next to Henry's, the greenery returned, almost before the casket came to rest.

By the time it was covered in earth again, a tension, an acrid smell in the air, a taste of revulsion that nobody had realized they were feeling, had faded completely.

Percy Hampstead would be a threat, they'd figured, until his own bones were dealt with. But for this sacred moment of the rebirth of the world, love would keep evil in check.

When the burial was complete, they joined hands around the graves, and Helen led them in a song about death, hope, and rebirth.

They were cold in their bones when they retreated to the bookstore for coffee and pastries, but the warmth and hope in their hearts eclipsed the physical discomfort—at least until Larissa's toes started tingling and she had to fight off a case of the giggles.

But the moment seemed to do more than give Tom and Henry some sorely needed surcease of suffering. By the time they'd turned away from the clearing, looking back only to see the gentle silhouettes of two men, sitting on the bench together, staring off into the horizon, the lot of them really were a family.

Not one of them doubted it—not even Ciaran or Otto, who were both very new.

And everybody got presents for Christmas.

Planning for Graduation

PIERS HAULED himself wearily across campus, oblivious to the first hints of spring in North Carolina. The stately old trees had unfurled tender green leaves, the sun was beginning to beam down on the green carpet of lawn, and the heaviness of summer had not yet set in like a blanket. Recent rains had washed the graceful white columns, and the pale bricks practically sparkled in the chill. It was the last Friday before Spring Break. The world was celebrating the coming of summer, of sunshine, and of joy.

He saw none of it.

His pocket buzzed, and Larissa's name popped on his phone screen.

I'm here. Everybody's sad you couldn't come.

Crap.

He'd been wrong during Christmas—he'd needed a special dispensation and *two* extra classes, in addition to the regular credit load, to catch up. He could graduate with his class in May, but the paper load had been absolutely crushing. It was late March, and he hadn't managed a single trip back to Spinner's Drift. He'd had high hopes for Spring Break, but one of his professors had spotted a requirement hole Piers had not yet filled, and he'd had to send Larissa on without him.

Although they found time for lunch or dinner together at least twice a week, it had still hurt to put her on the plane for Charleston knowing he was stuck here, writing his ass off, for the next nine days.

Miller had been patient and understanding—that was one of the nice things about dating a grown-up. He understood Piers wasn't absent because he wanted to be. Piers *wanted* to be done with school. He *wanted* to be job hunting in Charleston—or even hanging out his own shingle in Spinner's Drift. Hell, he'd even settle for sponging off Callan for legal scraps while building his own practice. Either way, he *wanted* to be with Miller, but he'd been working toward his law degree for a long time, and he finally actually *liked* the law. He needed to see this through.

Miller's phone calls and texts had been supportive—and they usually sported a picture of the tiny puppy he'd gotten before Piers had come back to school. The puppy—named Hopper—really *was* as cute as advertised, with a golden coat and wavy fur, a miniature noble head and calm little eyes, and a tiny body straight from a cartoon about Chihuahuas. According to Miller she *loved* riding in the boat in a special harness and lead, because Miller wasn't risking an accidental fall, or even an ill-advised leap from the moving vehicle.

Piers was half in love with the dog himself, but, goddammit, didn't Miller miss Piers too? Didn't he get frustrated, remembering their time together? How much fun they had, in bed and out of it? Didn't he miss Piers's smell? His touch? His eyes? The sound of his voice?

Because Piers almost couldn't breathe from missing Miller.

He shoved himself behind the wheel of his CR-V and carefully negotiated the thick traffic to his apartment building, trying hard to force his brain onto the papers he was supposed to be writing and not on what he couldn't have at the moment.

In contrast with the columns, arches, and aged brick and marble of Chapel Hill, the off-campus housing was gleaming, modern, and modular. His particular building had underground parking, and he glumly shouldered his backpack and took the elevator up to the lobby, staring at his phone screen hungrily as Larissa showed him pictures of their friends in the bright, breezy spring of Spinner's Drift.

Scout had cut his hair, and the curls made a disaster of whatever look he'd been trying to sport, but Lucky—whose own hair was long enough now to be held back in a ponytail—still looked at the wizard with his heart in his eyes. Otto, Marcus, and Helen looked adorable and oddly old-world, sitting on Kayleigh's patio, drinking tea from the pink flowered tea set she'd gotten for Christmas. Kayleigh—sandwiched between Desmond and Callan—looked tanned and radiant and confident, laughing at the camera, probably because her best friend was behind it taking the picture. Desmond was beaming down at her with obvious affection, and Piers was hungry for gossip about how that relationship had progressed. Callan looked leonine and self-assured, as he always did, but there was a spark of something… lonely in his eyes as he peered seemingly over Larissa's shoulder as she took the picture. Ciaran had his own picture as he held a tray of sandwiches in Kayleigh's kitchen. The young man had kept the long black fall of hair, but the pinched, lost look had faded from his eyes, and the grin he turned toward the camera was blinding.

And that was it—the sum of their friends in pictures, all of them happy and ready to take on a new spring and brilliant summer and all the forces of darkness.

Wait a minute.

Where's Miller? he asked, not seeing Miller in the corner of the bookstore, where everybody else—including Otto, who had come to the main island to greet Larissa—was meeting. Miller had been there during Larissa's two other visits, looking shyly away from the camera as Larissa had taken the obligatory shot.

Where are you? she asked, and he frowned.

In the elevator to the lobby, why?

You're stopping at the lobby, right?

He was a creature of habit, and he *always* stopped at the lobby to get his mail. That hadn't been a thing before, but the others had started sending him care packages—tiny things that mattered. A box of Helen's pastries one week, a little vial of sand from Miller the next. In his entire college career, his parents had sent him birthday cards and the occasional financial statement, but suddenly, checking the mail had become important to him. Even Callan had been sending him things— last week it had been a polo-shirt uniform with a card that said, *This would look great with a tie*, because apparently Callan *liked* the idea of Piers doing legal work for the hotel.

Text me when you get there, Larissa prompted.

And suddenly the long weekend, during which he'd *hoped* to go visit his home, didn't look like such a slog of homework after all. He wondered what was waiting for him at the lobby—fudge from the shop in the merchant's square? Scout had texted that Marcus was getting Great Gestalt T-shirts, as though Scout's magic act was a touring concert band. He'd promised Piers one.

Piers arrived at the lobby and looked toward the desk, hoping to catch the doorman's eye, but instead, he saw a midsized man with crinkles at the corners of his hazel eyes and a windburned nose, staring at the elevator like he was waiting for God himself.

As Piers stepped out of the elevator, Miller's face lit up in that beautiful smile, the tints of shyness still there, but a newfound confidence making it bloom even brighter.

"You're here," Piers whispered, his voice almost deserting him.

"My boss gave me some time off," Miller told him, taking a step forward. "I told him I missed my boyfriend."

And then he was in Piers's arms where he belonged, his head resting on Piers's shoulder.

The moment was so blissful, Piers didn't realize one of Miller's arms was not engaged in the hug until he felt the tiny wet nose investigating the hem of his jeans.

"Miller," Piers murmured into his ear, "my apartment doesn't allow pets." But the dog was wearing a little fleece hoodie with ducks on it from Doggie Duds, and Piers would make his father *buy* him a condo so they didn't have to leave her somewhere else.

"Can we tuck her in my jacket," Miller asked softly, "or should we get a hotel room?"

Piers looked up at the doorman, whom he'd gotten to know quite well with all the packages. Piers had spilled out his homesickness for Spinner's Drift in embarrassing quantities—and of course he'd shared the fudge and pastries too.

Clyde—a midfiftyish proud grandfather—looked around the empty lobby, put his finger to his lips, and waved them on.

"Quick," Piers whispered, "tuck her in your jacket and grab your duffel."

Miller gave a brilliant smile as a response, and together they made their way across the lobby to the elevator that reached the apartment floors.

TWO SWEATY, muscular, *heavenly* hours later, Piers collapsed on Miller's back, both of them wrung out, replete, and—for the moment—satiated.

"Wow," Miller breathed, his head turned to the side on the edge of the bed.

"You've ruined me," Piers agreed.

"You're the despoiler," Miller told him, but he sounded pretty happy about it, so Piers took it as a compliment.

"You're a fast learner," Piers said with satisfaction. While Miller might not ever be completely wanton, when they were in bed together, naked and aroused, he had become uninhibited, begging when he needed, pleasuring Piers without embarrassment, and taking pleasure from giving.

There was a happy silence then—or would have been—but Piers heard a tiny whimper, and an even tinier ball of fur and energy levitated into their vision and licked Miller on his sweaty nose.

Miller chuckled. "I think she needs a walk."

"But you brought pads," Piers said. They'd spread them on the tile in the bathroom and put her little bed next to the couch—which was maybe steps away from Piers's bed, because it was a one-bedroom studio.

"She tries not to use them," Miller said, pride in his voice. "She knows what good dogs do." He reached down to pet her, and Piers rolled off the bed and kissed his shoulder.

"We'll go for a walk, then," he said, happy to show Miller his town. "We can talk."

Miller pushed up and kissed him. "God, I'm happy to see you," he said, so naturally that Piers wondered how he hadn't known it in his bones.

They walked in the late evening shadows, listening to the slightly manic sounds of the students finding their ways to favorite pubs, restaurants, and cafés, giddy at the prospect of a week free of school.

Piers led the way to one of his favorite pubs, one in which he'd seen a professor take his calm and noble Labrador retriever while he had a few beers.

Little Hopper in her "Good Dogs Do" T-shirt barely rated an eyebrow raise, and they got to sit at a corner table and talk.

"How long are you here?" Piers asked, finally remembering to ask basic questions.

"I go back next Sunday morning," Miller told him, taking a pull from his beer. "So eight days, give or take. This is good—you forget what a tapped microbrew tastes like."

"I didn't even know you liked beer!" Piers told him, surprised.

Miller shrugged. "Only sometimes. Not worth it to haul it to my flat if I'm only drinking a bottle a week."

Piers nodded. "Well, when I move in, I'll buy beer or wine once a week." He took his own sip. "You're going to have a little bit of luxury."

Miller practically glowed. "I'll have you, I'll have the dog, I'll have the job—what more can a man want?" he asked.

"Beer," Piers said decisively. He thought, *And sex like that, at least three times a week*, but he didn't say it out loud.

"Fair." Miller sobered. "You really mean that? You, uhm, want to move in?"

Piers nodded, the ache of the last two months throbbing hard even though Miller was right there. "After I figure out my job situation, we can maybe get a house of our own. I've got money, and island residents get a break when they buy for development." He paused. "I miss Spinner's Drift. I wake up sometimes and wonder where the smell of the sea is, or why I can't hear the wind."

Miller nodded, meeting his eyes. "I'd go anywhere you are," he said, his expression naked. "But I love it too. I'd love to live there with you." He paused. "After we take care of Tom's bench."

Piers cocked his head. "What else do we need to do?"

Miller grinned. "Well, what are you doing on Summer Solstice?"

And Piers knew then that there was a plan. "I take it I'm going on an adventure with you?"

Miller grinned. "Yup. In fact, that's what I'm going to do here while you're doing homework so you can graduate."

"What?"

"Research." His voice dropped. "I need to find Percy Hampstead's bones, for one, and any other 'vessels' he might have used. You and me have a job to do on Summer Solstice so we can lay some of the pain in that place to rest."

Piers reached across the table and grabbed his hand. "And then? You and me and the dog, in Spinner's Drift forever and ever, happy ever after?"

Miller's grin upped its wattage, and his eyes went shiny. "Amen," he said, pulling Piers's knuckles to his lips and kissing them, right there in the corner of the pub.

It was a perfect promise, of adventure, of safety, of the two of them building their lives together doing things that they loved and that had meaning.

It was all the hope Piers needed to finish his studies, all the strength the two of them would need to finish the quest Scout had started, ensuring the protection of the place—and the family—they both loved with all their hearts.

Their future was there, in the Spinner's Drift sunset, and soon they would both return together to take part in everything they'd ever dreamed.

Eight Days and Twelve Hours Later

MILLER YAWNED and stretched, leaning into the wind in the prow of the ferry, yearning for sight of the main island, where he was spending his last day of his vacation to spill all the news about Piers before he took his skiff home to the dispatch apartment.

It had been a good week—the best of his life. Every day of working side by side in the day and making love at night a prelude of what they had to look forward to when this brief hardship was over. Miller had never, in all of his life, expected Cassandra would get a happy ending, but he was starting to think it could happen.

But something... something was off. His stomach had been buzzing since he'd gotten on the ferry—not with *danger* so much as with *power*. Something or somebody with enough power to be dangerous was on this ferry, and Miller had been surreptitiously scanning the faces of his fellow passengers to see if he could pinpoint the power to be aware of what was coming.

To his left, as he leaned against the railing, a man wearing an actual business suit stood. The suit was rumpled, and the man was... *exhausted* was the word Miller thought of. His hairline had just started to recede back in a widow's peak—it actually made the planes and angles of his face a little more pointed, a little more attractive. He had dark hair, slicked down, probably to contain the curl Miller saw escaping, and wide indigo eyes with bags underneath—and an unutterably weary expression at the bottom of their depths.

His face—the planes, the angles, the chin, the shape of the eyes— was familiar, but in odd ways. Some expressions almost made him look like... and others captured....

And then it came to him.

Scout. Kayleigh. This man could come from the same family.

The family of wizards that had almost killed Scout in front of their eyes back in October.

Miller's spine stiffened, and his expression hardened, and the tired man caught his eye.

"I'm not a threat," he said softly.

Miller didn't relax his spine, but he did open up his expression. "I'm sorry?" he said quietly.

"You... you recognized me? You looked angry."

Miller spoke carefully. "Not too long ago, someone who looked very much like you came to the island to try to kidnap a friend of mine and hurt her brother. It made me... cautious."

To his surprise the man's eyes grew limpid and red-rimmed, and his shoulders straightened, as though some of the exhaustion that had made him brittle and frail had slid off, leaving him stronger—and surprisingly young. Miller had first thought him to be in his midforties, but now he appeared to be in his early thirties.

And handsome in an understated way. He didn't have Scout's beauty or Kayleigh's vivacity, but he was surprisingly attractive.

"Scout?" he whispered. "Kayleigh? You're friends with them?"

Miller caught his breath. Scout and Kayleigh had spoken many times of being raised in a compound with an unnamed sum of half brothers and half sisters—an impersonal amalgamation from which two names only were mentioned. One was Macklin, who lived in California with his soon-to-be husband, and the other was the man who had risked their father's formidable wrath to slip credit cards and a phone into Scout's pocket when he'd been exiled from the compound.

"Josue?" Miller said cautiously, and the man dragged the sleeve of his suit coat across his eyes.

"Yes," he said on a shaky breath.

Miller's own breath caught, and he resisted the urge to hug this complete stranger and take all his burdens. If anybody needed that hug, that release, that care, it seemed to be this exhausted, worn-thin man.

Miller extended his hand and took a step forward, careful of Hopper, who had been sitting on alert at his feet. "My name is Miller Aldrun," he said quietly. "I can take you to your family."

Josue nodded and squeezed his eyes shut. "Forgive me," he said. "It's… it's been sort of a day."

"That's all right," Miller said. "I… I can take you to a good place. Where people will listen. Where they'll believe you. It'll get better." He gave a hesitant smile. "It did for me."

Josue Quintero swallowed, nodded, and seemed to get hold of himself. "Thank you," he said, pulling his dignity back on. Well, from what Miller had heard of Josue's life, dignity was a dear commodity, and Miller wouldn't begrudge him a cent of it.

With another fortifying breath, Josue noticed Hopper, still sitting at attention.

"What a dear little dog," he said, seemingly happy at the change of subject. "Do you mind if I pet him?"

"Not at all," Miller said. He bent down and pulled Hopper up into his arms. "Here—she'll lick your hand if you like. Her name's Hopper."

Miller's brain buzzed with questions, but he knew instinctively he wasn't the person who got to demand answers. Instead, he and Josue Quintero spent the next hour talking about small dogs and Charleston and Chapel Hill and waterways and police stations and anything else Miller could talk about, because his companion seemed to need a friend.

As Spinner's Drift appeared and grew larger on the horizon, and Miller felt the satisfying pull of being home, he wondered what Josue's appearance on the island would mean for all of them. If there was one thing his new family had taught him, it was that things happened for a reason, and the island sheltered her own.

Watching Josue Quintero's face open and grow peaceful as they neared Miller's home, Miller thought that this particular soul might need the island's protection more than anyone Miller had ever known.

But it was like that twilight evening when he'd first arrived in Chapel Hill and he and Piers had talked about their future, about riding into the Spinner's Drift sunset together, about having a life.

The details would come. The conflicts would be dealt with. The truths they knew were that their Spinner's Drift family would support them, and the island had taken them for its own.

He had faith that Josue Quintero would find his own way to his island home, and he looked forward to seeing his new friend lose his burdens and find the shelter he so badly seemed to need.

Keep Reading for An Excerpt from
All the Rules of Heaven
by Amy Lane.

For the Sake of Momentum

THE BED that dominated the center of the room was hand-carved, imported ebony, black as night, and the newel posts had been studded with an ivory inlay, random designs supposedly, dancing around and around in a way that made the unwary stop, lost in the intricacy of runes nobody living could read.

The wallpaper had once been an English garden jungle—cabbage roses, lilacs, mums—riotous around the walls, and the grand window was positioned strategically to catch the early morning sun overlooking what might once have been a tiny corner of England, transplanted by the cubic foot of earth into the red-clay dirt of the Sierra Foothills.

That same dirt was now the dust that stained the windows, layering every nuance of the old room in hints of bloody deeds.

The tattered curtains no longer blocked out the harsh sun of morning, and the wallpaper curled from the walls in crackled strips. The carpet threads lay bare to the hard soles of the doctor who tended to the dying old woman, but she had no eyes for the living person taking her pulse, giving her surcease from pain, making her last hours bearable.

Her eyes were all for Angel—but nobody else could see him, so he rather regretfully assumed that she appeared crazy to the other people in the room.

"No," she snapped contentiously. "I won't tell you. I won't. It's not fair."

Angel gave a frustrated groan and ran fingers through imaginary hair. This was getting tiresome.

"Old woman—"

"Ruth," she snarled. "You used me up, sucked away my youth, drained me fucking dry. At *least* get my name right!"

Angel winced. The old wom—Ruth—had a point.

"I'm sorry the task was so difficult," Angel said gently, containing supreme frustration. She was right. What Angel had asked Ruth Henderson to do with her life had been horrible. Painful. An assault on her senses every day she lived. But Angel needed the name of her successor—he needed to find the person and introduce himself. Angel really couldn't leave Daisy Place unless he was in company of someone connected to it by blood or spirit.

"You are not sorry," Ruth sneered. "You could give a shit." She looked so sweet—like Granny from a *Sylvester the Cat* cartoon, complete with snowy white braids pinned up to circle her head. She'd asked her nurse to do that for her yesterday, and Angel, as sad and desperate as the situation was, had backed off while the nurse worked and Ruth hummed an Elvis Presley song under her breath. The music had been popular when Ruth was a teenager, and it was almost a smack in Angel's face.

Yes, Angel *had* taken up most of her life with a quest nobody else could understand, and now Ruth's life was ending and Angel was taking the peace that should have held sway.

Her breath was congested and her voice clogged. Her heart was stuttering, and her lungs were filling with fluid, her body failing with every curse she lifted. She'd been a good woman, performing her duty without question at the expense of family, lovers, children of her own.

It was a shock, really, how bitter she'd become as the end neared. A pang of remorse pierced Angel's heart; the poor woman had been driven beyond endurance, and it was Angel's fault. It was just that there were so many here, so many voices, and Angel would never be released, would be trapped here in this portal of souls until the very last one was freed. Angel was incorporeal. Ruth was the human needed to give voice to the souls trapped in this house, on these grounds. If she didn't give a very human catharsis to the dead, they would never rise beyond the soul trap this place had become.

And now that she was dying, she needed to name a successor, or everybody trapped at Daisy Place would be doomed—Angel included.

"I'm sorry," Angel said, regret weighting every word. "It probably seems as though I didn't care—I handled everything all wrong. We could have been friends. I could have been your companion and not your tormenter. You deserved a friend, Ruth. I was not that friend. I'm so sorry."

Ruth blew out a breath. Her words were mumbles now—Angel understood, even if the doctor and nurse at her bedside assumed she was out of her mind.

"You weren't so bad," she wheezed. "You were in pain." A slight smile flickered over the canvas of wrinkles that made up her face. "You made my garden bloom. You couldn't prune for shit, but you did try."

"It gave me great joy," Angel confessed humbly. No more than the truth. Angel had loved that garden, loved the optimism that had laid the fine Kentucky bluegrass sod and ordered the specialty rose grafts from Portland and Vancouver. No, Angel couldn't prune it—couldn't hold the shears, couldn't hold back the tide of entropy that the garden had become—but that hadn't stopped the place from being Angel's greatest source of peace, even stuck here in this way station for the damned and the enlightened.

"I know it did." There was defeat in Ruth's voice. "Promise me," she mumbled.

"What?" Angel would take care of the garden until freed from this prison—there was no question.

"Promise me you'll be kind to him."

Oh! Oh sweet divinity. She was going to name an heir.

"To him?" Angel asked, all respect.

"I left him the house, but the boy hasn't had it easy, Angel. He'll be here soon enough. Be kind."

"I need his name," Angel confessed. "If I don't know his name, I'll never find his soul."

"Tucker," she whispered, her last breaths rattling in her chest. "My brother's boy. Tucker Henderson. Be kind," she begged. "He's a sweet boy…. Be kind."

Triumph soared in Angel's chest. Yes! Ruth Henderson's successor, the empath who could hear the ghosts and help exorcise Daisy Place! Angel wanted to cheer, but now was not the time. With invisible hands but tenderness nonetheless, Ruth Henderson's ghostly companion stroked her forehead and whispered truths about a glorious garden in the afterlife as the good woman breathed her last.

Blind Faith

TUCKER DIDN'T know how it happened—he *never* knew how it happened. One minute he'd be walking into a restaurant for dinner, and the next a stranger would stop by his table and strike up a conversation. Twelve hours later, Tucker would have a new friend—and a few used condoms.

It had cost him girlfriends—and boyfriends. He never planned to be unfaithful. He rarely planned to go into the restaurant or bar at all. He'd be strolling down the street, a bag of groceries in his hand and a plan for dinner with—once upon a time—friends, and he'd feel a draw, an irresistible pull, a rope under his breastbone tugging him painfully into another person's bed.

He'd tried to resist on occasion, back when he'd had plans for a normal life.

When he'd been younger—a green kid freshly grieving the loss of his parents—it had worked out okay of course. *Any* touch had been okay. He'd been alone in the world, and the empathic powers his aunt Ruth had warned him about had arrived, and suddenly he was seeing a host of people who shouldn't exist, wandering around in the world like everyday folk.

Sex had been comforting then.

He'd lost his virginity when he'd gone into a McDonald's for a soda after school and ended up trading blowjobs with the cashier—who happened to be his high school's quarterback—in the bathroom.

They had both been surprised (to say the least), but then Trace Appleby had broken down into tears and wept on Tucker's shoulder because he'd never been able to admit he was gay until just that moment. He said he'd been thinking about taking drastic measures, and although he'd never been more explicit than that, Tucker had gotten his first inkling of what was to come.

Given how lost he'd been, how heartsore, it had seemed like a karmic mission of sorts. He was kind of excited to see what came next.

Next had been right after high school graduation, when he'd been *working* at McDonald's—he and a friend had ended up doing it in her car in the upper parking lot. Afterward, *she* had broken down on a bemused Tucker and told him that her boyfriend had been cheating on her but she didn't have the courage to leave him.

Until right then.

Tucker started to harbor suspicions that *next* might not be as wonderful as he'd hoped.

Less than a month later, when he stood up a girl *he* liked because he'd wandered into a bar and slept with a guy who'd been thinking about going to a party so he could get high and woke up thinking about college instead, Tucker began to understand.

And the only comfort sex had offered him then had been the comfort he apparently gave others in bed.

He'd explained it to his friend Damien the next day. First, Damien had needed to get over the "Oh my God, you're *bi?*" But after that he'd been pretty copacetic.

"So you're saying God wants you to get laid," he'd concluded.

Tucker sort of frowned. "That does *not* sound like the Sunday school lessons I got growing up," he said. Of course, his parents had been gone for about two years at this point, and he hadn't attended a church service in a very long time.

Then he remembered something his father had said.

He'd been born late in his parents' life—they'd been in their fifties when their car had skidded off the road during their date night—but his father had been a kind man, active, with salt-and-pepper hair that hadn't even started to thin. He'd had laugh lines and kind brown eyes, and he'd told Tucker to go to church and soak up the feeling—the feeling of being protected.

"Ignore the words, son. Some people need them, but you're just there to know what it's like to find shelter from the storm."

Oh. Apparently Tucker *was* shelter from the storm. Maybe God really *did* want him to get laid. Or the gods, really. Tucker had already identified vampires and elves and ghosts and werecreatures among the hosts of not-humans who walked the city streets with him. In an effort to broaden his knowledge, he'd begun taking classes in comparative religion, ancient language, arcane lore, and anything he could find even remotely connected. School was fun at that point—but the broader lessons hadn't started to set in.

He looked at Damien, wishing that Damie was bi too, because he had a rich red mouth and dark blond hair and green eyes and freckled cheeks, and Tucker had wanted to kiss him for a long time.

But Damien was the kind of guy who always landed on his feet. If he got detention in school, he'd meet a pretty girl who'd want to be taken out Saturday night. Once when he'd been out of work, his car had broken down, and the Starbucks he'd gone into while he waited for the tow truck had been looking for a cashier.

Damien always found a sheltered path through life's difficulties, simply on instinct. He never needed shelter from the storm.

He'd never need Tucker.

Tucker had always been the guy with pencils when the teacher gave a surprise test, the guy with the extra sandwich when someone forgot their lunch, or the guy with the spare jacket or the shoulder to cry on. Even before the McDonald's blowjob and the sobbing quarterback, Tucker had a reputation as the guy people could talk to when life threw them a curve ball. He was a sympathetic ear.

Or an empathetic ear.

Talking to Damien, remembering his father's definition of religion in contrast to his college professors', it occurred to him that being the sympathetic ear might have become his cosmic mission in life—with the added twist of sex. Suddenly both the sympathy and the sex felt like a chore.

"Never mind," Tucker had said, his heart breaking for the things he was starting to see he'd never have. "I get it now. I'm an umbrella."

"And I'm an ice cream cone," Damien replied, because he thought that was the game.

Tucker hadn't been able to play, though. He was too busy thinking about how many ways being an umbrella could go wrong.

He'd found them. One night when he was in his twenties, he'd resisted the pull, sobbing from the wrongness in his chest, the displaced time, the pull in his blood and corpuscles to wander into a restaurant and come home with God or Goddess knows who. But he wanted to be faithful—his *heart* was faithful, dammit, why couldn't his body be?

He'd gotten home to a message on his phone—the father of the girl he'd fallen in love with had died, and she'd needed to leave town.

Tucker could have written it down to coincidence, but by then he didn't believe in coincidence. He'd given up on relationships for a while.

Not long enough, but a while.

And that had been many years and one eon of heartbreak ago.

So by the time he arrived at Daisy Place, he was tired, old at thirty-five, exhausted by his karmic mission, and so, so lonely.

But by then his gift, the empathic pull that led him to other people's beds and their cosmic epiphanies and karmic catharses, had been honed to a science. It had used him often enough that he knew what to expect.

The night the Greyhound dropped him off in the middle of what kind of passed for a town, suitcases in hand like a kid in an old musical, he didn't set about trying to find a ride to Daisy Place immediately. Sure, the press under his breastbone had started almost directly after he'd gotten the call from his aunt Ruth's lawyer, and it had been subtly building ever since, but he knew this game well enough to know that Daisy Place wasn't at critical mass yet. First, he needed a room to sleep in—and he'd felt the other pull, the older, more painful pull, for a mile before the bus had slowed at the depot.

Someone here would give him a place to sleep, and he could see to Aunt Ruth's inheritance in the cold light of day.

Sure enough, he was in the middle of a gi*normous* hamburger that had been cooked in an actual ore cart from the gold-rush days, when a tired-looking woman in nice comfy jeans, a skinny-strapped tank top, and flip-flops strode into the converted post office/restaurant and threw herself into a chair at the table next to him.

The restless, painful ache in his chest that had guided him there gave a little *pop*, and he could breathe again.

"Hey there, pretty lady," he said, shoving a plate of fries toward her. "Is there anything I can do to help?"

She had blond hair—artfully streaked and ironed straight—adorable chipmunk cheeks, and a full and smiling mouth. The girl took a fry gratefully and tried to put that mouth to happy use. She failed dismally, but Tucker appreciated the attempt. Putting a good face on things for other people was an unnecessary courtesy, but it was still kind. Thin as a rail, with a few subtle curves, she was in her late twenties at the most and seemed to have the weight of the world on her shoulders.

"It's been sort of a day," she said fretfully. "You know—a day?"

Tucker thought back to when he and Damien used to have this discussion, and his stomach twisted hard with regret. "I've had a few," he said softly. "What happened with yours?"

"It's just so stupid." She sighed and looked yearningly at the untouched half of his two-pound hamburger. Tucker cut off a quarter of it and put it on the fry plate for her, and her smile grew misty.

"Thank you," she said softly. "I mean, I was going to order my own, but eating alone...."

"Sucks," he said, nodding. "So, I'm Tucker Henderson—"

"Old Ruth's nephew?" she said with interest.

"Yes, ma'am." He hadn't seen Aunt Ruth in several years. She'd helped administer his parents' estate, sending him personal checks every month—ostensibly to help him through college, but the estate was more than enough to live on. He'd appreciated the gesture, though, and had called or written with every check, but she'd never asked him up to see her at Daisy Place, and Tucker....

Well, Tucker's entire life had become the inescapable knowledge, the pull under his breastbone, the pressing weight of being some sort of karmic tool. Quite literally. Leaving downtown Sacramento—where he didn't even have a car because he never knew when he'd get the call and stopping when walking or riding his bike was so much easier than driving—had been beyond him for a couple of years. Aunt Ruth didn't ask, and he didn't insist.

They'd barely spoken about the reasons—but she knew. He was very aware that she knew.

"I'd come to visit, Auntie, but I've got... uhm, things. Things I can't explain."

A sudden electric silence on the telephone. "Oh, honey. I'm so sorry. I know those... things. I have them living in my house. You be careful. Those things can be difficult on the soul."

"Folks are going to miss her," the pretty woman said in the here and now, her smile going melancholy. "Most of us played in her garden at one time or another."

Tucker remembered his own time there, stalking imaginary lions in the jungle of domesticated flowers that ran riot over what must have been ten acres of property. All of the people wearing strange clothes, walking through the benches and over the lawn. He was pretty sure he was the only one who had *those* memories, though. He'd eventually figured that seeing ghosts was part and parcel of the whole empathic gig. It had taken having a lot of "imaginary friends" until he'd been about thirteen and figured it out, but whatever. His parents had only visited Ruth a handful of times when he was a kid, but she'd always had cookies—the good kind, with chocolate. None of that persimmon crap either.

Ruth had been sweet—if eccentric. He'd always had the feeling that she had a particular ghost of her own to keep her company, but if so she hadn't mentioned his name.

"I didn't know the garden was a whole-town thing," he said. A town the size of Foresthill probably had a lot of close-knit traditions.

"Well, my grade school class anyway," the girl said with a shrug.

The skinny high school kid with spots and an outsized nose who was waiting the few tables in the place came up to them. "Hiya, Miz Fisher. Can I get you anything?"

She smiled again, but it didn't reach her eyes this time. "A diet soda, Jordan." She gave one of those courtesy smiles to Tucker. "Ruth Henderson's nephew seems to have taken care of my meal."

Jordan nodded, gazing at "Miz Fisher" with nothing short of adoration. "I'll get you the soda for free," he said, like he was desperate for her approval. "It's not every day your English teacher just strolls in on your watch in the middle of July."

Poor Miz Fisher. Her courtesy smile crumbled, and what was left made Tucker's heart wobble. There *was* a reason he hadn't quit on life after his second attempt to ignore his empathic gift had backfired so horribly. This woman was part of it.

"Former English teacher," she reminded Jordan gently. "Remember? They had to cut the staff this year."

Jordan's smile disappeared. "Yeah," he mumbled. "Sorry, Miz Fisher. I'll go get your soda." He wandered away, the dispirited droop of his shoulders telling Tucker everything he needed to know about how much this woman—homegrown by the sound of things—had been appreciated by her community.

"Lost your job?" Tucker prompted. "Miz Fisher?"

"Dakota," she said, taking another fry. "Dakota Fisher. And yeah."

Tucker knew that wasn't all there was to the story. He cut her hamburger into bites and handed her a fork. He might not have known squat about this town, but he was on his own turf now.

BY THE time they left the restaurant, he knew how much Dakota loved teaching. By the time they got to her tiny cottage and got their clothes off, he knew how much she loved her hometown and her parents and the kids she'd grown up with. And helping people.

By the time they fell asleep, sated and naked, she knew what she had to do. It wasn't what *Tucker* would have predicted, not at all, but it was right for her.

That's what Tucker did—what was right for other people. Because the results of doing what was right for him were too awful to face again.

WHEN THE simple white-walled room was still gray with predawn chill, he opened his eyes and blinked.

Damie?

No. It couldn't be.

But the young man sitting cross-legged on the foot of Dakota Fisher's bed *looked* like Damien Columbus. Dark blond hair, freckles, full lips, green eyes—so many superficial details were there that Tucker could be forgiven for the quick gasp of breath.

He blinked hard, then got hold of himself and took in the nuances.

No—this person had a slightly more delicate jaw, a pointier chin, and his eyes were… well, Tucker had never seen eyes the actual shade of bottle glass outside of contacts and anime cartoons.

And whereas Damie had worn skinny jeans and tank tops—looking as twinky as possible for a guy who'd professed to be straight until… *don't go there, Tucker*—this guy was wearing basic 501s and a white T-shirt. He looked like a greaser or a Jet, right down to the slicked-back hair.

Although—and this had been the thing that had first terrified Tucker to his marrow—this guy was also dead. Or astral projecting. Or something. Because his body wasn't depressing the frilly yellow-and-pink coverlet on Dakota's bed even a little. He just sat/hovered there, tapping the bottom of his red Converse sneakers with his thumbs, scowling at Tucker as if Tucker had somehow disappointed him.

"Can I help you?" Tucker mumbled, squinting at him some more. Oh yeah. The more Tucker looked, the less this guy resembled Damien. Which was good. Because he wasn't sure how to deal with… Damien. Watching him sleep naked.

Not after all this time.

But then the penetrating gaze of this stranger, this not-Damien, wasn't doing him any good either.

Tucker hadn't been with anybody of his choosing in a long time, and he'd assumed the part of him that *did* choose had been killed off by grief. Imagine his surprise when he felt his stomach flutter.

"You were supposed to be at the house last night," the young man said. "I waited up."

Award winning author AMY LANE lives in a crumbling crapmansion with a couple of teenagers, a passel of furbabies, and a bemused spouse. She has too damned much yarn, a penchant for action-adventure movies, and a need to know that somewhere in all the pain is a story of Wuv, Twu Wuv, which she continues to believe in to this day! She writes contemporary romance, paranormal romance, urban fantasy, and romantic suspense, teaches the occasional writing class, and likes to pretend her very simple life is as exciting as the lives of the people who live in her head. She'll also tell you that sacrifices, large and small, are worth the urge to write.

Website: www.greenshill.com
Blog:www.writerslane.blogspot.com
Email: amylane@greenshill.com
Facebook:www.facebook.com/amy.lane.167
Twitter: @amymaclane

Follow me on BookBub

AMY LANE

Sometimes the
best magic is just
a little luck…

THE
RISING TIDE

THE LUCK MECHANICS ⬥ BOOK ONE

The tidal archipelago of Spinner's Drift is a refuge for misfits. Can the island's magic help a pie-in-the-sky dreamer and a wounded soul find a home in each other?

In a flash of light and a clap of thunder, Scout Quintero is banished from his home. Once he's sneaked his sister out too, he's happy, but their power-hungry father is after them, and they need a place to lie low. The thriving resort business on Spinner's Drift provides the perfect way to blend in.

They aren't the only ones who think so.

Six months ago Lucky left his life behind and went on the run from mobsters. Spinner's Drift brings solace to his battered soul, but one look at Scout and he's suddenly terrified of having one more thing to lose.

Lucky tries to keep his distance, but Scout is charming, and the island isn't that big. When they finally connect, all kinds of things come to light, including supernatural mysteries that have been buried for years. But while Scout and Lucky grow closer working on the secret, pissed-off mobsters, supernatural entities, and Scout's father are getting closer to them. Can they hold tight to each other and weather the rising tide together?

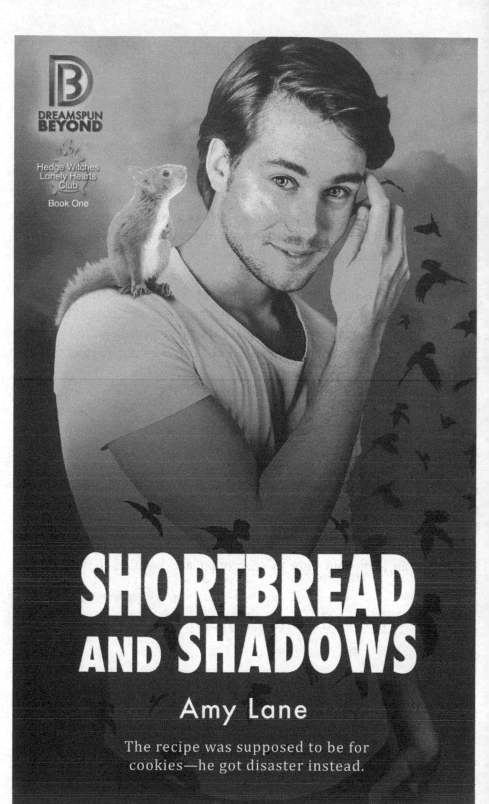

DREAMSPUN
BEYOND

Hedge Witches
Lonely Hearts
Club

Book One

SHORTBREAD
AND SHADOWS

Amy Lane

The recipe was supposed to be for
cookies—he got disaster instead.

Hedge Witches Lonely Hearts Club: Book One

When a coven of hedge witches casts a spell for their hearts' desires, the world turns upside down.

Bartholomew Baker is afraid to hope for his heart's true desire—the gregarious woodworker who sells his wares next to Bartholomew at the local craft fairs—so he writes the spell for his baking business to thrive and allow him to quit his office job. He'd rather pour his energy into emotionally gratifying pastry! But the magic won't allow him to lie, even to himself, and the spellcasting has unexpected consequences.

For two years Lachlan has been flirting with Bartholomew, but the shy baker with the beautiful gray eyes runs away whenever their conversation turns personal. He's about to give up hope… and then Bartholomew rushes into a convention in the midst of a spellcasting disaster of epic proportions.

Suddenly everybody wants a taste of Bartholomew's baked goods—and Bartholomew himself. Lachlan gladly jumps on for the ride, enduring rioting crowds and supernatural birds for a chance with Bartholomew. Can Bartholomew overcome the shyness that has kept him from giving his heart to Lachlan?

www.dreamspinnerpress.com

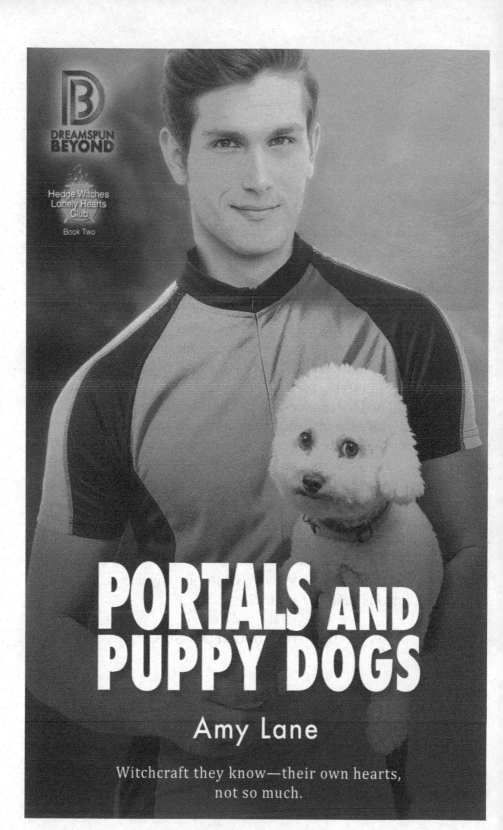

DREAMSPUN
BEYOND

Hedge Witches
Lonely Hearts
Club

Book Two

PORTALS AND PUPPY DOGS

Amy Lane

Witchcraft they know—their own hearts,
not so much.

Hedge Witches Lonely Hearts Club: Book Two

Sometimes love is flashier than magic.

On the surface, Alex Kennedy is unremarkable: average looks, boring accounting job, predictable crush on his handsome playboy boss, Simon Reddick.

But he's also a witch.

Business powerhouse Simon goes for flash and glamour… most of the time. But something about Alex makes Simon wonder what's underneath that sweet, gentle exterior.

Alex could probably dance around their attraction forever… if not for the spell gone wrong tearing apart his haunted cul-de-sac. When a portal through time and space swallows the dog he's petsitting, only for the pampered pooch to appear in the next instant on Simon's doorstep, Alex and Simon must confront not only the rogue magic trying to take over Alex's coven, but the long-buried passion they've been harboring for each other.

www.dreamspinnerpress.com

DREAMSPUN
BEYOND

Hedge Witches
Lonely Hearts
Club

Book Three

PENTACLES AND PELTING PLANTS

Amy Lane

He'll do anything to fix his coven—even
confront his own demons.

Hedge Witches Lonely Hearts Club: Book Three

A month ago, Jordan Bryne and his coven of hedge witches cast a spell that went hideously wrong and captured two of their number in a pocket of space and time. The magic is beyond their capabilities to unravel so, in desperation, they send up a beacon for supernatural aid.

They don't mean to yank someone to their doorstep from hundreds of miles away.

Once Macklin Quintero gets past his irritation, he accepts the challenge. The tiny coven in the Sierra foothills is a group of the sweetest people he's ever met, and he's worried—the forces they've awakened won't go back in their bottle without a fight.

But he also wants to get closer to Jordan. Mack's been playing the field for years, but he's never before encountered somebody so intense and dedicated.

Jordan might quietly yearn for love, but right now he's got other priorities. The magic in the cul-de-sac doesn't care about Jordan's priorities, though. Apparently the only way for the hedge witches to fix what they broke is to confront their hearts' desires head-on.

www.dreamspinnerpress.com

DREAMSPUN
BEYOND

Hedge Witches
Lonely Hearts
Club

Book Four

HEARTBEATS IN A HAUNTED HOUSE

Amy Lane

Never lie to magic about affairs of the heart.

Hedge Witches Lonely Hearts Club: Book Four

Dante Vianelli and Cully Cromwell have been in love since college, when Dante saved Cully from the world's worst roommate and introduced him to his friends. Seven years later, they're still roommates and they're still in love… but they've never become lovers.

Now a catastrophic spell gone wrong has cut them off from their coven. Wandering their suburban prison alone, separated by the walls of their own minds and gaps in the space-time continuum, Cully and Dante are as stuck as they have been for the past seven years.

And they'll remain lost in their memories—unless they confront the truths that kept them from taking the step from friends to lovers and trust their friends and coven to get them out. But it's easier said than done. Those walls didn't build themselves. Dante's great at denial, and Cully's short on trust. Can they do the work it will take to get into each other's arms and back to the sunlight where they belong?

www.dreamspinnerpress.com